ZERO
AVENUE

BOOKS BY LEONA GOM:

HOUSEBROKEN

PRIVATE PROPERTIES

NORTHBOUND

LAND OF THE PEACE

THE SINGLETREE

KINDLING

ZERO AVENUE

LEONA GOM

Douglas & McIntyre
Vancouver / Toronto

Douglas & McIntyre Ltd.
1615 Venables Street
Vancouver, British Columbia V5L 2H1

Canadian Cataloguing in Publication Data

Gom, Leona, 1946–
  Zero Avenue

  ISBN 0-88894-642-2

  I. Title
PS8563.083Z455   1989   C813'.54   C89-091133-9
PR 199.3.065Z455   1989

Cover illustration by Ron Lightburn
Cover and series design by Barbara Hodgson
Typeset by The Typeworks
Printed and bound in Canada by Gagné Printing Ltd.

For my mother

WEDNESDAY

PAT

When I look up, the only thing I see is the gun. It is large and black and pointed right at me. Sunlight from the window ricochets from the metal.

My heart begins to punch at my chest like a fist. On the television the woman is saying, her voice unnaturally clear, "You *know* I loved him! How can you think I'd want someone else?"

My eyes are fixed on the barrel, its perfect round opening from which I can imagine already the grey bullet emerging, growing larger and larger in my vision until it is too close for focus, for sight. Then I make myself look beyond the gun, at the hand holding it, at the arm stretched out straight, the other arm beside it bent slightly because that hand is clenched around the wrist of the arm that ends in the gun. The man himself is simply a thick dark shape against the window, a hole cut in the sunlight, his face a black moon. It is a scene from a police show, I think for one hysterical moment, nothing that I could really be seeing in my own living room.

"Open your mouth and I'll shoot!" The voice is shrill and loud, like an angry child's.

I nod. My fingers dig into the arms of the chair in which I am sitting as though I must save myself from falling.

I can see now that there are two of them, a second man standing by the door into the kitchen. He does not have a gun, but he is taller than the other man and thin almost to the point of emaciation. He is wearing a T-shirt that says "University of Oregon," and crumpled jeans that look several sizes too large for him; the belt that bundles the cloth together around his waist has so much leather left over it could nearly go around him twice. It droops down his crotch like an obscene brown tongue. I try not to look at his face, as though that will keep me safe, protect me. They aren't wearing masks —and the icy thought grips me, that they must not care if I see their faces, that they may intend to kill me. I can hardly breathe from the fear, the horrible, rummaging fear.

The thin man is waving his arms in the air as though the room were full of flies.

"For Christ's *sake,*" he says to his friend, "be careful with that thing!"

"You're coming with us," the first man says, ignoring his companion. His posture has remained absolutely rigid, the gun unwavering in his hands and extended towards me like some ugly handshake.

I open my mouth, say in a dry whisper, "What do you want?"

The second man comes forward then, holding his hands out to me, the way people do when they want to explain something. His voice is pleading, as though I am being a difficult pupil. "Now look. You'll be okay. Just don't make trouble. All we want is the money."

"Take what you want," I say. "There's my purse." I point to where it is lying in its usual place on the end table. "Take what you want."

The man with the gun gives a derisive cough. "Don't get cute, lady. You know what money."

I look at him dumbly for a moment, and then suddenly it is clear. It must be Stewart's money they want. My God. "You're kidnapping me," I whisper.

"That's right," the thin man says. "Get your coat." He comes up and grabs my arm, jerking me to my feet. "Where is it?"

I point to the hall closet. He pulls me along, his fingers like a clamp on my elbow. The man with the gun turns slowly, keeping me in his sights. "For Christ's sake, don't point that thing at me," the other man shouts. "She's not going to get away. Christ."

The one with the gun says something angrily that I can't hear, but he bends his arm at a right angle and points the gun up at the ceiling, his left hand still clutching his right wrist, the way I have seen it done in movies.

The man beside me jerks open the closet door, gestures inside. "Which one?"

I look at all the coats. Stewart's old blue windbreaker and Chris's summer jackets that she didn't need in Edmonton are on the left. Mine are on the right. How can I choose only one? It is as though the house were burning and I have time to save only one thing of the many I love. My hand reaches out, trembling. I touch the long fur, soft as water to my fingers, then the grey cloth coat, then the navy jacket.

"Is it cold outside?" I ask.

"Not bad," the man says. We could be acquaintances, making polite conversation.

"Maybe I should take a sweater, too."

"Okay, sure, come on."

I pull the grey cloth coat from its hanger, which falls clattering to the floor. The man with the gun says, "Jesus!" behind me but I don't turn around. I pull a wool sweater, too, from the shelf above the coats, and the man lets go of my arm so that I can put it on. I almost ask him if I could go change into another dress, or slacks, because I am wearing only a thin cotton housedress, but the thought of them following me down to the bedroom is too terrifying. He takes the coat and holds it open for me, a grotesque chivalry. I have to try two or three times before I can plunge my arms correctly into the sleeves.

"Let's go." He starts to pull me toward the kitchen, and perhaps for the first time I fully understand what is happening. My feet simply stop moving.

"You can't do this," I say, my voice sounding calm, although the panic is surging up in me like black water. "I can't just . . . leave," and I gesture around the living room, at my blue sofa with the two matching chairs and love seat, at the stereo in the corner, at the bookcase and buffet, at the TV

with the afternoon faces still talking on it, at the windows
with the sun pasting on them the perfect view of the north
shore mountains. "I can't," I say, as though it were obvious,
as though it were something they simply did not understand.

The one with the gun gives a nasty laugh. "Yes, you can,
sweetie. Believe it. Get her outa here," he says to the other
man, who gets a grip higher up on my arm and jerks me forward, toward the kitchen, toward the door outside.

"Wait," I say. I am taking deep breaths, trying to remain
calm. This is really happening. I have to deal with it. "I need
to get my shoes. They're by the TV."

The one holding me hesitates, as though it might be a trick,
but when he looks down at my bare feet he lets go of my arm
and pushes me back into the living room. I walk slowly to the
TV, my mind flying frantically around the room like a trapped
wasp, but there is no escape except through the doorway in
which they are standing. I put on my shoes, grateful that they
are not ones with heels, are ones I could run in. Then, I pick
up my purse and reach over and turn off the TV. "—what you
want—" Felicia is saying. I watch her face contract to a pin-
point. When the screen is completely blank, I look up at the
two men across the room, who are watching me as though
they might be amused.

"Come on." The one with the gun waves it at me, and,
clutching my purse, I walk toward them.

"The note!" the other one shouts. "Jesus, I almost forgot.
Where's a good place to leave it?" He is talking to me. A
ransom note. It must be a ransom note.

"The kitchen table," I say.

He goes into the kitchen, lays a piece of paper carefully on
the middle of the oak table. "Here?"

I can hardly stand to look at him standing there, his long
thin arms swinging like ropes at his side, looking at my im-
maculate kitchen without the deference of the visitor.

"Yes," I say.

"You better be right," says the one with the gun, moving
up beside me. "It's what'll keep you alive."

I nod. My fingers dig into the door frame so deeply I can
feel the wood mounding up under my nails. My pulse ham-
mers at my throat.

"He won't pay it," I blurt. "He won't. I know he won't."
Instantly I regret saying it. Did I think they would say, *Oh,
well, then, in that case,* and let me go?

The one in the kitchen looks at me carefully. "You better
be wrong," he says.

"Yeah," his friend says, snickering. "You better be
wrong."

"Hel-lo!" They both jump as the cheerful voice suddenly
fills the kitchen. I cringe as though I can already feel the bullet go through me. "Hel-lo!"

"What the fuck—"

"It's only Buddy!" I cry. "A budgie, a budgie bird!"

They stare at Buddy, hopping now excitedly, a blur of
blue, around his cage on top of the fridge. "Hel-lo!" he says.
"Want a beer?" I am the one who taught him to say that, although the phrase is one Stewart suggested.

They begin to laugh. "A bird!" the thin one says. "A bird!
Want a beer?"

"Want a beer?" Buddy says.

The one with the gun aims it at Buddy, squints along the
barrel.

"No!" I shriek. I have to stop myself from reaching for the
gun, trying to pull it from his hands as though he were a child
not realizing he was playing with something dangerous.

"Put it *down!*" the thin one shouts. "Jesus, will you grow
up?" He slaps the kitchen table so hard the note on it trembles. Buddy squawks in alarm. "You think he's going to give
an eyewitness account to the police or something?"

The one with the gun hesitates. "Maybe," he says. But he
lowers the gun, reluctantly.

"Let's get out of here." The one in the kitchen gives a last
glance around and then moves toward me.

They arrange me between them like orderlies escorting a
patient, and then we shuffle to the front door, which is standing open, with no sign of a break-in, although I am sure it was
locked. At the Neighbourhood Watch meeting a few months
ago the woman from the RCMP said we should all have dead
bolts installed, that locks like ours inside the doorknobs are
easy to open, and Stewart and I both nodded and said to each
other, "Yes, we'll have to get ours changed," but we never

did, we never did; too much else happened for us to even think about it again.

When we reach the door the one with the gun puts it into his coat pocket, but he leaves his hand there.

"Okay," says the other one, his voice panting a little, as though he had been running. "We're going out to the car now. It's right in front. Chuck will drive. You and I will get in the back."

"One false move and you're dead," says the one called Chuck.

"Shut up!" shouts the other one. "Jesus!" He turns back to me, his voice softening, almost kind. "Do you understand? Just walk slowly, and don't say anything. Anything."

I nod, swallowing. *One false move and you're dead.*

As we step outside, the sudden fresh air pushing at us makes me feel a little dizzy. They press up closer to me, and, slowly, like one multilegged organism, like some parody from a movie, we move toward the green Chevrolet parked in the driveway. I look around at the huge Douglas fir separating our property from the adjoining ones, at the lawn and then the pasture looping in green parabolas down the north slope, and I can feel, of all things, rage butting at my forehead, rage, because we have paid so much to have our privacy, our five acres as far south of city as possible, on Zero Avenue, the U.S. border a thick buffer of trees protecting us from noise, from neighbours. My eyes swing desperately at the trees like an axe, but of course they see no one, no one. In the pasture I can see Blackie raise his head and look at us, thinking perhaps we will come to feed him. Silky is lying in her favourite place on the hood of my car, and she stares at me with her large flat face and beautiful eyes. *Help me,* I think at her, *help me.* But she only curls herself up tighter and watches us impassively. Stupid thing, I think angrily. We should have got a dog instead, the way Stewart wanted, a nasty Doberman with lots of teeth and a possessive personality, who would come snarling now at the two men opening the doors to their car and shoving me inside.

The one behind the wheel, Chuck, slams the door and begins to laugh, thick hysterical "huh-huh"s of sound.

"Easy! Jesus fucking Christ, it was *easy!*"

The one in the back with me shouts, furious, "Drive, you asshole! You think it's over? Get out of here!" He pushes me over against the far door and slams his own shut.

My mind jumps with hope as I press against the door. They will probably turn down Pacific Highway, and when they reach the traffic light at 8th Avenue, where the store and service station are, if the light's red I could leap out. The man with the gun is in the front seat; he wouldn't be able to react quickly enough, or perhaps even see me, as I stumble into the store—its door opens inwards (I close my eyes visualizing it), and I can push the doorstop, which is just a box, out of the way and let the door slam shut behind me; maybe I can even lock it, and I will scream at the clerk to phone the police. There are at least three other people working in the service station this time of day; surely the kidnappers wouldn't take them all on—

My palms are sweaty with the excitement of planning it. Chuck pulls out of the driveway, makes a right-hand turn onto Zero Avenue. Yes, he is heading for Pacific Highway. He could, of course, turn south on it, but there is only the U.S. border that way, and surely they would want to avoid the stop at customs.

If the light is red: I've a 50 per cent chance. I reach for the door handle, getting ready.

The handle is gone. When I look down I can see where it has been removed. I touch the place, a moan pushing up into my throat, leaking from my lips the way stuffing is leaking like spittle from the hole in the door.

The man beside me must have heard. He looks at me, sees my fingers where the handle should have been. I jerk them away.

"I'm sorry," he says. I stare back at him. He sounds as if he really means it.

The car accelerates, a bullet speeding away. I turn so quickly to look out of the rear window that the man beside me tenses, reaches his hands up slightly as if to defend himself but drops them when he sees all I am doing is looking back at my house. It is not I being taken away; it is my home, my lovely safe home. Tears push up into my vision, and then I am crying, awful hiccupy sobs, the sounds of mourning.

CHRIS

When I step outside the Humanities Building the Edmonton cold splashes like acid on my face. God, I hate this climate. But I've chosen to be here. I've no right to complain.

I put on my thick Army & Navy mittens that make my hands look like two black clubs at the end of my arms, pull the belt on my coat tighter, and set out for home with that fast hunched walk people here have evolved. It certainly has smartened up my cardiovascular system; my pulse rate must be half what it was in Vancouver.

The snow snaps under my feet. I pass a yard where two children are trying to build a snowman; in their heavy coats they look like little astronauts wearing space suits so pressurized they can hardly bend their arms.

It takes me fifteen minutes to get to the basement apartment I share with Murray. The house is old but well cared for, owned by a widow whose husband was somebody important at the university. His portrait still hangs on the wall in the Rutherford Library, and twice I've seen her there pretending to read but really just staring up at the picture. The first time it almost made me cry; the second time it only embarrassed me.

As I head around to my entrance at the back she opens the front door and comes out, dressed for a walk, with her awful dog, Dickie. Dickie is almost blind, but he sees something now, probably me, and makes some grating noises in his throat that are supposed to be barks. The white frill around his neck, from which he got his name, looks yellowed with age in the sunlight that leans in from the west, sticking rags of light to the trees.

"Hi," Mrs. Appleton says, starting carefully down the icy steps. "Just taking my Dickie for a walk." Dickie winces down the steps with her, grunting a little.

"Is he wearing his make-up today?"

Mrs. Appleton laughs. I'm sure she wishes she'd never told me about that. Dickie has no melanin in the skin on his nose, a problem apparently common to his breed, whatever that is, so his nose will sunburn easily. The vet told her to put something on it whenever he goes out, and the only thing he won't lick off is ink from a felt marking pen.

"Not today," Mrs. Appleton says. "I didn't think there was enough sun."

Dickie licks at his nose, just to check. He's had everything on it from Revlon Touch & Glow to Paba Gel SPF 15. There's no accounting for taste.

"Well," I say, shuffling my feet until they point toward my door, "guess I'd better get going."

She nods. "Murray's home," she calls after me. She draws out the first syllable, Muuuu-ray, sounding coy and sly. I give her a little wave and keep on walking. I know she's dying to know more about our relationship, but I wish she'd mind her own business.

I met Murray last August when I answered his ad posted on the bulletin board in HUB. "Student wanted," it said, "to share basement apt. in Garneau. Separate bedroom. $290 mo." Although it was more than I wanted to pay (and I was determined not to ask Dad for money, even though god knows he could afford it), after last year's dreadful experience in residence, sharing a room with a girl whose snores frightened the paint off the walls, I was adamant about having a private bedroom even if it was expensive. The ad didn't give a phone number, just the address, so I walked over to see it. When I rang the bell and Murray answered the door, of course I was disappointed to see it wasn't a girl; I'd heard about guys who just wanted a sex partner or a free cook and housekeeper, a mommy. But I'd liked the apartment and I liked Murray. I thought we'd get along, that I could handle him if he had expectations I wouldn't fulfill.

My foot slips suddenly on a sneaky patch of ice hidden under the snow, and I tense myself against falling, although I know doing that is wrong, is just a way of getting a broken bone if I do fall. I regain my balance, take a deep breath, the air like sandpaper in my throat, and shuffle along the walk to my door.

I hope Murray's in a good mood. We have this agreement where we try not to be crabby at the same time, but Murray's used more than his share of crabbiness lately. I can't really blame him. But I don't find it easy.

Last week, for instance, when I came home from night class, he was just sitting there in the dark, and when I turned the light on I saw the ivy lying on the floor, its pot broken and the dirt strewn all over the carpet. I was afraid to ask what had happened, if it had been an accident or not, so I just began to clean everything up.

He watched me for a while and then he said, "I warned her. 'You won't like it out there,' I said. But, no, she wouldn't listen, she said she was sick of being stuck in a pot, watching life passing her by outside the window, she wanted out, so what could I do?"

So then I knew it was all right. Usually it takes longer. A whole day sometimes. But it's as though he knows when I'm at my limit, and he stops, and switches over to his funny self that everyone else thinks is so charming. It's only with me that he lets himself go, sinking into misery and self-pity so deep I sometimes think nothing can pull him out. Well, it doesn't really happen that often. If it doesn't get any worse I can handle it.

When I open the door and step inside, stamping the snow from my boots on the mat, I can see him at the sink washing dishes and wearing the earphones, the long thick cord winding around behind him into the living room, like a black umbilical cord growing out of the stereo, which is probably playing something by Glenn Gould. Murray's a music major (the only two classes I think he's bothering to attend this year), and he's recently become enraptured with Gould; I think it has something to do with Gould dying or it might be because, if I can believe him, they put one of Gould's records into the Voyager capsule they sent out into space.

"Hello," I shout, but I know he can't hear me. Last week when I came in and he had the earphones on I wound up frightening him so badly he let out a terrified shriek when I touched him on the shoulder. Mrs. Appleton came rushing down the stairs and banged on the door that connects our two apartments.

"What's happened?" she shouted. "Is it burglars?" I could hear Dickie trying to bark, sounding like rocks rattling down a drain.

Murray shouted back, clutching his heart, "It's only Chris, Mrs. Appleton. She scares me sometimes. I'm awfully sorry."

I get so pissed off when he says things like that. He told me I had no sense of humour. I told him he had no sense of decorum. "De*cor*um!" he hooted. "De*cor*um!"

I take off my boots and coat and come down the steps. In the kitchen I can see, to my relief, the wheelchair parked beside Murray at the sink. When he resigns himself to using the chair he seems able to handle everything better; it's when he's struggling along using only the cane or the walker that he gets into such rages or depressions. It won't be long before he'll have to use the chair all the time, and I suppose it's when he's trying to manage without it that he has to face the fact that soon he'll have no choice.

I walk over to the stereo. I was wrong; it's not Gould. It's his new Berlioz tape. When he first played it and I asked him what he was listening to and he answered, "It's Berlioz," I said, "It's barely *what*?" and now that's become one of those embarrassing anecdotes about me he dishes up to visitors.

I turn the volume down. Murray stops conducting the orchestra with the soapy fork he's supposed to be washing and cocks his head a little to one side, the way Mom's budgie does when something surprises it. Then he turns around and sees me and gives me a grin and yells, "Hi!" I see he's wearing his T-shirt that says "Up With Down's Syndrome," although of course it's not Down's syndrome he has. It's MS.

He's handsome when he smiles. When he doesn't, his face has a long droopy look, with no particularly prominent features, (except maybe for his ears, which he insists are so big they should move out and find a place of their own). When I first met him I remember thinking he looked a bit like a sheep. But when he smiles his whole face picks itself up, and even his eyes, which slant downward at the outside corners, lose their mournful look and seem to curl upward. He's flabbier than he'd like to be, the lack of exercise, I suppose, and whenever he steps on the scales he whimpers and whines, but after half a day of fasting he's back into the ice cream, saying he'll get into jogging when the summer comes. He's put a sign on the refrigerator saying "No Thyself," but it hasn't helped. "An ass only an upholsterer could love," he moaned yesterday, passing the full-length mirror. If I tell him not to put himself down like that, he'll say, "If I don't, who will?"

"Don't shout," I shout back now.

He reaches up with his left hand to pull the earphones off, and I can see his fingers have a hard time curling around the band. But I don't offer to help. Unless he's fallen flat on his face and is in total spasm he wants me to pretend there's nothing wrong. So I let him fumble the headset off on his own and finally he pulls it down around his neck like some high-tech collar.

I pick up the dishtowel and wipe up the flecks of soap suds on the wall and window above the sink.

"You're home early," he says.

"Boychuck let us out at half-past. I think he's getting sick of us." I reach for a plate on the drain board, and my hand brushes Murray's arm. A spark of static electricity snaps at us. Something else about this climate I've had to get used to. "I thought it was my turn to do the dishes," I say.

"Well, yeah, sure, but, you know."

"You're so articulate."

He wipes the wet fork on my arm. "Fork off," he says. I slap his hand away. "Are you having supper here tonight or what?" he asks.

"Here. I guess. Are you planning anything?"

"An omelette. Avec les oeufs." He pronounces it *oafs*. "Et pois." *Paws,* he says, holding up the can of peas on the counter. "You know. The pois that refreshes. But I don't know if we have enough oeufs."

"Stop."

"Had an oeuf, eh?"

I snap the dishtowel at him before hanging it back up on its hook. "Well. Thanks for doing the dishes. I owe you one."

He digs the plug out of the sink and then lets himself drop back into the wheelchair, which he backs out of the kitchen. "Out of my *way*," he snarls at the refrigerator as his right wheel snags on its door.

It's too early to think about supper, so I go into my bedroom, a large comfortable room that gets a lot of sun even though it's in the basement, and dig out my English 363 notes. I have got to get at that essay. The tragic hero in *Death of a Salesman*. "Surprise me," the prof said. "Give me something original I haven't read a hundred times before." Well, what's there left to say about Willy Loman? I keep shuffling thesis sentences through my head, but all of them sound banal. *Willy Loman introduces us to the modern tragic hero.* Puke. *Miller creates a tragic hero whose tragic flaw is less inside himself than in the society around him.* It's been done. At least a hundred times.

"Chris." Murray's at the door.

"What?" He mumbles something I can't hear, so I have to get up and open the door. "What?"

"I forgot to tell you," he says. "Your dad called. You're supposed to call him back."

"My dad? Did he leave a number?"

"No. He just said to phone home."

"So he's at the house."

"I suppose so. I don't know. He said it was about your mother."

"My mother? What about my mother?"

I suppose Murray hears the alarm in my voice because he gives me a careful look and says, "*I* don't know. Call him and find out."

But I only stand there in the doorway picking at my thumbnail. About my mother. My mother is one of the things I came to Edmonton to forget.

"What's with you and your mom, anyway?" Murray asks. "Whenever her name comes up you get this cramped look on your face." He wheels his chair a bit closer, making me feel pinned against the door frame.

Mind your own business, I want to tell him, but I know that would just encourage him. So I shrug and say, "Just, oh, the usual stuff." I run my fingers stiffly through my hair.

"Such as?"

"Nothing special. We just don't get along that well."

I feel like kicking at his chair to make him let me past. I clamp my teeth tightly together. We can stay here the whole bloody day, but he's not going to pry anything more out of me.

And then, mercifully, there's a knock at the door.

"Oh, shit," Murray moans. "That's Nadia. I forgot she was coming over. Let her in, will you?" He backs his chair away and lets me escape to the front door.

When I open it there's Nadia, all right, sweeping into the apartment in a swell of fresh air and perfume without waiting for an invitation. I've never figured out her relationship with Murray. She's in his French class and has a grant of some kind to help handicapped students, but she seems to show up only when she feels like it and Murray can't really count on her to get him to all his classes. He seems satisfied with the arrangement, though, and he manages well enough most of the time now that Mrs. Appleton has put the ramp in so he can get out by himself in the wheelchair to the Handi-Bus.

"Hiya," Nadia says, pulling her boots off. The heels are so high and spiky I can't believe she trusts them on the ice. She is obviously in what Murray calls one of her secular episodes, which alternate with her religious ones, the latter character-ized by a messianic determination to get Murray to join the Church of the Holy Redeemer, or whatever its name is (Mur-ray calls it the Church of the Wholly Depraved), where she insists he will be healed. He even went once, but Nadia said his faith wasn't strong enough to drive the MS from his body.

But today she's obviously not thinking about religion. When she sees Murray she trots down the steps to him and begins a confused babble about school and boys and movies. I think she has a black belt in the non sequitur. But Murray just gives her his big approving smile.

"And then Wayne's asked me out for the weekend—"

"He's forgiven you then?" Murray asks.

"Who?"

"Wayne. I thought you said he was mad at you because of Michael."

"Oh, *that*. That was last week. Jeez, it was awful. I was in West Edmonton Mall with Michael, just having lunch, right, no big deal, but then Wayne comes in and here I'd told him I wasn't seeing Michael any more. God, I could just have *killed* myself."

"Committing suicide in the West Edmonton Mall is redundant," I can't resist saying.

Nadia gives me a blank look, but then I guess she figures it out and protests, "Oh, hey, the mall's a great place to go."

"So's the bathroom, but I wouldn't want to entertain my friends there."

"Come on," Murray says. "Don't be so critical."

It annoys me, his taking her side, and then when we're alone he says things like she drives in neutral and that the ivy has a higher IQ than she does. Well, who knows what he says about me to her. But I suppose he's right about my being too critical; I'm no judge of what people should do for fun. According to Murray my brain is so overexercised from studying it probably looks like Schwarzenegger's pecs—but studying is what I'm here for, after all.

After high school I worked for a year as a secretary in Victoria for an aircraft charter service, which, someone told me later, was owned by the Mafia; this seemed to explain a lot of things about Victoria in general. But the good thing about the job was that it convinced me of the virtues of higher education. Next year I suppose I'll try to get into a Master's program—I'm still getting A's so I might as well go on until I reach my level of incompetence. I don't know what I'll do when that happens. When anyone asks me about "career" I feel as awkward as Murray must when someone, determinedly optimistic, asks him what he wants to be. He usually just gives silly answers like "Old" or "King" or "Jurgen Gothe." Once he said something about an old homestead his grandparents left to him and his brother, but even without the MS I cannot see Murray as a farmer, not Murray, who says things like, "I've never done any manual labour more demanding than masturbation."

I can't bring myself to think about his real future. I know it doesn't look good; even in the time I've known him I can see where he's losing ground, although when he goes into remission I tell myself he's getting better. He's so determined not to be seen as someone who's sick that I actually forget about it sometimes, and when people say "poor Murray" I have to force myself to understand.

"Yeah," I say, giving him and Nadia now a generous smile. "I know."

"Phone home," Murray reminds me.

"E. T. phone home," Nadia giggles.

"Right," I say. Nadia drops herself onto the couch as I go to my room, and behind me I can hear her going on again about some other sexual adventure she's had. I hate it when she does that, not even thinking it might bother Murray, treating him like some damned eunuch. *Don't be so critical*—I know, I know. I'm careful not to slam the door behind me.

I sit down at my desk, stare at the picture of Willy Loman's back slouching off into the cover of his book. Finally I reach for the phone. I try to make my mind calm, ready for whatever my father has to tell me. Something about my mother. I take a deep breath, exhale. Then I pick up the receiver, punch out the area code, then the number that was mine for so many years. E. T. phones home.

P A T

There is only one light in the room, from a table lamp with a dim bulb throwing a smear of yellow on the floor beside the door. A window that I think might look out to the west has been so carefully boarded up with thick slices of lumber that even if it were daylight outside nothing more than a few threads of sunlight would be visible between the boards. There is a bed with clean sheets still smelling slightly of fabric softener, a desk with an ashtray and some magazines on it, an armchair with a broken arm. One picture hangs on the wall, a framed print of *Blue Boy,* looking so like the one I had once in my house I can almost believe it is the same one, brought here to make me feel at home. The clothes closet is full of empty wire hangers. Beside the closet is a partial bathroom, with a toilet and a sink and two brown towels folded in thirds hanging on the rack. The door to the bathroom has been removed; hinges like stubby fingers reach out from the jamb. The door leading out of the room into the rest of the house is, of course, locked from the outside. I can see where a new dead bolt has recently been installed. Perhaps they went to the same Neighbourhood Watch lecture on dead bolts as I did.

It is a tidy room, a room prepared for a purpose, for me. I have been here for several hours now; I don't know exactly how long because for some stupid reason I didn't put my watch on this morning. I hate not having it—knowing the exact time has always been important to me.

We are somewhere in Burnaby, I think. We turned off the freeway at the Willingdon exit, and then the man in the back seat with me forced me down onto the floor. I tried to keep track of where we went: a left turn, a stop at a light (or maybe a stop sign), another left—it was too confusing, a cruel experiment where you are blindfolded and compelled to depend on the decisions of others. When I got out of the car we were in a garage, nothing to help me differentiate this house from what are probably others just like it for blocks around.

We came in through the kitchen, then through a living room, both of them square ordinary rooms, with ordinary furnishings, old but not really shabby or messy: the chrome kitchen table with four chairs; the brown fabric sofa with the cushions worn down on one side; the matching brown arm-chair pulled up in front of the TV; a coffee table and end tables, with a pizza carton and two unwashed plates on them; the stereo, which looked expensive but not new, with many complicated pieces and huge speakers; a stand for records and cassettes and books (I tried to catch the names of some of the books on it, but they rushed me past too quickly). These were not, I remember thinking, the kind of rooms in which one would expect criminals to live.

But neither of the rooms was as clean and tidy as the one I am in, the one that has been especially prepared for me. I tell myself it is because there is some decency in them, some basic kindness—surely it is not a room they have prepared for a murder, blood littering the freshly vacuumed carpet. I shudder, look away from the floor, where I have glimpsed the chalk outline the police will make of my body. I won't think that way. They are extortionists, not murderers. They don't want to kill me. I remember the way the one looked at me in the car, the way he said, "I'm sorry."

But Stewart won't give them the money. He will phone the police, and they will set a trap of some kind. For the police it is all the same, if I am killed or not; their job is simply to catch the criminals. It doesn't matter to them whether they catch kidnappers or murderers.

Perhaps he hasn't found the note at all. Perhaps he never will. My fingers pick at the blanket on the bed, puckering the coarse fabric the way I can feel my face puckering as it tries not to cry. A helpless love for Stewart pushes up in me, like a bubble of air working its deadly way through the intravenous tube.

It happened about a month before he sold the business. He'd come home from work and slapped down on the kitchen table the two plane tickets.

"Fiji," he said. "We're going to Fiji for a week."

"What?" I held the potato peeler in my hand as though it were something whose function I had forgotten. The potato I had just finished peeling lay white and fragile as an egg in my other hand.

"Fiji. Next Thursday. I've got the time off. A holiday. A surprise." He tapped the tickets with his forefinger. "Really. We can get passports in a couple of days."

"But—it's so soon—you could have asked me—"

"I know you. You'd have come up with a hundred reasons not to go."

"Well, that's right. It's so expensive—"

"I've got enough *money,* for God's sake—"

"But can you take the time from work?"

"We're not busy now. John can handle it. We're only doing the Willowbrook contract. The Brewsters are all that's holding us up. We got the big trucks from Seattle. Pre-Con are getting us the CB covers."

"Well," I said vaguely. "Are you sure you want to leave in the middle of that?" I understood so little of what he did at work. When he talked about it, it was like another language, close to my own but not the same, crucial bits of the grammar changed. But he didn't expect me to understand, would get impatient if I asked for explanations, and sometimes my questions seemed only like polite punctuation to a monologue. It seemed enough for him that I listen.

"Yes, yes," he said. "John can handle it."

"But the house, and the animals—we can't just leave them."

"I've already asked George. He said he'd be glad to come and stay."

"Well." I put the potato peeler down and picked up the tickets, carefully, as though that would be a commitment. I suppose it was. "If George can come—"

"George can come."

Oh, he was clever. He knew that if he had George on his side I would be persuaded. George is my older brother, and it has long been a joke between us that he could tell me to walk on fire and I would, because in fact I did once, when we were little. He had read about firewalking in a magazine, how people could do it if they believed they could, so he made a fire in the backyard and when it had died down enough I started across, quite calm, I remember, and unafraid. Of course I burned my feet miserably, and my mother was so furious she threatened to sell George to the jws, who, she said, went door-to-door collecting bad children. I felt awful for getting him into trouble, blaming only myself for doing it wrong.

"Does it hurt?" he asked, touching the bandages.

"Not really," I said. Of course it did, but I couldn't let on.

"That magazine," he said. "It was lying. It said anybody could do it."

Strange it is this story we always tell when we reminisce. I suppose we would find it uncomfortable to talk about less dramatic times, those years when my memories are full of his generous affection, his patience with the waifish sister who insisted on tagging along despite the taunts of his friends. When adolescence came, tugging at us, he seemed to lose interest in me and we drifted apart, but after I was married and had the children we became close again.

"So you're sure you don't mind?" I asked him on the phone that night. "It's such a long way to come every day."

"I'll enjoy it. Really. It's just for a week. Gives me an excuse to get out of the apartment."

The apartment: he complains about it constantly but refuses to move. He got it about ten years ago, after his divorce, some kind of punishment for himself, I thought, but what seemed like a temporary arrangement has never changed, and there he still is, living alone in his tiny suite in the West End, chafing at its limitations but too lethargic to move.

"Well, if you're *sure*," I said.

"I'm sure, I'm sure. Go."

So we went. To Fiji.

"It's *beautiful,*" I said, pulling open the balcony door at the hotel outside of Nadi. The ocean lumbered in practically to my feet. Far out I could see it catch on the reef. My skin sucked in the sun like a salve.

Stewart stood looking out at the ocean, drumming his fingers on the door frame. "Yeah, it's nice, isn't it? Are you having a good time?"

"Of course," I said. "If I were at home I might be shovelling snow."

"So aren't you glad you came, eh? Just do something different, to break the routine, do something kind of crazy?"

"I suppose so," I said. "Still, it's a lot of money—" I was sorry as soon as I said it, thinking, now he'll get annoyed. I had no idea, then, how much money there really was.

But he only shrugged and gave his funny little laugh that always sounds too high-pitched for his big muscular body. "Oh, come on. This is a holiday. That's what money is for. Now let's get changed and go down for dinner. Did you see those Fijian waiters? They all wear *skirts,* for God's sake!"

And so we went down for dinner, where the uniformed waiters, enormous men who did indeed wear skirts, were cheerful and friendly. The breeze, smelling of ocean and plumeria blossoms, blew in lightly through the open restaurant. Stewart had several drinks, which made him chatty and louder than I was comfortable with, but no one seemed to care, and when we talked it wasn't about his business; it was about things we had done together many years ago, about the time we left the children with my mother and rented the cabin in Lillooet, except it had no heat and after nearly freezing there for one night we gave up and came back home.

"Our vacations never amounted to much," Stewart said. He had ordered some brandy and kept swirling it in the large glass, until a few drops lolled over the rim and splattered the red tablecloth.

"This makes up for it," I said. I wanted to say something more, something like, *I've never been more happy* or *I love you,* but I was too embarrassed—it wasn't the kind of thing people who had been married as long as we had could say easily, and I didn't want to sound childish, sentimental. I wish I had said it, now.

After supper, back in the room and in bed, I reached out for Stewart, running my fingers down the curve of his throat the way I knew he liked, but he only caught my hand and held it there in his and said how tired he was from the flight and how we had to be up early the next day for the cruise. He fell asleep almost instantly, the way he can do, still holding my hand in his on his chest.

The cruise. Oh, yes, the cruise. I don't want to think about it.

And how ridiculous it *is* to think about it. When here I am, locked in a room in some strange house while behind that door my kidnappers are deciding whether I will live or die—but what is the point of thinking about that, either?

I get up and walk around the room, tiptoeing, as though I must be quiet, not remind them I am here. I touch the walls, the boards on the windows, the desk, the headboard on the bed. Marking my territory. Perhaps these are the last things of the world I will ever see. I take a deep shuddering breath. I mustn't let myself give in to the panic; I know it is important to keep calm.

I walk over to the door which separates this room from the rest of the house and behind which I have heard the two of them moving about, the blur of their voices, sometimes raised into shouts from which I think I can make out words: ". . . such an asshole!" ". . . telephone, for God's sake!" A door slammed once and I thought they must both have gone out, but then I heard the television go on, the applause and phony excitement of a game show, and I realized only one of them must have left. Then the other man came back and their voices mingled with the TV's, all of it jumbled together, as it still is now, into ambiguous fragments.

I go back over to the bed, lie down, look up at the yellowing ceiling, concentrate on my breathing, try to make my mind blank and empty. I stare up with such desperation a headache starts to tap at my forehead and a little push of nausea cramps my stomach. Like seasickness. Like the cruise in Fiji. I close my eyes.

We left from the pier in Lautoka, on a ship with the rust bleeding out through the fresh paint. Our room was impossibly small, not space for both of us to stand up together, a bed barely wide enough for one, a miniature bathroom with water that hiccupped coldly from the tap. Three days, I thought in dismay, watching the wake from the boat spreading out behind us like two arms held out to the land.

"It'll be *fun*," Stewart said, seeing my expression. "Once we get out to the islands we'll be going ashore."

"Sure," I said, smiling at him. "It's an adventure." He was so eager for me to enjoy myself it seemed cruel to refuse.

There were about twenty of us on the ship, mostly Australians with extravagant personalities and difficult accents. At dinner the captain made us all introduce ourselves, and my heart sank even further. It seemed clear that we would be expected to socialize. I am not good at socializing. I watched Stewart: how easy it was for him, sliding conversation across the table as smoothly as waiters slid in the food. He talked mostly to the man across from us, a cheerful drunk from Melbourne who worked as a garbage collector. He took out his wallet and showed us a picture of himself and his truck, on whose side was painted, in huge letters, GARBO. After dinner there were more drinks. Stewart found a middle-aged couple from Toronto and pushed me over to meet them.

"Do *not*," the woman shuddered, "try the Fiji Inn." I assured her I wouldn't. "But you'd *love* the Hyatt." I assured her I would.

Eventually we were joined by a thin young girl who seemed to be travelling with the couple, although not related to them. "I'm not a tourist," she said. "I'm a student."

I laughed, which was not the right response, and Stewart gave me a worried look.

It was impossible for us to get any sleep that night in the tiny bed. We lay there clinging to the edges of the mattress and listening to our breathing, to the faint lisp of water around us. Early in the morning we heard the anchor bashing its way up, and we headed out to the Yasawa Islands. I was seasick the whole way.

"Try to keep your eyes on the horizon," Stewart said.

"Easy for you to say." My stomach twisted again, contractions painful as childbirth, but with nothing left to deliver.

"Ah, so you're chundering," said the Melbourne man, lurching past to his own cabin. I only stared at him over another upswell of nausea, afraid to open my mouth to ask what he meant. It meant, Stewart explained later, to throw up, abbreviated from "watch out under," a nautical term used by seasick sailors.

When we finally stopped, in a sheltered lagoon beside one of the islands, the water was smooth as mercury. We were ladled into the two motorboats by the crew, black and energetic young men who shouted at each other in their own language, a rich and fluid sound, full of consonants that seemed always to pull "n" and "m" sounds along with them. I liked listening to it, although I wondered what they were saying about us, sunburned hedonists with too much money. On shore we were given snorkelling lessons. Stewart learned quickly and easily, diving right under and spewing the water up through the pipe the way the crew did it.

"It's fantastic," he said, wading ashore, not caring that his chest hair had picked up some seaweed, that his stomach drooped chubbily over his bathing trunks. "There's a million fish here, the water's clear as air—and the coral! It's just amazing, all the colours."

"Coral?" said two of the Australians, in unison, as they walked by.

"Yeah," Stewart said. "There's a reef over there—" he waved over to the west. "I broke off a piece but I lost it."

"You should watch out for the coral police," I said. "They don't want you even to touch it."

"What?" The Australians looked at me oddly.

"Well, not here, I suppose," I said, laughing nervously. "But somewhere, Florida, maybe, you can get fined for touching the coral. It's so fragile, you see. It would break. Even if you didn't intend it to." I wished I hadn't brought it up.

The Australians laughed. "Amazing," they said. "Truly amazing." I could tell they didn't believe me.

"It's true," I insisted. "It was on CBC radio."

"Well, we'll be careful," they said as they walked off, still laughing.

"It *is* true," I said to Stewart. "They must think I'm an idiot."

"Ah, well," he said. "What do they know?" He shook the

water out of the snorkel and wiped the face mask with one of
the towels I'd brought ashore. "Your turn," he said, handing
the apparatus to me.

"I don't know," I said dubiously. The whole thing looked
like some grotesque sexual appliance.

"Try it," he insisted. "They'll show you. It's easy."

But I couldn't learn. The first water that leaked into the
face mask and got into my eyes made me struggle to my feet
in panic, pulling the mask off and stumbling ashore for a
towel. "It's okay," I told Stewart. "I can see as much without
the snorkel. You go ahead."

"You shouldn't be afraid," he said. "You should try new
experiences." He looked at me with such sadness, such pity,
that I turned away, angry. He watched me settle down under
a tree with huge fleshy leaves and then he went back into the
water.

After a while the captain came ashore from the ship and
gathered us together for a walk to one of the local villages.
Stewart picked up frangipani blossoms that lay everywhere
along the path and stuck them in my hair, in his hair, in the
hair of the couple from Toronto and in the hair of the girl
who was a student not a tourist.

The village consisted of about a dozen grass huts spread
through a clearing. People stared out at us from them as we
walked by scattering chickens and the occasional pig. A
naked boy lifted a listless hand to wave. Someone from our
group picked up a chicken bone and curled it between his
nose and upper lip. "This is from the last tour group," he
said. We laughed, uncomfortable.

"They *did* used to be cannibals, you know," the woman beside me said. "Did you see those little carvings they sell everywhere of missionaries in cooking pots?"

"Oh. I thought they were just of a man having a bath," I
said.

"A man having a bath!" she exclaimed to her husband,
and they both laughed.

"This seems like such an intrusion," I whispered to
Stewart as we continued our slow tour of the village.

He shrugged. "They must want it," he said. "They must
have some kind of arrangement."

When we finished our circuit of the village and began heading back to the beach, I saw that Stewart was right. There was some kind of arrangement. Sitting along both sides of the path were about a dozen women, and spread out on blankets in front of them were shell necklaces, hundreds of them.

"We wait here for fifteen minutes," the captain said. "You can buy some things if you want." And he preceded us slowly down the path, exchanging greetings with the women, who smiled and laughed but kept their eyes on us.

Stewart raised an eyebrow at me. "Well, I guess we'll have to buy something." He bent down to the first woman in the row. "Ni sa bula," he said.

"Ni sa bula," she answered, giggling, looking at the woman beside her.

Stewart picked up one of the necklaces, a pink one with shells braided in an intricate way that must have taken hours. "How about this one?" he asked me. "It's only a dollar."

I nodded.

Stewart pulled out a dollar for the woman, who took it and murmured something. "Vinaka," he answered.

"When did you get so fluent in Fijian?" I asked.

"Just kidding around with the crew. You know. It seems pretty easy to pick up." Someone jostled him and he stepped onto the corner of one of the blankets. "Tulou," he said to the woman, who smiled back at him.

As we moved down the path, so slowly I wanted to scream, he bought two more necklaces, and then held up all three, spinning them in the seasonless sun. "We can give one to Chris and one to Sue," he said.

Sue is Mint's wife. Mint. Just thinking of him now warms me, like the hot sun, like a hot drink you close your hands around. Dearest Mint. I know it's silly to still call him that, when his real name is Martin and he is hardly a child any more. I think it started because he loved mint wafers and Stewart would only have to say "Mint" and he would come running. No one calls him by his real name except his wife, who tries hard to make him into Martin, into someone he has never really been. Strange, when I think of it, that we never

had a nickname for Chris. She wasn't the kind of child one
gave nicknames to, I guess, always independent and private
and pushing me away when I wanted to hold her.

On the ship that evening we had a spectacular meal, a buffet enough for several shiploads more. Stewart went back
twice, heaping his plate with the ham and lobster and buttery
salads. I don't know how much wine we drank. Enough. Too
much.

After dinner we went back down to our cabin, to wait for
the evening entertainment, a musical group that was rowing
over from one of the islands. I sat on the bed filing a nail I
had broken, waiting for Stewart to finish in the bathroom.

Filing a nail. I spread my hands out in front of me now,
looking at my fingers. It was the fourth finger on my right
hand, I think. What name does it have, the fourth finger?
There is the thumb, the index finger, the middle finger, the
little finger, but what is the other one called? It must have a
name, something I've forgotten. I forget the names of so
many things lately. Last week I forgot the word for parsley,
my mind bumping around against "asparagus" and "alfalfa"
and "celery," unable to find the label for the frizzy green
leaves lying suddenly alien without a name on my kitchen
counter. The verbs are okay, but the nouns, the names—
sometimes they just disappear, coming back casually later
when I don't need them, like thoughtless teen-agers. It terrifies me when that happens. I told Stewart about it once.

"What's the name of, you know, that disease when you
keep forgetting things?"

"Alzheimer's?"

"Yeah. Well, I think I've got it. I forget the names of the
simplest things."

So he said he would make up labels and stick them to
things, "fridge," "stove," "door," the way they have to do for
Alzheimer's patients, and I laughed, even though I was afraid
it wasn't really funny, and said he'd have to wear a name tag,
too, and he looked down at his shirt, with *Daniel Hechter*
printed on a manufacturer's tag over the breast pocket, and
for the next few days I called him Daniel, and it was a joke
between the two of us, the kind of intimacy closer even than

sex that exists between people who love each other, and all the time there was the other disease living there in the house with us, living there for years and my not knowing it.

I was filing a nail. The fourth finger on my right hand. I looked up and Stewart was standing in the doorway of the tiny bathroom, one hand braced against the wall as though he was afraid of falling. And he was crying. Tears were running down his face.

"Stewart!" I said, amazed. I had never in my life seen him cry.

"She's pregnant," he said.

"What?" Chris, I thought, it must be Chris. She would tell Stewart before she'd tell me.

"I'm sorry," he said, his face wet and crumpled as a used tissue.

"What are you talking about? Is it Chris?"

"Chris? God, no." He gave a harsh lurch of sound like an incomplete laugh. "It's Yvonne."

"Yvonne? Who's Yvonne?"

"She works with me. You know. You met her once. Oh, Jesus, can't you see? She's pregnant. It's my baby." He paused. "I have to leave you, Patty. I'm going to leave you."

I remember how every word slammed into me, like bullets, nails driving straight into understanding. In novels it says, *It took a moment for his words to sink in,* but it is not like that at all. There is no waiting, no moment during which you can tense for the pain. It goes in straight and immediate.

It is trapped in my mind, that awful moment, like a wasp buzzing in a bottle. Stewart standing in the bathroom doorway, one hand against the wall, tears running down his face, and crying out at me, "She's pregnant. It's my baby. I have to leave you, Patty. I'm going to leave you." If the kidnappers killed me right now I would die with his terrible words still rasping in my head.

Soon after we got back Stewart sold his business, determined to be fair, to give me a good settlement, to pay me off for my years of faithful wifehood. I should be grateful, I suppose, that he felt such guilt, that I have not, like other women I know, been left penniless. I have simply been left. I was too numb to care about the money, although George insisted I needed a lawyer and hired one for me. Stewart made a good deal selling the business, to some big German company for a little over five million dollars, and a reporter from Channel 13 even came to our door demanding a story of local success, a millionaire with a happy marriage, so what could we do but pretend, anchor our smiles onto our faces and tell the TV cameras that, yes, it was a very good deal and that, no, we didn't have any immediate plans for the money. After the loans for the equipment were paid off, it was closer to four million, but even so it was an astonishing amount. Until then, I had no idea at all how well Stewart was doing, how much, as they say, he really was worth.

I stare down at my hands, folded tightly into each other, as though they were lonely and seeking company. The posture of prayer. I curl the fingers of my right hand a little tighter so the nails pinch into the back of my other hand. It is what you do to wake yourself from a nightmare. But I have only another nightmare to wake to, I think, looking around this stark room.

I get up and go over to the window, try and peer through the tiny cracks, but they are too small. Outside I can hear the faint drum of traffic and what could be children playing, voices high-pitched and laughing. I try to push my fingers behind the boards but not even my fingernails can squeeze between them and the wall; they are hammered on with nails that look more like spikes, heads big as quarters and pounded in so deeply the wood around them is bruised into small semicircles.

I go back, sit down on the bed, and look at the door into the other room through which I can still hear the shrill voice of the TV, the shriller punctuation of the laugh track. I try to imagine what program it might be, what time it is, but I seem to have less and less of an idea how long it's been since I looked up from my own TV in my own house and saw my life turn as bizarre as any television plot. Three hours? Five? Eight? I can feel the panic start to gnaw at me again.

Will Stewart be home yet and will he have found the note? *Home.* When Stewart goes home now it's to Yvonne's. The house on Zero Avenue is mine alone, or at least it will be when the lawyers are finished. Stewart has still been coming by every few days after work, collecting his things which he's removing in ineffectual little armfuls, but his real purpose, I'm sure, is to check on me, to see if I've hung myself from the chandelier or something. George says I should tell him not to come, that the lawyer wouldn't like it and that it's too hard on me, and I nod and say, "Yes, you're right," ashamed to admit that is still a part of my day I look forward to, the sound of Stewart's car in the driveway, a habit of almost twenty-five years impossible to break so easily, perhaps for both of us.

"You're sure it's okay?" he asks whenever he comes, glancing furtively around as though he were looking for hidden weapons, clutching odd bits of clothing and papers, things he has every right to take, and, yes, I assure him as we slide past each other in the hall, yes. Oh, we are determined to be civilized, to stay friends.

And today—will he come again today? He didn't come Monday or Tuesday, so perhaps he will. I have to hope he does. He might call from work and when there's no answer he will drive by and there will be my car in the garage but no answer when he knocks and knocks, and at last he will use his key and come in shouting my name, expecting the worst. And what *is* the worst? Will he hold the note and think, well, thank God at least she hasn't killed herself.

I thought about doing it. Killing myself. A long, long sleep, not to wake any more to that horrible pain of knowing you are alone, abandoned by the one you have loved as much as your life, for most of your life. It doesn't even have a name, this pain. Mourning, grief: they are the words of widowhood, honest bereavement, not this, this grey world where your friends do not cry with you or send sympathy cards; they say things like "What a bastard!" and "You should find some young stud yourself" and "Make sure your lawyer makes him pay."

I close my eyes, take a deep trembly breath. Kidnap victims shouldn't think about suicide. Besides, I decided against it. I decided to live.

I reach my hand to my throat, an old nervous habit, to fumble with my pearls, which I'm not wearing, which I haven't worn for years, actually, although they were a wedding gift from my mother and once I wore them almost every time I went out, not as jewellery as much as for the comfort of them. Until the day Chris, watching me roll them absently between my fingers, said, "You should see what they do to oysters to make them produce those."

"What?" I had no idea what she was talking about.

"Pearls. What they do to oysters to make them produce pearls."

"They put a grain of sand in. And the oyster builds the pearl around it." I was pleased with myself for knowing. "It's not unnatural."

She laughed, her cynical laugh that was too old for someone her age. She was barely in her teens then. "Of course it's unnatural. They torture the oysters, pen them up between two layers of wire, for years, and then they kill them, just rip them apart, to look for the pearl. Sometimes there isn't even one. I saw it on PBS," she added, the touch of authority she knew I wouldn't dispute. When I didn't say anything, she continued, "It's only calcium, you know. Layers of calcium."

"Thank you," I said. "That was very educational."

When we came home that evening and I took off my pearls they felt cold and unfamiliar in my fingers. I put them away in my jewellery box and now wear them only with my black dress that has nothing else to match it. But sometimes, like now, my fingers still reach up for them at my throat, and I feel only my naked skin, soft and vulnerable and loosening with the years, something temporary, a dressing over a wound. I drop my hand, shove it into my pocket where it clenches itself into a fist.

Through the door I can suddenly hear the mutter of voices rising over the TV, and I get up and walk closer, straining to make sense of them.

" . . . *your* idea!" That is one voice.

" . . . not *my* fault if . . ." That is the other.

" . . . not a *car;* it's an experience!" That must be the TV.

Then I can feel a vibration on the floor, someone walking toward me. I step back from the door, look desperately around the room for somewhere to hide, although of course I know there is nowhere. I back into the desk and stand there pressed up against it as it cuts into my spine. If I stay very still perhaps he will not see me, I think absurdly, some animal instinct freezing me into the hopeless camouflage of desk and wall. When I blink it feels dangerous to raise my eyelids, every movement a risk.

The lock turns and then the door opens, inward. It is the man who was in the back seat with me. I am relieved at least that it's him, not the one with the gun. He has changed his clothes but these fit him as poorly as his others did, their looseness exaggerating the thinness of his body. His face is thin, too, with a long washboard of forehead. He is probably only somewhere in his twenties, but his hair is limp and receding, the way it can be with blond men. His eyebrows and lashes are so pale it makes his face look unfinished, a picture on which the artist forgot to put the highlights.

He stands for a moment looking at me pressed up against the desk. "Come with me," he says then. "You've got a phone call to make."

I simply stare at him and don't move.

"Come *on*," he says, gesturing at the door, sounding annoyed now.

I nod and move toward him slowly. When I am close to him he takes my arm and pulls me into the living room, pushes me into the armchair beside the telephone. The other man (did his friend call him Chuck?) sits across the room, where he has been watching the television. I can see the bulge in his pocket where the gun must still be.

"Turn that damned thing off," says the thin one.

"Fuck you," says Chuck, but he gets up and turns the volume down so that only the picture remains on the screen, people's mouths opening and closing for no apparent reason.

The other one pulls a chair up close to and facing me, so our knees almost touch. I push back as far as I can into the armchair. I can feel a loose spring nudging at my thigh. "Now look," he says, "here's the deal."

"Hey, what's your name, anyway?" calls the one by the TV. "Your first name. We know your last name." And he laughs a little.

"Patricia," I say.

"Pa*tri*cia." He tries it out, exaggerating the middle syllable. "I knew a Pa*tri*cia once. We called her Patsy. Okay with you if we call you *Patsy*?" And he gives another little woof of laughter. Obviously it does not matter if it's okay with me or not.

I hate the name Patsy. Most people call me Pat, sometimes Patty, although when Stewart calls me Patty it's when he is most insecure or manipulative. But no one ever calls me Patsy, which is why I am glad this man wants to use it. If he doesn't call me by my real name it's something less of me that he can own.

"Yes, that's fine," I say.

"Good. And you can call me Chuck"—he jabs his thumb into his chest—"and him Lyle. Of course, they're only pseudonames."

"Pseudonames. Jesus," the one called Lyle says. "Are you finished? Can we get on with it?"

Chuck shrugs, looks back at the silent TV.

"Okay." Lyle turns back to me. His voice is slow and careful. "Now this is what you do. I'm going to phone your husband, and I'm going to tell him where to leave the money. Then I'll give you the phone and you just say, 'Hello, Stewart. I'm okay, but just do as they say. Please.' Got that? Nothing more."

"What if he's not there?"

"What d'you mean, *if he's not there*?" Lyle looks at me suspiciously.

"I mean—if he's not home yet." I'm sweating so hard I can feel it running down my arm and between my breasts.

"How late does he work?" Lyle asks. "He should be home by now. Jesus."

"Sometimes he works overtime. Quite late. Past midnight, sometimes." It sounds like someone else's voice, pleading, making feeble excuses. My shoulders and neck are aching with tension.

"Well, we'll try him," Lyle says grimly. "We'll keep trying until he answers."

I nod. And what if he's not there, how can I explain, when there is no answer, and again and again, no answer—

Oh, all of this is all so mad. If they only knew that Stewart was divorcing me, that the last thing he must want is to pay money to get me back. Perhaps he has engineered this whole thing, a plot to get rid of me. I can feel laughter rising in my throat like some loosened part of my intestines. Stop it. Stop it. I take a deep breath.

Chuck gets up and comes over to us, rubbing his hands up and down on his pants. "What if he forgets where to make the drop or something?" he asks nervously.

"Stop worrying. He won't forget. Jesus, not everybody's got a brain like a drain board."

"Maybe you could give him the phone number here so he can call us if something gets screwed up."

Lyle looks at him incredulously. "Jesus Christ!" he shrieks. He turns to me. "Do you believe this man? Do you believe it? God, oh, God." He walks over to the TV, shouts at the face silently reading the news, "Do you believe this?" His hands bounce up into the air, as though they were juggling. Finally he walks back over to Chuck and says to him, enunciating carefully, the way you do when you talk to a foreigner, "You can't give them our phone number. It would be like giving them our address. The police can find out addresses from phone numbers in minutes."

Chuck shrugs. "Okay, okay."

Lyle sighs, calming down. "Jesus." He shakes his head.

Chuck takes out a cigarette, slowly, lights it with a match that he folds out of a matchbook. "Well, get on with it then, Mr. Know-It-All."

Lyle turns back to the phone, to me. "Remember now what you're supposed to say?"

I nod. *I'm okay. Just do as they say.* He's a poet and didn't know it. I clench my teeth, desperately. I can't let myself get hysterical. My palms are greasy with sweat; I press them down, hard, onto my thighs, the fingers splayed out as though I want to admire them.

He dials the number he has written on the cover of the phone book. I can hear from the clicks that it is my number he is dialing. I sit tense and stiff as a dried-out sponge.

"This is it," says Lyle.

The two of them are hardly breathing. Ash from Chuck's cigarette falls onto the carpet but neither of them notice. The room fills with the acrid smell of sweat, of fear. Lyle holds up one finger, then two—it must mean the number of rings.

"Hello, Mr. Duvalier?" His voice is shaking a little. He sits down quickly in his chair as though his legs have surrendered his weight. Stewart. He's there. Thank God. "I guess you've found our note, eh?" There is a pause of a few seconds, although it seems longer. "She's all right. You can talk to her. Here." He thrusts the phone at me.

"Pat? Pat?" I can hear Stewart's voice small and metallic coming from the receiver.

"I'm okay," I say clearly. "Just do as they say."

"Pat—" His voice twists away from me, even though I struggle to hear, desperate for any syllable, as Lyle jerks the phone back.

"That's enough," he says. "She won't get hurt if you cooperate. Now get this straight. Tomorrow at four P.M. you put the money, no bills over hundreds, in a brown paper bag and go to Granville Mall. Stand under the marquee of the Capitol 6 Theatre. Got that? Four o'clock. You'll be contacted there. Talk to the police and she's dead." He hangs up quickly. The word "dead" hovers in the air over my head.

"Well, what'd he *say*?" Chuck shifts from one foot to the other like a man who has to go to the bathroom.

"He kept saying, 'Don't hurt her.' " Lyle looks over at me, his gaze fixing on my right shoulder. For a moment none of us say anything. Chuck takes a long pull from his cigarette.

"But he's gonna do it?" he asks.

Lyle pushes his eyes up from my shoulder, focusses them somewhere on the wall behind me. "I'm sorry," he says to me, his voice low and dull. "God, this is shit. This is goddamned shit."

"Is he gonna *do* it?" Chuck shouts, grabbing Lyle by the arm.

"Yeah, yeah, I guess so."

"I don't think the bank can release as much as you want to him by tomorrow," I say timidly.

"Don't give me that, lady." Chuck whirls on me, making me cringe back into my seat. "We know you ain't invested the money."

"How do you know that?" It is terrifying, that they know as much about us as they do.

"That TV interview," Chuck says proudly. "And you said

you hadn't decided yet what to spend it on. Well, us is what you're gonna spend it on."

"Still," I say, "the bank usually requires several days' notice before it will release large amounts."

"We didn't ask for everything," Lyle says.

"Stupidest idea of the year," Chuck sneers.

Lyle gets up abruptly and walks over to the bathroom, which is next to the kitchen. He goes in and closes the door quietly behind him.

"Don't you fucking shoot up in there!" Chuck yells after him. "Goddamn junkie! Don't you fucking go to pieces now!"

There is no answer from the bathroom. Chuck glares at me, his eyes like big black stones. He has the look of something assembled from a kit with mismatched pieces: large and expressive eyes with brows so perfectly shaped they could belong to a woman, but with a mouth that slices at an angle across his face, lips so thin they look like rubber bands stretched around the rim of mouth; a thick and stocky lower body but the kind of weak and concave chest that belongs to an asthmatic.

He kicks at the chair Lyle has been sitting in, and it skitters clumsily across the room. "Son of a *bitch*!" he shouts. I stay still, still. I have seen Chris have such tantrums when she was a child but this is different; this is a man and an adult, and the anger is the kind that could kill.

"You just better hope the old man comes across with the money," he says to me viciously. His face is clenched tight as cauliflower. "Well, you might as well get back into your room. The show's over." He stabs his cigarette into a crumpled smear of tobacco in the ashtray beside the phone.

I pull myself out of the chair, keeping out of his reach. He walks behind me, a dog at the heels of a sheep. I can smell his cologne or after-shave, soured with sweat. Old Spice. I can see the TV ads for it scrolling in my mind: the handsome young man, his muscular torso naked, in a sterile curtainless room that the advertisers must think is appropriately masculine. He is alone, strong, confident, the kind of man all women must want, the kind of man all men must want to be. I got some Old Spice for Stewart once, but he never wore it.

Thank God. If he and Chuck wore the same cologne—the thought makes my stomach lurch.

We reach the door into my room. My room. For a moment I can see my real bedroom behind the door, the soft ferny wallpaper I put up last summer, the large framed portrait of the four of us, a family, hanging over the bureau, the queen-size bed with its blue down comforter and matching sheets and pillowcases. My room. I clench my teeth. It is all I can do to turn the knob, open the door into another room, not mine, a room sealed tight as a coffin.

But when Chuck slams the door closed behind me I feel only relief—it is at least private, away from him, his gaze on me the coldest I have ever felt.

I circle the room, once, twice, the way thought must prowl the perimeter of one's skull, looking for more space, a way out. Suddenly I stop, looking at the door into the living room. I did not hear the bolt slide into place. I go over to it, my heart beginning to bash at my chest. I turn the knob gently, pull it toward me. The door moves, moves. It is not locked. I can hear the TV flare through the crack, a violent show, the sound of gunfire. I push the door shut again, let the knob rotate back, slowly, until the door is latched again. Not now. It is too early; they are both still awake. But tonight, late tonight—my heart is beating so wildly I am sure they can hear it in the next room, like in the story by Poe, the tell-tale heart.

Unless they have other plans for me before tonight. But I cannot think that way. I am alive now, and that is the only rule I have to go by. They could have killed me after I made the phone call—that is how it happens in news stories, the victim having served her purpose and then too dangerous to let live. But I am still alive, and the way Lyle reacted after the phone call—it is like the door cracking open, hope leaning in. It was what Stewart said that affected him. *Don't hurt her.*

Don't hurt her. I see Stewart standing in front of me on the ship in Fiji, tears rolling down his cheeks like rain, telling me his horrible secret. *Don't hurt her.* Well, it must mean he cares, at least; he may want me out of his life but not at any cost.

My mind leaps ahead, before I can stop it: *maybe it means he wants you back; maybe there's still a chance; maybe this will make him realize*—foolish fantasies. I chop my hand onto my thigh. "No," I say aloud to myself. I am supposed to be trying to accept that it is over. What good is going to a counsellor twice a week if I cannot absorb even her most basic advice?

I sit down on the bed, between my coat on one side and my purse on the other, like faithful pets I have kept waiting. I close my eyes and take several deep breaths, cupping my hands lightly into each other on my lap. It is the way the counsellor showed me to relax. You are supposed to empty your mind of images, but it is impossible. I see face after face, Stewart's, Mint's, Chris's, my mother's, George's, the two kidnappers'—they melt into each other, Stewart with Lyle's albino complexion, Chris staring at me with George's eyes.

In the Old Spice commercial, there was a duck decoy on the windowsill. The only ornament, a duck decoy. It seems like an important detail for me to suddenly remember.

A noise. When I look up, I see Lyle standing in the doorway. He is holding in front of him a plate with a sandwich on it, cut in half. He sets it on the bedside table beside the lamp.

"Thought you might be hungry," he says, with a tight smile. His eyes have an unfocussed look, and as he backs away he stumbles a little, as though his feet were toys left on the floor by careless children. He catches himself on the door frame and then goes out. He closes the door behind him. I listen, listen. After the longest time, after I am sure it will not happen, I hear the dead bolt rasp into place.

T
H
U
R
S
D
A
Y

CHRIS

"Maybe I should have waited," I say for the tenth time. The sun is already squinting in our eyes from the west, and we're not even in Kamloops.

"You were only on standby, anyway," Murray says patiently.

I know he's right, and at least now I'm moving, not just waiting for the damn fog to lift at Vancouver International. With all the cancelled flights, who knows how long I'd have been sitting at the airport in Edmonton.

Driving down seemed like the only alternative. I knew I could make it in one day, but of course I got a flat tire, so that meant hanging around Hinton for over an hour before I could get it fixed. Murray said we should just drive on the spare, but I couldn't bring myself to do that, the thought of being stuck in the cold somewhere with him too scary to consider.

Oh, it was a mistake, taking him with me, but he insisted he'd be able to handle the trip, that he had a friend he could stay with when we got there. He doesn't care about missing classes, and when I reminded him about the MS study he's involved in at the hospital and for which he's supposed to check in tomorrow, he just waved away my concerns and said missing once won't matter and he knows he's getting the placebo anyway. "Doctors treat us like mushrooms," he'd said after the interferon experiment, when he was sure he was improving and then discovered at the end he was in the control group. "They keep us in the dark and once in a while they throw some shit on us." But I know he volunteers for any new studies that come along.

I *am* glad to have his company, someone else in the car to help push aside the horror of what's happened. If I really let myself think about my mother, about what might be happening to her right now, my hands start to tremble on the wheel and I can't stop the things I see in the shadows at the side of the road, crumpled in the ditches. As though it weren't bad enough that Dad was divorcing her (something I have tried hard not to think about, not to care about, something that in my secret, vengeful, nasty soul even made me think *serves you right*)—and now this. . . . Guilt rushes over me, and I have to take a deep shaky breath and focus determinedly on the road and tell myself, this is not my fault, this is not something I wished on her, if I could have her back now safe at home I would do anything, anything—

I reach for the radio, turn the dial back to the left as far as it goes, but all that percolates up from the speakers is static.

"So," Murray says, thinking I want conversation, "your brother's with your dad now?"

"I guess so. He lives close by. Him and his wife. Sue. And kids. He's got two kids."

"And his name's Mint? What sort of a name is that? Some local Surrey dialect?"

"Just a nickname. His real name's Martin but when he was little he pronounced it something like 'Mint' and of course Mom and Dad thought that was so cute they started using it. Mint was good at being cute. He had an extra chromosome for it or something."

"Yeah, my sister's like that," Murray says. "I think she's a mutant."

He starts telling me about his sister, his words pouring against the side of my head, and I try to listen, to be interested, but my ear might as well be a stoppered basin.

I think about the last time I talked to Mint. He'd phoned to tell me about the divorce.

"She won't even get out of bed. She just lies there full of Valium, staring into space. Sue went over and cooked supper for her last night but all she ate was the dessert."

"What was it?"

"What was what?"

"The dessert."

"*I* don't know." Of course he was annoyed, thinking I was being flippant. "You should phone her," he said.

"I guess so."

"You should. You should call her."

But I didn't. That night I picked up the phone to do it but somehow the thought of her depressed voice at the other end saying "Hello?" and then my having to answer and say something useful or reassuring made me just stand there numbly, the dial tone whining at my ear until the recording accused, "Your call cannot be completed," and I put the receiver back down. I decided to send her a card instead. I wandered through the drugstore for half an hour trying to find something appropriate, even looking at the "Feelings" line, designed by a psychiatrist for emotional illiterates. But what was the right message, what should an estranged daughter say to her mother on the occasion of her divorce? Finally I just picked some dreadful Hallmark with a cat on the cover and no greeting, and I scribbled a note that I don't think even mentioned the divorce.

I stare at the black road, the way it disappears under the hood of the car, reappears on the horizon. We are on a flat stretch now along the Thompson, and beside us the grey water folds itself into itself. The way my mother would make bread, kneading dough into dough. It wasn't until Mint and I were both in our teens that I can remember her ever buying bread from a store. I wonder what she thinks now, wherever she is, of all those years of dutiful wife-ishness. The river suddenly heaves up a huge tree branch like an arm, and I look quickly away. I clench my right hand on the seat, until it feels as if the vinyl is pushing back, pushing my nails into their roots.

I glance at my watch. "Shit," I say. "It's almost six o'clock. It'll be after midnight by the time we get in."

Murray nods, winces, as though I were blaming him. But even if I were home now what could I do to help, anyway? I told the policeman on the phone everything I could think of, which was nothing at all, really. (*Does your father have any en-*

emies you know of? No. *Have you ever seen anyone hanging
around the house, any suspicious cars?* No, but I haven't lived
at home for years. *Do you think your mother could have, you
know, done this deliberately?* No, of course not. *Is there anything else you can think of that might be useful?* No.) I'm going, I guess, because Dad wants me there, Dad crying and
saying, "Oh, please, Chris, I wish you would come," and so
what could I say except yes, of course I'll come, a part of me
glad he would want me there, even if he could have Mint.

"Wear your seat belt," I tell Murray, noticing he hasn't got
it on. "We could get fined."

Murray grumbles, but he reaches up for the belt with his
right hand. The metal clip has slid down slightly and he can't
get hold of it. He turns around a little to look, but he can't
turn far enough to see, and when he fumbles for the clip with
his other hand he only knocks it down further. I can tell by
the clumsy wooden way his left arm moves that it's gone
numb again, a new problem that's only developed in the last
few weeks. I can't stand to see him struggling, so I pull over
onto the shoulder and start to brake.

"Don't you stop!" Murray shouts, flailing around in his
seat like an epileptic. "I can do it myself!"

"It's a hard one to get," I say. "I have trouble with mine,
too." I let the car coast to a stop, but I don't reach over to
help him. His face is red with exertion and rage. "Maybe if
you open the door," I suggest, casually.

But he won't do it, keeps grabbing and pulling at the belt
without finding the clip. I fiddle with the radio, engrossed in
the various frequencies of static. I pull up the sock on my
right foot, rub a little at my eye for an eyelash that may or may
not be there. I remember once, when he'd climbed up on a
chair to get something out of the cupboard above the fridge
and would have fallen except that I was there to grab him, he
said he had anosognosia, which, he explained, was a kind of
dementia where people forgot they couldn't do things any
more. Anosognosia: not knowing you don't know. Maybe we
all have it.

Finally Murray sinks back, panting, and then he opens the
door, and I can hear the clip rattle against the door frame. He

picks it up, jerks out a long sweep of belt and slams it into the fastener.

"All set?" I ask.

"Yeah," he snarls. I pull back onto the road. "Damned thing," he adds, giving the belt a contemptuous tug with his thumb. "It probably doesn't work, anyway."

"Well, at least now if I have an accident and smash us up you can sue me."

"If I got smashed up nobody could tell the difference."

"Probably not."

"Bitch." He gives me a punch on the arm, then leans his head against the headrest and looks down at his hands, which he arranges deliberately and tidily in his lap. "How many people with MS does it take to screw in a light bulb?" he asks.

"How many?"

"All of them. And then it falls out. They have to start over. It's very Sisyphusian."

"Uh-huh."

"Maybe God isn't really evil. Maybe he's just an under-achiever. That's a quote. Nietzsche. Or Woody Allen. I always get those two confused."

We drive for a while without talking, watching the car suck up the road.

"I should phone again," I say. "Maybe Dad's back by now."

And, as though I had only to ask, a service station appears up ahead on the right, and even from here we can see the phone booth outside it. I pull in and order a fill-up, although you should be able to buy a whole new car for what they're charging, and then I go into the phone booth and pile the counter full of coins. I took everything we had in our grocery-money jar, and all day I've been saving up change, wherever we stopped. I'm not sure how long I'll have to talk. It depends on what's happened.

The cold pulls itself up into the soles of my feet. I can't stop shivering. On the glass in front of me someone has written in felt pen: *Help! Being held prisoner on the* Tardis! It's some joke, I suppose, but it only makes me more apprehensive.

I give the operator the number and begin hurriedly plugging in quarters, as though she'll disconnect me if I'm too slow. I feel suddenly as though I'm standing in front of the vending machine in SUB pushing in coins, and somewhere inside the machine the mechanism is starting to turn, getting ready to deliver what I've paid for. By the time I've inserted enough money, I've spilled about as much on the floor as I've put into the machine. One ring. Two rings. I can see the phone sitting in its little kitchen nook, the extensions in the bedrooms, and Dad getting up to answer, with what news for me; what words have my coins bought?

"Hello?" It's not my father. It's Uncle George. Shit. I pull the receiver away from my ear, stop myself just in time from hanging it up. I'll have to talk to him.

"This is Chris. Is Dad back yet?"

"Chris! Where are you?"

"Is Dad back yet?"

"No, no, he's not. I'm waiting to hear something, too."

"Is there any other news?"

"No, nothing, I'm afraid. The police say they're doing everything they can. One of them is here now."

"Well, tell Dad I called and that I'll call him again later."

I can hear his voice making some reply, but I shove the receiver back onto its hook. My hands feel like chunks of ice, clumsy and numb, at the ends of my arms. They try to open the door of the booth but have forgotten how; they push instead of pull. I can feel panic, black and breathless, pouring over me. My teeth are clenched so tight I'm afraid I'll break them. At last I'm able to rattle the door open and lurch outside, gasping, as though I've been imprisoned somewhere with diminishing oxygen. I can see some of the coins I've spilled still lying on the floor inside the booth, but I decide not to go back for them.

I stumble over to the car, and Murray asks me anxiously, "Are you all right? What did he say?"

"Nothing. He wasn't home yet."

"Well, you can try again later," he says. I just sit there staring through the windshield. "I paid for the gas," he prompts. "We can go."

"Oh. Okay." I start the car, pull back out onto the high-way.

I'm so cold I can't stop shaking. I turn the heater fan up as high as it goes and the car lathers on the heat until finally Murray begins to pant histrionically.

"The horror," he wheezes, "the horror."

"All right, all right." I turn the fan back to where it was. Murray rolls down his window and the fresh air rushes in, the car a huge mouth inhaling. Murray sucks in a deep breath, lets it out, in visible, thin white ribbons.

"The air, apparent," he says. He closes the window.

We say nothing for several miles, just letting the landscape stream past our windows. Murray massages his legs, but when I ask if they're cramping up he says no, they're fine, and leans back. After a while he begins to sing, songs from old musicals, "Oklahoma" and "The Sound of Music," songs he knows all the words to and which he exaggerates absurdly, gesturing with both hands. Between songs he grins and says, "Pretty good, eh?"

"You have a dimple," I say, pointing at it on his right cheek. "How come I've never noticed it before?"

"Oh, I don't use it unless I have to," he says.

About an hour from Kamloops Murray offers to drive for a while, and I laugh, thinking he's joking, because he could never manage my Honda with its manual transmission, but he snaps back, "Okay, okay," and I realize he was serious. He sulks for a few minutes and then puts his seat back and yawns and tries to sleep. He does look tired, his eyes puffy, but not as bad as this morning when I dragged him out of bed and in-sisted we had to leave early. When he crawled into the bathroom he screamed so loudly he probably woke Mrs. Appleton upstairs. "Aaaaagh—a face worse than death!" Murray is not a morning person.

He finally gives up on sleeping now and jolts his seat back to a ninety-degree angle. "Entertain me," he demands. "I'm bored."

"What would you like?" I ask. "I can't sing like you can."

"Well, that's true." I make a derisive face for him. "So, let's see. Tell me about your first sexual experience."

"What?"

"Oh, come on. I've told you about mine."

"Ladies have more class than to talk about theirs."

"You're no lady. Come on, come on."

And for a moment I really want to do it, can feel the story rising up in my throat, the words shaping themselves around my tongue. I shut my teeth on them, bars clanging down on a prisoner about to escape.

So I tell him about Brent instead, the kind of story he's expecting, how in high school we went out a few times and then one weekend his parents were away so we made love in his room. Brent Waspinski. Wasp, his friends called him. God, I haven't thought of him in years. I remember lying there under him, staring up at the ceiling with the fish mobile slowly swimming around and thinking how his name suited him, how I was a piece of ripe fruit and he was a wasp, digging at me. It wasn't very satisfying for either of us.

"I think he was a virgin," I say. "He really didn't know what to do so I had to, you know, pretend."

"Pretend?"

"You know. Pretend. That he was, well, turning me on when he really wasn't."

"Faking orgasm! You sleazy women!"

"We do it for the guy's ego," I protest. "Would you rather have us get up and yawn and say, 'Wow, was that ever boring'?"

"Well, no, but, well, how are guys supposed to get any better unless you tell them?"

"It's not fair to expect girls to educate you. You'd resent it."

"How do you do it, anyway? I mean, how do girls fake an orgasm?"

"Well, let's see." I drum my fingers on the wheel. I think about Brent and then the guy I met at the college—god, what was his name? Jason. "First you act sort of uninterested, shy maybe or cold, depending on what the guy seems to prefer. When he begins, you just stay rigid but then, when he touches you one particular place, your breast, probably— most guys like breasts best—you just catch your breath, as though you were suddenly surprised. A little gasp or moan—

nothing overdone, mind you, just barely audible—is a good touch. Once he, you know, penetrates, you should writhe around more, turn up the sound effects, dig your fingernails into his back—we're assuming, of course, the old missionary position. And be sure to pretend to come just as he does— that's important to him. Afterwards, what you say to the guy depends on what he seems to expect. There's, let's see, a) the aggressive response, like, 'God, that was good'; or b) the shy response—a petite little 'Thank you'; or c) the witty response, such as, 'Have you patented that?' "

Murray is staring at me, his mouth actually hanging open, as though it's lost the fight against gravity. "Jesus Christ," he says. I don't often get the chance to nonplus him.

"Well, you asked me." I shrug.

"Is that *really* what girls do? Have *you* done that?"

"Sometimes."

"And there's no real way of knowing, I mean short of coming right out and asking her if she's faked it?"

"You could hook up a polygraph to the bed, I suppose."

"Well." Murray leans his head back against the headrest. "This has certainly been educational. The real difference between men and women. I'll have to tell my French prof. He asked us the other day, Quelle est la différence entre un homme et une femme?"

"Well, what?"

"La différence entre."

"I don't get it."

"It's a pun. On *entre.*"

"Oh. Okay, I see. And he told this in *class*? I think that's pretty poor judgement."

"Why? Everybody laughed. He's a good teacher."

"Well, you think the prof who told you how to play compusex is a good teacher, too."

"That's not something you play. It's not a game." His voice is suddenly serious, defensive. I glance at him, but he pretends not to notice.

"Oh?"

"You type out your fantasies on-line while you masturbate," he says, trying to sound casual. "What's wrong with that? Like *I'm* not into it—you need a modem, for one thing—but I don't see anything wrong with it. Handicapped people do it."

Handicapped. I don't think I've ever heard him use that word. Even now he's said it as though it didn't apply to him. He prefers the uglier words, *cripple* or *spaz* or *gimp.* Once when I left him waiting for me by my car in a spot labelled "Disabled Parking," I came back to find he'd drawn on the sign a picture of a banged-up car with a missing wheel. "You just make things worse by doing that," I said, and so he got mad and said what did I know about it, and a week later I noticed he'd written "Enabled Parking" on Mrs. Appleton's garage where I usually park.

So I'm tempted to call him on *handicapped* now, but I realize it would just provoke an argument, so I only say vaguely, "I suppose so."

"At least I would trust my machine not to fake it," he sighs.

"You and your machine," I say. Murray has more computer disks than he has books. He'll spend hours in front of his Apple with the "Caution: User is Unfriendly" sticker on the side, playing games which are pirated so he doesn't know the names or rules and has to keep guessing until he finds the right keys or makes the right move. Even when he does know the rules, he plays at too high a level for his skill. His favourite is one he calls The Game of Life (he says it's the generic name), which he plays at Level Six or, if he's really depressed, at Level Eight. If I walk past his room I can tell by the number of electronic explosions what mood to expect when he comes out. I can't stand to watch him playing, seeing his little green man on the screen get destroyed over and over by insurmountable odds. He says his physio recommends computer games to keep his fingers exercised. I say he plays to keep his brain unexercised. Sometimes he says we're both right.

It begins to snow lightly, then more heavily, flakes dabbing sucky wet kisses on the windshield, the wipers fending them off. Gusts of wind push snow like surf across the pavement. Soon it begins to stick on the highway, oncoming vehicles leaving tracks that look as if the road has just been travelled for the first time. The car is a warm envelope carrying us like messages into the dark. I put on the headlights. The wipers swing back and forth, back and forth. My mother, I think, my mother.

"We must almost be in Kamloops," Murray says finally, checking his watch.

I look at the mileage gauge. "A few more miles. Kilometres, I mean. I want to phone again. Dad must be home by now."

"You want to stop for something to eat?"

"Maybe we can get something to go. I don't really want to take the time to stop."

When we get into the city I watch for a phone booth and he looks for a place to eat, and we both see what we want at the edge of a shopping centre outside of town. Murray insists he wants to get out and get us the food while I phone, so I park in front of the restaurant, really just a tiny deli.

"Do you want the wheelchair?" I ask.

"No, it's so close. I can use the cane. There's no ramp anyway."

I go around and open his door, and he lifts his legs out. It doesn't look to me as if they'll be able to hold him but I know enough not to say so. I hand him his cane, and he lifts himself up, holding onto the car with his other hand.

"Go on," he says, annoyed, as I stand there watching him nervously. "I'm all right. The place is just two steps away, for god's sake."

"Okay. Get us something good." I make myself walk away, over to the phone. The parking lot is lacquered with a spray of ice, but I don't let myself turn around to look at how Murray's doing. At least the snow has died down, only a few thin flakes trickling through the air, skating across the parking lot.

I'm prepared this time to have Uncle George answer. I can feel my body straighten and tighten, the pores of my skin contract, getting ready for his voice.

But it's my father this time.

"Dad! It's Chris. I'm in Kamloops. What's happened?"

His voice is blurred and cut with static. "They didn't show up. I had the money and I waited and waited, over two hours and there was just nothing, nothing—" He breaks off; I can't tell if it's him or the poor connection.

"Did they see the cops, maybe, and get scared off?"

"I don't know, I don't know. *I* didn't even see them. They were, like, in plainclothes. But there was this patrolman in uniform who I guess didn't know what was going on and he was wondering why I was loitering around and he came up and asked me some questions and by the time I got rid of him, well, maybe they saw that and thought it was a setup, hell, I don't know, I don't know what to do now—" This time it is definitely his voice that breaks off, collapsing into awful little sobs.

"You'll just have to wait until they contact you again," I say, uselessly. I lean my head against the cold black plastic of the phone, trying to think of something else to say. "Is it more than one?"

"One what?" His words sound harsh and raspy, but under control again.

"One kidnapper. I notice you've been saying 'they.' "

He's silent for a moment. "I think it's more than one. I think the one I talked to said 'we.' 'We' is more than one, isn't it?"

"Yeah. So I guess there's more than one." A shiver sweeps over me, so intense the phone almost shakes from my hand. *Someone walking on your grave,* Mom used to say. God. This is all just some ugly nightmare. How can it really be happening, to people like us? I close my eyes and I can see my mother in her kitchen, the way I remember her, the way she should still be. I clench my free hand into my scarf, so tight my nails go right through, digging into my palm.

The operator comes on, wanting more money, so I plug more coins into her uninflected voice and she lets us continue.

"Why didn't you phone collect?" Dad asks.

"I don't know," I say. "I thought maybe you wouldn't accept the charges."

It's supposed to be a joke, but of course it doesn't work and Dad only demands, "Why wouldn't I accept the charges, for God's sake?" I mumble something which he doesn't bother asking me to repeat and then he says, "Look, are you still planning on getting in tonight? It's so late. And if you're only in Kamloops. I don't like you driving in the dark— there's been a lot of snow and some slides on the Coquihalla.

Maybe you should stay overnight there and come down in the morning. You could make it before noon even if you went through the canyon."

I bite down on my disappointment. It sounds as if he doesn't care when I get in. But of course he's right—it *is* a dangerous drive in the dark. Maybe we *should* stay over. He's my father again—the man in charge, the man who knows what's best.

"Well, if you think so, Dad, okay, maybe I will."

"I just don't want to have to worry about you, too," he says.

"I know," I say. "Is Uncle George still there?"

"No, he's gone home. He was just watching the phone. But Mint is here. He's staying the night."

"Oh. Well, I'm glad Mint's there."

Then there's silence on the line, static snapping up stray syllables from other conversations. I can hear the word "franchise" break through from another connection.

"I'll see you tomorrow, then," Dad says. "Phone before you leave if you want. Collect."

"Okay." I wait for him to hang up, but after he has I just stand there holding the receiver, waiting stupidly for something more, anything. My head feels tight, thoughts revved up but with no place to go. Gridlock of the brain.

Finally I hang up and mince my way back to the car, where I can see Murray sitting with his door open and his legs sticking out. I get in and he hands me one of the ham and cheese sandwiches he's got us; I've chewed ends of pencils with more flavour, but we gobble them hungrily as I tell him about the phone call. He shrugs and says, "Fine," when I suggest we stay here overnight.

I swallow the last of my sandwich. "Close the door, will you?" I say, wanting to hurry him along. "It's freezing in here."

He sets the remainder of his sandwich on the dash and says, carefully, "Well, I can't, you see. My legs have gone into spasm."

"Well, why didn't you say so?" I can't keep the frustration from my voice. I get out of the car and go around to his side, and together we tug and strain at his legs, which refuse to bend. It's like trying to fit two logs into too short a box. Finally one knee bends enough for us to shove the leg past the door frame, and then Murray leans sideways so we can push the other leg inside. When he straightens up, the pressure on his feet from the floor of the car bends his knees slowly into a normal sitting position.

Both of us are sweating with exertion, but we don't say anything and we don't look at each other. I hope he doesn't see how frightened I am—what if he gets worse? I was barely able to manage him this time.

I get back into the car and we slither out of the icy parking lot and onto the Trans-Canada.

"I was just sitting too long," Murray says finally.

"Well, we'll stop soon," I say. The truck in front of me fishtails on the ice, and I have to stop myself from slamming on the brakes. The truck straightens out, and I ease my foot back onto the gas. An accident—shit, that's all we'd need now.

"So, anyway," Murray says, resolutely calm. "If the kidnappers didn't get the money, will they set up another rendezvous?"

"I don't know. Dad doesn't know. He's just waiting by the phone hoping to hear from them again."

"So what does this mean for your mom, do you think?"

"I suppose it's possible they've killed her." Before I can stop them the words are out, at their most brutal and unambiguous, and they fill up the car like words said by someone else, a news bulletin on the radio.

"God," Murray says. "Surely not. You can't even think that."

I nod. Of course he's right. It's as though I had to voice the most horrible thing possible. *What's the worst that could happen?*—it's what Dad would always ask when as children we were afraid to try anything new, and of course the worst we could conceive of never happened, kept at bay by our imagining it.

My need for the worst not to be true now surges up in me so strongly I start to shake. *Please be all right,* I plead to the god I don't believe in, *be all right Mommy and I'll forgive you forgive you forgive you.* I can feel sobs bunching up in me,

and Murray reaches over and spanks at my arm a little, trying
to be comforting.

"Yeah," I say, giving him a skinny little smile.

"It'll be okay," he says. "Try not to worry."

On the long hill outside the city I pull into a big motel with
a splendid view out over the city and river valley; the mountains jag sharply along the horizon like a child's scribbled
drawing. I ask the clerk for a room that's wheelchair acces-
sible and has twin beds, and she looks at me in alarm, as
though I were proposing something illegal.

"My friend is handicapped," I explain patiently.

"Like Rick Hansen," she exclaims.

"I guess so."

"He came through here, you know. In a wheelchair."

"Oh. Really."

"Your friend know him? Rick Hansen?"

"Of course. All people in wheelchairs know each other."

She misses my sarcasm, of course, which is a relief; her
kind of prejudice is after all better than the other kind. Now
that she has us figured out, she becomes excessively helpful
and assigns us "a really neat room" on the ground floor, only
forty dollars. I pay with my credit card, as though I were an
expert at this.

After I park in front of our unit Murray doesn't complain
when I hoist the chair out of the trunk and wheel it over to
the passenger side. On the back of the chair is still the sticker
I bought him a month ago, thinking he'd find it funny. Originally it said, "Life is hard, then you die," but Murray said it
would be funnier if you left off the good part, and he tore off
"then you die" before he stuck it on.

He manoeuvres himself into the chair, and, although his
legs are bending now, I can tell by the way he has to lift them
with both hands that they're not as good as they should be,
and I doubt he can walk at all with just the cane. He wheels
himself into the room as I collect our bags, and we exclaim at
the size of the place, which has two double beds and seems
larger than our whole apartment. Maybe it's only because
we've been trapped in a car for ten hours.

"Well," Murray says, "too bad we ate. We could go down
to the restaurant."

"There was a bar," I say. "Maybe we could go have a drink."

Murray looks surprised; I'm not exactly a big drinker. But he's eager to go, so we head down and order some beer, which I temper with tomato juice, and we listen to the band, a country and western group which throws in the occasional old Beatles song to sound, I suppose, more modern. The band is so loud that when we try to talk the music only seems to blow our words back into our faces.

"Qu'est-ce que babblez-vous?" Murray shouts, cupping his ear, but it seems too much effort to keep shrieking at each other, and eventually we give up. I sit and let the beer numb my stomach, the music homogenize my brain.

It's eleven o'clock by the time we head back to the room. We're both a little drunk, and Murray uses it as an excuse to make atrocious language mistakes; it's like listening to a foreign movie without subtitles. Outside our room he has a collision with a bush, to whom he apologizes profusely. I hope the manager isn't watching; this isn't the way Rick Hansen would have behaved. Inside, we move aimlessly around the room, not sure how to go about getting undressed and going to bed now that we have to sleep in the same room. Murray tosses me one of the mints in the ashtray on the table, and unwraps the other one for himself. The cellophane crackles in our hands like static.

"You know," Murray says, "the first time I ever stayed in a hotel, I think I was seventeen, it was at one of those bizarre Christian youth conferences at some fancy hotel in Jasper. Well, some of us cut out to the bar and got drunk and when I went back to my room I just passed out on my bed, and the next morning when I got up and looked in the mirror I saw the side of my face and neck was all covered with this ugly brown growth. Now I'm talking fear. I thought God had got me good, that he had moved in one of his mysterious ways. My roommate came in and screamed at the sight of me and so on. Well, eventually we discovered it was the chocolate mint they'd left on the pillow. That's why," he says, tossing the cellophane about two feet short of the garbage can, "they no longer leave chocolate mints on the pillow."

"You made that story up," I say.

"Now think about it. Who could make up a story like that?"

I throw my cellophane at him, and he wheels away, in exaggerated evasion, over to the window, where he starts to pull closed the curtains, which are the dull grey colour of rotting raspberries. "Oh, oh," he says. "Freddy Krueger's out there getting a manicure."

"Ha, ha."

"I'll protect you, doubting damsel. Conan the Cripple has a black belt in wit. His tongue is licensed to kill. It goes straight for the jocular." He gives me his lizard-lips smile and goes over to the TV and turns it on.

It's an old set, and when it finally warms up we discover it's not on cable so only two channels come in clearly enough to watch. Both of them are showing news. A fire is burning on one channel and on the other a woman is reading something from a piece of paper while a small white square on the screen behind her shows a picture with numbers on it and an arrow pointing down. Something is falling, interest rates, the dollar, the sky, who cares. Then another picture flashes into the square and suddenly I'm terrified to watch, can imagine the next square or the next showing a photograph of my mother, the announcer saying, " . . . was found on a logging road with—"

"Turn it off," I demand.

Murray does, reluctantly, giving me a puzzled look.

"It's just . . . I'm afraid of seeing news about Mom," I explain. I won't let myself think about her—you can choose what to think about. I stare around the room. Wallpaper. Suitcase. Window. Murray.

He slaps his hands down onto the arms of his chair. "Well, then maybe we should just go to bed."

"I suppose."

I leave him fiddling with his alarm, a complicated tiny travel clock, and take my suitcase into the bathroom and put on my pyjamas, watching myself in the large mirror above the sink. The silver has started to chip in the bottom corner, and my throat looks like an old painting, full of tiny dark cracks.

Whenever I see my reflection in a mirror I try to make my thoughts neutral, unevaluative. It started when I was thirteen.

A lot of things started when I was thirteen. I turn out the light and go back into the other room.

"I'm finished in the bathroom," I say.

"About time." Murray wheels over with his pyjamas on his lap but the bathroom door is too narrow to let the wheelchair through, so he leaves it there and pulls himself into the room with his hands on the door frame. I can see his legs are stiff and unco-operative.

I go back into the other room and crawl into one of the beds; the top sheet is tucked in so tightly it must be stapled to the mattress. I realize I haven't brought along anything to read except textbooks. I check the drawer in the bedside table but of course there's only the black Bible lying there and that desperate I'm not, so I get up and dig around in my suitcase until I find *Death of a Salesman,* and then I insert myself back into the bed and begin to flip through it. Tragic hero. I have to find something original to say about the tragic hero. *Willy Loman's tragedy arises from his inability to realize he is a dime a dozen in a society that . . .* That what? . . . *that rewards excellence but . . . needs mediocrity.* Well, that's not bad. I could talk about Biff and Happy and Bernard then, too—

"Chris." His voice is so faint that at first I'm not sure if I really hear it.

"Murray?" I jump out of bed, *Death of a Salesman* tumbling from my lap, falling with its pages squashed onto the floor. I step over it to the bathroom. I don't know if I should knock or what, so I just stand staring dumbly at the door. He must have been in there at least twenty minutes. "Murray?" I ask, pressing my ear to the door.

"I could use your help, Chris."

"Okay. I'm coming in." I open the door, slowly, dreading what I will find.

He's sitting on the toilet wearing his pyjama top and, thank god, his shorts. His pants and shirt lie in a lump on the floor, and one leg of his pyjama bottoms is twisted around his ankle and the other is up only as high as his knee. He's just staring straight ahead and he says, his voice cracking only slightly from what I recognize as pure rage, "I can't seem to get these fucking things on. My left arm is numb and I can't even stand up."

"No problem." I hate the phony cheeriness I hear in my voice. But it's better than having him know I'm frightened and embarrassed and repelled, and angry at myself for feeling any of these. I untangle the pyjamas and work them up as high as I can above his knees, and then he holds onto me with his good arm and manages to stand so that I can pull the pyjamas up all the way, over his shorts, to his waist. My fingers tremble as they touch his thighs, his shorts, beneath which I can see the outline of his genitals. I've never had to touch him like this, and it's all I can do to keep myself from giggling, or crying, or pushing him away, saying, *I can't, I'm sorry, I can't.*

When we are ready we lurch back into the living room, and I don't bother with the chair, just take him straight to his bed, pull the sheets back and let him collapse. Before he can turn his face away I see his eyes watery with tears.

I go around and turn out all the lights, even the one on my night table, and then I fumble my way into bed. The brittle sheets rattle as I move.

We haven't said a word since I went into the bathroom, and now we both lie here, still not knowing what to say, hiding in the dark.

"Do you want me to get you anything?" I ask finally. "A Valium or something?"

He doesn't answer, and I think, oh god, it's going to be a bad one. I close my eyes and make my breath squeeze in and out of me, thinking, *sleep, sleep,* although I know I can't. The night presses against my face like heavy fur. *Willy Loman is. . . .* It doesn't work. I'm too conscious of Murray lying there across from me, the way he looked as I let him down into the bed.

"It's just so goddamned humiliating. To just have no control like that. You don't know what it's like. You've no damn idea what it's like."

My eyes jerk open. I know that if he'll talk about it he'll get over it sooner. "You're right," I say. "I can only imagine."

"It's hell. It's bloody hell. I feel like a thing. A vegetable."

"It's the trip. And the alcohol. You just had too much stress today. It's no wonder you're cramping up so much."

"It's not the trip. It's the disease. This ugly piss of a disease."

"This was a bad spell—you'll be better in the morning—" This is always what I say, what I think he expects. Sometimes I'm even right. A headache butts at my forehead, and I press my finger hard on the pressure point right between my eyes, pushing the pain back, back.

"In the morning. Sure. Every morning I'm worse."

"That's not true. You have remissions."

He sighs. "Remissions. Christ. I'm a brain grafted onto a coffee table."

And I can't stop myself, I start to laugh, stupid little boozy giggles that contract out of me like speeded-up hiccups. And then, mercifully, Murray begins to laugh, too, and when we finally stop, only a stray snicker escaping occasionally, we feel comfortable again, almost at home. The night seems to have lightened, but I suppose it's only my eyes adjusting. I listen to us breathing, almost in sync, but not quite.

"Are you awake?" Murray asks softly after a while.

"No."

"Me neither."

The night is powdery around us, grey from moonlight straining through the curtains.

"What I told you in the car. About my first sexual experience. It's not true. It wasn't with a kid in high school. It was when I was only thirteen and it was my Uncle George."

It's my voice that said that, it must be, thick words bumping into the darkness, memory caked up inside me suddenly being broken up and dumped into the room.

"What?" Murray fumbles up in bed, his sheets crackling.

"Don't turn on the light. Please. My Uncle George. He raped me."

I hear my door creeping open, the scar of light from the hallway along the foot of my bed and Uncle George a black shadow saying "Shhhh" and how I'm relieved it's him not some burglar but he only says "Shhh" his hands pushing up the nightie and I scream but Mommy and Daddy are away "Shhh you'll wake Mint" his hand over my mouth and he is breathing hard and uneven and I am full of such pain and terror the screams bubbling up against his hand. And afterward there was blood and he took the sheet off and said, "Don't tell anyone now, okay? They wouldn't believe you and they'd take you away somewhere."

And later, crying and crying, and Mint standing frightened at the foot of the bed hugging himself and saying, "Are you all right? Chris? Are you all right?"

"Go back to bed," I said, curling into myself tight as a flower against night. "It's okay. Go back to bed."

"Oh, Chris," Murray's is the voice that is trembling. "Oh, Chris."

"It happened five times, every time Mom and Dad were away and he stayed with us. I believed him, of course, that they would take me away if I told—Jesus, I was so *young*, I wasn't one of those worldly thirteen-year-olds, I was dumb as a stick. But after the fourth time I said to him, 'I'm going to tell Mom on you, I'm going to tell,' and he just laughed and said, 'No, you won't.' "

"And when you did tell her, she didn't believe you."

"Yeah," I say, not surprised that he's figured it out. "I told her, as well as I could, god, it was hard, and I can still see her standing in the kitchen wearing her apron with the red strawberries on it and holding the colander with the water dripping out of it onto the floor and saying, 'What an ugly, ugly thing to say! How can you make up such a horrible story about your Uncle George, your Uncle George who loves you like his own? Who told you to do this? One of those Friedlander kids, I bet, those awful people, those gutter people—'

"I'd never seen her so upset, hysterical really, shaking and her voice all high and squeaky. She was holding the colander at an angle so bits of broccoli were rolling out and onto the floor. Finally she put the colander down and came over to me and put her hands on my shoulders, digging her fingers in, and I was crying, and she said, 'Don't ever make up anything like this again, Chris. Ever. Ever. Promise me.' And she wouldn't let go of me until I said, 'I won't.' "

"Oh, god, Chris. But she was just ignorant. I mean, that was ten years ago and people couldn't believe it was happening as much as it was—"

"She's my mother. It was her responsibility to listen to me. To believe me."

"What about your dad? Did you try to tell your dad?"

I shake my head. "I should have, I suppose. Uncle George was Mom's brother, after all, and I knew how she adored him. But, I don't know, when you're a kid you think all adults are, that they think the same, so it never occurred to me to go to Dad. And he was a man, so he would believe Uncle George. Mom was the one who should have been on my side, who should have understood. Even now. It's not important to me that Dad know. It's Mom. It's always been Mom."

"So what happened finally? What made it stop?"

"*I* made it stop. I took a knife from the kitchen and hid it under the bed and the next time he did it and after he was finished and had turned over onto his back beside me I rolled out of bed and grabbed the knife and held it in both hands in the air right over his stomach and I screamed, 'I'll kill you if you ever do it again! I'll kill you!' God." I give a little rabid bark of laughter. "I was just so blind with rage, at him and Mom both, just so blind with it that I believed I could do it. Maybe I would have. Anyway, that was the last time. It was over. That was the last time."

(And Mint later standing frightened at the foot of my bed saying in a small voice, "Are you all right, Chris?" and me, curled tight as a stone into myself saying, "No, no. I'm not.")

And now I'm crying, like a kid, shoving my face into my pillow, stupid wet noises soaking into the pillowcase. Ten years I've kept that story frozen up inside me, ten years since I've told anyone, and now it's spilled out as easily as a glass of water spills when it's set too close to the edge of the table. The sobs run out of me until my throat aches.

"Oh, Chris, I'm so sorry." I can hear Murray getting out of his bed and pulling himself clumsily over to me. He pets my hair, as though I were a cat he's trying to calm.

"I'll be okay," I mumble into the pillow. I take a deep breath and sit up and give him a crumpled damp smile. "Sorry I dumped all this on you. Must have been the beer."

"I'm glad you did. I'm glad you felt you could." He sits beside me on the bed and puts his arms around me, something he has never done, and he holds me against him, stroking my shoulder. I reach my arms up around him and hug him back. It feels right to have told him. The only other person I told who believed me was my best friend in high school. She believed me, all right. She said the idea made her sick. Murray strokes and strokes my shoulder. It's like ice is breaking up inside me.

And then I feel something uncomfortable pushing at my thigh, and I know instantly what it is. I jerk away so quickly I haven't time to think about it—all I feel is revulsion and anger, and the words pour out of me, unstoppable.

"How can you even think about that?" I cry. "I think you're being a good friend and all you want is to fuck!"

Murray pulls back, pushes himself away from the bed, almost falling. The night table clatters as he grabs it for support.

What have I done? How could I say that? Stupid, stupid, stupid. I'm sorry, I take it back—

"Oh, shit, Murray," I say, "I didn't mean it." But my words just sound guilty and insincere.

"It's all right," he says, his voice strained.

We lie there miserably, the silence like a wall bricking up between us. Finally Murray says, his words so careful and uninflected it's as though he's printing them out on a typewriter, "Well, I guess we should try to get some sleep."

But it's hours before sleep opens its white chute and lets me slide down into dream. And there it's only Uncle George I see, standing monstrous at the foot of my bed, saying my name.

PAT

It must be four o'clock by now.

Stewart's watch was always fast so surely he would be there on time, if he were coming at all. I can see him standing under the theatre marquee, holding the empty bag, and around him loiter the policemen. One is dressed like a businessman and looking through records in the window of the Kelly's next door. Another is wearing frayed jeans and a torn shirt and sits on one of the benches pretending to read a newspaper. A third is disguised as a panhandler. A fourth has replaced the ticket seller just inside the theatre. Now Lyle comes walking along the street trying to look casual but with his eyes darting everywhere, seeing but not seeing the danger. He approaches Stewart, reaches quickly for the bag and they are on him, a wild grappling and then he is shoved, hard, up against the wall, his arms wrenched behind him and handcuffs snapped on. And half a block away, in the doorway of one of the porno shops, Chuck watches it all, clenching his hand in rage on the gun in his pocket, and he turns and walks quickly away to his car, not looking back once. He will come back to this house, I can hear his key gnawing at the lock, and when he opens the door into my room the gun will no longer be in his pocket, and he will say, "I don't need you any more, lady—"

I give a little whimper of denial and leap to my feet, as

though it were really happening, Chuck standing there in front of me holding my death in his hands. A long shudder grips me by the shoulders.

I walk over to the door, pull uselessly at the knob. I have already tried to pry out the bolts anchoring the hinges but they are rusted in so tightly they are no longer separate pieces of metal, and all I have succeeded in doing is scraping my fingers and ripping one nail so badly it bled. Fortunately I had a Band-Aid with me in my purse, and after I put it on I took out everything else I had in my purse and laid it out on the bed in a careful row, like a burglar taking out his tools, taking inventory, but there was nothing of use. The wallet with about forty dollars, not enough to buy my life; my set of keys to the house, the cars, the safe deposit box; the comb, whose pink plastic tail broke off almost immediately when I used it to pry at the boards on the window, making me think, absurdly, well, I never liked that comb much anyway and now I've an excuse to throw it away; my address book, full of names of people I hardly know, business friends of Stewart's —Frank and Beth, Tom and Ursula, Lester and Anne; a compact; the linty Kleenexes; the pen and pencil; the crumpled credit card receipts I always intend to file more carefully but never do; the letter from my old high school friend Ellen, who's just moved to Toronto. I picked the letter up, intending to read it again, but I didn't even take it out of its envelope. What is the point of reading of someone else's freedom, someone who has the right to do something as simple as step out of her house and go to the store to buy a carton of milk, and perhaps even then to complain of that as a kind of enslavement? I tossed the letter angrily back onto the bed. Who cares, Ellen, I thought bitterly, if you *are* working full-time and if you've met some wonderful new man across the street?

I let my things lie on the bed for some time, looking at them periodically to see if anything had changed, if suddenly I could see how to use something there to help me escape, but they remained only what they were, a wallet, a comb, a compact, keys, bits of plastic and paper. In ancient Egypt these were the kinds of things they would bury with you in your tomb, things you might need, things of which you were fond. Well, I thought grimly, picking them up and putting them back into my purse, perhaps someday they'll dig them up with me, artifacts of ancient Canada. I hesitated over my wallet, then took out a ten-dollar bill and slid it under the insole of my shoe. Just in case. Then I put the wallet back into my purse and snapped it shut, like a suitcase, all packed up and ready to go.

I pace the room like an animal. My steps slap hard on the carpet, as though they might be able to break through the floorboards, plunge me into the basement from which there will have to be another exit. I remember seeing a nature film on TV of polar bears that biologists had caged and were trying to relocate. The bears did not attack the bars as most animals would, seeking a lateral escape, but bounced stiff-legged on the floor of the cage, trying to break out the bottom because that is what they could do to ice, smash their weight on it until it gave way into water. Prisoners of our conditioning, I think, going again to the boarded-up window and pressing my face to the tiny crack so thin nothing of the outside can seep through, only the simplest electrons of light that carry no image, no information.

I go lie down on the bed, try to rest. I lie on my back, my legs straight out, my hands clasped on my chest, but it seems too much the way a dead woman would lie, so I turn over onto my side, snap my eyes determinedly shut, watch the black-and-white afterimages crawl over my eyes for a while. I breathe in, out, in, out, long slow breaths. Relax. Relax. Sleep. I try to find that floating feeling I used to be able to create as a child. It's what they call an out-of-body experience now, what people who have clinically died and then come back report. Well, that's not something I want to practise for. I pull my thoughts carefully back in out of the ether, curl my legs up to my chest. Breathe in, out. Relax. Sleep.

I start to compose in my head the letter to Elaine I've been struggling with. Hundreds of such mental letters have put me to sleep at nights: *Dear Manager: I am writing to complain about the service I received at your store— Dear B.C. Telephone: I am still being billed for a phone I don't have—*

Dear Elaine,

    As you know, at the last Hospital Auxiliary meeting I was assigned to the fundraising committee. However, I had made it clear at the previous meeting that I only wanted to be on the gift shop committee, and that I wanted to *cut* my hours at the Superfluity Shop, so I really must insist that—

That what? That if they put me on fundraising I'll resign? No, I don't want to go that far—

Oh, it's no good. I'm too tense; the letter is just making it worse. I turn over angrily onto my other side. Now it feels as if something is crawling up my leg, but I know even as I reach down to scratch there's nothing there. It's a sign of some disease, feeling things crawling on you. I'm such a hypochondriac. Well, if I have Alzheimer's at least I'll forget about it. I turn onto my back again, stare up at the ceiling, listen to my breath, the slow chant of my heart.

Finally I give up. How can I expect to sleep, with all my senses on red alert, waiting for Chuck and Lyle to come back and tell me whether I will live or die? Last night I don't think I slept at all, and I know I am physically exhausted, but still my body insists, *danger, danger, stay awake.*

I go over to the boarded-up window, press my face and hands against the boards. I can feel the tears begin to well up.

"Why me?" I whisper to the boards. "Why me?" Oh, of course it is whining and self-pitying and banal, but I have a right to that, surely. As if it weren't enough that my husband should abandon me—

"Why me?" I scream into the boards. "Why *me*?" And then I cry, loud, thick sobs tearing out of me, my mouth contorting until it hurts, tears streaming down my face.

When I get myself more or less under control again, I shuffle off to the bathroom and reel off a long roll of toilet paper and blow my nose and mop at my eyes until it seems I'm finished emitting liquids. I wash my face with cold water, avoiding the image of myself in the bathroom mirror—I've seen my face looking this way often enough in the last few weeks not to want to see it more than I have to. I go back and sit on the bed, for a long time, staring at the corner where two dead and

desiccated flies lie against the baseboard. You need a special
vacuum attachment to suck up things so close to the wall, I
think dully, the dutiful housewife.

Finally I get up and walk around the room again, pausing
at the window and squinting at the cracks as though suddenly
I might be able to see something. I go over to the desk and
flip again through the magazines, from which the address
labels have been carefully cut. An odd assortment: four old
*TV Guide*s and one each of *Sports Illustrated, Playboy, Vancouver, Douglas College Calendar,* and *Psychology Today.*
Only *Psychology Today* and the college calendar did not originally have address labels, so they must not have been bought
by subscription.

I pick up the *Playboy,* gingerly. On the cover a woman lies
on a bed, covered, barely, by a satin sheet and looking out at
the reader with her red mouth open, the tip of her tongue
protruding slightly from the side. I flip through the magazine,
page after page of undressed women in painful postures, staring out at me with flat eyes and pouty mouths. At least the
women all seem to have their pubic hair—I remember
Stewart, when we began sleeping together, wanting me to
shave mine off because he said the women in the magazines
all did, but I couldn't bring myself to do it.

The first time we made love, in a greasy motel room in
Nanaimo, its walls the colour of old celery, he whispered, as
finally his eager fingers unbuttoned me into nakedness,
"Your body's as good as those in *Playboy.*" (Except for the
pubic hair, I guess, but he didn't bring that up until later.) I
supposed he meant the comparison as a compliment, so I
said, as I thought he expected, "Oh, no, it's not," but inside I
cringed away from him, his man's eyes that were evaluating
me the way I suppose most girls were evaluated then.

He made me sit on the bed for several minutes and just
looked at me, then at last he began stroking my breasts with
icy fingers that trembled as though he were afraid.

"Jesus," he breathed, when my nipples contracted under
his touch.

He wouldn't get undressed himself until he turned out all
the lights, and it wasn't until we'd slept together a dozen
times that he let me see him, the penis that stuck out in front

of him at such an impossible angle I couldn't believe that gravity allowed it, that there wasn't a collapsible bone in it that could be folded up like a walking stick when it wasn't being used.

Stewart is the only man I have ever slept with. Of course I have been attracted to other men but the thought of acting on it was as impossible to me as the thought of going out in public with my hair dyed purple. Marriage and monogamy were simply the same thing, each a reason for the other. It is different for young women now, I suppose, sexual relationships so much easier and more casual. Chris lives with a boy without marrying him. I shut my mind against the sudden image of her making love with him—there is something obscene about parents imagining their children's sexual lives.

My thumb lets drop the middle page of the magazine, and it uncurls, dangles down in front of me like a big fleshy tongue. When I was a teen-ager I heard that boys would masturbate onto the centerfold. I set the magazine quickly back onto the desk, rub my hands on my dress as though the paper were covered with semen.

I pick up the *Psychology Today* and go over to the bed with it and sit down, although I know I won't be able to concentrate enough to read. I stare across the room at the two flies, willing them to leap up and fly, but they remain resolutely dead. On the wall above them a crack is beginning to spread across the plaster. It looks like a child's scribble, like Chris used to do repeatedly when she was little. She'd stand there with the blue crayon still in her hand, look me right in the eye and say, "I never did that." I was so exasperated I had to restrain myself from spanking her. That is something I am proud of, anyway, never spanking my children. With Mint of course it was easy, but Chris, well, Chris was more difficult. The way she would lie.

I sigh and look down at the magazine in front of me, begin flipping through it, although I have already done so earlier this afternoon. It is full of summaries of experiments on college students. "Seventy-one per cent of men increased their self-esteem after weight training twice a week." Fascinating. On another page I read of a theory that facial muscles act as tourniquets; when we smile we squeeze an artery, which

sends more blood to the brain and makes us feel good. Therefore, I think, it mustn't be that we feel good and then smile;
we smile and then we feel good. I look up from the magazine
at the picture of Blue Boy on the opposite wall and I give him
a generous grin, letting it sit on my face for a full minute,
giving it a chance. I do not feel blood diverting to the brain. I
do not feel suddenly happy.

When Chris was going to college in Surrey, I used to sneak
looks at her textbooks, wondering what it was like being a
college student, learning things from thick books like those. I
remember liking her psychology books best, perhaps because
the things it taught were only common sense, things I could
understand, that would make me sit up, excited, and say to
the empty air, "*I* knew that!" Sometimes Chris would catch
me reading her books and I would know she was annoyed by
the way she would say nothing about it. Except once.

"Why don't you go back to school yourself if you think this
stuff is so interesting?" I don't think she meant it, but the
idea stayed in my mind for a while, an exciting possibility,
me, with my background, going to college, to university. In
the logging camp where I grew up even getting to high school
was an unusual accomplishment, *university* a word that
meant *far away,* that meant *smart,* that meant *rich.* Rich. I
almost laugh out loud. I am here now because I am rich,
because I married a rich man.

I mentioned the idea of college once to Stewart, who said
casually, "Sure, go if you want to," but somehow that only
made me see how foolish it would be, me, going back to
school, at my age, as though it would be as easy as going out
to buy a new toaster.

I have always resisted change. I remember once, when the
children were still quite young, I had gone away for the
weekend, probably to visit my mother, a widow by then, in
the Okanagan, and when I came back I saw to my dismay that
Stewart, with the help of the children, had rearranged the furniture. I can still see their three eager faces looking for my
surprise and pleasure, as though they had bought me a gift.

"Oh, isn't that nice," I said. "It looks fine that way."

And it did, I suppose. There was no logical reason why the

sofa couldn't be against the east wall instead of the west, why the flokati rug had to lie with its long side instead of its narrow side against the fireplace, why the big lamp couldn't be moved to the other end of the love seat. But I hated it. Every time I walked into the living room my eyes moved things back the way they were, the way I had left them.

And so I changed things back. I didn't intend to, really; I just suddenly found myself the next day setting down the glass of milk I'd poured myself and tugging like a madwoman at the sofa, jerking it inch by inch across the room back to where it belonged, and when I finished I did the same to the other things until the room was mine again. I sank down, exhausted and sweaty, and drank my milk and felt at home. The children didn't even notice what I had done, but Stewart did, of course. Guilty and apologetic, I tried to explain it to him.

"Well, you're the one who has to spend most time here," he said. "Have it the way you want. It doesn't matter to me. I just thought you'd like something different, that's all. A change."

"If it ain't broke don't fix it, my father used to say."

He shrugged. "Okay. Sure. I just like to keep in practice. For when things do get broke."

Well, he had a point, I think wryly. When things did get broke I was definitely out of practice.

I turn my arm over, look at my wrist where my watch should be. I hate not knowing the time. But whatever encounter there was between the men negotiating my life must be finished by now. I look up at the door as though it is already opening, the foreman of the jury coming back in with the verdict. Perhaps these are the last moments of my life.

I am overwhelmed suddenly with such desire for all the good things of my life. All the memories. I reach for one—my father pulling me on my silver sled; George coming up and taking my hand at recess the day the teacher made me cry; Mint, Mint on his fifth birthday; my wedding day—

But what is the memory I clutch like an amulet against what will come through that door for me? It is Stewart standing in the doorway of the tiny bathroom of the ship in Fiji. I glance down at the nail I am filing on the ring finger of my right hand (of course, it's called the ring finger—yesterday I couldn't remember that); one more stroke and I will be finished. I look up and see tears pulsing down Stewart's cheeks. It is like a scene in a movie, the camera leaving the face of the main character for a second and then cutting back and now there are tears running down his face; you know it is only a trick, that some make-up man has run in with his eyedropper and dribbled on poignant streaks of water; it cannot be real. But a voice is saying, "I have to leave you, Patty. I'm going to leave you."

Those words trapped in my head like music on a record: the needle comes down and it plays, over and over and over.

I pull my knees up to my chest, hug them tight, my arms the lid of a jar I am sealing shut. I rock a little back and forth, desperate not to lose control, not to give in to the poisonous whisper of *if,* if I had been more loving, if I had had another child, if I had lost ten pounds, if I had, if I had—all too late, let them kill me, without Stewart I am dead inside anyway—

A door slams. They are back.

I jerk to my feet, my heart banging like a drum in an empty room. I may think I don't care, but my body doesn't believe it—life, ka-thump, goes my heart, life, life. I press close to the door, listen; if they come toward me I can jump back for the bed, pretend I was asleep. Their voices are loud and angry. It must mean they didn't get the money. I close my eyes for one sickening moment—they didn't get the money. I tell myself it was what I expected, but still—

Phrases dribble through the door: Chuck's voice, ". . . *waited* . . ."; Lyle's voice, ". . . *you're* the one. . . ."

Then suddenly there is another voice, a woman's. It is only when I hear the laugh track that I realize it is the TV, and the voice is Marion Cunningham's on "Happy Days." Mint used to love that show when he was young. I find myself listening for the words of the script, the comforting half-hour problems that were always solved by someone admitting he was wrong, Fonzie betraying a generous normalcy under his tough-guy façade.

Then someone is coming to my door, and I stumble back to the bed, sit down quickly and spread the magazine on my lap, as though I am trying to cover nakedness. I want to look innocent, innocent, not responsible for what happened in the city. The bolt retracts. Already my eyes are seeing Chuck come inside, one step only, the gun ready in front of him for what it must do. My hand grips the bedspread as though it is all that is keeping me conscious. There is nothing in my mind but fear.

The door opens. It is Lyle. He steps inside. My hand loosens on the bedspread.

"What happened?" I ask.

"Nothing happened." His voice is thin, like something squashed flat with a rolling pin. "He was there, and he was carrying a bag that could have had the money, and we had the pickup all arranged and then this cop showed up." He sinks down into the armchair as though he were too tired to stand. "It could have been coincidence—I mean surely the cops aren't that dumb, but we couldn't chance it, either."

"So you just . . . left."

"Yeah. So we just left."

It is like a program you are involved with that suddenly cheats you, flashes *To Be Continued* on the screen.

"So what happens now?"

Lyle sighs. "God knows." He runs his hand across the top of his head, as though he has forgotten he no longer has hair there. "What would *you* suggest?"

"You could just let me go. We could pretend it all just never happened."

Lyle gives a little bleat of laughter, but he is clearly not amused. Well, what did he expect me to say? I notice how the sleeve of his shirt has ripped under the arm and been carefully sewn up again, small parallel stitches. But the thread is black and his shirt is green, and the sewing is all on the outside when of course it should be on the inside, along the seam. He has done the sewing himself, I assume, and its errors seem like such an intimate thing for me to see that I pull my eyes away quickly in embarrassment.

Maybe he has felt me staring, because he stands up abruptly, then points at the magazine on my lap. "Psychology," he says. "That was my major."

Major. I cannot imagine what he is talking about. Then I remember it is a word Chris used, about the courses she was taking.

"You mean, you went to university?" My voice must sound incredulous. University is not a place for kidnappers. I remember the T-shirt saying "University of Oregon" he wore yesterday, but I didn't think he had actually gone there.

"Surprise, surprise." He sounds angry. "Now ask me what an educated guy like me is doing in a job like this."

"Well—what *are* you doing here, then?"

"He's an aaaa-dict, Pat-sy." Chuck is standing in the doorway, watching us. I don't know how long he has been there, listening. He jerks back a swallow of beer from the can he is holding.

"Fuck off!" Lyle whirls to face him. "Mind your own fucking business!"

Chuck giggles and takes another swallow of beer. "So now poooor Mr. Ivory League has to hang around with such low-life like me."

"Get out!" Lyle starts toward him, his hands up to push. His face is turning pink, white patches standing out on it as though someone has thrown bleach at him.

"Want her to your*self,* eh?" Chuck throws me a look so full of hate I shrink back from it as though he has tried to hit me. "So you can talk about psy-*chol*-o-gy, maybe."

Lyle has reached the door and he shoves at Chuck, who walks backward with no effort to resist.

"Just sit down and watch TV," Lyle says, his voice under control again. "It's all your amoebic brain can manage." He walks stiffly away toward the kitchen.

"Says who, eh? Says who?" But I can see Chuck through the open door go back to the TV and pick up a remote control and switch angrily around the channels. He finally stops on one that has sports on it, hockey perhaps. He sits down on the chair he has pulled up only a few feet from the screen. Not taking his eyes from the set he shouts, "You just better figure out what we're going to do now, Mr. Smart Guy."

He takes the last swallow of beer and then crumples the can slowly in his hand. I can hear the moan of metal even above the noise of the game. He tosses the can at a corner out of my sight and as he glances up to see if he has hit what he aimed at he sees me watching. Our eyes meet for a second before I look away. He lurches to his feet and comes over to the door and slams it closed. I do not hear the bolt click shut but this time I do not let hope excite me; if it is not locked now by tonight it probably will be.

It is over an hour later when Lyle comes back, holding out to me a plate of something pale and runny with chunks of green in it. I am too effusive in my gratitude. This time he closes the door behind him and sits down in the chair facing me, watching me eat, saying nothing. I am nervous, as though he will judge me on my table manners, the way I must hold the plate clumsily to my face and scoop the food (I guess it is an omelette) with the fork into my mouth. It does not taste as bad as it looks.

"About tomorrow," he says finally. "We've decided. We'll phone your husband again then and arrange another drop."

I nod. "Couldn't you phone tonight? Just so he'll know that . . . that nothing's happened?"

"In the morning. I don't want to give them time to set anything up. Another trap. If it was a trap."

"Okay." At least it is one more night I am guaranteed safety, a reprieve. "Do you . . . did it look like he had the money?"

"He had a paper bag. *Some*thing was in it. I guess we both just have to hope it was the money, don't we?"

I look down at the crumbs of green pepper and shreds of egg left on my plate. Suddenly they look inedible, nauseating. I make myself look up, directly at him, his pale face the colour of the omelette.

"What will you do with me if the bag is full of shredded newspaper?" There. That's it, the bottom line.

He picks at the frayed cuffs of his shirt, then tries to smooth them back down into a tidy edge. "I don't know," he says in a low voice.

There is a strained silence in the room. *Strained silence:* I remember when I first read that phrase in a book and wondered what it meant, could imagine silence being poured through a sieve, sifting impurities. Lyle gets up, abruptly, and takes my plate from me and turns to go.

I have to keep him here a little longer, I think with a sudden clarity. He is my only hope.

"Why are you doing this?" I ask, making my voice gentle, soft, the way I would with the children when I wanted them to tell me something they didn't want to.

He stands with his back to me. "Don't think I'm better than Chuck," he says. "I'm worse. I don't have Chuck's excuses." He turns back to me so suddenly the fork shuffles from the plate and falls to the floor. It makes no sound at all on the carpet. "Well, you heard the man. I've got a habit. I'm doing it for the money. I need the money."

"I could help you," I say, not even sure what we are talking about, desperate not to let the conversation end. "There are places you could go that would help you—"

"That's another of my problems, you see. I don't want help. I don't want to quit."

"Why not?"

"It feels too good, that's why not. It feels better than being alive." He gives me a smile that seems genuinely happy. "I'm what you would call 'half in love with easeful death.' See what I learned at the big kids' school? All kinds of good things. You should try it sometime," he says, still smiling. "You'd like it."

"Death," I say. "But I'm not in love with death."

"We're *all* in love with death." His smile suddenly drops from his face as though it had landed there by mistake. He bends down and picks up the fork and then reaches for the doorknob.

The door will not open.

"What the hell—" He jerks at it. "Chuck! Open the goddamned door!" He pulls at it in a frenzy. "Chuck!" I am afraid to say anything.

Finally, after several moments, I hear the slither of the bolt and the door lurches open. Chuck is standing there with his scar of a mouth pulled up into what looks like a grimace of pain but must be a grin. He says sweetly, "Well, hey, I thought you were going to spend the night in there, so, hey, I just locked up."

Lyle slouches out, waving the fork like a weapon. "Don't be such an asshole. Jesus Christ."

Chuck pokes his head into my room before he closes the door. "Good night, Patsy. See you in the morning." His voice is still sugary sweet.

"Good night," I say, the polite hostess.

F
R
I
D
A
Y

CHRIS

We must have been sitting in this line-up for nearly an hour. If there'd been an accident surely it could have been cleared by now. It's probably just some bloody construction. No traffic is coming through from the west, either, so both lanes must be blocked.

Murray's resigned himself to the wait, and he sits with one leg propped on the dashboard and his book on his knee. He looks like a spider contemplating a meal. It doesn't seem to bother him, being stuck here like this. At least his legs aren't seizing up on him today, and the arm that went dead on him yesterday seems to be bending obediently again.

All morning we've been very careful with each other, not talking about what happened last night. I feel so guilty and ashamed for the way I pushed him away, but I'm afraid that anything I say now will only make it worse. Maybe I just don't want to admit that he could think about me in any sexual way at all. I like Murray more than any guy I know, and it's not that he isn't attractive, but to sleep with him—oh, god. Even if it weren't for the MS—and that's an "if" big enough to become a whole new planet—I can't consider it. We're friends; why risk spoiling that? Maybe he's not able to have sex any more, anyway—just because he can get an erection doesn't mean he can ... do the rest of it. Or even want to. Maybe what happened was just purely physiological and had nothing to do with me, or even with him, or how we feel about each other. Oh, hell. Everything is so complicated.

But I'm glad I told him about Uncle George. I guess it was the right thing, to talk about it, after all these years of keeping it fisted up inside me. Maybe I should jump out of the car and pound on the windows of the vehicles around me, shouting, "I was raped! By my own uncle!" If it feels better to have told one person maybe it will work in reverse geometric progression: telling enough people will diminish my anger to nothingness. Well, at least it would diminish the boredom of the people in the line-up.

It diminished Tracy's boredom, that's for sure. Tracy. She was supposed to be my best friend. The very *idea* made her sick, she said. "Your own *uncle*? It's so *creepy*!" I guess she decided I must be creepy, too, because she found a new best friend by the next week. I cried my damn heart out.

At least Murray didn't say it was creepy. Although I suppose that's as good a word for it as any.

"I'm getting a bit chilly," I say, more just to make conversation than because I'm cold. "Mind if I start the car?"

"Sure." He glances out the window at the Toyota unmoving in front of us. "Anything look promising out there?"

"Uh-uh. The holdup must be miles ahead. You were right, we should have stopped in Yale to eat. I'll starve to death if we have to sit here much longer."

"You can munch on my book. Chapter Three was pretty good."

"I've brought along a term paper, thanks."

"So you can eat your words."

I smile. "Yeah. I can eat my words."

I settle back in my seat, let the warm air pulse up at me from under the dash. And wait.

When I phoned Dad this morning he was crying. I hung on to the receiver so tightly my hand was numb afterwards. The kidnappers had phoned, he said, but before they could really say anything they were cut off. "But I talked to her," Dad kept saying. "I talked to her. She was okay. They let me talk to her."

"It doesn't make any sense," I said to Murray. "Yesterday they set up a rendezvous and didn't show, and then today they phone but they don't say anything."

"Their copy of *The Kidnapper's Guide to the Galaxy* has a few pages missing," Murray said.

"What're those kids doing out there?" he asks me now.

A little way ahead the highway branches out into three lanes for a hill, and a couple of car lengths in front of us is the sign saying Keep Right Except to Pass. Two teen-agers from a green Datsun are carefully defacing the sign, and when they're finished it says Keep Right Except to Piss.

"Vandalism," I say. "That's what they're doing."

"God, Chris. I've had enemas with a better sense of humour than you do."

Before I can answer, a car horn sounds somewhere behind us, and I realize the traffic has begun to inch forward. Murray lifts his leg hurriedly down from the dash, grimacing as it hits the gearshift, and I jerk the car ahead, relieved just to be moving. When we come to the point where our lane branches into two, Murray asks, "Taking the pissing or non-pissing lane?"

"Piss off," I say, but I have to grin.

I swing into the passing lane, persuading my pinging Honda past the Toyota which is straining just as hard to keep up. Some idiot in a big Chev sucking my bumper flashes his lights and, although I'd like to stay here just to thwart him, I cut back in front of the Toyota.

"So much for life in the fast lane," I say.

"Life in the fast lane," Murray snorts. "I don't even have life in the slow lane. I have life in the parking lane."

When at last we come to what has delayed us, we can see it's a large yellow tanker truck lying on its side across both lanes of the highway. The cab is detached and lying about twenty yards away, like a fly some huge hand has batted into the side of the mountain. The cab's been burned, and smoke still blurts into the air as the men working there prod at it.

I pull onto the shoulder to squeeze past the yellow tanks from which some clear fluid is leaking. There's a chemical smell in the air; my eyes start to itch. Of course, trying to get a better look, everyone slows down even more as they pass the cab.

"God, people are such ghouls," Murray says, but we can't

stop ourselves from looking, either, looking for the worst we can see. But there are no bodies, no stretchers with sheets pulled up over them. Everyone drives carefully after that for a while, no tailgating, slowing down on spots that could be black ice, but by the time we get to Hope they've already forgotten. Someone roars past us on a solid line.

We stop in Hope to eat, at a real restaurant this time, and Murray orders enough for three loggers and a horse, but my appetite has disappeared. This will be our last stop before home, and the thought makes me so nervous I can only nibble at my french fries, which look like squashed fingers. The waitress walks by and I ask her for more coffee.

"Just bring her the carbon coffee of the original," Murray says. She smiles uncertainly but brings me a refill. Murray winks at her and then crosses his eyes, which he does with such expertise his eyeballs nearly disappear.

"Honestly," I say. I know he's just trying to cheer me up. The waitress giggles and moves off.

"Ah, yes," Murray sighs, watching her go. "A critical success but a flop at the box office." He rubs at his eyes as though he needs to push them back into place.

I take a slow sip from my coffee and nudge a french fry around my plate.

"We should frappez la rue, don't you think?" Murray asks, poking at the last of his Greek salad. Actually he wanted the Caesar, but he said "Seizure salad" to the waitress, so it serves him right if she misunderstood, and he felt too guilty to send it back.

"I suppose."

He spears the last piece of feta cheese and pops it in his mouth. "Feta compli," he says.

We split the bill and go back to the car, and soon we're on the last miles of the winding road bringing us into the Fraser valley. I remember Professor Boychuck in Geology saying, "Nature abhors a straight line." So does the B.C. Highways Department. Maybe I should have taken the Coquihalla road; even if there had been slides, as Dad said, it couldn't have been slower than this. But I've lost my desire to hurry, anyway; the closer to home I get the more uneasy I become. I try to picture Mom there, opening the door as my car pulls into the drive, the years of strain and mistrust between us miraculously gone, but I know the reality is something else, that she will still be missing and only Dad will be there, sitting beside the phone as the house, no longer even his, disintegrates around him.

I won't let myself think about it; I squeeze it from my brain, reach for something else to absorb, fast. *Willy Loman is a tragic hero.* What was it I came up with last night? *A dime a dozen, in a society that likes success but wants mediocrity,* something like that.

"Murray," I say. "Would you write something down for me? It's a thesis sentence for my English paper. There's a pen and notebook in the glove compartment."

"Don't you ever stop working?" he demands, but he gets out the paper and writes what I tell him. "Willy Loman. *Death of a Salesman,* right?"

"Yes—I didn't know you'd read it."

"Television. Starring Dustin Hoffman. You know I can't read."

"Well, what do you think of the thesis? Does it sound original?"

"Tragic hero. Let's see. You have to die at the end, right?" I think about it for a minute, not sure. "I guess so."

"Oh. Because I remember the two boys—they seemed more interesting than the old man. One because he knew he was a bum and the other because he didn't. And they had to go on living. Willy just offs himself—that's easy, that's not tragic. Tragic is knowing the future and living with it."

I'm surprised to hear him come up with something so thoughtful. Biff and Happy as tragic heroes. It's a possibility. I'll have to check and see if you have to die at the end.

"That's not bad," I say. "But a tragic hero has to have some tragic flaw. You know, like Macbeth's was ambition."

"Well, that's easy. Everybody's got a tragic flaw. Mine is MS. My French prof's is Edmonton. My mother's is me. Your mother's is being dumped by her husband and kidnapped."

I have to laugh. I'm trying not to think about my mother and Murray manages to bring it all around to her, anyway.

"And my tragic flaw?" I ask. "What's mine?"

"Oh, yours. Too numerous to mention."

But I can see I've embarrassed him so I won't let it go. "Come on. What's my tragic flaw?"

"Your driving."

I rein the car in from where it's wandering over the white line. "Now what is it?"

"You don't like sex."

I feel as if he's punched me in the stomach. My foot drops back from the gas pedal and I can't seem to make myself press it back down.

"Oh, shit," Murray says. "I'm sorry. I had no right to say that."

I watch the road come at me more and more slowly through the windshield.

"Pull over," Murray says. The car has almost rolled to a stop and a truck bleats at me. "Come on, Chris. Pull over and we'll talk about it."

So I pull over, numbly. I don't want to listen to what else he has to say; he's said everything he needed to. I just stare straight ahead, my hands clenched on the wheel as though I need them there to hold me up.

"I know what you think," I say tightly, not looking at him. "That because of what happened with Uncle George I hate all men or something. But that's not true. I've slept with lots of guys since—"

"I know, Chris. You don't have to explain."

"I've got sexual feelings like everybody. Don't make me out to be some prude—"

"Aw, Chris—"

"It's really because of last night. Isn't it? Because I pushed you away and said those stupid things to you, now you say I don't like sex. That's it, isn't it?"

"No. That's bloody well *not* it." He sounds angry, but then he takes a deep breath and twists himself clumsily to face me, his hands held out in front of him as though he were offering me two handfuls of air. "Look. I swear to god—I swear—" he picks up the novel he'd been reading and slaps his right hand flat on it "—I swear on Isaac Asimov that's not what I meant. Of course I was upset when you pushed me away. But

at least you didn't patronize me. You didn't act like you had
to be nice to the horny cripple. You treated me like just a regular guy. You always do."

I give him a sideways look and decide that if he's shitting
me it's a pretty good job.

"Look," he says, "I don't want you to feel guilty about me,
okay? I get enough sex. I sleep with Nadia sometimes."

"Nadia!" I forget I'm mad and stare at him open-mouthed.

I can actually see a blush creeping up his neck. "Amazing,
isn't it? Bimbotic Nadia." He rubs at his left arm as though it
were cold. "Maybe she feels it's part of her job, keep the
gimp happy, you know."

"Don't be silly. She wouldn't do it if she didn't want to."

I can't believe it, him sleeping with Nadia. And to my
amazement I feel a surge of jealousy—that's what it is, all
right, *jealousy*. It doesn't make sense, of course—I've made it
clear I wanted our relationship to be strictly friendship, so
why do I feel this sudden possessiveness, this sense of
betrayal? A few hours ago I was thinking sex with him would
spoil everything, and now I feel as though I've been jilted.

"I know I shouldn't put Nadia down the way I do," he
goes on. "No pun intended. We have fun together. You
know. She can be really . . . affectionate. I appreciate it. It's
nice to feel that I can, that I'm still, you know, normal that
way."

"Well," I say, fumbling for words. "I'm glad you told me
about it." I'm not sure if I mean that or not.

I don't know what else to say, and neither, apparently,
does Murray, so finally I just put the car in gear and pull back
onto the highway, the fan belt whinnying as I accelerate. I
have got to get that fixed.

Murray and Nadia. Images of the two of them together
flare in my mind and I have to keep snuffing them out.

The traffic has dropped to almost nothing, and we twine
smoothly on, west, going west, the Fraser galloping along beside us.

I realize that I never did make Murray explain what he
meant about my tragic flaw. It sounds like a movie. *My Favor-
ite Year. My American Cousin. My Brilliant Career. My Tragic
Flaw.* It's not as simple as Murray says, but it's not as simple

as I say, either. I *don't* dislike sex, but. *But* isn't just a conjunction; it's a whole phrase, a whole sentence, a whole bloody essay of argument that can't be ignored but that can't be articulated.

Maybe everything does go back to Uncle George. How do I know what I'd feel if he hadn't been the first? Maybe I'd be sexually insatiable. Maybe I'd be the same as I am now. Whatever that is. Oh, shit, I don't know. What does "normal" mean anyway except the average of all the abnormal people?

By the time we get to Abbotsford the clear cold weather has changed and the sky turns the colour of sour milk. Rain slurs down, the wipers making their bored trips back and forth across the windshield.

"Rain!" Murray exclaims, as though I hadn't seen it.

He rolls the window down suddenly, gives me a guilty grin with all his teeth showing. He has perfect white teeth, all lined up like a row of Chiclets. They are so even I suspect he might have a denture, but it's not the sort of question I ever felt I could ask him.

"About that chili I had for lunch," he says.

"Oh, god."

"Sorry. A fart worse than death." He pulls the air in the car in fast handfuls toward the open window. "A fart leaving a stinking ship. Or a sinking shit. Or a—"

"You're demented."

"Of course. It's listed on my passport under 'distinguishing marks.' "

Only half an hour later we're turning off onto Pacific Highway. Almost home. I haven't lived here for five years, yet I still say "home." When can you stop calling it that, how long do you have to have lived away before you're really free of it, before you make your own home? Maybe never. I remember Dad only last year talking about going home to Manitoba.

We take the by-pass around Cloverdale, and I point out my old high school to Murray. He asks me questions about it, but there's little I want to remember. I was a diligent student, I worked hard, I graduated, what more is there? We pass the Seacrest Homes development, the huge houses on their stingy lots replacing the Singhs' blueberry farm. A bush has grown subversively in front of the "Com" in the sign that says, "Seacrest: A Community Without Compromise." I almost point it out to Murray, but then we're past and explaining seems like too much effort.

I rub my palms on my slacks as we head up the hill at Grandview Heights. Only a few more miles. For a second I close my eyes. What if Uncle George is there? Shit.

It's been over two years since I saw him. Christmas, the last Christmas I spent at home. The next year I stayed in Edmonton, with some limp excuse about having to study, and last Christmas I spent in Grande Prairie with Murray's family, a loud and chaotic bunch, the opposite of mine. His aunt, he warned me, was a glossolalic, which I discovered meant she was prone to unexpected vocal seizures. As Murray's father was passing me the turkey she suddenly stood up and burst into ecstatic syllables, in a language unknown to any of us, including her, an incredible gush of unrestrained babble. It lasted for only a minute and then she sat down, glancing up at us, shy and confused.

"Turkey?" Murray's father asked.

"Yes, please," I said.

After dinner Murray's father said he'd play some carols for us on his handsaw, and I thought, oh, god, it'll be dreadful, but when he sat down, holding the saw carefully between his knees, the jagged edge toward him, and began to play the other side with a bow that looked as though it belonged to a violin, the sounds were amazing—beautiful, haunting notes that trembled in the air. He played about three or four pieces and when he stopped I actually had tears in my eyes.

Anyway, being with Murray's family was a lot more fun than being at home, with Mom tackling a Christmas dinner beyond the scope of a major restaurant, Dad sneaking off to his study to work on his year-end reports, Mint so carefully apportioning to everyone his ration of nice, Sue getting in Mom's way in the kitchen but trying to help so Mom could hardly ask her to stop. And Uncle George. And me. Awful. Awful. I swore it would be the last time.

We had drawn names so that we would have to buy only

one gift, Sue's suggestion, and it was fine with me. I half hoped I'd get Uncle George. I could see myself choosing the perfect gift, a dead rat, a hangman's noose, a donation in his name to Rape Relief. But it was worse than that. He got my name. Christmas morning, all of us sitting around the living room, exclaiming over gifts that were too expensive and nothing we would ever have chosen for ourselves, Mom handed me mine, a large rectangular box beautifully wrapped, and when I opened the lid and lifted up the tissue I saw at the same time the rich leather coat and the card saying, "To Chris, from Uncle George. Merry Christmas."

Of course I had to lift the coat out and hold it up for everyone to see. I felt like throwing up.

"Try it on," Dad was urging.

"Oh, George," Mom said. "It's beautiful."

"The receipt's in the bottom of the box," Uncle George said. "If it's the wrong size. Or you don't like it."

"Oh, how can she not like it!" Mom exclaimed. "It's lovely."

"Well," Uncle George said.

"That's what you can get *me* next Christmas," Sue said, snuggling closer to Mint, putting her hand on his knee. He reached around the back of the sofa and put his arm around her. The baby, Stephanie, was playing around their feet, tearing the wrapping paper into mouth-size portions.

I bit my teeth together so hard my fillings must have started to crumble.

"Try it on," Dad was urging, a bit nervously now, pushing his words across the room to fill the empty space over my head that was supposed to have the words *Thank you, Uncle George* printed on it. *Damned* if I'll say it, I thought.

I tried the coat on. It was a perfect fit. The leather was soft and supple under my fingers.

"It's a nice coat," I said. I pulled my lips straight back a little from my teeth.

"You can return it if you want," Uncle George said.

"Oh, no," Mom said. "Why, it looks perfect on her. It looks perfect on you, Chris. Don't you think so, Stewart?"

"Perfect," Dad said.

I wanted to scream, to rip the damned thing off and throw
it at them, but I held myself closed, shut tight, not even
breath escaping from me as I turned slowly and took the coat
off and sat down again, and Dad picked up his present and
said, "My turn next!"

As he started to tear off the wrappings, saying, "Now who
can this be from?" I got up and went into the kitchen. I sat on
one of the kitchen chairs and put my head down on my arms.
But I wouldn't cry. Damn him, I wouldn't cry. I squeezed my
eyes shut tight and pushed my hands hard against the table.
The embroidery on the tablecloth under my fingers felt like
Braille. *What you don't see won't hurt you,* my mother would
say. No, that's wrong; it was, *What you don't know won't hurt
you.*

I heard the sound of another chair being pulled out from
the table. I didn't have to look up to know it would be Mint.

"Chris," he said softly. "Ah, gee, Chris."

"Please, Mint. Just leave me alone."

"I know it's hard."

"Do you?" I said. I wouldn't lift my head. I wouldn't look
at him.

"It's Christmas, Chris. Please . . . try. Just try to make the
best of it."

"Don't spoil it for the rest of you, you mean."

"Ah, gee, Chris." I could imagine his unhappy face, the
way he would be squirming in his seat. "I *don't* just mean
that. I mean don't spoil it for yourself, too."

"How do I do that?" I said into my arms. "Should I gush,
'Golly gee, *thanks,* Uncle George, you're the best uncle a girl
could have!' ? Is that what I should do?"

"Of course not. You don't have to overdo it. But . . . now
everybody thinks it's you, that you're the one not being nice."

"You want me to be nice?" I lifted my head, finally. "Well,
I don't want to be *nice.* When I die, I don't want *She was nice*
carved on my tombstone."

"What would you like? Carved on your tombstone, I
mean. Just so I'll be ready."

"Oh, something like *She was a bitch but she was interesting.*"

Mint laughed nervously—he was always a little shocked
when I talked tough; maybe that's why I did it so much. He
picked at the tiny cross-stitched rose in the tablecloth until
he'd loosened the thread, and then he kept trying to smooth
it back down.

"I know it must be hell for you," he said. "You must hate
him."

"Yeah. I do. Merry Christmas, Uncle George, I hate your
guts. Merry Christmas, Mom, I hate your guts. Merry Christmas, Mint."

He was quiet for a long time. The refrigerator clicked off
with its awful rattling finale. I could hear the others in the
living room, the awkward laughter and the rustle of the baby
in the wrapping paper.

"You don't hate her guts," he said finally.

"No," I said. "I suppose not."

"And me? You hate me?"

I didn't answer for a while, as though I had to think it over.
My brother Mint. My mother's perfect son.

"What do you think?" I said.

We're almost there. I recognize the houses now. The
Goldsteins—their alcoholic daughter Katy was in my class.
The Petersons, whose two Dobermans used to strain at their
chains whenever I rode by on Blackie, terrifying us both. The
Vanderpols, who set up an ultralight field in their back pas-
ture until we all signed a petition about the noise.

And here we are, the Duvaliers. I wonder what the neighbours said about us.

We're turning into the drive, to the beautiful house with
the view that made us all exclaim when we first saw it fifteen
years ago, the perfect house on Zero Avenue. It doesn't look
as impressive as it did then, not with all the huge new houses
being slammed into subdivisions elsewhere in Surrey, but
Mom has kept it up well, and the property and view, in spite
of the cloudy weather, are as splendid as always.

"Wow," Murray says. It shouldn't matter to me that he's
impressed, but it does. "Very picturesque." He pronounces it
picture-skew. I can see Blackie raise his head in the far pasture.

I get out of the car, slowly, a salesman not sure what to expect, what dangerous things will leap out at me. I notice a scrap of wet newspaper blown up against the cedar hedge on the west side of the house—it gives the place suddenly an abandoned look. Silky comes and rubs my leg, and I pick her up, pleased that she seems to remember me, although I imagine she'd do the same to anyone who came by. Perhaps she did it to the kidnappers. I let her drop abruptly to the ground. She was my cat originally. I'm surprised Mom kept her because she's allergic to cats. We had a fight about it, I remember. ("We can't give her back! It's not fair!" "I get sick around her, Chris." "She's mine—it's not fair!") Guilt scraping its shrill nails on my skull.

I go over to Murray and open his door. "You want to use the chair?" I ask.

"Yeah, I guess so."

I hoist the chair out with one heave, slam the trunk lid closed. My car is so dirty from the Edmonton winter my fingerprints look as though I had someone in the trunk clawing to get out. I pull the chair open, wheel it up to Murray. He has some trouble, but not as much as yesterday, getting into it, and then slowly I push him along the walk. The wheels squeak at every revolution. "You need to oil this thing," I say.

"That's me, not the chair."

I'd forgotten how quiet it is out here. But far away I can hear a chain saw, the beep of a truck backing up, the developers moving in.

"I feel so grubby," Murray says nervously, looking down at his jeans with the mustard stain on one thigh, the knee with a hole that looks as if it's been bombed out from the inside. He lifts his right arm and bends his face into his armpit. "*Mon Dieu*," he moans, crossing his eyes and slapping his arm back down to his side. "Wayne Gretzky's jockstraps can't smell this foul."

"You look fine," I say, although I can smell what he means about his armpits. "Just don't reach up for anything."

"Maybe you should hose me down," he says, gesturing at the green garden hose wrapped neatly around the tire rim at the side of the house. I notice a raw circle of rust has filed through the metal.

"Don't worry," I say. "Dad won't care."

"Have you noticed, incidentally, how much Wayne Gretzky looks like Princess Di? I think they're the same person."

"What?"

"Nothing, forget it, hysterical babble." He fumbles closed the top button of his shirt, something he always does when he's nervous about meeting people. He has a wild pasture of hair on his chest that grows right up onto his neck if he doesn't shave it back, and I know it embarrasses him, makes him feel he isn't completely evolved or something. "I need a goddamned machete," he moans sometimes. His collar looks so tight now he must feel he's being garroted.

"By the way," I say. "I haven't told my family you have MS."

"What?" Murray pulls the brakes on so abruptly I walk into the back of his chair. He wheels sharply to face me. "What do you mean, you haven't told them?" he demands.

"Well—" I play nervously with my thumbnail. "The subject just never came up. It doesn't matter, does it?"

"Jesus. Of course it matters. How are you going to explain this wheelchair? As my suitcase?"

"It was just none of their business," I say.

And, oh, I suppose that's true enough, but I know it's also because I wanted them to imagine other things about us, things that would change if they knew about the MS; I enjoyed listening to Mom ask her cautious questions, the way she was dying of curiosity but determined not to show it.

"Well," Murray says grimly, "I guess it's their business now. Push on."

The wheels crackle on the walk as we go up to the front door. I take a deep breath, like someone preparing to drink something medicinal, and then I lift the big knocker in the shape of a bird and let it drop. The noise makes me jump. My palms are sticky with sweat. I feel as though I'm about to introduce a pit bull to a baby, although I don't know which is which.

Dad opens the door.

"Chris."

"Dad."

We hug and cry a little and I'm suddenly flooded with my

love for him, hang onto him like a kid.

When we finally pull away, I introduce him carefully to Murray.

"Well," Dad says, "what happened to you?"

I wince, because I know how Murray hates that question, how he'll give sarcastic answers such as that he has a cerebral hemorrhoid or that his dink fell off.

So I say quickly, although I know he doesn't like people answering for him, "Murray has MS."

"Ms," Dad says vaguely. "I've heard of that." He steps back to hold the door open for us, and I know it looks as if he's backing uneasily away, but Murray doesn't say anything about not being contagious, the way he usually does if he thinks someone's afraid of him.

We're moving into the kitchen. And I hear my mother's voice. "Hel-lo!"

I stop, stare at Dad, my mouth rounding into the childish O of surprise, and even as I start to exclaim I can hear the same voice saying, cheerfully, mindlessly, "Want a beer?"

"God," I say, feeling ridiculous, my smile still stranded on my face. "Buddy. It sounded like Mom. I actually thought it was Mom."

Dad gives a little "uh" of sound. "No. No."

I notice how old he looks (despite or maybe because of all his grim workouts at the health club), how his skin has that loosening, frayed look, how his eyes seem to have sunk deeper into his head. His hair is over half grey, and, even though he parts it farther over on the side than he used to, it can't hide the scalp showing through, the shine of baldness a few years away. One of his shirt buttons is undone, and when he moves his arms his shirt pulls open like a lens, exposing a fleshy oval that my eyes keep being drawn to.

"Could I use the phone?" Murray asks, his best company-manners voice. "I have to call my friend and tell him where to pick me up."

"Oh, sure, yeah." Dad gestures at the phone, which is sitting not in its little nook but on the edge of the counter.

"Don't talk too long," I say, as Murray wheels over. "I imagine we should try to keep the line free."

Dad nods, watches Murray as he picks up the phone. He

has to dial twice before he gets through. After he says hello, I try not to listen, but I can hear him repeating, more or less, the directions I gave him. I hope his friend has a map. Well, we're not hard to find: go south until you hit the border.

"Any more news?" I ask Dad, although I know already what he'll answer.

"No. No. All I can do is wait. At least . . . at least she was okay when I talked to her." His voice begins to thicken. I squeeze his arm.

"Well, that's got to be good news. If they haven't hurt her so far—" The sentence dangles horribly in the air.

"I just don't know why they didn't call back," Dad says. "There was some noise in the background, someone shouting, maybe, and then the line went dead. The police didn't know what to make of it, either."

"And they didn't call back?" Of course I know they didn't, but still it seems necessary to ask.

"No," Dad says, dropping into one of the kitchen chairs as though he were exhausted. I suppose he is. He sits in that strange way he has, his knees and toes pressed together and his heels sticking out to the sides. When he walks it is the opposite, bowlegged, his toes splaying out as though he's wearing flippers. "I mean, it finally looks as though we're going to pull through this divorce thing—your mom was really starting to accept it, and Yvonne and me, well, and then *this* has to happen. It's just incredible. Like I'm being punished."

"It's no picnic for Mom, either, I expect." Dad looks up at me, surprised and hurt that I've taken her side. Well, I'm surprised, too.

"Of course, of course it's not. She must be going through hell."

Murray's finished his call and he pulls his chair clumsily forward a little, its squeaking making us look over at him. He's biting at his cheek as he does when he's nervous. I notice he's keeping his arms clamped tightly to his sides. His chair seems to take up the whole kitchen, which looks suddenly small and cluttered—a cheat of memory, space collapsing to fit an adult perspective.

"Tom's on his way," Murray tells us. "He says half an

hour. He's in Richmond. I guess that's not too far."

"Richmond," Dad repeats, the way someone will when his mind is elsewhere and he's trying to fake attentiveness. He rubs absently at his cheek, and I can hear the bristles from his beard snap and rasp against his palm.

"Maybe I can wait for him outside," Murray says.

"No, no." Dad clutches the kitchen table and pulls himself to his feet. "Don't do that. I can make us some coffee or something—"

"No, really—"

"And you haven't met Mint."

"Mint?" My voice sounds like a creaky hinge. "Is Mint here?"

"Oh, yes. Him and Sue and the kids. They're just putting the baby to sleep." He herds us both toward the living room.

And there is Mint, just coming down the hallway from his old bedroom.

"Chris!" he says. "I didn't even hear you drive up."

He is handsome, as he always was, lean and tall and blond, not wearing the glasses he used to in high school. Maybe he's got contacts now. His eyes are large and blue, his brows arching over them in perfect little steeples. He had a moustache for a while, too, I remember, but it's gone now. His mouth is the only part of him not symmetrical, but it only makes him look more charming, the way it narrows and turns up a little at one side, giving him always a slight grin. The scar by his right ear from where the swing hit him on the playground when he was ten is almost invisible now, something you have to look for to find. Mint, my little brother. The favourite.

He comes over and gives me a careful hug. When he sees Murray I can tell he's surprised, but he recovers perfectly, goes over and extends his hand.

"And you must be Murray."

"What's left of me."

They shake hands, as though some transaction has taken place.

"Can I get you anything?" Mint asks, too solicitously. "Coffee? Dad, were you going to—"

"Sure. I'll make some—" Dad gestures vaguely at the

stove, which is piled with dirty pots and plates.

"No," Murray says. "Really. My ride will be here any time."

And then Sue and Stephanie, who's three now, come out of the bedroom and join us and we all contribute to a nervous fumble of greeting. Sue is a small anxious woman, blonde like Mint, with skin so pale it looks painful. We have tried hard to become friends although it has never really worked.

"Are you hungry?" she asks me. "There's a casserole in the fridge it would be easy to warm up."

"No, no," I say. "We're fine. We ate on the plane. I mean on the *way*." God, I'm babbling. But if I let the tension ease up in me I'm afraid I'll collapse and roll across the floor like a ball.

"Were the roads icy?"

I take a deep breath. "Not bad. But there was an accident the other side of Hope. It held up traffic for quite a while." There. I sound almost normal.

Stephanie is tugging at Sue's slacks, saying in that repetitive and irritating way children have, "Mommy. Mommy. Mommy. Mommy."

"*What*, dear?"

But now that she has our attention she's afraid to speak and she shoves her face into Sue's legs and throws her arms around them. Sue bends down and pulls her arms away and picks the child up. She whispers something into Sue's ear.

Sue smiles and says, "Yes. Your Aunt Chris. The one you've been waiting so anxiously for and now are too silly even to say hello to."

"She's just cautious," I say.

The girl giggles and gives me a little sideways look. She has large blue eyes, Mint's eyes, and fine blonde hair that Sue has tied up with pink ribbons into two ponytails.

"Is she doing her shy routine again?" Mint asks, turning to face us.

"Oh, you know how she gets," Sue says.

Stephanie reaches over to Mint and struggles to climb out of Sue's arms and into his. Mint picks her up and holds her easily in one arm. Of course he would be good with the kids. Of course they would adore him. Safe now with her father,

Stephanie stares at me with the bold frankness that is the other side of shyness. I can't remember at all what it was like, being that young.

"Did the police talk to you?" Mint asks, pulling Stephanie's hand out of his shirt pocket.

I nod. "But I couldn't tell them anything. I guess they've really nothing to go on."

"Just the phone calls. And the note. It's something."

"What did the note actually say?"

Mint looks away from me, and then he leans down and sets Stephanie on the floor where she makes angry noises at being planted again into a forest of legs.

"Just that they had Mom and that we'd be contacted. It was made from words and letters cut out of a newspaper."

"God. Right out of a bad movie." And I laugh, stupid inappropriate laughter that I can hardly stop.

Stephanie has discovered Murray's wheelchair and she's trying to thread her fingers through the spokes. Murray rocks the wheels a little and she laughs as her fingers flap up and down. He shows her how the foot pads work, how they flip up, and then he tucks his feet in behind them and lets Stephanie sit on one. When he begins to move the chair she shrieks with delight, and as soon as he stops she demands he continue. She sits with her feet stuck straight out in front of her, and Murray gives her a little ride around the living room.

Sue goes over and picks her up. "Now don't you bother the man," she says, smiling kindly at Murray.

"It's okay. She wasn't bothering me."

Stephanie struggles to get down, but Sue won't let her go. "Oh, she's such a nuisance sometimes," she says. She backs over to stand beside Mint, who, without looking at her, reaches an arm across her shoulders.

Dad seems determined to make coffee so he's gone into the kitchen and started to run water and shove pots around. It's possible he knows what he's doing, but I decide I should go in and offer to help.

Then Murray says, "I think I hear a car. It's probably Tom."

"Already?" I say.

"I didn't hear a car," Dad says.

But I know Murray can hear things beyond the range of most mammals, so I don't suppose it's just wishful thinking that makes him hear a car in the yard. "I'll go out with you," I say.

"He can stay overnight here, too, you know, if he wants," Dad says. "There's lots of room."

"Or he can stay with us," Sue chimes in.

I glance at Murray; I know how he hates it when people talk about him in the third person, as though he weren't present. "That's okay," he says. "My friend is expecting me." He bounces his hand stiffly on the wheel of his chair.

"*Well*—" I say, the word sounding louder and shriller than I intended. Everyone looks at me as though I were a teacher demanding order. "Let's go then," I add weakly, grabbing hold of Murray's chair. He takes his hands off the wheels, folds them tidily in his lap, and lets me guide him through the house to the front door. Behind us I can hear the others follow in clumsy lurches, Stephanie beginning to cry a little because she knows someone is leaving.

When I open the door I can see the orange Firebird in the driveway, and a man who must be Tom, wearing a huge red moustache that clashes with his car, getting out of the driver's seat.

Murray wheels himself over the doorsill. "Hey, Tom!" he shouts. I follow uncertainly behind as he pushes himself over to Tom, and they slap at each other a little the way men do.

"I didn't know you were in a *wheelchair*," Tom says. "Do you have to bring it? I don't know if I can fit it in the car."

"Chris can get it in. She's an expert."

So I come up and collapse the chair and hoist it in one motion into the trunk. It makes me feel good to see Tom watching me rather helplessly, and even Mint, who comes to help, is able only to give the chair an unnecessary nudge and close the trunk for me. I get the rest of Murray's things from my car and hand them to Tom, who fits them into his back seat.

"Call me," Murray says. His car door is still open.

"I will. Tomorrow. Or as soon as I hear something."

Mint goes over and takes hold of the door and says, "It was good to meet you, Murray. I hope you can come out again before you go back."

"Thanks," Murray says, giving him a rather congested smile. Murray waves at the others on the porch and they wave back, whatever they might be saying drowned out by Stephanie's screaming. She reaches her arms out dramatically to the Firebird, as though it were her parents in it about to drive away. Mint leaves go of the car door at the same moment as Murray reaches for the handle to pull it closed, making it seem as if Mint is in exact agreement that the visit is over. Oh, my brother with the perfect timing.

Then they are gone, the Firebird spitting a pebble toward us as it turns onto Zero Avenue. I watch the car until it dips below the first hill. Stephanie is still crying; I know how she feels. Sue and Dad go back inside with her, leaving Mint and me standing awkwardly, leaning on my car. Mint kicks at the pebble which has rolled down the driveway to us, and Silky jumps down from the hood of Mom's car and begins to bat at it, too, winning it easily away from Mint and chasing it up and down the drive, silly as a kitten.

"You haven't seen the baby yet."

"How old is he now?"

"Six months. He's homely as a horse."

I give a little laugh. "I'll bet. Mr. and Mrs. Perfect don't have horsey kids."

"I'm not Mr. Perfect."

We are silent for a minute, scuffing our shoes on the driveway, not looking at each other.

"Is Uncle George likely to show up when I'm here?" Even though I'm not looking at Mint I can see him wince, see him look down at his hands as though he were a student cheating on an exam, searching for the right answer written on his cuffs.

"I don't know. Probably not."

"Do you see him? Do you have nice family get-togethers on Sundays? Do you bring the kids?"

"Chris, come on."

"Well, do you? Do you ever leave him alone with Stephanie? Does she sit on his knee while he tells her the story of the little engine that could?"

Mint looks toward the house, afraid, as though it's me that's going to hurt his Stephanie. "I don't, Chris. I'm careful.

It's all . . . we should try to forget all that. We've got to get on with our lives."

I take a deep breath. "Good old Mint," I say.

Then the front door opens, and my father stands there and stares at us, stiff as two trees frozen up into winter postures.

"Hey, you two," he shouts. "Don't know enough to get in out of the rain."

And then we notice it *is* raining, a thin mist of it clinging to our clothes, our skins, our hair, the air smelling heavy and yeasty. I don't know how long it's been like this. I run my finger down my forearm, surprised at the path I plow through the moisture.

"Rain!" I say, sounding like Murray. "Rain."

P A T

The air in the car is almost opaque with smoke but neither of them seems willing to open a window and I don't intend to ask, even though I'm starting to get dizzy. I can't roll down my window because the window handle, like the door handle, has been removed. Maybe they're afraid that if they open a window I'll begin to scream hysterically. Maybe they only want to conserve the heat.

We've been waiting in the line-up for almost an hour. Lyle thinks a snowslide has closed the canyon, but if that had happened surely we'd all have been turned back by now. Chuck is convinced it's the police, that they're searching all the cars, working their way back to ours. He wants to pull out of the line-up and turn back to Hope, but Lyle has convinced him that would only draw more attention to us. They are both of them almost as frightened as I am. Chuck takes out his gun and drums it on the steering wheel and when Lyle yells at him he only sets it on the seat beside him and picks it up again a few minutes later. Lyle sits beside me and stares out at the thin rain, at the Fraser eating its way through the narrow canyon below us. He bites at his hangnails until he makes one of them bleed. His fingernails look ugly and chewed-up, too, growing in thick little lumps at the ends of his fingers.

I am still not sure why we are here. Maybe they aren't, either.

This morning they came in early to wake me. I can't believe I was asleep, but I must have been. I remember opening my eyes and seeing them both in the room, hearing Chuck's voice saying "Pat-sy," and my struggling awake.

"You have to make the phone call," Lyle said. "Hurry up. I left you a cup of coffee on the table."

And then they went out, so suddenly I thought they must be part of some strange nightmare, but then I realized I was wide awake and remembering everything, and that sleep had never inflicted on me nightmares like this. It's Friday, I thought, visualizing the day on my calendar in its tidy second-from-the-right column. Wednesday. Thursday. Friday. My third day with them. (This is the first day of the rest of your life, it said on a sampler my mother began embroidering once, only she got bored with it and it lay around the house for months saying only "This is the.")

I knew I had no time to waste, so I got up, quickly, and went to the bathroom. The underclothes I'd rinsed out the night before were dry so I slipped them on again under the dress I hadn't dared to take off; I've slept in it two nights now. I wouldn't have thought I'd be able to do that, sleep in clothes I wore all day. At least I didn't have my period. The thought of it, of having no tampons, no protection against the determined blood, made me shiver. I rubbed at my teeth with my finger, and the coffee, which was surprisingly good, helped to get the taste of something dead out of my mouth.

Stewart. I was going to talk to Stewart. What could I say? What ambiguous message could I slide into the few words they would allow me? I knew nothing that would be helpful; I didn't know where we were.

When I was ready I went to the door, which opened to the slightest turn of the knob. I held the coffee cup carefully in front of me in both hands, like something I was carrying in a procession.

They were sitting by the phone, arguing over who would make the call. Chuck said he wanted a turn, and Lyle said that would only help the police get a fix on his voice, but Chuck insisted, and finally Lyle said, exasperated, "Well, it's your funeral."

"All *right*," Chuck said. "Where's the number?"

Lyle pointed to it. "Now you know what to say? Just the same as before only now it's eleven A.M. and the meeting place is the corner of Bute and Davie. Got it? And first you let her talk. And make it fast."

"Yeah, yeah, yeah." Chuck licked his lips and rubbed his hands up and down on his greasy jeans, as if his palms were gritty with sand he was trying to remove. He picked up the receiver and dialed slowly, carefully, his lips moving as he read off the number written on the phone book. My number.

Stewart must have answered on the first ring. "Hello, there, Mr. Duvalier," Chuck said, his voice high-pitched as a woman's. "I guess you know who this is." There was a pause, and then Chuck continued, his voice picking up speed, like something dropped from high up losing out against gravity. "Now you brought the cops in last time, Mr. Duvalier. That wasn't so smart. But we're gonna give you one last chance. You bring in the cops this time and it's game over. You got that?"

He reached over and grabbed my arm and pulled me to the phone, but instead of handing me the receiver he only held it a little away from his own ear so that I had to bend close to him to talk. His breath, smelling of coffee and cigarettes, pushed at my face. The pores of his nose looked large as potholes.

"Stewart?" I shouted. "Stewart?"

"Pat?" I could hardly hear him, but I couldn't bring myself to lean closer to Chuck. "Are you okay?"

"Just do as they say, Stewart," I said. "I love you."

"Don't worry. Don't worry. It's all under control here. Don't worry."

Chuck pushed me back and I stumbled into the wall, stood there scarcely breathing. "It's all under control here." Why would he say that? He didn't say, "I'm giving them the money." He didn't say that because it wasn't true. And why did I say, "I love you"? I hadn't planned to do that. It wasn't something I was allowed to do any more. But my life was at stake, I thought; surely the rules must be different then.

Chuck was saying, "Now you—"

"Hang up! Hang up!" It was Lyle, standing over by the window and suddenly yelling wildly at him.

Chuck just stared at him. "Hang *up*!" Lyle raced across the room, tore the phone from Chuck's hand and slammed it into the cradle. "Cops! The cops! They're coming up the walk! Jesus, Jesus, Jesus!" He was almost crying. "Take her into the bedroom. I'll try to stall them."

He grabbed Chuck with one hand and me with the other and propelled us both with quick jerky steps into my bedroom.

"Just—" Chuck finally recovered enough from his astonishment to say something, but Lyle cut him off, slamming shut the door in our faces. The second before it closed I glimpsed the top of a policeman's hat moving past the kitchen window. They've found me, I thought, calmer than I expected to be, but what difference would it make? Chuck would kill me, anyway.

Chuck motioned me as far back into the room as I could go, until I was pressed up against the towel rack in the bathroom. He took out his gun, holding it in both hands and pointing it up at the ceiling. He leaned against the door, listening, not moving. His face was tense as glass. Under his arms scoops of perspiration were forming on his shirt.

Without looking at me, he said, "One word, lady, that's all, and you're dead." I believed him.

I don't know how long we stood there, the breath moving into, out of, us. As I watched Chuck a sudden sense of . . . what? comradeship? touched me. We were both on the edge of death. What would it matter, finally, exactly how it happened? I could feel my mouth open, wanting somehow to articulate it, to give us both some comfort, but then, thank God, the moment passed and I was again only a terrified woman huddling in a bathroom.

There was a noise at the door, a voice saying something, and Chuck backed slowly away from it. When he was about halfway across the room and directly in front of the door, he said loudly, "Okay, come in."

He stood with his legs apart, crouched slightly, the gun extended rigidly in front of him. The fingers of his left hand flexed twice on his right wrist.

I closed my eyes, waiting for the explosion. But I only heard Lyle's voice, shrill and excited. "Put it down! It's only me, for Christ's sake, it's only me."

When I looked over at the door, there was no policeman,

no one walking into a trap to rescue me, only Lyle, standing with his arms raised, like a caricature, shouting, "They've gone! They've gone!" He came into the room and closed the door, and only then did Chuck pull at something on the gun, the safety catch, perhaps, and lower his arm.

"What happened?" he demanded.

Lyle sank down on the bed. He held his hands up in front of his face, watching as they trembled like those of someone with a disease.

"They had her picture," he said. "They were going door-to-door. To see if anyone knew anything."

"Oh, fuck!" Chuck shouted. "How did they know to look here?"

"How do I know? Somehow they've zeroed in on this neighbourhood. Maybe they followed us back yesterday. Maybe they traced the phone call and got part of the number that identifies this area. Maybe Mr. Annenheim across the street told them you threatened to shoot his dog. And if he hasn't told them yet he will. Who knows? Who knows? But they're close. Too close. We've got to get out of here. Now."

"And her? What about her?" Chuck didn't look at me, only waved the gun in my direction.

"She comes with us," Lyle said. He turned to me, nothing in his eyes I could understand at all. "You'll come with us," he said.

"All right," I said, as though it were necessary for me to agree.

"Phone the kid," Lyle said. "Tell him it's off." The kid. I'd heard them mention him before, and I wondered what his role in this was. The one who would actually pick up the money from Stewart, perhaps. A buffer.

After they put me back into my room I could hear them shouting furiously at each other as they packed up to go. "You don't need *that*!" "How am *I* supposed to know?" "Oh, for Christ's sake!" "Hurry *up*!" I was almost getting used to it, the violence of their language that was only normal conversation to them. Except for the obscenities, it could have been children squabbling, could have been Chris and Mint fighting over what to watch on TV, over whose turn it was to do the dishes.

I sat on the bed with my coat on, holding my purse on my lap, waiting, like someone who had called a taxi. My fingers reached up to fumble for my pearls.

And now here we are, stuck in a traffic jam outside of Hope. I am afraid to ask where we are going, what their plans are. I don't think they know. I don't think they have any plans at all. Everything now is—what does Stewart call it?—*ad hoc*.

Chuck lights another cigarette from the end of his old one. In profile he looks as if he doesn't have any lips at all, only a hole under his nose from which smoke drizzles in dirty grey streaks.

I look away, down at my hands, folded prayerfully into each other on my lap. *Our Father Who art in Heaven, get me out of here.* I wish I *could* pray; I was raised a good Lutheran, after all, but religion seemed even then only something we were expected to abandon eventually, only one of the warnings adults give children against growing up. Yet when it came to raising my own children I felt compelled to stumble through the same old rituals with them, as though it were an obligatory part of parenthood, like changing diapers or becoming an advocate for broccoli, and I began to read to them from *Bible Stories for Children,* the same book my mother used with George and me. But the children were restless, Chris anticipating more interesting plot developments than the stories could provide or else challenging their logic.

"Is that really *true*?" she would demand.

"Well, yes—Jesus was a real person—"

"But nobody can walk on water."

"Daddy-longlegs can," Mint said.

"You think God is a Daddy-longlegs?" Chris sneered.

When Stewart, who didn't care one way or the other, asked how I was doing with the religious instruction I said, "Oh, fine. I think I've turned them both into atheists."

"So it's working out okay then," he said.

I considered sending the children to one of the Sunday School classes that abounded in the neighbourhood, and Chris was eager to go because her friends went, but finally I decided against it, probably less afraid of what they would learn there than of the disgrace of having Chris sent home with a note pinned to her coat saying she was beyond redemption. Actually, that did happen to her, more or less, later, when she was in high school and the principal sent her home for selling stickers that said "Born-Again Pagan" to the other kids. I don't think he objected to the stickers as much as to the fact that she was selling them, whereas Betty-Ann Lumas was giving out her "Born-Again Christian" ones for free. Stewart said Chris should be commended for her entrepreneurial spirit, but of course it was all just a joke to him; I was the one who had to phone the school and try to mollify everyone.

Well, I shouldn't be surprised that she chose disbelief. It is, after all, the logical choice, the intelligent choice. But religion would be a comfort now, I can see that, a promise of reward for suffering, hope against all reason or argument. I glance down again at my hands, the fingers stacked piously together, but they only look like two fists clenched into each other.

I wish they would open up a window. *Open up.* That doesn't make any sense. It should be, *open down* a window.

I must be getting giddy. Maybe it's oxygen deprivation.

Still, for a woman who couldn't even stand to have her furniture moved, I am coping pretty well. No one will ever dare tell me again I haven't had enough adventure in my life.

"Hey!" Chuck yells. Through the steamy windshield I can see the cars in front of us are beginning to move. "All *right!*" He jerks the car into gear. We move slowly but decisively forward. This time it's more than just gaps closing from cars turning around and heading back west.

"Holy shit," Chuck says, excited. "Look at that. Somebody offed himself there for sure. It's just an accident, just a fucking accident." I've never heard him sound so cheerful.

Out the side window I can see part of a tractor-trailer smashed up against the rock face. Lots of people are standing around but there are no ambulances. I suppose they have all come and gone. I shudder and look away. Ahead of us is a police car with its lights flashing, an officer standing beside it waving traffic onto the narrow shoulder and past the huge yellow tanks lying on their sides in the middle of the road.

"Take it easy," Lyle says, leaning forward onto the front seat. "Don't look at the cop. Don't tailgate."

"Yeah, yeah." Chuck takes a firmer grip on the wheel, as

though it were someone's head he has taken by the ears. We ease by the tanks. I stare desperately out at the policeman, willing him to look, to see me, but of course he does not, only waves his arm repetitively at the cars that are moving too slowly for him.

And then we are past it, the traffic like released animals picking up speed, running from what has frightened them.

"We've gotta get gas," Chuck says. "Less than a quarter tank left. How much cash you got, anyway?"

"I told you. Only about a hundred."

"Jesus. That ain't taking us too far, is it? How's about you, Patsy? How many buckniks you got in that purse of yours?"

I open my purse and take out my wallet. I start to count the bills but Lyle takes it away from me and does it himself. "Thirty," he says. "Not a helluva lot. But, hey, what's this?" He pulls out my two credit cards and waves them in the air. Chuck adjusts the rearview mirror to watch.

"Yeah? So? We can't use those."

"Why not?" Lyle turns the cards over and looks at my signature. "Pat Duvalier. Hell, I could be a Pat Duvalier. God bless androgynous names."

"And what kinda names?"

"I mean, *we* could use this card, asshole. We can learn to fake her signature and as long as we don't buy anything over a hundred bucks they don't do any checks. It's like cash, man—it's like goddamned cash."

"I dunno," Chuck says. "Sounds risky to me."

"No sweat. Remember, I used to be part of the establishment once. I had one of these babies. So long as we keep moving, keep our purchases small, it'll take a month at least before it gets dangerous. And in any case you can bet the cops—or Duvalier—didn't think to call and report the cards stolen. Because they weren't, were they? Just the owner was stolen."

Chuck laughs. "The owner was stolen. Hey, that's good. The owner was stolen." He points at a service station up ahead clinging to the side of the road only a few yards away from the sheer drop into the Fraser. "How about you try it out there?"

"I have to practise the signature first," Lyle says. "But she

can sign it. You'll sign it for us, won't you, Mrs. Duvalier?"
Lyle turns to me and grins, as though he is asking a favour.

"I don't have any choice, do I?" I say coldly, surprised to
hear my own voice that does not sound deferential or frightened, that has an edge of anger. Careful, I tell myself.

"Touchy, touchy," Chuck snorts, but Lyle looks uncomfortable, looks away from me out the window.

We pull up at the pump, and Chuck stares at me in the
rearview mirror. "Not a word, Patsy. Remember what I got in
my pocket."

"I better do it," Lyle says. "I know how to use the card."

He opens the door, gets out, and the rush of cold, clean air
into the car is wonderful. I hear him at the side of the car, un-
screwing the gas cap, pushing in the nozzle. An attendant
comes out and I can hear their blurry voices. I look over at
the seat beside me, the door with the handle.

And I feel something against the side of my head.

"Don't," Chuck says.

I don't move. I know it is the gun, nuzzling my hair. I don't
move, my muscles so tense they feel as though they are tearing under the strain.

"Please," I whisper. "I won't try anything."

He pulls the gun back, slowly. "Remember this, Patsy," he
says, his mouth close to my ear. I can smell his scalp, stale and
unwashed. My eyes focus on the hairs on his neck, sticking
out straight and coarse, like cat whiskers. "I got nothing to
lose. Now, Lyle, he thinks he's smarter than me but he still
don't know something that simple. But me, I know it. I got
nothing to lose. Believe it or else."

Then something touches my throat, and it's not the gun;
it's his hand, the fingers crawling like insects under the collar
of my dress. It is worse than the gun, worse, worse. I feel a
scream snagging in my stiffened throat. Not this, I think, not
this. I thought I was safe from it, that all they wanted was the
money.

Then the car door opens and Chuck pulls back, quickly.
Lyle shoves the little clipboard with the credit card slip toward me. "Sign it," he says.

The attendant stands outside, within range of my voice. I
scribble down my signature, trying to make it look different

from usual, as though it would matter. I realize that the attendant who filled out the slip has written down the car's licence number—of course, he has to do that. So here is my name with their licence number. A perfect clue for the police. But it would be at least a month before Stewart received a statement and even then they might not think to check. And the car might be stolen. Still, it is something Lyle has overlooked, and it gives me a shiver of excitement. The police came to the door, after all, with my picture; they are not incompetents; there is a chance.

"Come *on,*" Lyle hisses, reaching in and pulling the clipboard from my hands. He tears out my copy and hands the rest back to the attendant. Then he jumps into the car and slams the door.

"That's it?" Chuck asks.

"Yeah. Go." Lyle folds up the credit card receipt and puts it in his pocket. I am so relieved to have him sitting beside me again I want to thank him for coming back, for not leaving me with Chuck. But maybe it won't happen again; maybe it was just a warning. This is my third day with them, and they have left me alone. Rape. I make myself think the word. Oh, God. I can feel nausea contracting my stomach. Then I remember how quickly Chuck drew back when Lyle came; he knew Lyle would be angry. Lyle wouldn't let it happen. If Lyle is the one in charge. Most of the time I think he is. But Chuck is the one with the gun.

The road pulls us along, a toy on a string. A couple of times I see signs saying Runaway Lane and a gravel road branches away from the highway, heading uphill and then stopping suddenly in a dead end; it seems so funny I have to stop myself from laughing. The weather suddenly turns clear and sunny, although sometimes we hit chunks of fog wallowing down out of the mountains or lying like large sofa cushions along the river. Chuck doesn't even slow down. I used to love going for rides like this with Stewart and the kids, the landscape moving past our windows as though it existed purely for our enjoyment.

It seems to relax Chuck and Lyle, too. Chuck makes noises in his throat that could be humming and he dabbles his fingers occasionally on the steering wheel as though he is beating time to music. Lyle folds his arms across his chest and dozes off. Snores putter from his mouth at about every fifth breath. A dream twitches across his face and under his lids his eyeballs race back and forth. I stare at him, fascinated. We are just outside of Lytton when he jerks awake, looking at me and then at Chuck in confusion.

"Jesus," he says. "What a nightmare."

Yes, I almost say. It is.

He yawns and stretches. "So, Mrs. Duvalier," he says suddenly, "tell me about yourself."

"I thought you knew everything about me you needed to," I say.

"This is just for fun. Conversation."

"Well, what would you like to know?"

"If I knew that then I wouldn't have to ask." He sounds annoyed. I don't want to make him annoyed. "Yourself. Tell me about yourself."

I smile nervously. "Myself. Well, I married Stewart when I was nineteen, and we have two children, a boy, he works in New Westminster and he's married with two little children, and a girl, she's the oldest, about your age, I guess, and she's a university student."

"Which university?"

"Edmonton."

Lyle makes a face. "I've been to Edmonton. It's so cold I froze my gonads off. Why'd she go to Edmonton?"

"I suppose she just wanted to get away from home." The truth doesn't sound odd. Getting away from home is, after all, what children are supposed to do.

"Edmonton!" I remember myself exclaiming, hurt and surprised. "But—you won't know anyone there."

"I'll know myself," she said.

Will you, I wondered, will you? "Well, I still wish you'd go to UBC—it's so much closer."

"I don't want to go to UBC, okay?"

"You always know better," I said bitterly, turning away from her.

"Not better," she said stiffly. "Just different."

I turned back to look at her, Chris, my only daughter, grown up and leaving home and with so much unsaid and unresolved between us. *Don't go,* I wanted to plead. *Not yet. Please.* But all I said was, "Well, it's up to you."

"I know," she said.

"Does she like it? University?" Lyle asks.

"Yes. I think so. She gets good grades."

"That doesn't mean she likes it."

"Oh, well, I suppose. . . . Where did you go to university? Oregon?"

Lyle grins. "The T-shirt, right? No, no, that was just to confuse you. And I'm supposed to be asking the questions."

"I thought this was supposed to be a conversation."

Chuck slaps the steering wheel and gives a hoot of laughter, as though I had said something hilarious. "Hey, she got you there, eh?"

"Oh, fuck off," Lyle says, glaring at Chuck, whose disembodied eyes, beautiful now that they are cut from the rest of his face, watch us from the rearview mirror. No one says anything else and I wonder if that is it, if the conversation is over. But surely, I think, it is better for me to talk to them than not, to establish whatever human link I can with them. With Lyle, anyway. I don't want to establish anything with Chuck.

"But you did go to university somewhere, didn't you?" I say timidly.

"Yeah. Somewhere."

"How long?"

"Two years. A little knowledge is a dangerous thing."

"Why did you stop?"

"Money. I told you. Money. They wanted it. I didn't have it. Everything comes down to money. Ideas are an expensive habit. And I was getting seduced, as they say, by other expensive habits. But they're all the same. They lift you up—oh, yas, sweet Jesus, they lifts you up—and then they show you the black hole of the cosmos, the whole fucking existential fraud—oh, yes, lady, I mean death, the big Bergman boogeyman—"

I stop understanding what he is saying. It must make sense. Death, he says. I remember him talking about it before. Death. We're all afraid of death.

"We're all afraid of death," I say.

Lyle takes a deep breath, calming himself. "We're not all afraid of death. We love death. Necrophilia. Our society worships death. War. Religion. Evolution. Television. Money. It's all a love of death. Who are our big heroes? People who die young. Remember the one-legged kid who did that marathon run and then died of cancer? Perfect hero. Handsome and young and dead. When Presley died one of his managers said, 'Good career move.' Whose pictures did your generation have on the wall when you were my age? James Dean? Janis Joplin? Che Guevara? Jesus Christ? Death. We love it."

He reaches into his shirt pocket and takes out a small plastic Ziploc bag that is about a quarter full of something that looks like icing sugar. "Death," he says, waving it lightly in the air. "I love it."

"Oh, shit—" Chuck says. "Don't you do any of that now." His eyes in the mirror are flat and hostile.

Lyle ignores him, opens the bag and spoons out thin crescents of the powder under three of his fingernails. "Want some?" he asks me.

"What is it?" I ask. A drug of some kind, obviously.

"Heaven," he says. "Hell." He turns slightly to the window and moves the fingers with the powder to his face. I try to see what he does with it but he has turned too far away from me. I have seen a syringe in his suitcase, but apparently he doesn't need it now. When he turns back the powder is gone.

"You should try it," he says. "Getting addicted doesn't happen from just doing it once."

"That's what Stewart said about getting pregnant." I can't believe I told him that. I can feel a blush, a foolish girlish blush, pull at my cheeks. Stupid, stupid thing to say.

Lyle begins to laugh, a funny braying sound that he seems unable to control. "Beautiful," he gasps. "Atta girl. Don't you believe us. Cynics live longer than anybody."

"Is that the point then? To live longer than anybody?"

"For some people," he says. He turns to look back out the window. Apparently he doesn't want to talk any more. Perhaps the drug makes it impossible. Or perhaps it only makes me less interesting than the conversations he can have in his own head. I try to imagine what it is like—like alcohol, I suppose, although alcohol has never made me feel much more than dizzy.

"Death," Chuck says suddenly. "You wanna know what death is? It's nothing, man, no heaven, no hell, just nothing. It's like you pull the tab off a beer can and there's a little pop and that's it. Nothing."

Lyle gives a little laugh. "That's not bad, Chuck. The tab off a beer can."

"Yeah." His voice sounds pleased. He shifts around in his seat as though he wants to continue talking, but he only reaches for the radio and turns it on and finally pulls in a station. Country and western music rolls wavily into the car, a song about a trucker's wife and a CB radio. ". . . Never hear your voice again," sings a woman, her voice so sad and real it makes me swallow, makes tears sting at my eyes.

"Oh, turn it off," Lyle says, irritably. "It's maudlin."

"Never heard of her," Chuck says. He runs the dial quickly back and forth, but there is nothing but the crackly voice of static so he tunes in the country and western song again.

"Sounds like a sick cat," says Lyle.

The song ends, the last quivering guitar note reaching out from the speaker. The announcer comes on and tries to sell us outboard motors, and then there are a series of community announcements: a dance tonight at the high school gym, a whist drive tomorrow afternoon at the Happy Pioneers meeting, Reverend Fellbad speaking on "The Devil and You" Sunday at the Holy Redeemer Tabernacle. I listen carefully, as though I might have to go to one of these and must remember the details. Then the announcer puts on another record, but we turn a corner around a steep embankment and the radio stutters with static.

". . . west Texas town of El Paso, I fell—" and then the words crumble away.

"Shit," Chuck says, turning the volume up.

". . . as the west Texas wi-i-i-i-ind," the radio surges up, then dies again.

"Dum dum, da dum dum," Chuck fills in. "Out where the horses were ti-i-i-i-ied." He does surprisingly well on the high notes. "Dum dum da dum dum, it looked like it could run—"

"Up on its back and away I did ride," says Lyle, his voice not quite singing, but keeping the rhythm, rising up on the right notes.

Chuck and I turn to stare at him.

"Shouting and shooting I can't let them catch me," exclaims the radio suddenly as we turn east again. "I have to make it to Rosa's back door—"

And both of them are singing along now, the three voices a bizarre blend, and because it is a song I remember I feel my lips moving a little, too, the old melody tugging at my throat.

The radio retreats again into static by the last stanza, and when Chuck fiddles with the dial he loses the station completely.

"Oh, fuck," he says.

"From out of nowhere Felina has found me," Lyle sings, "something, something, she kneels by my side, cradled by two loving arms that I'll die for, one little kiss then Felina good-bye."

"Hey, yeah," Chuck says. "I thought you didn't like this stuff."

"A vestigial remain," Lyle says. He grins a little, apologetically. "How'd I do?"

"Pretty good," I say, assuming he's addressing me. "I thought her name was Selina, though."

"I thought it was Helena," Chuck says.

"Felina," Lyle says.

"Huh," Chuck says. "Lot you know."

We drive on, the landscape unrolling perfectly past our windows. Chuck, giving up finally on the radio, begins to drive faster, impatient, taking the left-hand turns by moving out into the other lane even when his vision is impaired. I clutch onto the seat whenever it happens, tensing for an oncoming car. I suppose there are seat belts curled up in the crack in the seat behind me, but I don't want to start rummaging around there now. Lyle stares dreamily out his window, unconcerned, beating his fist gently on his knee. Either he doesn't care how Chuck is driving or he trusts him to be able to manoeuvre safely. I'm surprised Lyle doesn't seem to want to drive, but I suppose I prefer it this way, him instead of Chuck in the seat beside me.

"I gotta take a leak," Chuck says suddenly.

He slows down and turns off at the first pull-over he sees on the narrow road, a little gravel crescent that slices down sharply into the Thompson; the bank is ragged with exposed tree roots, making me think of dental X-rays and abraded gums. There is a picnic table at the edge and parking for only about three cars. Chuck pulls so close to the bank that Lyle screams at him, "Stop! Christ. What's the matter with you? Jesus, I've met plankton smarter than you."

Chuck only grunts and gets out of the car. He walks behind it and I try not to imagine what he is doing.

"I have to go, too," I say to Lyle.

"Okay," he says. "Just wait until Chuck's finished."

When we hear the crunch of gravel under Chuck's feet Lyle opens his door and I slide over and we get out.

"Hey—who said she could get out?" Chuck demands.

"Oh, get off it, eh? She has to take a leak, too. Come on over here, give her some privacy, for Christ's sake."

Chuck makes a derisive noise but he comes over to where we are, and Lyle says to me, "Go ahead. We won't look."

"Thank you," I say.

"Don't try to run," Chuck says. "You got nowhere to go."

I walk around to the other side of the car, the clean, cold air, the open space around me like a gift I don't deserve. I inhale deeply, the air scraping the smoke and dirt from my lungs. Then I remember what I am here for, and hurriedly I squat down. I need to go badly, but it won't come. Hurry up, hurry up, I plead with my body, but it takes forever before I feel the warm release. I have brought my purse and I use the toilet paper I took with me from the room in Burnaby, and then I straighten my clothes and stand up. I wish I could wash my hands, but the river is inaccessible. When I turn around I see Chuck has wandered off and is skipping stones into the water and Lyle has sat down on the car's front bumper and is staring vacantly into the thick grey water.

A truck goes by on the highway, and I consider my chances of rushing out and trying to flag someone down. The traffic is going so fast, and there is a curve limiting visibility—I might only get myself killed. But it could be worth the risk. I might never get another chance. My thoughts dash around furiously in my head, banging into my skull as though there is not enough room to decide. And then Chuck sees me standing up and he saunters back toward the car and I know that it's too late. I am actually relieved; the decision on the side of cowardice has been made for me.

I make no move to get back in the car; I want to stay out here as long as possible, until I am summoned, even though I can feel the cold sucking up through the thin soles of my shoes. I suppose I am like most people on the coast, pretending there is no such thing as winter, as snow, as cold. I notice patches of ice frozen into the gravel, water with its soft molecules all sealed up tight.

And suddenly there is a memory. Of Chris. She was so young. Three, perhaps. She had found a dead bird on the lawn in the fall, and I saw her, from where I was weeding the roses, as she picked it up and held it in the air, as though she were putting it back on a shelf, replacing it from where it had fallen, where it should be. When she released it and it fell back down to the ground, I could see her face twist up in frustration, and I thought, how do I explain it when she asks?

"It felt funny," was all she said. "All stiff."

"That's death," I said.

And that winter, when the frost came and covered the water on our driveway with a thin skin of ice, she prodded at it with her toe and said, "It's all stiff, Mommy. The water's dead."

Years later, when she was a teen-ager and fell off that stupid motorcycle and broke her arm, she said flippantly to the doctor as he was putting on the cast, "Well, will I live or die?" and he answered cheerily, "You'll do both, my dear." I wish I could have made up answers like that.

When I think of Chris it is always so confused. She is my daughter, my first-born, but when I had Mint she pulled back even further from me, into a private dark corner full of her own fantasies, slapping out at me when I reached for her with whatever she knew could hurt me most.

"I hate you," she would scream, crouching in her bedroom like a cornered animal. "Leave me alone" and "You can't make me!" and crawling into Stewart's lap as he laboured over his business reports because sometimes he would let her stay; it must have pleased him to see her choose him over me, to see her cling to him and look out at me with her face closed and angry.

And the worst, the worst, the story I cannot even think about, about George—how did she come to hate me so much, that she could say something so ugly and cruel? For days afterward I couldn't even bear to look at her.

The old anger and outrage rise up in me as I think about it, but they are duller now, numbed by time—I feel them more as a loss, a failure, mine and hers both, perhaps. Oh, I have admitted to myself that I did not love her as I loved Mint, but which mother can tell you honestly she does not love one child over another? Especially when one child is always eager and open and the other struggles from the moment of birth for separateness? I think my mother loved my brother more than me, but I did not use that as an excuse to become bitter and hostile, to make up dangerous lies about people who loved me.

When my counsellor asked me if I'd discussed my divorce with the children, I said, "Mint is sympathetic and consoling and says I've been treated dreadfully. Then he'll talk with Stewart and be sympathetic and understanding to him. He's not insincere. He's just very . . . empathetic. Like a counsellor."

She ignored that and asked, "And your daughter?"

I hesitated, trying to think of something noncommittal to say. "Well, I don't think she really cares a lot."

"But don't you think it's worth talking about with her? You need her support now."

I didn't tell her that my need might be all the more reason for Chris to back away. You didn't support *me,* I can hear her saying; why should I support you? And she's right, of course —I tried to believe her, but I couldn't, I simply couldn't. If it had been anyone but George, perhaps—I knew such things did happen, after all—but not George, not my brother, who, when Daddy was killed, became like my father, the one I could count on, the one who was strong when my mother retreated into her widowhood and misery.

I was ten when I opened the door to the policeman and he told us about the accident, the tree falling the wrong way, and

Daddy was dead. Daddy. I have always called him that in my memory, Daddy, a child's name, but that is still what he is, someone never allowed to grow up into Dad, Father, Grandfather. He was forty-three when he died. The age I am now. It sends a shiver through me. I read somewhere how children have a difficult time when they reach the age at which their parents died, how it is hard for them to accept that they can live beyond it. Well, I can accept it. If I'm given a choice.

I look around for Chuck and see he is still in no hurry to go. But then he shouts at me, "Are you ready?" and I have to say yes.

Lyle gets up from the bumper on which he's been sitting and stretches and walks over to the water's edge, nudging a stone over the side with his shoe.

"Are you guys hungry?" he asks. "Let's have a sandwich."

"Good idea," Chuck says. He goes over to the trunk and opens it and takes out a brown grocery bag. "Over there?" He ducks his head toward the picnic table.

"Sure," Lyle says.

They go over to it and set the bag down. A red-winged blackbird, the crimson on its wings like a flow of blood, flies over and watches us hopefully from a branch a few yards away.

"Damn crow," Chuck says, picking up a rock and throwing it at the bird, which flutters away but lands again on the gravel close by, eyeing us in its sharp birdy way.

"It's a blackbird, for Christ's sake, not a crow," Lyle says.

"It's a crow. I know what a goddamned crow looks like." He picks up a handful of pebbles. The bird hops further away.

"It's a red-winged *blackbird*. Look at the size of it, the red tips on the wings. Jesus."

"Caw. Caw," says Chuck. He throws one of the pebbles. The bird flies back to the branch.

"What do *you* think it is, Mrs. Duvalier? It's a blackbird, isn't it?"

"I don't know much about birds." *Don't take sides,* Stewart would say when I complained to him about the children's fights. *Then Chris will always win,* I'd protest. *Maybe she's always right,* he would say, or something equally glib.

He didn't really think things were that simple; he just didn't want to get involved.

The bird finally decides we are unlikely to be generous with our food and flits off across the river.

"See that red?" Lyle demands. "Red-winged blackbird."

"I don't see no red," Chuck says, not looking at the bird. He begins to take things out of the bag, and Lyle, with an exaggerated sigh, starts to help. I am amazed at all they finally unpack. There is cutlery, a loaf of bread, cheese, peanut butter, canned meat, beer, napkins. How could they have packed this all up so quickly this morning? Perhaps it is something they have had to do in a hurry before. I move over to them, some early conditioning telling me I should help.

"I'm impressed," I say.

Lyle grins, as though I have said the right thing. "What would you like?" he asks, holding his arms out over the table like a priest. "Place your order."

"Well . . . whatever you're having." It sounds so silly I almost begin to giggle. It is the kind of conversation that people really could be having in a restaurant, lazing over their menus.

Lyle picks up the can opener and attaches it to one of the cans of meat, ham, it looks like. "How about this?" he asks.

"Fine."

Chuck has opened one of the cans of beer and he takes a mouthful, flicking it around inside his cheek before he swallows. He hands another can to Lyle and then he opens the bread bag and lays out six slices side by side on some of the napkins. "Brown bread," he snorts. "What'd you get this brown shit for? White tastes better."

"Brown is healthier," Lyle says.

"Huh," says Chuck. "It's just white bread with some brown colour added."

"Jesus Christ, don't be so goddamned ignorant. The flour is brown to start with and then it's *bleached* to make white bread."

"Says you. My way makes more sense."

Lyle winces his head to the side, raises his eyes skyward. "Brain dead. I swear to fucking Christ you are *brain dead.*"

"Mr. Know-It-All. Mr. Smarty-Pants." Chuck sits down on the bench with his back to us and glares out across the river.

Lyle drops thick chunks of ham on three of the slices and then he opens the cheese and cuts enough to fill the other three. He squashes the sandwiches together, hands one over to me, nudges Chuck who half turns and picks up his, and then we all begin to eat.

It is delicious. I have never tasted anything so good. I eat slowly, savouring it. "Mmmmm," I say to Lyle, who grins back at me, his cheek bulging out comically from his thin face.

We sit and eat. If anyone drives by and sees us, they might smile a little to themselves, thinking we are a mother and her two sons, a family, having a picnic. My feet are numb from the cold, but I pull them up beside me on the bench and cover them with my coat and it seems to help.

In the river a fish twists out of the water, like a silver coin tossed spinning into the air. I want to say, *Look,* that most wonderful of first words in the Dick and Jane reader, *look:* that simple urge to share with a companion something beautiful. But I don't, of course.

Chuck finishes his sandwich and makes himself another one. "That wasn't bad, man," he says, sounding so normal, so human, that I almost forget about the gun in his pocket.

Lyle makes himself another sandwich, too, saying, "Help yourself," and when I finish mine I do.

Chuck takes a last swallow from his beer can and then hurls it in a high parabola down toward the river. I can hear its thin clatter as it hits the rocks on the bank.

"Litterbug," Lyle comments.

"Mr. Law-abiding Citizen."

"That can's got your prints all over it. Now one of those cars going by—" he gestures back at the road where there are indeed two cars going by at this very moment "—just might remember seeing us here, will tell the cops that the woman they saw could just be that missing woman they've heard about, and so the cops will come down here looking for evidence, and what do they find but that can with your prints plain as hell all over it." Lyle takes a careful drink from his own can, sets it down slowly in front of him, keeping his fingers cupped around it.

"Oh, yeah?" Chuck says, but his eyes shift nervously to the edge of the bank.

"Yeah," Lyle says. And then, and I can hardly believe it, he gives me a blatant wink.

"Well, I ain't crawling down there to get it," Chuck declares, giving us both a surly glare.

"It's your funeral," Lyle says. He takes the last swallow from his can and drops it into the grocery bag with the left-over bread and cheese which I assume we will take with us. "Well, I guess we can go then." He takes out my credit card from his pocket and waves it in the air. "Garçon!"

"You learned to fake that signature yet?" Chuck asks.

"Oh, hey, no. You got a pen?" he asks me.

I hand him one from my purse, and he tears off a piece from the grocery bag and starts to copy my signature. His first attempt is awful, and it all seems so funny, him trying to steal my name, and doing such a poor job of it, that I start to laugh.

"That's terrible," I say.

Chuck leans over and looks and says, "Yeah. It sure is."

"Everyone's a critic," Lyle says, but sounding amused himself.

He tries several more times, and at last he seems to master the correct slant and the right proportion of the capitals to the small letters. Finally he pushes the card away and covers up his first attempts, and it is only then that I feel fear, as I see his hand writing smoothly, no longer copying, my name. Pat Duvalier, writing my name in my script, as though it were his.

S
A
T
U
R
D
A
Y

CHRIS

Dad and I are doing the lunch dishes, him drying and me washing, both of us pretending we don't see the automatic dishwasher built in right beside the sink. It's sort of a friendly thing to do, I guess, cleaning up the dishes with someone, and it makes me miss Murray, because we sometimes do this together. I wanted to call him this morning, but Dad was too nervous about tying up the phone, and, besides, the thing is tapped and I don't really want them to record Murray talking about farts or fornication, which he would do on purpose if he knew the police were listening. Phoning him from somewhere else will give me an excuse to go out this afternoon.

Dad has been telling me about Yvonne, who, I realize with distaste, will soon become my stepmother. He glances repeatedly at the phone on the counter as though its silence will shame him into not talking about her. I don't care about Yvonne, I want to snap. I turn the hot water tap on, hard and loud.

But what's the point of coming home if I'm not going to try to be agreeable? Maybe I'm just afraid to see Dad so vulnerable, needing me, wanting my approval, one adult to another: parents shouldn't do that to their kids. I turn off the tap.

"She's pregnant, you know," he says.

"What?"

"Yvonne. She's pregnant."

"Oh, Dad." Pregnant. God. "Are you, you know, happy about that?"

He picks at the glaze on the cup he's drying. "I don't know. Not a whole lot, I guess. But Yvonne wants it. I have to stand by her."

How noble of you, I want to say, but I stop myself. "So. I'm going to have a stepsibling. You're going to start a whole new family." I hand him the casserole bowl.

"Well—you and Mint turned out so well, I can't lose, eh?" It's a feeble joke, but I give him the smile for it he expects.

"How far along is she?"

"Three months. Maybe four. You should meet her, you know. She's a nice person. People always like her. Maybe if you've time tomorrow—"

"I don't know how long I can stay. It depends on what happens with Mom." I drop her name deliberately, like the spoon I drop into the dishwater, watching the soapy ripples as it disappears to the bottom.

"I know," he says. "I know."

And then he's crying, oh, god, he's crying, and what am I supposed to do now? He turns away from me so I won't see, and I stand there holding the dishcloth, flicking it miserably against the drain board.

"It's okay," I say. "It's okay. They'll let her go. They usually do." I've no idea if they usually do. In the cases you hear about they usually don't.

We finish the dishes awkwardly in silence, Dad periodically hunching his shoulder in what he thinks is an inconspicuous gesture to wipe tears from his face. We put the dishes away together, my fingers remembering where everything goes. Dad props the big platter up behind the stack of dinner plates in the buffet, the way Mom always did, although it leans farther forward than it should, nudging the rims of the cups. I don't let myself go over and fix it, although it wouldn't matter to Dad if I did, not the way it would matter to Mom. To her any change was criticism.

As I'm putting away the glasses in the cupboard I glance at the calendar hanging on the side of the refrigerator, Mom's tiny handwriting noting appointments. I can remember some of the abbreviations: *Hos. A.* means her hospital auxiliary meetings, *Claire, l.* means lunch with Mrs. Fraser. I reach my hand up, touch the days she's been gone. Wednesday. Thursday. Friday. My fingers move to today, Saturday, the last day in the row, but I drop my hand abruptly, as though if I don't touch it it won't count—I take a deep breath, lean my hand for a moment against the cupboard wall where Dad can't see. Then I turn determinedly back to the sink, pick up two more glasses from the drain board.

Claire, l. Sunday. This Sunday.

"Dad," I say. "I think Mom's arranged to have lunch with Mrs. Fraser tomorrow. Look at the calendar. Maybe you should call her and cancel."

Dad peers at the calendar. "*Claire, l.,*" he reads. "Well, that's tomorrow, all right." He turns the saucer he's drying around and around in his dishtowel as though he were filing it down.

"Maybe you should call her," I prompt. "You don't want her showing up here and finding out what's happened."

"I guess not." He doesn't sound convinced. "But what will I tell her?"

"Tell her Mom's sick, or out of town. Anything."

"Could you do it?" Dad pleads. "You're better at this kind of thing."

At lying? I almost ask. "It would look strange if I called. I'm not even supposed to be here." I try not to sound impatient.

"Mom might be home by then. By tomorrow." Dad finally sets the saucer down on the counter; the friction must have started to burn his fingers.

"Well, even if she is I doubt she'll want to go out for lunch with Mrs. Fraser."

"I shouldn't tie up the phone."

"Look, if you don't want to— I only thought—"

"No, you're right. I'll call her. The police would want me to call her."

We finish putting the dishes away, and Dad, with a final plaintive look at me that I ignore, goes over to the phone, fumbles in the book until he finds the number, and begins to dial.

When I hear him say, "Hello? John? Is your mother

home?" I go down the hall to my room; I don't want him to think I'm eavesdropping. I run my hand along the wall as I walk, feeling the faintly raised pattern in the wallpaper repeating itself under my fingers. Suddenly, my eyes snag on the closed door to Mom's bedroom. I'm not even conscious of going over to it, but here I am, opening it gently, as though someone might be inside, asleep.

The room looks as I remember it, the large closets with mirrored sliding doors, the walnut dresser with matching bedside tables and reading lamps, the queen-size bed perfectly made and covered with the blue comforter Grandma gave her. The family portrait we had done about five years ago hangs over the dresser, all of us looking so happy and handsome, Mom and Dad sitting on the studio settee, him covering her hand with his, Mint and me standing behind them, smiling at the camera, making the kind of picture the photographer would want to display in his window. My eyes flick down to the dresser top, across the small framed photos there: Mint and me as toddlers, holding hands; Mom's wedding picture; Grandma and her and Uncle George—I jerk my eyes away.

The only thing that looks even slightly disorderly in this room is the dressing gown tossed onto the bed, as though whoever wore it were coming back soon, to put it on or hang it up or have it laundered. I go over, cautiously, touch my fingers to it, draw back almost immediately, a chill shivering up my back. I picture absurdly a scene from "Star Trek": someone has been vaporized and all that remains are the clothes, collapsed emptily inwards, and Captain Kirk draws his phaser and looks nervously around at the landscape that is suddenly sinister, dangerous. What if the kidnappers came in here, her bedroom— I close my eyes, refusing to see anything at all, and turn away from the bed. I take several deep breaths, can feel my lungs filling, pushing my chest against my blouse, keeping me alive.

When at last I open my eyes, the thing they focus on is a book, a thick hardcover, lying on one of the bedside tables, with a bookmark protruding from it like a tongue. Curious, I go over and pick it up. It's a novel, I see, flipping through the pages, called *Married Alive*. On the flyleaf is the inscription, "Hang in there. Love, George." I close it quickly and set it down and back away, like a voyeur afraid of being caught, until I'm out of the room entirely, standing in the hall. When I turn and reach for the door and start to pull it closed, the last thing I see in the room before the door snaps shut are the photos on the dresser, smiling behind glass. Mint and me as children, holding hands; Mom and Dad on their wedding day; Grandma and Mom and Uncle George in Kelowna. All of them incomplete stories. All of them telling lies. I lean back against the closed door.

I don't hear anything from the kitchen so I assume Dad's off the phone by now, and when I walk back down the hall I see he's gone into the living room and is fiddling half-heartedly with our old 400-day clock that hasn't been working right for the last five years.

"What did you tell her?" I ask, dropping myself into the love seat.

"I said my sister in Victoria was sick and that Pat has to go over and look after things for a few days."

"That's pretty good." I'm surprised that he's come up with something so inventive. His affair with Yvonne has probably sharpened his skill with believable alibis.

He pokes at the clock, says "Damn!" when the screwdriver slips.

"I think I'll go out for a while. If that's all right," I say.

"Sure. Fine. Take my car if you want."

"Okay. Thanks." I stand up, feeling guilty, as though I'm abandoning him. "I'll make us supper when I come back."

Dad gives a little grunt, doesn't take his eyes from the clock.

It feels good to step outside. I take big lungfuls of breath, the air sweet with the ferment of spring. Blackie nickers at me from the pasture and trots over to the fence. Blackie is something else that used to be mine and that I've abandoned. Guilt, guilt, guilt. I walk over to him, across the lawn that feels sharp as steel wool under my feet, and I rub my palm up and down his long, flat face. He paws a little at the ground, bounces his head up and down impatiently, expecting the sugar I always used to bring him.

"It rots your teeth," I tell him, what Dad always said and I always ignored.

I look over at the barn. Maybe I could go for a quick ride, just in the pasture, bareback; it's been years since I've done that. He could probably use the exercise. He follows me to the barn, nuzzling at my pockets, finally shoving me irritably in the back. I pick up the bridle and slide it on, but he clamps his huge yellow teeth shut and won't let me push in the bit. We struggle for several minutes but he won't give in. I almost decide to let him win but then I try putting my hand in my pocket, bringing it out closed and then opening it up right under his nose. It takes him off guard, and as he rummages greedily on my hand with his big horsey lips he lets his jaw relax and I slide the bit in fast between his teeth. He doesn't seem surprised. It must be nice to be so stoical.

I swing the reins up, climb on the fence and then heave myself onto his back. He moves off with me still draped across, graceful as a stocking filled with sand. I hang desperately onto his mane until finally I'm able to get my leg up and over, and then I get hold of the reins and manage to urge him out of his lurching walk into a trot. I try to get into the rhythm, but he always seems to be coming up when I'm coming down, and it feels like a hammer on my spine; I can imagine my vertebrae fusing. When I bang my heels into his sides he finally concedes me a gallop, but that's even worse. Now I'm not only getting smashed up, I'm in danger of falling off. I tug back on the reins and he skids to a halt, almost tossing me over his head. My face jars into his neck, my mouth fills with his coarse mane hair.

It's very depressing. I remember how I would draw pictures of Blackie into the margins of my school notebooks, how I thought *The Black Stallion* was the greatest book ever written, how nothing was as exciting as taking Blackie for a run. And now I only feel like a tourist at a dude ranch. Or a grownup playing a child's game.

"Grow up!" my mother used to snap at Mint and me when we were young and squabbling, "why don't you grow up!" as though grownups would never fight; and so "Grow up!"

we'd shout at each other later, only partly in parody, clever children rehearsing the weapons of adults, "Grow up, will you!"

I slide off Blackie's back, don't even want to ride him back to the barn.

I take the bridle off, and he ambles away across the pasture. When he gets far enough out he grunts as he drops himself clumsily down to his knees and then onto his side. Lie Down always *was* his favourite gait. He rolls over onto his back, twisting and kicking his legs as though he has to rub himself clean.

I brush myself off, hang the bridle back in the barn, and head for the house. I hope Dad wasn't watching. He's probably wondering why I haven't gone for my drive. I get into his Lincoln, back it carefully out of the garage, along the driveway. I watch my hands on the steering wheel, the way the slightest touch turns the wheels, the slightest pressure on the gas pedal means acceleration. Horsepower. Only it's more than that, something dangerous, something we learn to want. Luxury.

I drive down to the beach at White Rock, full as usual with teen-agers and their loud radios. A few years ago I was one of them; now I feel like someone of another generation. Only the music sounds the same, electricity, drumming my fingers on the wheel. Murray insists he can taste music. Glenn Gould tastes like chocolate, he says. I turn the radio up louder.

The sports car in front of me wears a bumper sticker that says "White Rock means never having to say you're Surrey." Snob. What's White Rock anyway except that little chunk of Surrey sliding into the ocean? Marine Drive is so crowded I finally give up and turn right up the hill, the Lincoln not giving a ping as it starts up Johnston, which must be nearly at a ninety-degree angle. Johnston won't go through, so I turn onto Fir, and then Pacific, left on Dolphin, and I wind up going east on Semiahmoo, but that's okay because if I turn on Balsam it'll become Finlay which will take me straight to the King George Highway. It surprises me, that I still remember where to go, that the grid of Edmonton hasn't stamped itself permanently over this map. Amazing what can live side by

side in your mind: toleration of contradiction. It's supposed
to mean you're creative ... or else it means you've been
brainwashed. Both things are true. Both things are false. Isn't
education wonderful?

I turn onto the old boring King George, head up into the
middle of Surrey, although it's hard to know where the
middle is. The real centre of Surrey is still Vancouver, almost
an hour away.

I don't know why I'm wasting time like this. I should be
doing something useful—shopping for groceries, working on
my essay, getting the fan belt fixed—but I feel as if I'm in
suspension, the day a waiting room where nothing is possible
except waiting, the waiting a kind of task in itself, that has to
be finished before I can go on to something else.

I drive up to the community college, where I took my first
year of university transfer courses. The parking lot is almost
empty because it's Saturday, but I park and go into the cafe-
teria, buy a Coke. A pregnant girl in a dress like a nightgown
asks me where Admissions is, and I'm pleased that I can
point her in the right direction. She thanks me warmly and I
watch her waddle away, the huge swell of her stomach seem-
ing to pull her along as she leans back from it, apparently re-
sisting. I suppose she has to walk that way, that it has something to do with a new centre of gravity.

I wander through the 400 building. There's a creepy feeling to the place when it's so deserted, like one of my father's
warehouses. Well, I suppose that's all it is, a big warehouse,
empty today of what is usually stored here. The hallway still
looks as if it's set up for a gymkhana, garbage cans everywhere for the leaky roof.

I find a pay phone and call the number Murray left me. No
answer. I feel stupidly annoyed—he should *be* there when I
want him. There are other people I could call, I suppose,
people I met in college, but I don't want to talk to anyone
else. Selfish: my mother's favourite adjective for me.

"The world doesn't revolve around you," she'd say.

"Yes, it does," I'd snap back. I can hear my voice now,
bratty and sarcastic, and it makes me wince, realizing how
often I must have sounded like that, not even hearing what

she was saying, contradicting and challenging her almost by instinct, no matter how illogical I sounded. Was it worse after what happened with Uncle George? Maybe not. Maybe after that I just tried not to talk to her at all.

I wander back outside to the parking lot and then over to the playground of the elementary school next door. I sit down in one of the swings, my legs dragging under the seat which isn't made for somebody my size. I feel big and clumsy, but I walk myself back far enough to give me some momentum and then I let myself go, tucking my legs tightly under the board. The air rushes at me. Back and forth, back and forth: my legs pump in the old rhythm, higher and higher. I'm the tongue of a bell, banging into the air, tolling.

Finally I let the arcs subside, smaller and smaller, until I drop my legs and they scrape me to a stop. I sit there fiddling with the ropes and feeling silly. I never even liked swings. They always made me dizzy.

A woman walks by with a tiny fuzzy dog on a leash, and she stops and waits while the dog has a dump on the playground lawn. When it's finished it kicks at its pile with its rear legs, a behaviour that seems to be entirely rhetorical, and then the woman bends down and picks the dog up, dabbing it at her face like a powder puff and whispering effusively.

"Such a *good* doggie," I hear her say.

People have got to be the strangest things in this world.

When the woman has gone, still pressing the dog at her face, I get up and walk back to the car, and, because I can't think of any more excuses to stay away, I head back home. I drive so slowly that twice cars beep angrily at me, wanting to get past. A guy in a TransAm, with a girlfriend welded to his side, accelerates indignantly past me, and the girl throws me that smug look that girls with guys give girls without guys. Well, she can have him, I think, as the TransAm spins back into my lane so sharply I have to brake; his car is probably more interesting than he is.

I ease over the last hill before the house, and then I let the car coast up to the driveway. It has just enough momentum to take the turn smoothly. But as I pull around the corner of the house, my heart gives a sudden jump—there's a strange car parked in front of the door. I feel myself starting to tremble. It's a police car, I'm sure of it, an unmarked police car. Oh, please, god, no, don't let him have bad news.

I don't bother pulling the car into the garage; I just shove the gear handle into Park while the car is still moving and I jump out and run to the front door. When I reach up to brush the hair from my eyes, I can feel my forehead greasy with sweat, as though I'd been running for miles. I take a deep breath and reach for the doorknob.

The constable is a young and apologetic-looking man, his uniform a size too small for him, his hair cut so short it must hurt. He stands in the kitchen holding a cup of coffee that is probably still left from what I made this morning. His gun hangs along his thigh like a heavy black frying pan.

I barely give him a chance to turn around before I say, "What's happened? Is there any news?"

"This your daughter?" the cop asks Dad, as though I were too young to answer for myself.

"Yes, this is Chris." To me Dad says, "No, no news, really, nothing. Chris, this is Constable Persky. Constable, my daughter, Chris." My father, never forgetting his manners, the good businessman. But I can see his eyes are red and watery and I'm sure he's been crying. I can't bear to look at him; it seems so shameful, to see your father crying, and in front of a stranger.

The constable extends his hand and, reluctantly, I let him take mine. I hate shaking hands—someone offering you something and you reach for it and it's nothing and your hand comes away empty. His handshake is hard, authoritative, the way they taught him, I suppose; my own hand feels like a jumble of bones in a glove of skin as he squeezes it, incapable of returning any pressure even if it wanted to. He holds it so long I'm beginning to feel we're glued together.

"I was just telling your father," Constable Persky says, "that we were able to do a partial trace on the first call and we narrowed it down to a section of Burnaby. We started doing some foot patrol work there yesterday. We might come up with something. We're doing all we can."

Doing all we can. Yeah. Sure. That's what they all say. "Is there anything we should be doing here?" I ask, just to have something to say.

"Just make sure someone's home all the time. Keep the phone free. If they call keep them talking as long as you can. Agree to anything they say."

I nod.

"We do wish you'd not keep the money in the house, Mr. Duvalier. We could arrange with the bank—"

"No. I want it here. I want to have it ready." Dad inhales deeply a couple of times and passes the back of his hand quickly under his nose. I think absurdly of the joke about how the RCMP got the yellow stripe down the sides of their pants, the answer being the nose-wiping gesture Dad used followed by another wiping motion along the trousers. I glance quickly over at Constable Persky, swallowing a stupid giggle that bubbles up in my throat. God, what's wrong with me? Nothing about this is funny.

"Well, it's up to you. But then we should have one of our men stay here."

"I'd rather not," Dad says. "If anyone's watching the house—no, I'm okay here. I'm doing what I have to." I'm surprised at how firm he sounds.

"Well—" The officer sets down his cup. "I guess that's all then. Someone'll be driving by every half hour or so, anyway. And if you hear anything, anything at all—"

"You'll be the first to know," I say.

Constable Persky smiles, a little uncomfortably. "I suppose we will be," he says.

"I have to move the car," I say, as he opens the door to go out. "I think I'm blocking you in."

We walk down the steps together, but instead of going to his car he follows me to the Lincoln. "How long you here for?" he asks.

"I don't really know," I say, getting in the car. He holds onto the door so that I can't close it. I notice how his jacket fits him tight as upholstery. He still hasn't let go of the door. "It all depends, I guess."

"Well, I sure hope we can find your mother before you go."

"So do I." I reach for the door handle and give it an unmistakable tug.

"Maybe if you're not busy tonight I could come over and we could go out for a coffee or something. Just for a break, you know. To take your mind off it."

Oh, god almighty. The man is, no question about it, hitting on me. "Oh, that's really generous of you, but no thank you. I promised my father I'd stay here with him and he's counting on it."

"Okay, sure." He lets go of the door. "Well, I'll probably see you before you go."

I give him my nicest smile and close the door and back the car, faster than I should, into the garage beside Mom's car. When I get out, I go into the house through the garage so I don't have to walk past Constable Persky. Silky gallops up and leaps inside just as I'm shutting the door, a silly habit she has, and some of her tail hairs don't make it. Judging by the hair on the door frame she's lucky she has a damn tail left at all.

"What were you and the constable talking about so long out there?" Dad asks.

I throw down his car keys, as though it's all their fault. "Would you believe it? He wanted to take me out tonight. For coffee. Just for a break to take my mind off it."

"Are you going?"

"What do you mean, am I going? Of course I'm not going. I think he's got some nerve to ask."

"Well . . . he thinks you're attractive. What's wrong with that? Aren't you flattered?"

"Oh, Dad, come *on*. It's so sleazy. I mean, he's supposed to be trying to find Mom—it's his job, for god's sake—and he uses it as an excuse to hit on me."

"Don't be so hard on the poor guy. Maybe he really was just trying to be nice."

"Yeah. Sure." Now I'm annoyed at Dad, too, that he doesn't seem to see my point.

"Have some coffee," he says. "I made some fresh."

He pours us each a cup and it doesn't taste as bad as I thought. He never used to be able to make anything besides instant. We take it into the living room and sit down facing the TV. Every chair in the room faces the TV, I realize. Murray and I don't have one, and it's strange to remember living in a house where it was so important, where we spent more time listening to it than to each other.

"You know," Dad says, "today was the first time I really considered the possibility that she was dead." His voice trembles but doesn't break.

"She's not," I insist. "You talked to her yesterday."

"But why didn't they call back? Why didn't they set up another meeting? Why did they just hang up in the middle like that? It doesn't make any sense."

"I know," I say helplessly. "We just have to keep hoping."

"'Do you think she told them about the divorce? Or maybe they found out some other way and think that now I wouldn't want to pay."

"Oh, I—"

"When it's not true. It's really not true. I'd pay anything. The police say I shouldn't, that I could have gone with an empty bag."

"But it's you who has to decide."

"Yeah. It's me who has to decide." He leans back and closes his eyes. "You know what Yvonne said to me yesterday? She said, 'Maybe Pat's faking all this, just to punish us or to get more money.' Isn't that wonderful? Isn't that great?"

"What did you say?"

"What would *you* say? I told her she was full of shit." He sighs, harshly; it sounds as though he's coughed up a clot of air. "It didn't go over too well, I can tell you that. She wants it to be so *simple,* you know, for Pat just to be the wicked old wife who's easy to sweep out of my life."

"Well, isn't she? Just your wicked old wife?"

"What?" He snaps his eyes open. "Of course not. Jesus, Chris. She's your mother. She's a good person."

"Just testing," I say, with a tight smile. Maybe I was. Testing us both. Wicked old wife. Wicked old mother. I want it to be simple, too.

"I don't know," Dad says. "I don't know."

"Are you having second thoughts?"

He sighs, pinches his thumb and forefinger on the bridge

of his nose. "No, not really. I've *had* second thoughts. But I've made my choice. I won't change my mind."

"Maybe Mom wouldn't take you back, anyway."

He smiles a little, although it's more like just a twitch at the corners of his mouth. "She shouldn't," he says. "But I'm afraid she would."

I don't know what to say to that, so I just sit there pulling at a thread that's worked its way out of the padded arm of my chair.

"People live too long," Dad says.

"What?"

"I mean, marriage was invented for when people died off by forty, not for us, for people who live to twice that. It's a long time to stay with only one person."

"Except usually both people in the marriage don't feel that way."

Dad sighs. "Yeah," he says. He stares down into his coffee cup, tilts it a little from side to side, as though there were something at the bottom he was trying to see.

"Was that cop right," I say, "about your keeping all the money in the house? Do you have five million dollars in cash here?"

"They didn't ask for five million. They only asked for half a million."

"Oh. Nice guys."

"Yeah, it's here. In the house. In the refrigerator."

"The *refrigerator?* As in, cold hard cash?"

"I read somewhere that was a place thieves probably wouldn't look. There or in the oven. But I was afraid I'd turn the oven on by mistake and burn it up."

The whole idea seems so ridiculous that I start to giggle and then Dad does, too, and soon we are both bellowing with laughter, until tears are running down our cheeks.

After supper we drink brandy and watch TV. "Hockey Night in Canada." It's a poor game that degenerates into fights every ten minutes, and Dad says "Oh, shit!" when it happens, but he watches the fights, doesn't switch to another channel as he does when the commercials come on. And I watch, too, carefully, as though I have to, the way the players smash each other into the boards and then start punching, the way sometimes they just hug, as though they were greeting each other or dancing. Usually the other team members get involved, too, and it looks like a big party on the ice, everyone acting drunk and loud and silly.

"This guy at work," Dad says, "has this tape of all fights, a whole tape of nothing but hockey fights. Can you imagine?"

I suppose I can. I remember the accident on the highway, how we all wanted to see. Violence. As long as it doesn't affect us. As long as we can feel safe, just be the onlookers, the audience.

"Maybe we could watch something else," I say.

Dad switches around and finds a police show that is just starting so we watch that. Eight people are killed in the first five minutes, but this is only simulated violence so it's not supposed to bother us. I doze off in the middle of the show.

The phone jerks me awake. Dad has already leapt up to answer it.

"Turn the TV down," he yells at me, and I push the volume button of the remote control to zero. In the picture the police are chasing a black man through a car lot. There's a close-up of faces shouting, making no sound.

"Hello," Dad says.

"Hel-lo," Buddy answers from the kitchen. "Want a beer?"

"Oh, Frank. . . . Yeah, sure. . . . No, use the regular size. . . . Warnchuck's. . . . Pete, Pete's the one. . . . Yeah, yeah. Look, I'll call you. . . . Yeah, I'll call you. Bye."

He comes back and thuds down into the chair. "Just Frank. From work. Business."

"I thought you sold the business."

"They got me as part of the deal. I hang around, as sort of a consultant. What the hell, I don't mind, they pay me." He picks up the remote control and turns up the volume again. Then he sits back, grunting a little. He sounds like an old man.

The picture has just switched from a woman shouting at a policeman, "And I'm glad I did it!" to a picture of another woman, beautiful and young, with a husky voice, holding up a bottle of shampoo. She shakes her glamorous head in slow motion.

Silky jumps up into my lap and begins to butt her furry cat face at my mouth, purring and kneading at my thighs with claws that feel like spiked shoes running over me. I grimace and lift her off, her claws catching on my slacks, but as soon as she hits the floor she jumps up again, walking up onto my chest as though it were a ladder. I give in, finally, and pet her down into a reclining position, until she lies slit-eyed and happy on my chest, draped down the front of me like a white scarf. I pet and pet.

"Pretty puss," I say. "Pretty puss." She purrs and purrs. When old cats are dying, they start to purr: I read that somewhere. Maybe people purr, too, in their own way, when they're dying. It's a nice thought.

Her loose hair rises like steam into the air from under my hand. I still have clothes into which her hair has woven itself so tightly it's become part of the fabric, a sort of mohair effect. I try not to think of the fleas probably burrowing joyously into my sweater. One year we all had bites on our ankles. It was the year Dad got phlebitis in his leg because of his stupid smoking, and Mint thought it was spelled flea-bite-is.

Dad looks over at us and smiles a little, waving his hand to clear away the hair that floats over to him. "Long-haired cats," he says. "They should be illegal."

The phone rings. We only stare at each other. This must be it. It's too soon after the other call to be someone else we know. Like the woman in the commercial, Dad gets up slowly and walks to the phone. He's still carrying the remote control, as though it's something he needs, so I untangle Silky from my clothes as quickly as I can and get up and turn the volume down on the set, and then I stand there beside it, my hands clenched in each other as though they were afraid to be separated.

"Hello? . . . Oh, it's you."

Oh, it's you. You don't say, "Oh, it's you" to someone who might kill your wife. I go back to my chair and sit down.

"No, not a thing. . . . Okay. . . . Sure, of course. . . . That's a good idea, that'd be nice. .... Sure. .... Sure. See you then."

When Dad comes back he says, "That was Mint. Martin, I should say."

"What do you mean, 'Martin, I should say'?"

"Oh, Sue thinks we should call him by his real name. And she's right. Mint is no name for a grownup. We should never have started that. It's all your fault, you know."

"*My* fault?"

"Sure. When you were learning to talk it was the way you said his name. And we all thought it was so cute we started saying it like that, too."

"Are you sure? I thought it was Mint himself who started it."

"No, it was you. But maybe I'm wrong. It was so long ago."

"Well," I say, reluctant to concede, "I thought Mint started it."

"It doesn't matter."

"Anyway. What did Mint-I-should-say-Martin want?"

"Oh, he just said he'll come over tomorrow. He said maybe I could go to, uh, to see Yvonne. That you two could watch the phone. That okay with you? I wouldn't stay long."

"I guess so." Spending the afternoon alone with Mint: just the thought of it depresses me.

Dad picks up the *TV Guide* and asks me what I want to see at ten o'clock, but the choices all sound the same, like wallpaper patterns I'll have to stare at for an hour.

"Maybe I'll just go to bed," I say.

Dad says fine, that he'll wake me if there are any developments. So we say our awkward good nights, and I go off to my bedroom, which is still too much the way I left it four years ago, some of my old clothes hanging in the closet, the Bruce Springsteen poster on the wall, my books in the bookcase. Mom has moved some of her sewing things into the room, but they look like immigrants in a hostile neighbourhood, not fitting in, not pushy enough to look like more than visitors. Mint's old telescope is here, too, staring at the wall from the top of the bureau. It looks like a cannon. I suppose Dad's put it here, since he's sleeping in Mint's room.

I pull one of my old high school textbooks from the bookcase. English Literature. I did well enough in it, although it wasn't one of my favourite subjects. I had a teacher who said she couldn't read Dylan Thomas without getting a lump in her throat. Well, I could. It was just words on a page, nothing to cry about. I wanted to make myself tough, hard, masculine. That was where it was safe. You couldn't like poetry and be safe.

I put the book back without opening it, turn out the lights, go to the window and look out at the night, the thin wink of moon. I push open the window and feel the dark on my face, soft as a felt eraser on a blackboard. I breathe, in, out, long pulls. In, out. The air smells of spring.

Finally, abruptly, I close the window, lock it, and then I lie down on the bed. I look up at the ceiling, the patterns the shadows make. I should get undressed, I suppose. I reach my hands up to my chest, begin to undo my blouse, feel the buttons tug loose from their holes. One. Two. Three. Under my fingers my breasts feel hot and tight, hurting around the nipples the way they do before my period begins. I let my hands rest on them, feel the soft push of breath, of heart, the skin keeping everything in. On the ceiling the shapes of trees move, the way I remember, my mother telling me when I was little and afraid that she could pull the curtains, but no, I said, I didn't want that, I liked the moon shining through, and she said, if you don't want shadows you can't have light.

This is the room in which I grew up. I don't want the memories to come but I know they will, cells I've tried over and over to scrape from my mind but that always grow back—I squeeze my eyes shut. Don't think about it, don't think—

Willy Loman is a tragic hero because he dies at the end. No, I had something better than that, an idea Murray gave me. *Biff and Happy are tragic heroes because they don't die at the end.* There was more to it than that—

The door cracked open and Uncle George was standing there. Right there. At the foot of this bed, saying my name.

Damn you, I whisper. You bastard. I sit up, sweat itching at me, running down between my breasts. It disgusts me. I get up and go back over to the window, lean my hot forehead against the glass.

Tomorrow Mint will come. I can see him now, too, eleven years old, standing at the foot of my bed, frightened and saying in a small voice, "Are you all right, Chris?" and me, curled tight as a stone into myself saying, "No. No, I'm not."

He came over to the side of the bed, his arms wrapped around his chest. "What did he do to you, Chris?"

I reached down and pushed the knife back under the bed. "Leave me alone."

"What did he do, Chris?"

"You know what he did. You saw it."

"No, I didn't."

"Yes, you did. Every time. You came into my room every time and you saw it."

He began to whimper a little, afraid. "I didn't."

I sat up, snatched hold of his wrist. "Don't lie. I know you were there. And you have to tell Mom about it, Mint. You have to. I told her and she didn't believe me. But you saw it. If you tell her she'll believe you."

He kept trying to pull away, but I didn't let go. "I didn't see anything. I don't know what you mean."

"You saw what he did. Just tell Mom what you saw."

He was almost crying now. "I didn't! I didn't see anything." He tried to pry my fingers off but I was too strong. I dragged him forward, skidding on the carpet.

"You little baby! You did too see! You know what it meant!"

"No," he was wailing. "No!"

"Tell her. You'll have to tell her. Promise me!"

"I didn't see anything!"

"Liar!"

"I didn't see anything!"

"You did too!" It was useless and I knew it, but I didn't care, about anything, if I hurt him or if Uncle George could hear. "How would you like it if he did it to you?" I began jabbing at his crotch in the dark with my free hand, could feel his soft genitals through his pyjamas. "How would you like it? How would you like it?"

He was crying miserably now. I let go of his arm and dropped back onto the bed, exhausted, sick with myself for what I was doing. Mint ran back to the door and when he was safely away he shouted at me, "I hate you! I hate you!"

"Yeah," I said. "I know."

Awful hiccupy sobs are wrenching at me. I turn over and shove my face into my pillow, but they don't stop. My lungs feel as though they're tearing loose from my chest.

There is a knock at the door and Dad's voice, faint, as though it comes from another house, saying, "Chris, can I come in?"

And I say loudly, desperately, "No. No. I'm okay. Please don't worry."

And he waits for a long time and then he says, "She'll be all right. Really she will."

The light under the door goes out and I can hear him closing the door into his room, Mint's room. All I can do is try to sleep.

P A T

I just have to sit here, waiting for evening, when I
suppose they will tie me up again. At least for now my hands
and legs are free. I didn't think being tied up would be so
awful—a violation of the simplest human right to move your
hand up or down or to flex your ankle, a terrifying claustrophobia so much worse than the room in Burnaby with its
boarded-up window and locked door.

It was Chuck who tied me up last night, although it was
Lyle who told him how. The ropes were in the trunk of the
car, in a brown paper bag next to the bag with the groceries,
so they must have expected to need them. While Lyle carried
the two bags up to the room, Chuck took me up, holding my
arm so tightly it went numb. I could feel the gun in the small
of my back. It was late when we checked in, Lyle using my
credit card just as he had planned. No one was around, and
even if anyone had been, we wouldn't have looked unusual,
just a young man escorting an older woman, his mother perhaps, up to the room, holding her arm tight so she wouldn't
slip on the ice.

The room is actually two rooms, each with a view of the
lights of Kamloops and the mountains slouching against the
night sky. The main room has two single beds, an armchair, a
desk and a TV, and the other room, the one that became
mine, has only a double bed and a night table. A door with no
lock connects the two rooms. They argued about tying me
up, but even I could see that unless they took turns sleeping

to guard me I might be able to slip out, if not through the doors then through the window. But I didn't expect it to be as horrible as it was.

They let me go to the bathroom first, and I took a quick sponge bath, never getting completely undressed, watching the door nervously, as though they could see through it. I wished I could wash out my dress, which smelled of sweat and smoke, but obviously that was impossible.

Finally Chuck banged on the door. "You homesteading in there?" he yelled. A prairie expression. My father had used it sometimes when I was young.

"Coming," I said. Ready or not. Before I went out I tore off several feet of toilet paper, although I still had some left, and stuffed it in my purse. Be prepared.

When I came out they had decided how to handle it. Lyle gave the directions, but Chuck was the one who wanted to do it. I suppose he didn't trust Lyle to tie the knots tight enough. First he did my hands, winding the rope, a heavy white cord, around and around my wrists.

"Is it too tight?" Lyle kept asking.

"Forget it," Chuck would answer, exasperated. "Of course she'll tell you it's too tight."

"You can cut someone's circulation off," Lyle said. "It can cause gangrene."

When Chuck was finished and my hands were lashed in front of me as though they were heavily bandaged, with several feet of rope dangling free, Lyle came over and examined it, poking at the spaces between the rope and my skin.

"Does it feel too tight?" he asked me.

"It's pretty tight," I said. He couldn't expect me to say it felt all right. "I don't know how it's supposed to feel."

"Flex your fingers," he said, and I did. It seemed to satisfy him that they were still connected to my wrists underneath the layers of rope.

"Sit down on the bed," Chuck said. "I'll do your legs." And he took the second rope and tied it around my ankles, just two easy loops this time and a double knot. Lyle bent to check it, wedging his forefinger partway down between the rope and my ankles. The touch of his fingers was cold, clinical, a doctor prodding you where you don't want it, saying, "Does it hurt?"

"Lie down," Chuck said.

I looked at him uneasily. I thought they had finished. "Do I have to?" I said. "I'm not tired enough to sleep yet."

Chuck snickered. "Yes, you hafta, Patsy."

"Just a minute." Lyle pulled back the covers on the side of the bed I wasn't sitting on, exposing the white sheets like something naked. "You can sleep on top if you want to," he said. "But I'd get in if I were you. You'll probably get cold."

Chuck picked up the extra feet of rope dangling from my wrists. "This gets tied to the bedpost, you see." And he tugged at it, jerking my arms up, toppling me like a doll onto the bed.

That's when the panic started, I think, when I understood how helpless I really was, a toy at the end of a string. Hysteria clawed at my throat.

"Roll over," Lyle was saying. "Get under the covers." And Chuck was pulling my arms up, up, tying the other end of the rope onto the headboard.

My dress was up on one side around my thighs and there was nothing I could do. I could see Chuck looking at me.

And then I could feel his hand sliding slowly down from my wrists at the headboard, along my arm, pretending to be pulling the blanket and top sheet out from under me, but not doing that at all, passing his hand heavily against my right breast and lingering there, moving on to my waist, my hips, down to the edge of my dress, and then his hand was on my naked thigh, a touch that clenched my body so tight I felt it would break, shatter into wild screams.

"Ah, jeez, man, give her some decency, eh?" And Lyle jerked my dress down, over my knees, and flipped the covers over me, efficient as an orderly. I don't know even now what he saw, what he thought. Perhaps he thought only that Chuck was being insensitive. Perhaps he knew exactly what was happening.

But all day today I have stayed as close to Lyle as I could, locking myself in the bathroom when he went out to McDonald's across the street to get us food. When Chuck even comes near I can feel myself tensing, the cells of my body squeezing closed, wanting to make myself hard, impenetrable. I can't even look at him without revulsion. And he knows it. He comes up to me, close, and just stands there, a sneer on his face that is revulsion, too, that has nothing to do with real sexual desire, that has to do with sexual hate.

I don't know why we are still here, in this same motel room. Last night they had planned to check out in the morning. But when the morning came, and after Lyle went out and brought us Egg McMuffins and coffees, they argued about it, shouting and then shushing each other with nervous looks at the walls, and finally they decided to stay another night. It was safe here, Lyle insisted; why risk driving around? So he called the office and told them to put another day on the card and not to bother with maid service. I had thought of leaving some kind of clue, a piece of toilet paper with a desperate message perhaps, under my pillow or between the sheets, but now it will have to wait until tomorrow.

It has been the hardest day yet. They seem to have no plans at all. I can't even look forward to a phone call to Stewart; to anything that will give me a sense of future. Even though they untied me as soon as they got up, my wrists still feel sore, my arms stiff from being pulled up tight against the headboard all night. My temples throb with a headache like a crack across my forehead.

And worst of all is them. I think of the picnic we had yesterday, how there was a lightness to us all, something like a sense of adventure, perhaps. But today depression oozes from us like body odour. I can imagine people asking me, "What was it like?" and my saying, "Boring." I can just see their incredulous faces. But it's true: right now I am as bored as I have ever been. It's what purgatory is supposed to be like, a holding pen, giving you time to worry about hell.

Well, I shouldn't complain. There are far worse things than being bored. The devil is supposed to find work for idle hands. I glance over at Chuck and Lyle. They're like children tiring of a game. I'm the toy they're going to have to get rid of, one way or another.

Chuck has been sitting all day just watching TV, although twice now he has complained about a toothache, getting up and squeezing something from a little tube onto one of his molars.

"I told you you should have gone to the dentist before we got into all this," Lyle says.

"Yeah, sure," Chuck mumbles, rubbing at his cheek. "He'll tell me what he told me last time. A root channel, he said. You know what one of them things costs?"

"We could have gotten the money," Lyle says. "You're just scared of the dentist."

"I ain't scared of the fucking dentist. We ain't got the money, that's why."

"We could have gotten the money."

"We get five cents in the house and it goes to your god-damned dope."

Lyle looks away, at the window with the curtains pulled so tight they overlap. "I told you you should go," he says. "You were the one who said it wasn't that bad, you could live with it."

"Because there was no fucking *money,*" Chuck shouts.

"We could have gotten the money," Lyle says.

And they go on, the kind of argument I remember my parents having about money, the angry accusations, their two faces clenched and hard at the end of the day and my praying at night, *Please, God, give us enough money.* But with Stewart there was always enough money, enough to go to the dentist as often as I wanted and say, "Do anything that's necessary," the bill simply something we never discussed, that went to the company accountant and disappeared. Couples fight more about money than about anything else, I read in the paper last year, and I remember how lucky I felt, folding over the "Lifestyles" section and going on to Ann Landers: smug, that's what I was, exactly the kind of person God's eye snags on, some morning when he's tired of meddling in the Middle East, and he thinks, *She's got it coming.*

Chuck and Lyle's argument seems to be drizzling away into their usual final "fuck you"s and noncommittal grunts, and then they sit there staring at the TV again. This is the second western movie Chuck has found to watch today.

"How can you watch that trash?" Lyle demands, but he's watching it, too. So am I. The hero has just been shot by the cattle baron's foreman, but now he is being nursed back to health by the cattle baron's daughter, so things do not look as desperate as they did before the last commercial.

"Movies full of dead men," Lyle insists. "Fonda. McQueen. Wayne. Reagan."

Another commercial jumps onto the screen and Chuck turns to look at Lyle. "They're not all dead," he says. He stubs out his cigarette, hard, keeping his fingers pressed down on it even after it is out, as though it were the head of a man he is trying to drown.

Lyle gives a derisive snort. "What do you mean, they aren't all dead? Jesus, how dumb are you? Of course they're all dead. Fonda. McQueen. Wayne. Reagan."

Chuck turns back to the TV, where a loud man in a cowboy hat is showing us rows of used cars. "Okay. So what?" Chuck says.

I try to make sense of their relationship but it's not easy. I know it's important that I understand, because I am sure that I need Lyle if I am to survive. But I need to understand what ties him to Chuck. Perhaps it's only the money. I've tried to talk to Lyle today, to nudge him into conversations like the ones we had yesterday, but he seems so uninterested, only answers me monosyllabically, and Chuck is the one who is deciding the little things like where I should sit and if the drapes should be closed. Perhaps he will be making more important decisions soon.

It's almost six o'clock, and I can hear Lyle's stomach rumble, although it is really less a rumble than a tinny clatter.

"I suppose we should get something to eat," Chuck says.

"Yeah," says Lyle. "Maybe I should go get something." But he makes no move to get off the bed. "Maybe we can fix up a sandwich or something from what's left." But he makes no move to get the groceries, either.

"Well, there's no rush," Chuck says. "We've still got the whole night to kill. Ha—" He turns to look at me. "That's pretty good, eh? The whole night. To kill. Get it?" He laughs, a hissing noise that sounds like pressurized air suddenly released. "*Get* it?"

"Yes, I get it," I say. I am a puppet on the knee of a

ventriloquist, my mouth moving woodenly with the words I
am given.

"Well, you want to eat now or what?" Lyle says, sitting up.

"I dunno. You want to eat now?"

"Yeah, I guess so."

Now that they are talking about eating I realize how hungry I am, too, and I can feel my own stomach make its little
gargly sounds, its odd little movements in search of food.

"A restaurant meal," Chuck says. "That's what I'd like. A
meal in a real restaurant." He yawns, stretches his arms high
above his head, and his T-shirt rides up, exposing a coil of
pink skin around his waist. I turn quickly away, look back at
the TV.

"Why not?" Lyle says.

"Eat in a *restaurant*? What about her?" He tosses a hand in
my direction.

Lyle sits up. "She can come along," he says to Chuck, but
he is looking at me. "She won't make trouble."

Chuck turns to look at me then, too. I can actually see his
eyes narrow, the skin at the corners puckering as though he is
squinting into sun. "Okay," he says finally.

"Well, let's go, then." Lyle jumps off the bed with more
energy than I have seen in him the whole day. He slides on his
shoes and laces them up and then reaches for his jacket.

"I'll get my coat," I say, since it is apparent we are really
going out. Chuck grunts something which I assume is his
permission.

When I come back out of my room they are both standing
by the door, waiting. I walk nervously toward them, and
when I am close enough Chuck clamps his fingers on my arm
and says, "No funny stuff, Patsy." He jiggles his right hand in
his jacket pocket.

"Oh, Jesus," Lyle says. "Will you stop with that macho
stuff? You're going to shoot your pecker off."

"I'll shoot yours off, you don't stop bugging me."

We shuffle out to the car, Lyle and me going in the back
seat as before. I look around for people, for someone to see
us, but there's only a woman hitchhiking beside the highway,
not exactly someone I can expect to help. A dirty pickup

truck veers abruptly off onto the shoulder to give her a ride, and she runs to meet it. I feel suddenly as much afraid for her as I do for myself. Don't get in, I want to shout. As the truck pulls away, its tires spraying gravel from the speed of acceleration, I see an empty gun rack through its rear window.

"Well, where should we go?" Chuck asks, pulling out onto the highway.

"Just drive around," Lyle says. "Until we see a place. Somewhere not too crowded."

"How about there?" Chuck points at a Pizza Hut. Even from here we can see the line-up inside the door.

"Too busy," Lyle says. "Keep going."

We turn off into the downtown area, and Chuck winds up on a dead-end street. His curses sound routine now, nothing in them able any more to shock me.

"There," Lyle says, pointing at a run-down building with a sign in one of the windows saying Angelo's Coffee Shop. If it weren't for the card in the door saying Open the place would look abandoned.

Chuck skids the car to a stop right in front of the door. "Looks like a dive," he says, ducking his head up and down like a bird to get a better view of the place.

"We don't want the Hilton," Lyle says. "So long as they take credit cards."

"Want I should go in and ask?"

"It's on the door. I can see from here." Lyle turns to me and reaches out his hands, cupped slightly together, holding an invisible globe of air. "Okay," he says. "Now when you go in there, Mrs. Duvalier, you take it easy, right? Remember Chuck will be right behind you."

"Believe it," Chuck says, turning around and fixing me with a cold stare. He is one of the few people I have known who can look you straight in the eye for as long as he wants.

"I won't do anything," I say. But my heart is starting to beat faster, getting ready for something. Sweat itches at my armpits. In the restaurant there will be other people, close to us, a waitress who will ask me what I want. And I will have to decide, will have to choose between what is on the menu and what I really want to order.

Chuck and Lyle both get out and wait for me beside the open car door. When I slide across the seat Chuck grabs my arm again and jerks me out. I almost fall right out of the car, unable to get my feet outside and on the ground in time.

"Jesus!" Lyle hisses. "Take it *easy*! Don't draw attention."

Chuck loosens his grip on my arm but only to take a firmer one higher up, squeezing my arm so tight it feels as if he's going to amputate it. We walk carefully to the restaurant, one of them on each side of me, the gun as strong a presence as a fourth person.

Lyle pulls open the door. The greasy warmth of the restaurant folds around us. A bell attached to the door by a string jerks awake, tinkling a warning to the owners. Carefully, we step inside, the door twitching shut behind us. Chuck throws a quick hard look at it over his shoulder, as though he has to make sure it hasn't turned into a wall, sealed off the exit.

No one is in sight, although we can hear dishes clattering in the back. It is a small restaurant, fewer than a dozen tables, with three wooden booths, painted the colour of old carrots, lined up against one wall.

"Perfect," Lyle whispers. "We're the only customers."

Chuck pulls me over to the booth nearest the door, pushes me in and sits down beside me, closer than he has to. I squeeze against the wall, the muscles in my thighs contracting away from him. Lyle slides in across from us and sits with his forearms on the table and his hands clenched in front of him, as though he were preparing to say grace. When I glance over at Chuck I can see his right hand, inches from my side, is still in his jacket pocket. His eyes shoot around the room.

A Chinese man comes out from the back and nods at us. "Menus?" he calls.

"Yes, please," Lyle says. His hands on the table clamp so tightly on each other it looks as if the bones are about to pop out through the skin.

"Jesus," Chuck hisses. "A Chink. I thought this was supposed to be wop food. Angelo's, shit. He ain't no fucking Angelo."

"Shhh," Lyle whispers desperately.

The Chinese man is almost at our table, holding the menus

out to us. I try to catch his eye, but he doesn't look at us; he may have heard what Chuck said. When we've all taken our menus he turns and goes back to the kitchen without saying a word. We all watch him go. Behind the cash register I notice a shelf full of small red dolls huddling together like a flock of frightened birds. They are all of somewhat different shapes, but alike enough to have a common ancestor. I have an absurd urge to ask Lyle to go and see if they are for sale.

We open the thick padded covers of the menus. Looking at the lists of food, so much to choose from, I am suddenly ravenous, not caring who I am with or why, wanting only to eat. I decide on spaghetti and meat balls, perhaps a legacy of the missing Angelo. Maybe it will give me garlic breath, something to help ward off Chuck.

"What are you having?" Chuck asks. I assume he's not talking to me.

"The halibut, I guess."

"Fish!" Chuck snorts. "Steak, that's what I'm having."

"You should eat more fish," Lyle says. "At least twice a week. It keeps your cholesterol down."

"It's *fish*," Chuck insists. "It ain't real meat."

"Of course it's *real meat*," Lyle snaps, and then he takes a deep breath and lays his menu down carefully, setting his fingers neatly on either side of it, as though he were preparing to type or play the piano. "Have what you like," he says, his voice neutral. "What are you having, Mrs. Duvalier? I'll order it for you."

"The spaghetti," I say, a bit apologetic. Maybe I should have the fish, too.

The Chinese man comes back over to our table with a tray of cutlery and glasses of water and, still without looking at any of us, he lays them down in front of us, each of us getting one knife, fork and spoon, one glass of water, a careful frame for the plate of food we will only have to ask him for and he will bring. I stare at his pale, delicate fingers as they move in front of me.

"Are you ready to order?" he asks, drawing back and pulling out his order pad. He has no trace of accent, and it surprises me; he was probably born in this country, but all his life he will be identified by people like me as Chinese.

"I'm having the halibut," Lyle says, "and she's having the spaghetti. And he's having the steak, I guess."

"Yeah," Chuck grunts.

The waiter writes it down. "How do you want your steak?" he asks.

"Cooked," Chuck says, snickering. The waiter looks impassively at his order pad, waiting.

"Medium," Lyle says. "He wants it medium."

"Anything else?"

And I realize that any minute he is going to turn around and leave, and how easy it would be for me to simply open my mouth and cry, *Phone the police, phone the police—*

As though Chuck is reading my mind, he leans slightly toward me. I can feel the gun pressing solidly into my side. *I won't,* I think at him. *Please.*

"Not right now," Lyle answers.

The man turns and goes back to the kitchen, and the tension seeps out of all of us. Chuck shoves a cigarette between his lips but when he reaches for a match he can't find one. He slaps angrily at his shirt pockets as though fires had started inside them.

"Shit," he says. "Fuck."

"Shhh," Lyle says.

Chuck jerks the cigarette from his mouth and throws it on the table, where it lines itself up beside Lyle's fork like another piece of cutlery.

"You don't need one now," Lyle pleads. "Come on. Don't make a scene."

Chuck doesn't answer, but eventually he picks up the cigarette and stuffs it back into the pack. I have matches in my purse, I realize, but I'm certainly not going to offer them to Chuck. He curls his hand into a fist, lifts it to his mouth, and coughs harshly into it.

We sit and wait for our food. Chuck pulls a napkin out of the dispenser and begins to pick at it, peeling off little pieces that he rolls into balls and piles up around his water glass. Lyle fidgets in his seat, scratching at himself as though he were suddenly infested with fleas.

Then we hear the door beside us open, the bell jingle, and when we turn quickly to look we see an older couple come in, a man with a face so weathered the wrinkles seem like separate features, the woman with him short and fat, with a sad drooping face supported by a large lower lip like a cushion.

"Shit," Chuck whispers.

"Don't worry," Lyle says. "It's okay. Isn't it, Mrs. Duvalier?"

I nod. But my heart has started to beat faster again, as though these people have come here especially to save me, as though they are policemen in disguise.

They move over to a table in the middle of the room, which seems odd—usually it is the tables against the walls that fill first. The man is so bowlegged he has to throw himself from side to side as he walks. The waiter comes out and smiles at them.

"Don, Eva. How're you folks this evening?"

"Fine, fine," the man says, rocking his way over to a chair and dropping himself into it with a sigh. "How're you, Pete?"

"Can't complain." He brings them menus, and they talk some more, the woman saying something now, but her voice so soft I can't hear, although my ears are straining. Chuck and Lyle are listening, too; I can tell from the way their heads are half turned in that direction and the way they are conspicuously not looking at the couple. Lyle has picked up his fork and he presses his thumb repeatedly on the tines. When his thumb lifts up, I can see the dents, deep enough that surely they must hurt, but he doesn't seem to notice.

The waiter writes down the order and goes off into the back. I stare and stare at the couple, willing them to look at me, although what I could do then I don't know. The old man has something, a small dead leaf, perhaps, caught in what's left of his hair, and I don't know how his wife can stand to sit opposite him and not reach over and pick it out.

"I have to go to the bathroom," I say.

"Like hell you're going to the bathroom." Chuck turns and glares at me.

"You can't go," Lyle agrees. "You can understand that, can't you? We'll be back at the motel soon. You'll just have to wait."

"Pinch it," Chuck says, giving a silly little giggle.

I look down at the table, embarrassed, wishing I hadn't brought it up. Still, it was worth a try.

I look back at the old couple, a desperate kind of claustrophobia grabbing at me, trapped here beside Chuck. I have to grit my teeth to stop myself from leaping up and screaming. My breath stretches out, snaps back, like an elastic.

I can hear the woman's voice now, in a sad monotone to her husband. "—Winnipeg. So she said Christmas, maybe, if they have the money, Eric doesn't like to drive—"

I clench my hands tight on my lap, try to get my breathing under control. *Christmas, maybe*—where will I be at Christmas? Dead, probably, dead, no children or grandchildren coming from Winnipeg to see me, and I will never be able to grow old and sit with an old husband in a restaurant, and the hysteria rises up in my throat but I swallow and swallow; if I shout I will be responsible not just for myself but for the old couple and the waiter and I have no doubt no doubt whatsoever that Chuck could take out his gun and kill us all.

I turn my face to the wall, close my eyes. There is only white in front of my eyes, an afterimage, as though I have been staring at darkness.

"Pat? Are you all right? Pat?"

At first I cannot place the voice; who would be calling me Pat; it must be someone I know, and then I realize it is only Lyle, for some reason not saying *Mrs. Duvalier* now, saying *Pat,* as though he were my friend.

I turn quickly to face him, and the emotions in me fly out into words I cannot seem to control.

"I hate you," I hiss at him. "I hate you. How can you do this to me, how can you? What have I ever done to you— what gives you the right—"

"Shhhh—" Lyle leans across the table. My eyes are filling with tears and I can hardly see his face.

I feel Chuck's fingers biting into my arm and his words are right in my ear. "You shut up, you fucking bitch, you shut up, or I'll shoot you, believe it, I'll spread your fucking guts on the wall—"

I blink and blink and the tears start to clear. My body sags
back in the seat, as though someone has opened a valve and
let all the pressure out.

"I'm okay," I say quietly, dully. "I'm sorry. Please don't
spread my fucking guts on the wall."

And then the waiter comes with our orders and sets them
in front of us and we eat.

It's almost ten o'clock, and I suppose soon they will turn off
the TV and tie me up again. I shudder at the thought, Chuck's
hands on me and then the long night cramped on the bed,
sleep like a tourniquet I can only stand for so long. Lyle has
been dozing off on the bed and I watch him anxiously. If he
falls soundly enough asleep and I am left alone with Chuck I
can't think of what will happen, what he will try to do to me
in the other bedroom. If I cry out, it might be all the excuse
he needs to kill me. I can feel already the hands around my
neck, choking off the scream.

"Hey," Chuck says suddenly. "Wake up. I'm gonna go out
and change the plates." He grabs Lyle's foot and gives it a
shake. Lyle jerks awake, brushing at something invisible in
front of his face. I notice he has a nosebleed and it's left a red
stain on the pillowcase. It should be soaked with cold water, I
think automatically, or it will set.

"What?" he asks, sitting up. The blood trickles onto his
upper lip. I reach for my purse and pull out one of the two
Kleenexes I keep there and hand it to him. He takes it without any acknowledgement and presses it to his nose. If I'd
known he wouldn't thank me I would just have given him
some of the toilet paper. Maybe he is still angry over my out-
burst against him in the restaurant, but surely he must understand. If I'd apologized it would have sounded insincere and
manipulative.

Chuck is putting on his shoes, heavy hiking boots. "The
plates. I told you this morning. We should change them."

"Oh, yeah. Sure." Lyle reaches over to the bedside table
and takes a drink from the beer can sitting there.

Chuck is only wearing his undershirt and he rummages

through his bag for a shirt to wear. He pulls out a sweatshirt and, turning his back to me, at where I am sitting in the armchair beside the bed, wriggles it on over his head. He turns around.

"Like it?" he asks me, grinning.

The slogan printed in big letters on the sweatshirt says "If men weren't meant to eat pussy, why is it shaped like a taco?" And there is a picture of a large drippy taco with a woman's legs attached to it. I don't think I have ever seen anything so repulsive.

The expression on my face must have satisfied him because he laughs and says, "Yeah, so do I."

"Oh, Jesus, Jesus, Jesus," Lyle moans. "Why did you bring that damn thing along? You can't wear it, for Christ's sake."

"Why not?" Chuck faces him belligerently, his hands on his hips.

"Because we don't want to do anything to draw unnecessary attention, that's why not. Jesus."

"I'll have my jacket. And it's night. Nobody will see."

"Then why wear it?"

Chuck looks down at his feet. I can almost see his mind fumbling, determined to win. "Because," he says. "Because I want to."

"Shit. That's no reason. A town like this, it might even be against the law to wear something like that. You want to get picked up? You want them to check you out?"

"Fuck you," Chuck says. "Fuck you. Okay, I won't. If it makes you happy." And he twists the sweatshirt up over his head, where it gets stuck; I can hear his enraged curses tangled in the cloth. When he finally frees himself of it he throws it against the wall with such fury I cringe. "Fuck!" he shouts after it. He picks up from the floor the shirt he wore earlier today and puts it on, glaring at the TV. Then he pulls on the jacket, sliding his hand into his pocket to make sure that what he expects to find is still there.

"Are you gonna be okay here with her?" He dips his head in my direction. "Should I tie her up?"

"Oh, for Christ's sake. No, you don't have to tie her up. You think she's going to beat me up and take off?"

Chuck grunts, looking suspiciously from Lyle to me. "You

never know," he says. "You can't be too careful." He goes to the door, still looking distrustfully at us both. I notice he holds his right shoulder higher than his left. It's supposed to be a sign of some cardiac disorder. His hands hang from his sleeves like two cocked guns.

"Go, for God's sake! It'll be all right." Lyle jumps from the bed, waving his arms, the bloody Kleenex still in one hand.

"She's a sneaky bitch. Don't you take your eyes off her for a minute. Don't you let her get close to the door."

Lyle opens the door. "Go," he says wearily. "It'll be okay."

"Lock up behind me." Chuck points at the lock that is just a part of the doorknob you have to give an extra twist. "Jesus. I could loid that in two seconds."

When he is gone Lyle comes back to the bed and drops himself down. Without looking at me he says, his voice flat and even, like the print on a typewriter, "Don't try anything, Mrs. Duvalier. You may think I'm not as tough as Chuck, but we're in this together. I'm not going to let you escape. Don't test me."

"I wasn't planning to," I say.

And I suppose it's true. I cannot imagine myself leaping up and trying to overpower him, to claw my way past him to the door. Maybe that means I have stopped believing escape is possible. Maybe I have become like battered wives and prisoners of war, who will not leave their prisons even if the doors are left open because they cannot believe any more in their own free will. I remember how I stood unmoving at the side of the road yesterday, how my mind did not trust me to act. No, I tell myself firmly, I have not been so brainwashed; I am simply waiting for the safest time. Fight or flight, it said in one of Chris's textbooks: every animal chooses one or the other to survive. I cannot fight them. My only hope is flight. The book did not, I remember, give "Wait to be rescued" as an option.

"If you want to get up from the chair," Lyle says, his voice less hard, "just ask me first."

"All right." The chair suddenly feels like a trap, something I might as well be tied to.

We are quiet for a moment, staring at the tv. I should talk

to him, I think; I should try, now that Chuck is out. The more
we can talk with each other the harder it will be for him to
hurt me. The Stockholm syndrome. I saw a movie about that,
a bank robber holding a teller hostage and finally letting her
go because he had gotten to know her.

"What did Chuck mean," I say, "about changing the
plates?" He probably won't tell me, but it doesn't hurt to ask.

"You don't miss a thing, do you? Changing the plates." He
pauses, as though he's deciding whether to go on. "Well, you
see, instead of stealing a new car periodically like most bad
guys do when the cops are after them, we just steal new licence plates. Not even steal, just exchange. This must be
about our fifth set. So even if anybody makes our car it's got
plates on it belonging to God knows who, some tourist from
Prince George. Most people wouldn't even notice they had
different plates. How often do you go out and check to see if
your plates are really the ones Motor Vehicles assigned you?"

"That's pretty clever," I say. I think of when we first
stopped for gas, how I thought, now there's a record of their
licence. I feel foolish more than anything. I almost wish he
hadn't told me.

"It was Chuck's idea," he says. "Sometimes I want to
strangle him because he's so stupid, but he has his moments."

"How did you meet him?" I ask.

"I don't even remember. Somebody my dealer knew, I
think. I've about a year there where my memory went on
holiday. Probably just as well. Besides, as they say about the
sixties, if you can remember them, you weren't really there."
He jerks back another swallow of beer. The blood from his
nosebleed is a red smear above his upper lip.

"Chuck . . ." I think of how I should say it, "terrifies me."
Not that you *don't,* I want to reassure him quickly, but of
course it's too late to add that now.

"He should."

There's a dark silence between us for a moment, only the
TV murmuring to itself, the way Buddy does sometimes, looking at himself in his little mirror.

"You have to understand about Bill," Lyle says finally. "If
you'd had the kind of life he's had you'd be a pretty brutal
person, too."

Bill. He called him Bill. Lyle doesn't seem to be aware of his slip. And I mustn't be, either. Chuck, his name is Chuck. Bill is the name I will file away for when I need it, for the police. Unless it wasn't a slip at all. Unless he has done it deliberately, to mislead me. Or, I think with a sudden pinch of fear, unless it no longer matters if I know their real names. I wonder what Lyle's real name is. It's surprising that Chuck hasn't let it slip. It seems important for me to know, not for the police, just for myself. The Stockholm syndrome, I remind myself firmly—it works both ways, the victims empathizing with their captors. The bank teller testified for the defence at the robber's trial.

"What kind of life has Chuck had, then?" I use his name casually, to see if Lyle will correct me. He doesn't.

"His dad started beating on him from the day he was born. He's got more broken bones than Evel Knievel. His mom got hit a lot, too, until one day she just took off. Then there were the usual foster homes, a little sexual assault in this one, a little beat-the-hell-out-of-them Christianity in that one. How do you expect anyone to grow up normal with a past like that?"

"It *is* pretty dreadful," I say. It's not anything I can even comprehend, such violence, against children. I think of Mint and Chris. What would they have become, if that had been their childhood?

Stewart said more than once that perhaps we raised our children *too* free of knowledge and experience of life's brutalities, too protected, leaving them vulnerable and easy victims to the exploiters of the world—as happened to Claire's son Bobby, who disappeared for a year into a bizarre religious cult, which, the police told her, specifically targeted nice middle-class kids because they were easier to recruit and convince.

But a childhood like Chuck's—what defence would such a child learn except hate and violence? The suspicion that would protect him from a religious cult might also define the world forever as his enemy.

"Yeah," says Lyle. "Pretty dreadful."

"But don't you think," I say, trying to convince myself, too, "that people can overcome such obstacles, even such terrible ones as Chuck's? That they can take responsibility for what they are right now? Don't you think they can overcome their pasts?"

Lyle laughs bitterly. "Sure they can, lady. Look at me. I overcame my past."

"What was wrong with your past?"

"Everything. My parents loved me. We had enough money. I was bright. I had lots of friends. And I overcame it all. Look at me. I overcame it all." He opens his hands into the air over his chest, as though he were releasing something. There is such horrible self-loathing in his voice I am afraid to speak. He twists another beer from the few remaining in the plastic holder, jerks the tab open and drinks down about half of the can before setting it back on the bedside table. I wonder why he is drinking beer, if he has run out of the other drugs. Perhaps he's saving them. Perhaps he only reaches for what is closest. I pick for a while at the worn fabric on the arm of my chair, trying to think of what I should say.

"Lyle." My heart starts to beat faster, warning me of danger.

"Yeah?" He turns his head to look at me. In the yellow light from the bedside table his skin looks worn-out, thread-bare as thin, old cotton.

"If it were the only way you could stop me from leaving this room, could you kill me?"

He looks at me for a long time, saying nothing.

"I don't intend to try it," I say, trying to sound sincere. "I'm just curious, that's all."

"No," he says. "I don't think I could."

And he gives me a slow smile, a bit crooked, like Mint's, the kind of smile you have to return. "But," he continues, still smiling, sitting up a little straighter, looking at me carefully, "I could hurt you. I'd do what was necessary to stop you. I'm capable of doing anything this side of killing you."

"Oh," I say, my smile turning limp. "Just checking."

He gets up slowly from the bed and stands beside my chair, looking down at me. I tilt my head to look up at him, my heart starting to hammer with apprehension. Oh, God, what is he going to do?

Suddenly he squats down beside me and grabs a handful of

my hair, twists it. I cry out in pain, my head helplessly screwed tight onto his fist. It feels as if he is ripping off my entire scalp.

"It hurts," I whimper. "It hurts."

"I know," he says.

"Please let go. I won't try to run away."

But still he holds on, even tightens his grip a little. Tears pop from my eyes as though he is wringing them out of me. "Please," I whisper. "Please."

Abruptly he lets go, flinging his hand open and snapping my head against the back of the chair. My scalp burns as though it is on fire. Trembling, I reach up to touch it, press my hand gently against it.

Lyle throws himself back on the bed, stares at the TV. I cower back in my chair, trying not to feel betrayed. Well, he warned me, right at the beginning—*I'm no better than Chuck,* he said, but, still, he was the one I was counting on, the one I thought I could trust. Disappointment wells up in me like tears.

We stay as we are for several minutes, me with my hand pressed to my throbbing scalp, him staring at the TV.

At last he says, not looking at me, his voice deliberately flat, "I'm sorry. I shouldn't have done that. But I wanted to be sure you understand. I can't kill you but I can hurt you."

"Yes," I say, my voice meek and chastened. "I understand."

"Inflicting pain, you see, is a permissible, even encouraged, activity in our society. Committing death, on the other hand, because it is probably the most pleasurable of human experiences, comes with more rules and taboos, as do all our most pleasurable experiences."

I only stare at him, confused. What does he mean? Would he actually enjoy killing me? Or is he making one of his nasty jokes, the way he does with Chuck? I can see him looking at me out of the corner of his eye, to see my reaction, I suppose. Then he sighs and says, "Just don't test the theory, okay? As Oppenheimer should have said."

"I'm not . . . underestimating you," I say, hoping it is what he wants to hear.

"Just don't *over*estimate me," he says, turning to look at me again.

I nod, as though I understand. Why did I bring any of this up in the first place? I've only made things worse between us. He's not as bad as Chuck, I won't believe that, but he's shown me what he's capable of. But it's better, surely, that I know what I can expect. I was naive to think I could manipulate him, make him take sides with me against Chuck, to let me go. He is a criminal, after all, he is desperate, he would go to jail for a long time if they caught him. To say he's not as bad as Chuck might only be like saying the man who beats up his wife isn't as bad as the one who kills her.

We both stare at the TV, not wanting to look at each other. The news is on, pictures of a war somewhere, people who look too much like us firing machine guns or lying facedown on cobbled streets.

Lyle sinks back further against the pillows, his hands folded on his chest, the lids half down on his eyes like those of the dolls Chris used to have, lids that slid down as the doll was moved from vertical to horizontal.

"I have to go to the bathroom," I say. "Is that all right?"

"Okay. No fast moves." He turns his head, watches me.

I get up slowly, walk the two steps to the bathroom, which is right beside my chair, about as far from the front door as it is possible to be. I close the bathroom door and lock it. I don't really have to urinate, but my body is so stiff it needed to move. I bend down from the waist, touch my forehead almost to my knees, then I straighten and pull my legs up one after the other to my chest. I do a few more stretching exercises that I remember from my aerobics class, but they don't make me more relaxed, only slightly dizzy. I've missed two classes now, I think—when I go back I might have to go into the beginners' group for a few days. When I go back. If I go back.

I look at my face in the mirror. It doesn't look like the face of a kidnapped woman. My scalp is tingling a little on the left side, and my hair is limp and getting greasy, but the face is still the same one I left home with, no more wrinkles than before, no bruises swelling out my eyes. A nice enough face, making its peace with middle age, a nice enough body, no more than five pounds overweight, well, ten at the most, not the kind of body a husband should be repulsed by. I close my eyes quickly, turn my face to one side as though I have seen something in the mirror I do not want to. Stewart. Stewart is leaving me, for someone else.

I looked up. I was filing my nails. He stood in the doorway into the tiny bathroom, steadying himself against the easy rocking of the ship. And I was amazed, to see the tears bulging in his eyes, magnifying them, and then the tears ran down his face, and some of them collected in his moustache, which stopped them like a little hedge. I could only stare at him, astonished.

"Stewart!" I exclaimed, my voice full of surprise. Stewart doesn't cry, I thought. Stewart never cries.

"She's pregnant," he said.

"What?" It was Chris, I thought. I thought it was Chris.

"I'm sorry," he said.

"What are you talking about? Is it Chris?"

"Chris? God, no. It's Yvonne."

"Yvonne? Who's Yvonne?"

"She works with me. You know. You met her once. Oh, Jesus, can't you see? She's pregnant. It's my baby. I have to leave you, Patty. I'm going to leave you."

I stood up slowly, understanding it the way you understand pain or joy or fear, by instinct, without questions. "I see," I said.

"I still care about you, Patty," his voice was weak in my ears, the way it is in a bad telephone connection. "I really do, but Yvonne— Oh, God— Forgive me for doing this to you—" He was sobbing like a child, his face red and ugly.

I walked carefully out of the cabin, stepped to the railing, stood there looking at the soft black water cuffed by the wind, the curl of moonlight on each wave. There was no horror, no despair, nothing, just a great blankness, like amnesia must be.

The couple from Toronto and the girl travelling with them were coming down the passage and when they saw me they smiled and waved and the woman said, "Are you coming up now?"

"In a few minutes," I said, smiling back. "You see, my husband just told me he's divorcing me so I have to, you know, collect myself a little before I go up."

They simply stared at me, all three of them. "Really?" the girl said finally. "No joke?"

"No joke," I sighed. "I'm afraid it's true. It's quite a shock, really. I thought we had a good marriage." It was the most articulate I had been for the whole trip. Stewart should have been proud.

He came out of the cabin. Of course he had heard us. His face looked raw and bruised. "Patty, please," he whispered. "Come back inside."

"Is there more?" I asked. "You haven't changed your mind, have you?"

"Sorry about this," Stewart said to the couple from Toronto and to the girl, who were standing glued to the deck, watching us with their mouths open in little ellipses. He took my arm, gently, and led me back inside. I remember stumbling on the step into the cabin, the way his arm tightened on mine to keep me from falling.

"Oh, Patty," he said. "Oh, Patty."

"That's it?" I said, my voice still calm. "You've made up your mind?"

"Yes," he whispered, not looking at me. "Yes. I've made up my mind."

I pushed into the bathroom, nausea suddenly cramping my stomach. I put my head down into the sink but there was nothing to heave up. Cry then, I told myself. You're supposed to cry. But there were no tears, either, not for days, not until we came home. And then it was as though they would never stop.

I look into the mirror here now, into my own blue eyes. I'm not crying, I realize, but the tears are there, ready. At least now they're waiting for permission.

"Stewart," I whisper into the mirror. "It wasn't fair. It just wasn't fair." The tears jostle each other impatiently, but I take a deep tense breath and pull them back. My God, how long will this last, this one terrible memory waiting to shove itself into my mind every time my guard goes down? Maybe it's something I'm going to be stuck with for the rest of my life, a condition, like epileptic seizures. The rest of my life. It might not be that long.

I suppose I had better get out of the bathroom or Lyle will think I am planning to stay here for the night. There's no point annoying him. I splash some water on my face and dry myself with the thin motel towel and then I open the door and step back into the main bedroom.

My foot freezes in mid-air. On the bed, Lyle is lying as I left him, but the lids have fallen all the way down on his eyes now and they flinch with dreams. From his mouth are coming the soft gargly sounds of a man asleep. He's *asleep*.

I stand there and stare at him, watch his chest slowly rise and fall. So he's asleep, part of my mind says, so what? He could wake up any minute. Chuck might be just outside the door by now. Sit down. Don't be foolish.

But the other part of my mind has turned hard and clear. You'll never get a better chance, it says. My eyes measure the route to the door. My purse is sitting beside my chair but for once I will have to leave without it; picking it up takes time and it is only something that will get in the way. The same with my coat and sweater.

Slowly, slowly, I move across the room, my eyes flicking from Lyle's face to the door and back, alert for any change, any movement. It is hardest to walk in front of the TV picture, as though then I will be noticed for sure, interfering with what Lyle must be watching even through closed lids. I am at the door. My hand closes on the doorknob, turns it carefully to the left until the lock snaps out. My lips grimace as though that could cancel the noise. Then left again, further, further. I can feel the mechanism retracting from the slot, and when it is as far as it will go I pull the door open. It sticks a little on the frame but I have no choice but to force it further. Suddenly it lurches inward, grating on its hinges. I am certain Lyle must hear, but the TV has blotted up the noise and he lies as oblivious as before.

I step over the sill, outside. Only now does my heart begin to race, adrenalin shooting through me like electricity. I gently pull the door closed behind me, only to the point where it sticks, not caring if it latches shut. Outside. I am outside. Free. Now it is only a question of where to run. The of-

fice, of course. It is to the right, I remember, and around the
corner. It can't be more than eleven o'clock; surely they will
still be open. I can see the Vacancy sign still lit on the road
where traffic lumbers loudly past, straining up the hill.

I run. Down the dimly lit concrete sidewalk, flying past the
other units, my breath pushing out in front of me in a grey
cloud. I am at the corner of the building now; I slow down,
stop, peer around the corner. It looks safe. It looks wonderful. I can see the general office, someone behind the desk, a
car with people in it idling under the overhang.

There is a change in the light. I whirl around and I am
blinded by headlights. I stumble back, against the wall. I
know who it is. I turn again, push off from the wall—the office is so close—I should be able to make it before he can get
out of the car—

But it is too late. He must have jumped out the instant he
saw me. He manages to grab hold of my wrist and although I
hold on to the corner of the building with my other hand and
pull myself fiercely away, toward the office, the people, he is
too strong. His other hand is on my upper arm now and my
feet are skidding toward him no matter how much I lean
away. I can't see his face—he is only a thick chunk of black
silhouetted against the headlights, but I can hear his voice,
not loud, saying, "You fucking bitch," and I have never been
so terrified.

I scream, a shrill birdlike noise I did not know I could
make, but even reverberating in my own head it does not
sound loud enough against the traffic, loud enough to save
me. And then I feel the pressure gone from my wrist, and,
even as I start to pull more desperately, thinking I have a
chance while he is shifting his hold, I can see the fist coming
at my face.

SUNDAY

CHRIS

"Now you two behave yourselves," Dad says, and then he nods, as though he were agreeing with what someone else had said.

He fumbles with one of the buttons on his shirt I had to fix for him this morning. When he'd gone to get dressed, he discovered the button he'd left lying in the bathroom a couple of weeks ago had been sewn back on, by Mom, obviously. Except that she had sewn it on to both the button side and the buttonhole side. He handed the shirt to me, baffled as a child that he couldn't open it. I took the scissors and cut loose the threads, a thick mat of them, far too many for it to have been a mistake, and I thought of my mother having done this, such a small rebellion, but I had to smile a little and think, *Good for you.*

Mint and I sit at the kitchen table and assure Dad that yes, we'll behave ourselves, that he shouldn't worry. We listen to the Lincoln back out of the garage, stop, then pull up the driveway and onto the street.

It's been years since Mint and I have been alone together. How do a brother and sister talk to each other, when they're adults and equals, but with the past not outgrown and sitting like a third querulous child between them? The silence arranges itself around us as though we were actors in a play.

"You haven't met Yvonne, have you?" Mint says, taking a sip of coffee. The light from the kitchen window turns his hair white, lays a soft pencil of sun along his cheek. He's wearing blue jeans and a T-shirt, and on his arms I can see the pale downy hair that looks sun-bleached but isn't. A vein tugs gently at his wrist.

"No," I say. "What's she like?"

He shrugs. "Okay, I guess. She tries to be friendly. I think she'll do her best to make it work."

"How old is she?"

"Not old. Thirty, maybe."

"Jeez."

"It's all so unfair to Mom. Twenty-five years and this is what she gets."

"He told her about it on their holiday in Fiji, didn't he? A real class act, Dad. Why did he do that?"

"I don't know if he really planned it for then or not. I think he just wanted to do one last nice thing with her. She's been seeing a counsellor, you know. For her depression. Although she keeps insisting she's accepted what's happened." He gets up and pours himself another coffee. "I don't know why they haven't called." He sounds like Dad, the same voice, the same words, *Why don't they call? Why haven't they called?* as though someone would give him an explanation.

"They will." And my voice, all morning, saying the same thing, too, over and over, *They will, They'll call.*

Mint sighs, sets the coffeepot back on the stove and starts to stir the sugar into his cup. "Oh, god."

"What?" I look up, startled.

He points at the side of the fridge with his spoon. "There. Mom's got a lunch date with Claire. Jesus, what if she comes over here—"

"It's okay. I fixed it. I got Dad to call her yesterday and cancel." I hate the way I've made it sound, so smug, *I fixed it, I got Dad to call,* even at a time like this wanting Mint to see how capable I am.

"Well, that's a relief." He lets his spoon clatter into the sink. "You know how Claire is. She'd freak right out."

"Yeah. Well. There's no problem." He called her Claire. To me she's still Mrs. Fraser, Mom's friend. How did Mint learn to call her Claire? Maybe he's just showing off, the way

I did, children trying to impress each other with their grown-up skills.

"What did Dad tell her?"

"He said Mom went over to stay with his sister in Victoria."

"He doesn't have a sister in— Oh."

He comes back over to the table, tapping on Buddy's cage as he goes by.

"Want a beer?" Buddy sings out.

"No thanks," Mint says. We give awkward little chuckles.

"I still think he sounds like Mom," I say. "The way he says 'Hel-lo.' "

Mint goes back over to the cage and opens the little wire door. He holds out his forefinger and Buddy steps onto it without hesitation, Cleopatra onto her barge, and lets himself be carried over to the table. He ducks his head rapidly up and down, making happy gurgly sounds, and then he walks up Mint's arm and settles on his shoulder, mumbling at his ear.

"Remember how he used to imitate the toilet flushing?" Mint asks.

"And the coffee percolator?"

"And the way Dad used to cough before he quit smoking?"

"Have a beer," Buddy says. He walks around the back of Mint's neck as though it were not a gravitational impossibility, like the bumblebee that flies, ignorant of the scientific fact that its wings are too short to do so, and appears on Mint's other shoulder, murmuring to himself.

"You want a sandwich or something?" I ask. "There's a paper bag of lettuce in the fridge we could use."

"Lettuce?"

"You know. The money."

"Oh, yeah." He smiles. "Isn't it funny, that he wants to keep it there? Well, maybe it's as safe as anywhere. Oh, god, I wish they'd call. I can't stand this just not knowing."

We sit there in silence, holding our coffee mugs tightly between our hands, our eyes skimming the room looking for a safe topic of conversation to land on. A headache is starting to jerk at my temples, something inside wanting to get out. I push at the circle of moisture my cup has left on the table until all that remains is a damp smudge on my fingers. The kitchen begins to smell stale and dusty, the way it does just before the furnace kicks in.

"Murray seems nice," Mint says finally. "Considering."

"Murray is nice. Considering."

"That disease he's got. There's no cure, is there?"

"No."

"Oh. That's a pity."

We are silent again, not looking at each other. It's going to be a long afternoon. The heat comes on, a long shuddery exhalation. Mint draws a rectangle onto the table with his thumb and then traces his index finger around and around it.

"Maybe I *will* have a sandwich," he says abruptly. He gets up, Buddy still clinging to his shoulder, and goes to the fridge. He reaches inside and gingerly lifts the brown paper bag with the money out of the way. "Putting your money where your mouth is," he says. He sounds like Murray. He takes out the bread and cheese, which is stippled with white mould around the edges. He cuts it off. "How old is this, I wonder?"

"I guess it's still something Mom bought," I say. I can almost hear him counting back with me, to Wednesday. Four days.

He brings the sandwich back to the table and begins to eat.

"Stephanie's turning into a nice kid," I offer.

"Oh, yeah, she is. Real nice. Sue's got her enrolled in a ballet class now."

"Ballet. Well."

"You think you'll ever have kids, Chris? You should. They're good for a person."

"I don't know. They might turn out like us." Of course it sounds snide. I suppose I intended it to.

"What's wrong with us?" Mint says lightly, but he swallows the last bite of his sandwich in a bigger lump than I think he intended.

"Nothing."

That only makes him more uneasy. He crosses his right arm over his chest, grasping his left shoulder, a funny protective gesture I remember from when we were kids. Maybe

he sees me watching, because almost immediately he un-
clamps his hand and slides it down his chest into his lap.

I get up and pour myself another cup of coffee. A banana
with large black freckles lies on the counter beside the sink,
and, without thinking about it, I begin to peel it, biting off
little pieces that melt to chalky mush in my mouth. Through
the kitchen window I can see the forsythia in bloom, its
branches spraying up like a yellow fountain in the sun.

Without turning around I say, "I was thinking about Uncle
George last night."

Behind me I can hear Mint shift in his seat. He makes a
small sound, not quite a word.

I turn and go back and sit down. The sun from the window
lays a thin parallelogram of light on the table in front of me. I
set my banana skin carefully in its centre, where it looks like
the petals of some large dying flower.

"Do you think he's going to come over while I'm here?"

"I don't know. Probably not." Mint picks up the banana
skin and lays it down lengthwise, carefully arranging the three
yellow strips on top of each other. "Did you know that
people eat more bananas than any other fruit?" he says.

"Great. I'd like to shove one up his ass. Unpeeled."

Mint sighs, pulls his hand back from the banana skin.
"Chris. Why can't you just . . . let it go? Try to forget."

"Be*cause*!" I slap my hands on the table so hard Buddy
gives a frightened squawk and flies up, back to the cage. He
opens the door with his beak and pushes inside, where he
feels safe and makes indignant noises. "Because I'm not like
you," I say, trying to get calm. "Because I can't pretend it
didn't happen."

"I don't mean pretend it didn't happen. I mean—don't let
it destroy you. Decide it's over and that the past is done with.
You have to get on with your life."

"It just doesn't work that way with me, Mint. It's not that
easy."

"The trouble is," he says, "that you wind up hurting yourself more than anybody."

"Yeah. Poor Chris. She's such a masochist."

He frowns, running his fingers in small aimless patterns on
the table. "Have you . . ." He hesitates, as though he's al-

ready regretted his question, but then he plunges ahead, "you know, gotten over her not believing you?"

Gotten over. Like a fence you have to jump. "No."

"But you must understand why she didn't. She adores Uncle George."

"And what about me?" Me, me, me. "Maybe it's just the thought of losing her," I sigh. "I don't know. But I can't stand to think that she and I are never going to be able to be close. Because of that bastard."

"She made one mistake. Can't you forgive her for that? Will that have to come between you forever?"

I think about it. He makes it seem so trivial. One mistake, for which I won't ever forgive her. "I can't help it," I say. "I thought it would all go away in time, that it wouldn't matter to me any more. But it does matter. It matters more than ever. Unless she can believe this one thing about me, this one crucial thing—"

I lean suddenly across the table toward him. "Mint, listen. You can tell her now. You're not a kid any more. You know what happened. If you tell her she'll believe it."

It's the first time since that awful night that I've actually put him on the spot like this. But I'm sick of his evasiveness. I know he wants to forget about it, but I can't, I can't. I find I'm holding my breath, waiting for his answer.

He pulls back against his chair as though I've thrust a rotten egg under his nose. "Oh, Chris—it would, it would be devastating to her. The divorce, the kidnapping, then I tell her . . . this—"

"I don't mean *immediately.* I mean, it has to be done. Sometime."

"It's too cruel. I can't."

"You *can.* She has to choose between me and Uncle George. That's what it comes down to. The way it is she's chosen Uncle George and written me off. Don't you see how terribly unfair that is?"

He twists in his chair as though it were growing increasingly warmer. "She hasn't written you off. Don't exaggerate."

"I've a *right,* Mint—goddamn it, I've a right to have her know the truth. You owe it to me. Please, Mint."

"She wouldn't believe me. She'd think I was saying it because you wanted me to."

I open my mouth, full of ready arguments, but what he says makes sense. Maybe he's right. If Mom's determined not to face the idea she might discount Mint, too, think I put him up to it; she knows how easily I could persuade him to do what I wanted. And Mint would be hating the whole business so much I can see how he might back down, might decide he has no right to force her into believing something so awful. I can see him now, squirming away from her horrified eyes, saying anything to make it better.

But if he really wanted to he could do it. He could convince her. My god, surely it wouldn't be that hard. He just has to tell her the truth.

"You can make her believe you. If you really want to."

He won't look at me. He says in a low, miserable voice, "Then I guess I don't really want to."

So there it is. I stare at him, such anger building up in me I feel like throwing my coffee in his face. "Damn you. You're as bad as he is. God damn you."

I push my chair back viciously and get up and walk into the living room. I can't stand the sight of him, the bloody coward. I throw myself down on the sofa, pick up the *TV Guide* and leaf through it so savagely I tear one of the pages, a rip going right through the nose of a soap star smiling ingenuously up at me. I don't hear anything from the kitchen for a long time and then finally there's the sound of a chair being pushed back, then of the refrigerator door opening, closing. After a few minutes I can hear him coming into the living room. I don't look up. I'm absorbed in the interview with the star of the disease-of-the-week movie.

He sits down in the chair opposite me. "Chris," he says.

I slap the magazine back down on the coffee table. "Yes?"

He's holding a glass of milk, from which he takes a careful swallow and then sets it down on the end table. He looks so calm I could scream. He leans forward, clasps his hands together and rests his forearms on his knees. "I know you won't believe this, but I honestly think I'm doing what's best for you. This thing with Uncle George, it's . . . an obsession with you. Bad things happen to all of us and we get over them, but you, you hang on to it and on to it—you just have to forget. Bringing it up now will only hurt everybody, including you. Don't you see that?"

"No, I don't damned well see that."

He takes a deep breath, ready to try again. "And it's best for Mom. We just don't have the right to hurt her like that."

"And it's best for Uncle George, of course. And let's not forget Mint. It's best for Mint. Sweet little Mint who doesn't want anything to upset his safe little world. Something not nice happen? Oh, well, we can just pretend it didn't! See how easy life is?"

"That's not fair." His lips tug tight, as though he'd pulled a drawstring around them.

"Damned right it's not fair."

"Now, Chris—"

"All your life you've wrapped Mom around your little finger—anything Mint wants Mint gets—so what if you have to stretch the truth a little here, outright lie a little there—"

"You've no right to say that!" At least I've finally provoked him into some real anger. "Just because you were always picking fights with Mom didn't mean I had to," he snaps.

"Picking *fights*! Since when did I pick fights with her? Just because I had a little backbone—"

"You acted like a spoiled brat."

"*You* were the spoiled brat—always whining and wheedling to get your way—"

"That's a damned lie and you know it—"

"It's the damned truth and you know it—"

"Oh, really?"

"Yeah, really."

A grim silence settles around us. God. Fighting like kids, pathetic Mother-liked-you-best arguments.

Finally Mint says, his voice calm and reasonable again, "I know you think it was hard being my sister, but it was hard being your brother, too. You got to do everything first—I came second."

I give a bitter little laugh. "You never came second, Mint. Not from the moment you were born."

He sighs, and shrugs, as though he knows there's no point arguing, and of course there isn't.

"If you really thought you came second," I say, aware of how I'm twisting this, "you'd support me in telling Mom about Uncle George."

"I can't, Chris. I just can't."

"You can't. Oh, yeah. I forgot."

He looks at me with such misery and hurt I almost relent. I can see myself that night ten years ago, jabbing at him, *Tell her, tell her,* trying to bully him into it, but it didn't work then and it doesn't work now. That night he screamed at me that he hated me; now I think he pities me. I'd prefer the hate. I understand hate.

"You know," he says, and then he pauses.

"What?"

"Well, after one of the . . . the nights, I heard Uncle George in the living room. I heard him crying."

"So did I." And I'm surprised to admit that, but it's true, I did hear him. At first that was all I wanted to remember, telling myself it meant he was sorry. But later I tried to forget it; all I wanted to remember was my anger. "It doesn't change anything," I say. "It makes him even more to blame. Because he knew it was wrong. And he did it again."

"You've a strange way of reasoning," Mint says.

"So did Uncle George. So do you."

Mint sighs, and rubs his hands slowly together. They sound like pieces of paper sliding on each other. "Anyway," he says softly. "She may never come back. We have to face it. They might have killed her."

"No, they haven't," I say. "They haven't. They can't have." Selfish Chris. Mommy can't die until she gives me absolution. Until we give each other absolution.

But it's true, I think fiercely. I don't just want her back, the way it was. I want her back and able to love me.

We stare at the phone, willing it to ring. I wish Mint would leave but I know he won't. He'll stay here visiting dutifully with his sister, because that's what he said he'd do, until Dad comes home.

"When do you have to go back?" Mint asks.

"I don't know. I'm trying not to think about it."

"Oh. Yes. Of course. I just thought that, you know, maybe you had exams or something."

"I do. I have one on Wednesday." I run my fingers through my hair, which needs a wash; I can feel my fingernails plowing up flakes of dandruff.

Mint finishes his glass of milk, slowly, rolls it in his hands for a while, then sets it down on the coffee table. "Do you want to come over before you go? Have supper with Sue and the kids? You're the only aunt Steffie has. She'd like to get to know you."

I consider my answer for a minute. "Mint. Listen. I'm mad at you, okay? Don't pretend I'm not. You don't invite someone who's mad at you home for supper with the wife and kids."

He rubs his palms up and down on his thighs, as though they were wet or cold. "We're brother and sister, Chris."

"That's got nothing to do with it."

"Yes, it does."

"Look. I don't care who you are, I'm pissed off at you. Okay?"

"You can be mad at me forever but I'll still be your brother." He refuses to understand, his logic so doggedly simplistic that I throw my hands in the air in exasperation.

"I swear to god, Mint, sometimes your head is so hard they could use it to drill for oil."

He laughs. "That's good," he says. "Drill for oil."

"I meant it." But I concede him a smile. My anger against him is seeping away, anyway, into something else, disappointment, I suppose, a sense of failure, his and mine both. I feel tired, worn-out, sick of arguing. "You think I'm a bitch, don't you?" I sigh.

" 'She was a bitch but she was interesting.' "

I laugh weakly. "You remembered that."

"Of course," he says. "I thought I had to."

And then we just sit there, for how long I don't know, the silence around us like some soupy grey pond we are trapped in. I'm just about to suggest we turn on the TV, anything to push back the gloom, when Mint says, relieved, "Dad's home." Thank god. I hear the car door slam, the fumble of feet on the walk.

"Any news?" Dad asks, as soon as he opens the door.

"No," we say together.

"How's Yvonne?" Mint asks. I turn away a little so that Dad won't see my ironic smile, but of course Mint isn't being sarcastic. He'll probably invite the two of them to dinner after they're married, and they'll talk about the children and everyone will be so civilized, everyone will adjust. Toleration of contradiction.

"Oh, she's fine," Dad says. I can feel his eyes sneaking nervously my way. "It's pretty hard on her, of course. With the baby and everything."

"Of course," I say, trying out Mint's neutral tone, but it doesn't work; I still sound snide.

"I called the police again," Dad says, "but there wasn't any news. They had a couple leads from that house-to-house in Burnaby, but nothing definite."

Mint and I nod sombrely, not knowing what to say. We slide our eyes past each other, fix them on the stolid white appliances. I can smell the stale basement air the furnace is starting to shove up at us. Finally Mint says, "Well, I should go. I told Sue I'd be home by three."

"Sure," Dad says. "I'll, you know, call you if I hear anything." He goes out with Mint and, because it'll look odd if I don't, I trail along.

Outside the sky has thickened with clouds the colour of glue, and the occasional drop of rain is coming down. Silky trots up to me, tangling around my legs like underbrush. I finally pick her up and toss her across my shoulder, which seems to satisfy her for the moment. Her purrs snore into my right ear.

"Will I see you again before you go?" Mint asks me, his hand on the car door. He knows I can't be rude now that Dad's here.

"It depends."

"Well," Mint says, lingering, fiddling with the door handle.

"Well," I say, "I'll see you then." And I turn and walk

back to the house. Silky bounces on my shoulder. I can feel
her claws digging in to my back to hold on. I fumble open the
door and close it quickly behind me. It seems important to
have done that, to have gotten inside before I hear the slam of
Mint's car door and the grunt of the motor, the wheels turning on the pavement, the final acceleration onto Zero
Avenue.

P A T

"Maybe this time we can send him something," I can hear Chuck's voice through the door. "A finger, maybe." And then a sound that might be a laugh, and Lyle's voice, low, saying something I can't hear. It doesn't even horrify me. My head lies on the pillow like something that doesn't belong to me, a thick ball of pain. I think dully, *I have another day at least, then, to live.* Because sometime before that, when I first struggled to consciousness, the voices weren't talking about going back. They were talking only about killing me.

"So what difference does it make?" Chuck was shouting. "You said yourself she might have a concussion. She's damaged now. She's dead weight. We gotta off her."

"One more try with him before it comes to that, that's all I'm saying."

"Sure. One more try. You fucking asshole. You goddamn fucking asshole. You're outa this now, you're outa this."

"I'm sorry, I said I was sorry—"

Then the voices drifted away, and I was aware only of the beat in my head, ta-dum, ta-dum, ta-dum. The fist coming at me: I remember that, and the eruption of stars somewhere behind my eyes, just the way they describe it in books—*I saw stars.* But it is the back of my head that hurts the most, not the front. Perhaps he hit me again, or perhaps my head slammed into the motel wall. I reach up to feel my face but my hands jerk against the rope and I realize they have tied me up the way they did the night before. I try to turn my head, to see if I can, but it only tips the darkness over me again.

Then Lyle is sitting on the side of the bed, saying something to me. It must still be night; neon lights are leaking through the split in the curtains. I feel I am coming out of anaesthetic, the nurses saying, "Time to wake up now, Pat." Opening my eyes is like prying apart two drawers rusted together. Slowly I focus on the ceiling.

"How do you feel?" he is saying. His voice sounds far away, as though it's coming from a telephone receiver off the hook somewhere. "Can you talk?"

"I don't know," I say, the words rattly in my throat.

He reaches over and turns my head slowly on the pillow, prodding gently at the back. "Does that hurt?"

"Yes," I say. "All over."

"The skin isn't broken," he says, "but there's a lump. You took a good whack there." He rotates my head back to where it was. "Why'd you go and do that, anyway, Mrs. Duvalier? You asked for this, you know. I warned you." His voice doesn't sound angry or even accusatory, only resigned. "Now you've got Chuck good and mad, you know. Mad at me, too."

"You'd have done the same," I say.

He sighs. "Yeah."

Then I hear the door open and although I don't turn my head to see I know Chuck is standing there. He looks at us both for a long time before saying anything.

"So how is she?"

"Conscious."

He comes over to the bed and looks down at me. His face hangs over my head, something that has descended from the ceiling, a spider on a thread. I try to look at him but my focus is still stuck to the ceiling.

"You stupid bitch," he says. "You goddamned stupid bitch. I should have beat you to bloody death." But his voice is not as full of hate as I expected. There is a kind of ugly cheerfulness to it.

"It wasn't her fault," Lyle mutters. "It was mine, okay?"

Chuck whirls, pushes a finger into Lyle's chest. "Damned rights it was your fault! You're a goddamned stupid bitch, too." He turns back to look at me. "You better be ready to move at the crack of dawn, lady. You ain't, you stay behind. You got that?"

She's damaged now. His voice from earlier floats into my head. If I am to stay alive I am not allowed to be damaged.

"I'll be ready," I say.

"And you," he says, turning to Lyle, "get the fuck out of here. I don't want you talking to her. At all. You got that, Mr. Bigshot, Mr. Thinks-He's-Better-Than-Me?"

And Lyle only turns his sad look at me and says, "Try to get some sleep," and he follows Chuck out.

When the door closes behind them I shut my eyes in relief; it is too much of an effort to remain conscious. I can feel sleep like a cushion being pushed in around my body. There is a dream, all confused, the kind of dream you get with a fever, and George is in it, looking as he does now, a pudgy business-man, and I am in it, too, except that I am only a child, and there is Lyle, what is he doing in this dream, we are all run-ning to catch the school bus.

Then I hear voices in the next room, it must be the Grade Fours going on their field trip, and there is a toilet flushing, and I realize slowly that I must be awake and that I am in a motel room in Kamloops and that my head is aching because I have been punched in the face by a man who has kidnapped me. And it must be morning. Pale transparent light is drib-bling in through the curtains. My mouth tastes sour, metallic.

I turn my head slowly, cautiously, and the pain in the back seems to be better, although my jaw is starting to pound; when I try to move it back and forth it feels soldered shut.

As though he knows I have just woken up, Chuck opens the door and stands looking in at me. "You still alive, Patsy?" he calls from the doorway.

"I'm okay," I say, but the words have trouble getting through my lips. The skin of my face feels stretched tight, like cloth held in embroidery hoops. *She's damaged now.* I don't want to be damaged.

Chuck walks slowly over and looks down at me. He puck-ers his thin lips and sucks in a raspy whistle. "You don't look like no prize today, Patsy. I don't think your old man would pay ten cents to get you back the way you look."

He runs his finger along my cheek. I want to turn my head away, but I am afraid to have him see me cringe. Finally he lifts his hand away and reaches up and unknots the rope from the headboard and then unties my hands. When I rub them they are icy cold, blue and numb. Gangrene, I remember Lyle saying. It is unlikely Chuck would have let him check the ropes last night. I realize for the first time that my feet aren't tied, although they feel as cold and numb as my hands.

Chuck stands watching me. Then he reaches down and jerks the sheet and the blanket off me. By reflex my body curls up, protecting itself, as though I had been suddenly attacked. He only stands there, looking down at me. I lie still, not breathing, trying to make myself shrink into invisibility.

"Get up and go to the can," he says at last, stepping back. "You got five minutes." He splays one hand in the air, five fingers, as though I were a foreigner who needed sign language.

The breath releases from me like an opened faucet. Thank God, I think. Thank God. When I stand up a wave of dizziness almost pushes me back down, but I clench my teeth and steady myself on the night table. Chuck stands watching me as I shuffle across the room to the door into the main bedroom, then around the corner to the bathroom.

Lyle is sitting on the bed turning the pages of a newspaper. It looks like a copy of one of the Vancouver papers, too large to be just a local. He looks up when he hears me but his eyes seem cloudy, like someone with cataracts. His eyelashes are stuck together in little gluey clumps.

"You okay?" he says, his voice not raising up at the end the way it should, as though it were too much effort.

I nod, not trusting my mouth to provide more than a whimper if I open it. My head feels like a glass beginning to ring; one touch and it will shatter.

When I reach the bathroom and pull myself inside I almost scream at what looks back at me from the mirror. That's not me, I think, remembering the face I saw here only yesterday, the face that was still attractive, still pretty when it smiled. What I see now is something with a jaw bulging out, a blue stain starting to spread under the skin. There is a cut on my bottom lip extending down to my chin, dried blood smeared almost to my ear.

I turn on the hot water and let it run, scalding, over my cold hands until I feel some circulation return, and then, carefully, I wash my face. It looks better with the blood washed off, and the cut isn't as bad as it looks, but the swelling is. At least I can move my jaw a little; it doesn't seem to be broken. I feel the back of my head, and, yes, there is a lump, the size of a small potato, simmering with pain.

Chuck pounds on the door. "We're outa here," he says. "Come on."

I look at my face again, with such love the tears come to my eyes. This isn't how I want to remember myself.

I leave the bathroom and walk back to my bedroom, keeping my head down, embarrassed at how I look, even to them. I put on my sweater and coat and pick up my purse and go back into the other room. Lyle has already left with their bags, and Chuck takes my arm and pulls me close to him and we step out the door. In the sudden light his skin looks the colour of mushrooms.

"Why don't you try to run again, bitch?" he whispers in my ear. "Why don't you?" And he shoves the gun in his pocket so hard into my side that it feels like a knife, the kind of weapon he might prefer to use on me. I am curiously numb to everything, my head feeling dull and mushy in the crisp morning air.

"I won't run," I say.

We shuffle down the walk to where the car is, only a few steps from the door. I look down the sidewalk to the end of the building where I ran last night, expecting to see some evidence, bloodstains on the wall, perhaps. But it is only another anonymous motel, made for people who leave nothing of themselves behind.

Ours is the only car here. It is later in the morning than I thought, and the other people must have already checked out, anxious for their real destinations. Lyle has loaded the luggage into the trunk and opened the car doors, and Chuck pushes me into the back seat. He stands there blocking the door, as though he expects me to try to lunge past him, until

Lyle comes up. Even then Chuck just stands there, and Lyle
has to pull the door open further and squeeze past him.

"You sure you can *handle* it back there alone?" Chuck
asks. "You sure she's not too *much* for you?"

"Let's just go," Lyle mumbles.

"Jesus," Chuck says. He slams the door closed so hard the
whole car shudders.

I lean my head back against the seat and half close my eyes.
It feels good to sit down again. Chuck gets in and starts the
car, but before we leave he adjusts the rearview mirror to
check out first Lyle and then me, and only after he has glared
at us each for several minutes does he adjust the mirror the
way he needs it for driving.

He pulls out onto the highway, and the sudden motion
makes me nauseous. I swallow and swallow, and finally the
feeling goes away, although my head begins to ache worse
than it has since I woke up. I think vaguely about dying. It
has to happen sometime. Perhaps even now there is a cell
somewhere in my body smouldering with something awful,
igniting another and another, beginning the flame that will
become the fire that will become my death. It's just a question of how and when, not if.

I close my eyes all the way and watch the strange shapes on
the inside of my eyelids, moving in waves now, and bringing
me sleep.

The scenery chugs dully past my window. Ahead I can see a
sign saying Vernon. What are we doing in the Okanagan? I
thought we were going back to Vancouver, that they were going to try Stewart one last time. Chuck wanted to send him
one of my fingers. Or was that the option they discarded?
Perhaps the one they chose was to kill me. It hardly matters.
Cut off a finger, kill me, drive me around forever in this car
reeking of cigarettes and stale sweat—I cannot sort out which
is the best alternative. My brain feels as though it's wrapped
in thick layers of wool. I lean my head against the seat and
close my eyes again.

Chuck has been able to find several radio stations and it

seems to invigorate him. He finds one playing rock music and he turns it up, loud, shouting, "All *right*!" and singing along to the few repeated lyrics. The bass shakes the back seat, batters at my ears. I try to imagine it is Mint and Chris I am with, the radio on so loud, the music wild raw energy going through them and through them. I remember when it felt like that to me, too, before I became old, before the music became noise.

Lyle has hardly spoken at all since we left. He sits looking out the window with his eyes seeing something else, pulled tight inside himself like mercury. Twice now he has taken the little bag out of his shirt pocket and scooped out some of the powder and, not bothering to turn away, inhaled it up his nose. It surprised me, to see it done that way. I had assumed it would be taken in through the mouth.

The second time, when he saw me watching, he held the bag out to me and said, "Want some?" And the strangest thing is, I almost said yes. The thought was so clear in my mind: why not? I'm going to die anyway, why not try it? But then he pulled the bag back and put it away. Of course it wouldn't even have occurred to him that I might say yes.

We drive and drive. Chuck stops in Vernon for gas and hands the credit card slip in to Lyle to sign. I notice his signature no longer resembles mine. But maybe mine no longer resembles mine, either; it seems so long ago since I was that person. The clerk pays no attention. I wonder under whose licence plates we are travelling now. Nothing seems to be of much consequence. My head throbs and throbs, like another heart growing behind my eyes.

Chuck brings back some bags of potato chips and candies for us and throws them into the back seat. I expect that will be lunch. Neither Lyle nor I open ours. We are both sulky, listless children, staring out our windows at a world we are excluded from. Before, the white powder seemed to relax Lyle, but today it only seems to pull him more into himself, the way the leaves of a fern contract shut at the slightest touch, a breath. Chuck drives now with his right arm draped along the back of his seat. The arm looks deceptively relaxed, the ropy muscles still, but it reminds me of a garden hose the moment before the water is turned on.

Outside of Vernon, Kalamalka Lake opens up its brilliant colours to us, and Chuck pounds the wheel excitedly. "Hey, ain't that *something*!" It seems incongruous that he should appreciate beauty, but then they say that even Hitler loved the mountains.

He pulls the car over at one of the scenic lookouts and jumps out and goes around to the trunk. Lyle rouses himself enough to roll down his window and look out, too, at the sun silvering the water far below. Chuck comes around to Lyle's door and opens it. I see in astonishment that what he is holding is a camera.

"Stand over there," he says to Lyle, pointing at the railing.

"Oh, jeez, you've got to be kidding."

"Come *on,* eh, before somebody comes. I never been here before. I want some souvenirs."

And so Lyle stumbles out and goes to stand at the railing, and Chuck takes three pictures of him. Behind him the lake poses as beautifully as it has for thousands of tourists before us. The water is so still and dense it looks like endless layers of glass.

"Now one of me," Chuck says, and they change positions.

I can feel laughter crackling up in my throat, but I choke it back. It is mad, it is all mad. Perhaps they will want me to get out, too, to stand first with my arm around one, then the other, smiling for the camera. But, no, my face is not photogenic today. My old man wouldn't pay ten cents to see it.

Finally they get back in, Lyle giving me a weak smile as Chuck goes to put the camera back. "We're on holiday," he says. He shoves some of the white powder up his nose before Chuck comes back and we drive on.

In Kelowna Chuck makes a wrong turn and we wind up on a gravel road heading east instead of on the bridge going across the lake. He curses at Lyle, who has the maps and is supposed to be navigating, although he hasn't looked at them since we left this morning and they have fallen in a crumpled heap around his feet. He gathers them up without a word and hands them to Chuck, who pulls over to the side of the road and broods over them for a while. Finally he turns around and heads back.

"Watch for Highway 97," he instructs us. "Got that? 97."

Back in Kelowna we seem to drive around for hours until we come to a sign for Highway 97, and then Chuck misses it. I have to bite back the eager "There it is!" Why should I help him? It is easiest for me just to sit here; I am in no hurry to get anywhere. At least here, driving around in circles, I am alive; I look out the windows at people in other cars, people walking casually on the streets looking in shop windows and enjoying the unusually warm day. I am in an airplane in a holding pattern, safe from the dangers at both ends of my trip.

It's Sunday, I realize as we pass a Catholic church with people just leaving it, clustering in little groups on the lawn to discuss the weather, the sermon, their new clothes. . . . Sunday. At home I would be starting dinner, a roast, I suppose— no, wait. I would be out for the afternoon with Claire. I smile a little to myself as I think of it. What will Stewart have told her when she came to pick me up? I can see her shocked face, aghast but also excited, the way it was when I told her about the divorce. Claire is the kind of person who likes you best when you are miserable. It makes her feel useful, I suppose, to be able to offer consolation. But I am grateful for her interest, at a time when my other friends are drawing back from me as though I have something contagious.

Chuck slams on the brakes as the car in front of him skids to a stop on the orange light. "Goddamn idiot!" he shouts. When the light goes green, he tailgates so closely we must be only a few inches from the car's bumper, but then I can see him take a deep breath and ease up on the gas.

He turns right on a street that looks as if it might be a highway, but obviously if he wants to get to the bridge he's going the wrong direction. I lean back, say nothing.

It is strange to be in Kelowna again after so many years. My mother lived in the Okanagan, in Kelowna and then in Oliver, for about ten years before she died. Neither George nor I wanted to move here with her so we stayed on in Vancouver, made our lives there and our obligatory annual visits to her here. At the end sometimes she didn't even recognize us.

Once when we came down together she thought I was

George's wife and kept calling me Cathy. It was right after George's divorce and I could see him wince every time she said it. I wondered if she knew better and was doing it on purpose; she was like that sometimes.

"Look at this, Cathy," she said, picking up the old family Bible from the kitchen table and waving it carelessly at me. "They keep sending me these in the mail and then want me to pay for them. What do I need condensed books for? I don't read them."

"That's the family Bible, Mom," I said, taking it from her, showing her the first page with Grandma's and Grandpa's names, then her own, and George's and mine.

She stared at it intently. "Well," she said, pulling it from my hands and setting it back on the table, "they keep sending them to me."

"How's your recipe book coming?" George asked. I shot him a warning glance, which he ignored; her recipe book was something I didn't want to talk about. At that stage it consisted of a large cardboard box containing about fifty handwritten recipes, some inherited from her mother; a huge number of clippings from magazines and newspapers, recipes mostly but not exclusively; and a great variety of other bits of paper like bank statements and personal letters that may have fallen into the box by accident or because it was the only place she had to file things. She wanted me to take all this and have it published. It was useless to say it needed to be organized first or that I knew nothing about publishing. I knew the day would come when she'd remember to give it to me before I left, and the thought of actually taking it home with me, accepting the responsibility, filled me with something close to horror.

This time, thank God, she just squinted suspiciously at George and said, "Well, that may be, but I won't pay for them. They keep sending them but I won't pay for them."

"I'll write them a letter, Mom," I said. "I'll straighten it out."

When we left, her neighbour old Mrs. Elmchuck pulled us over to her porch and whispered to us that it was time to "do something."

"You mean, like have her put to sleep?" George asked. It had been a difficult day for him.

I laughed, to show her it was a joke, but I don't think she believed him. She addressed the rest of her comments to me, sliding a quick critical look at George occasionally. "She gets this slingshot, see, and she sits on her front step and everything that goes by, zing, gets it. She's got a whole pail of little rocks and sometimes she's there the whole afternoon, zing, zing. Cats, birds, dogs. Once or twice even people—teenagers, old men. And she's a good shot, she gets better all the time."

"The army should draft her," George said.

"It's no joke!" Mrs. Elmchuck snapped, turning her fierce blue eyes on him.

"Of course it's not," he said, chastened. "I know it's not. Thank you for telling us."

"You should do something," she said, as we walked away. "Somebody should do something."

On the way home we were quiet for a long time. We must have been nearly in Keremeos, and then George said, "Zing, zing."

"Zing, zing." And we began to laugh, so hysterically that I finally made George pull over until we had ourselves under control. He found a couple of Kleenexes in the glove compartment and mopped his streaming face.

"Oh, God," he said. "What the hell are we going to do?"

"I don't suppose you want to take her."

"I can't—I work all day—just that little apartment—"

"I know," I sighed. "I don't want to take her, either."

"She wouldn't want to go, anyway. She's happy where she is."

"Well, I suppose we should check out the nursing homes in Kelowna next time we come. Just to see what there is."

But the next time I came down, with Stewart and the kids, she seemed fine, her old self, saying why didn't I find someone for George so he could get married again.

"He doesn't want to get married again, Mom," I said.

"Well, I don't blame him," she grumped. "Being married is a pain in the ass."

And the next time I came, with George, it was because she'd died, a heart attack, mercifully quick, the way she would have wanted to go. We sat, in our black clothes, in her living room with the curtains drawn, thinking about what it meant. Neither of us cried, I know that; perhaps we were trying to be brave for each other.

"Look," I said, pointing at the coffee table with the tape pulling closed its cracked leg.

"God. That's still from the logging camp, isn't it?"

"The cracked leg," I say. "Remember how it got that? Dad was still alive. They were dancing across the living room, and the loose hem of Mom's dress caught on the coffee table and made them fall and then Dad—that's right, he did—he fixed her hem with the stapler and she fixed the table leg with Scotch tape. We were all laughing so much."

"They were drunk. They were drunks."

"That's not true," I protested, shocked. "They drank, of course, everyone in the camp drank, but they didn't, they weren't *alcoholics*."

"They were drunks. Both of them. Mom passed out on the couch, stinking of it, with vomit on her dress. How could you forget?"

"They weren't," I insisted. It astonished me, that he could think of them like that, as though we had not lived in the same household at all. I had no idea he felt this way, that this was what he remembered. "But we had basically a good childhood. Don't you think so?"

He leaned forward and started picking at the tape on the broken leg. "You don't remember all of it," he said.

"Neither do you."

He only sighed and leaned back in his chair, let his eyelids droop, almost closed. I sat there helplessly, feeling our two different memories sag in the room.

"I wonder what the coffee table remembers," I said.

He gave a little laugh, but in a way I was serious, wanting there to be some objective truth, an impartial witness. But maybe the coffee table wouldn't have been unbiased, either; it was, after all, what got broken.

We were quiet for a while. The Valium I'd taken was starting to wear off, and I could feel the crying it had suppressed pushing up in my throat; I kept swallowing, determined not to let it come, not yet, not here.

"We'll have to pack up and sort everything," George said finally. "And put the house up for sale."

"I guess so." It was too depressing to think about. "Maybe we could sell it furnished. Unless you want the furniture—"

"No, no. If you want it—"

"No, I'd have no place to put it."

"Maybe we should sell it furnished."

We sat there a while longer, staring at the walls full of old pictures and framed embroidery. There was a picture of Blue Boy, I remember suddenly, done in petit point.

"I'm going outside," George said abruptly. "It's so stuffy in here."

He walked out, and I heard the front door slam behind him. After a while I got up and went out, too, and sat beside him on the front step. It was a beautiful summer day, the sun warm but not hot, a little breeze wandering up from the lake. George bent down and pulled up a blade of grass and began chewing on it, so I reached down for one, too. My hand grazed something and when I looked I saw the old cottage cheese container that was sitting beside the step, hidden in the grass and filled with rocks. Slowly I lifted it out and set it down in front of us.

"Zing, zing." One of us must have said it, and then I put my arm around George and leaned my head against his shoulder and we sat that way for a long time.

We have left the downtown area and are in a residential district now. I look out at the houses, intently, noting the details, the things people display in their picture windows and gardens, things that seem to be less for the people in the houses than for us, the ones who drive by and look in. A white cat lies like a sculpture in the window of the blue house with the beige trim. A plastic duck with three ducklings walks across the lawn of the modern pastel house with a wavy tile roof. A sun deck is agog with red patio furniture. I note the way the sun touches the trees, the unexpected patterns their shadows make. It gives me such peacefulness, this gazing carefully at the things of the world outside myself. They will continue when I am gone. I remember a program I saw on the stages people go through when they are dying; the last stage is acceptance. No, I correct myself—the last stage is death.

"Ly-el," Chuck's voice cuts in, plaintive. "Help me here, will ya? I can't get out of this fucking place."

And Lyle sits up a bit straighter and looks around as though he has just arrived here and tells Chuck exactly how to get to the bridge.

We are there in less than five minutes. Chuck says nothing at all. I look at Lyle from the corner of my eye. At least he is still here, I think with relief, damaged, like me, but still here. He sinks back into himself, looking out the window with his eyes half-closed, his shoulders folding forward into his chest like a collapsed coat hanger.

As we wind around Okanagan Lake, so lovely it is hard to believe it is just a huge fissure in the earth filled with water, Chuck stops several more times to take pictures, not bothering to ask Lyle to be in them now. I have been here so often it is hard to remember what it was like the first time, the landscape suddenly so flagrant with beauty it seemed to expect acknowledgement.

We drive with the windows open now, it is so warm, the sun raising crinkly waves from the hills. The trees lining the draws look like dark veins running down into the lake. I take off my coat, but the movement seems to jar loose again the nerves in my head which had been knitting themselves back together, and I sit back gently, telling the headache which has rushed up to punish me that I didn't mean it, that I'll be quiet. If I sit perfectly still, there is almost no pain at all. The sun is hot on my face, healing. I close my eyes and watch the geometric patterns on the inside of my lids. My head feels large as sky, thoughts floating around like a giant nebula. I doze off a little, into that top layer of sleep that is only dream and image.

I can see myself at home, in my kitchen, doing what I have

been intending to for about a year, repapering the walls, only this time making sure I get rolls all from the same dye lot, not like last time, for the bathroom, discovering too late that the last roll was paler than the others, that the last two panels beside the sink had lighter yellow flowers than the others. Everyone said you couldn't notice, but I did; I noticed. Every morning as I stood there brushing my teeth my eyes would slide away from the mirror and linger on those flowers, like a confirmation, a checkpoint, that I was back in the unasleep world again, that here was reality, those flowers, refusing to be perfect. For the kitchen I will be more careful. I have already picked out a pattern at the store, violets twining up slender blue stripes. And I will order some fabric in the same pattern and make pot holders. Perhaps place mats, too, yes. (Somewhere far inside of me I can hear a mocking voice, one I have never heard before, sneer, *Place mats! That safe little world is gone forever! The rest of your life will have to involve more important things than place mats.* No, I protest weakly, afraid. Why do I have to give up what makes me happy? *Because it won't,* the voice says. *Not any more.*)

The car has stopped, and I snap open my eyes. Chuck is standing by the side of the car, urinating. He has his back to me, but I can see the stream arching out in front of him in a thin parabola. I turn my head, look at Lyle, who is watching Chuck, too, or watching something in that direction.

"Are you awake?" I ask.

He is silent so long I decide he has not heard me or is ignoring me. "No," he says at last, and turns his head so he won't have either Chuck or me in the field of his vision.

When we are moving again I see the sign for Osoyoos. It is as far south as we can go before the U.S. border. At Osoyoos we either have to head east, toward Alberta, or west, back to Vancouver. My heart starts to beat a little faster, something my head does not appreciate. Which direction will he choose; what will it mean? We are in the outskirts now, entering the reduced-speed zone.

And then I remember something about Osoyoos that startles me, because I have not thought of it before this.

"I was married in Osoyoos," I say, unable to stop the sur-

prised words. It was Osoyoos instead of Oliver because of
some problem with the church or the minister, I forget
which. All those years ago. Where I got married.

"What?" Chuck says, his eyes flicking up into the rearview
mirror.

"Osoyoos. It's where I got married. My mother used to live
around here," I mumble.

"That so?" Chuck says flatly. His eyes bend away from the
mirror back to the road.

Oh yes, I want to say, the past like a dangerous vision pulling me forward in my seat, handing me the apple of memory,
the poisoned apple of fairy tales, one bite and you sleep forever, oh, yes, I want to say, see that intersection? Well, the
church is straight down that road, and it was a perfect sunny
day in May, everything was in bloom, and, it's true, it was the
most wonderful day of my life. George, that's my brother,
George, he gave me away, and I walked down the aisle on his
arm. The "Wedding March" burst around me, and I moved
slowly, slowly, doing the little step with the hesitation, and I
thought, it is all happening the way it is supposed to, the man
up at the front, looking so handsome now in his black tux-
edo, is the man I love, and he has chosen me, little ordinary
Patricia Ferguson. Let me remember this forever, I thought
fiercely, going step, pause, step, pause, let me remember this
forever because it is everything my life has been made for,
turning out perfectly. And finally, at the front of the church
there was Stewart, beside me at last and smiling, choosing
me, and our trembly voices were saying we would love each
other forever and ever until death do us part.

"Marriage," Chuck says, turning west onto the Crowsnest
Highway, the road back to the coast. "It's a pile of shit."

M

O

N

D

A

Y

CHRIS

"Well, I *thought* there was something weird about this club, you know, all men, and then when I saw them dancing together of course I *knew*. And god *damn* Tom, he didn't give me a *clue* before we got there. I suppose he thought it'd be easier to tell me in the club, or have me just suddenly realize what it was and that he was—you know—but *god,* can't you just see it, naive little Murray thinking, where are all the girls—oh, I tell you, a farce worse than death—"

Murray's voice circles around my head, not really finding its way in. He's upset; I should be listening, of course I should; this is important to him. But my brain's so sluggish today, crawling around inside my skull, not wanting to work, a run-down watch. My whole head feels numb; even my ears feel like glued-on pieces of cardboard. I can't stop brooding about my fight with Mint yesterday, and then all morning, sitting with Dad in the living room waiting for the phone to ring, and there was only silence and the noises the house made as it tried to take care of itself, waiting, too—

"And he treated it like just another little shopping trip for souvenirs down Robson Street—"

I shake my head a little; maybe the watch will start ticking again. Murray. All right. His friend is gay.

"I just felt so out of place, you know? Like if there was a riddle asking, who feels more uncomfortable than a straight gimp from Edmonton at a gay club in Vancouver the answer would be nobody. And I just feel so awkward around Tom now. He might have AIDS, for god's sake—"

"Oh, Murray, stop overreacting."

"Well, how would *you* like it if you suddenly found out one of your best buddies was gay?"

"If the friend was important enough to me I'd try to work it out. There's nothing wrong with being gay."

He sighs, rubbing his arm absently. "I guess so. God, life is so complicated. It's enough to drive a man to dink."

"Ha," I say halfheartedly.

"Are you sure you want this lane, by the way?"

And I realize I'm on the exiting lane from the bridge, taking us onto the convolutions of the Marine Drive West interchange. "Shit. Shit." It's too late now to do anything.

"Lord have mercy," Murray whimpers, as I squirt us finally past the stop sign on the by-pass and into the line of traffic, accelerating frantically away from the car I've just cut off. "Kafka must have designed that intersection," he says.

But after that the road pulls us along in easy meanders, and we curve around it as though this were exactly what we'd planned. We didn't have any plans at all, actually—Murray just suggested I come out to Richmond and pick him up, so that's what I did. When I asked him where he wanted to go, he said, "Lourdes." Well, if I'm not more careful I'm going to drive us right into the holy waters of Georgia Strait. I should have asked Dad to let me use his car again; the fan belt in my Honda sounds as though it's ready to take off and start a life of its own.

We reach the entrance to UBC, and I point out to Murray what little I know of the place. It's where I should have gone, I suppose, instead of U of A, Edmonton like some distant sanitarium I thought would heal me. Looking for Lourdes. Aren't we all.

Murray says he wants to stop and go inside for a while, so finally I find a parking place beside the rose gardens, and I get out and bring him his chair. The wind from the ocean smells briny and wet, but it's stopped raining, and the sun is even starting to butt in through the clouds. We're quiet for a while, just taking deep breaths and listening to the cawing sea

gulls and looking out across rows of spiky bushes still several
months away from blossom. A sign in one corner of the
grounds says "Please—do not pick roses."

I wander down an aisle, reading the names embedded
above the plants like little headstones, and when I head back
toward Murray, I see him leaning down from his chair in
front of the sign. He's carefully filling in the bottom loop of
the "r" so that it looks exactly like an "n."

"If god hadn't meant for us to deface signs he wouldn't
have given us felt-tip pens," he grins, straightening up.

"What if somebody *saw* you?" I demand. "We could get in
trouble."

Murray shrugs. "Nobody *saw* me," he says, irritated. He
twists around and starts to wheel back to the car.

Oh damn. Now he's mad at me. Why didn't I keep my
mouth shut? I slouch along behind him, kicking at the gravel
on the path as though it were to blame. When we're back in
the car, Murray just sits there glaring out the windshield, and
I feel like screaming at him not to be so childish, but I know
it's as much my fault as his.

"I'm sorry," I say carefully. "I'm just in a bad mood. I had
a fight with my brother yesterday and it's still bothering me."

He doesn't quite look at me, but he stops staring so grimly
out the window. "It's all right," he mumbles, not sounding
convinced.

I start up the car and we head off, but I can't stand the
grouchy mood hanging over us, so I arrange my face in what I
hope is the right expression and say, " 'Do not pick noses'—
oh, you are bad!" I even manage a little laugh.

He grins. It's like someone's lifted up his whole face and
pulled its features upward. "Naw," he says. "I just smell that
way." I can't believe that's all there is to it. He may feel better
but I just feel I've manipulated him.

We drive around the rest of the UBC rim, then drop down
into Kitsilano, Murray moaning over the view as English Bay
with Vancouver floating in it comes at us around a corner.
Eventually we wind up on the Burrard Bridge, the city its
usual flagrant self below us, the ocean flat as a plate. I scrape
the car against the curb as I point out the landmarks, and

Murray yelps at me to stop driving by Braille, but at last we get across the bridge and find a parking lot just off Hornby, and then we get out and meander down Granville Mall.

Murray buys another Glenn Gould album in a record store and, because the clerk is busy or ignoring him, he finally just puts his money down by the cash register. When we start to leave, the clerk yells after us, "Hey, this isn't enough," and I realize Murray's probably forgotten the sales tax.

"He's from Alberta," I tell the clerk, a muscle-laden kid with a neck thick as my thigh; he only watches us suspiciously, waiting for his money. We slink from the store like thieves.

"He's from Al-*bird*-a," Murray complains at my back as I walk quickly away. "He's from Al-*bird*-a." He lifts his leg from the foot pad and kicks me in the calf.

Finally we find a pub with a wheelchair ramp, although it's so steep I can hardly stop the chair from getting away on me as we head down. Murray hangs on to the arms and moans with apprehension, and although I tell him it's okay I realize how helpless he is, having to trust me completely to control the chair. If I lost hold he'd pitch forward flat onto his face.

When we get settled we're only at slightly below sidewalk level, squinting up like ground hogs at the people walking by outside in the sunshine.

"They're gay," Murray says gloomily every time two men go past together. He's probably right; who cares? I watch the legs of the women, trying to guess the colour of their nylons—*medium taupe* there; *charcoal:* that was easy; *light beige* on that one. I cross my own legs, feel my right knee press up against the hard knots of gum corrugating the underside of the table.

We order another round. The beer, even mellowed out with tomato juice, tastes like raw potatoes, but it spreads some anaesthetic over the bruises in my brain.

"What do you get when you cross an alcoholic with someone who's got MS?" Murray asks.

"What?"

"Multiple cirrhosis."

"That's pretty good."

"What do you get when you cross me?"

"What?"

"Wheelchair tracks on your face."

I give him a constipated smile and take another drink. I look across the room and let my eyes slowly go out of focus, see people doubling, transparent.

"So—what did you and your brother fight about?" Murray asks suddenly.

I'm not prepared for the question, my mind reaching immediately for the evasive "Oh, nothing," but I decide I might as well tell him. "Uncle George. I want Mint to tell Mom what he knows, but he won't."

"What *does* he know?"

"Enough. He saw it. He doesn't really deny that. He just doesn't want to talk about it. He says I should forget about it." I take a large swallow of beer, can feel it dropping coldly down my throat. "I've tried to put it all behind me, honest to god I have, but I hate that bastard as much now as I ever did. Not just for the rape, but for the way he came between Mom and me. I mean, we were never all that close, but he's made it impossible for that ever to change. Kids fight with their parents all the time and then they grow up and get along fine, but we can't, we won't ever to able to—"

I stop, anger locking the words up in my chest. If Uncle George were here now I could smash this beer glass and cut his lying throat. My hand clenches around the glass. God—it scares me, the rage still there, a door I open and it blizzards in, as though what he's done were only yesterday and like hell does time heal all wounds, or wound all heels, as Murray would put it.

"Well," he says carefully, "you should do something about it. Talk to somebody, a counsellor, you know."

"There's nothing they could tell me I haven't told myself."

Murray starts to say something but stops himself. He probably has some profound comment like don't knock it 'til you've tried it, but I guess he can tell it wouldn't do any good. He rubs at the moisture on the side of his glass for a minute, and then he says, "Did you see him this time?"

I shake my head. "I'm sorry in a way. I'd like to tell him to his face how much I hate him. I've never actually done that. Not since that night."

"I knew a girl once who was raped. She went to high school with me. He was a city alderman. A real dork. She was baby-sitting for him. Anyway, she went to one of these support groups and they said sometimes it can make you feel better if you confront the man about it in front of people he works with. I mean, that's really a way of getting to him."

I stop my glass of red beer on its way to my lips. My mind has suddenly jerked taut. "Did she do it?" I demand.

"Yeah, she did it. She went right into city hall."

"Did she feel better afterward?"

"I don't know. I didn't know her all that well. She was just somebody in my Math class."

I take a slow sip of my beer, put it down. My heart has begun to bang away in my chest as though it's revving up.

"Murray," I say.

He stares at me. "Oh, hey—I wasn't suggesting—"

"He works only two blocks from here. I know exactly where. I was in his office lots of times with Mom. It would be perfect." I lean across the table. "Perfect. He's such a toady, sucking up to his boss, trying to weasel promotions for himself although I don't think it ever works. I could just saunter in to the second floor—it's a big open area with just a couple of room dividers and his office and his boss's at the end. Four or five secretaries—"

"Chris, Chris—" Murray reaches over, handcuffing his hands on my wrists. "Wait a minute. You want to walk into this roomful of people and say, 'My Uncle George is a rapist'? What would happen then? They'd call the police and have you taken away to Looney Tune land."

"Okay, okay, maybe not in front of everybody. Maybe just his boss. I could just tell his boss. It was *your* idea."

Murray gives a little whimper. "Aw, Chris—"

"I want to do it."

"You're drunk. It's the beer."

"I've had a glass and a half. I'm not drunk. I mean it. I'm going to do it. If I don't I might go out and buy a gun and shoot the bastard." I push my chair back and stand up, careful not to look like a lunatic. "You want to come with me?"

Murray slumps back in his chair. "I'll just wait here until you're in remission."

"Fine." I don't crack a smile.

"It could all backfire on you," Murray pleads. "Think about it some more."

"If I do, I'll chicken out. I'm going. Right now. I'll be back in half an hour. Just wait here for me."

I ignore his whines of protest, what he's saying about bail money, and get up and head for the exit, not looking back. I take the steps two at a time, and then my reflection is walking toward me in the glass door. I reach out my hand, push.

The air is damp as a wet sponge on my face. I start to walk quickly down Georgia, bumping into oncoming people as I overtake others. "Sorry, sorry," I keep murmuring, a chant, a mantra. I turn onto Burrard, then Melville, one block more and there it will be, the telecommunications firm for which Uncle George has worked ever since I was a kid. I walk fast. If I think about it I'll be too afraid; I walk fast.

And here it is, just as I remember, from the very first times Mom took Mint and me here, to show us where her brother George worked, her dear brother George, who let us play with the adding machines on the desks while the secretaries were at lunch, who introduced us proudly to his boss as though we were all his own. After his divorce it was us he asked to the company picnic, Mom and Mint and me, his family.

My hand is on the outside door. I hesitate, planning it out, a terrorist attack, a rushing in and throwing the bomb and rushing out before it explodes, always a risk that you'll be caught, that the bomb will go off with you still inside. And it's been years since I've been here. Things will look different. I'll have to be prepared for that. Through the glass doors I can see the elevators and the big board beside it listing all the departments, employee names. I can check there first. I tug open the door, which resists as though it knows why I'm here, and go inside.

There are lots of names on the board, but I look for the two I'll recognize. George Ferguson, Assistant Regional Manager. Yes. And the other one, the name I couldn't remember but that slides now like a bolt into memory's slot, P. L. Levitt, Regional Manager, his boss, a man with a face like a pecan. Second floor.

"Levitt," I say out loud. "Hello, Mr. Levitt."

I push the elevator button.

The elevator dings and the door opens. Two men in dark grey suits get out, arguing vehemently about a transmission break. My ears strain to hear their conversation, as though they might have clues I need. The doors start to close and I jump inside, the way Silky leaps through the second before the door closes, as though she's timed it for the last possible moment. Maybe by the time I leave there'll be pieces of me that didn't make it stuck to the door corners, too: bits of hair, clothing, blood.

The elevator begins to go up although I haven't pressed any buttons; someone from another floor must have called it. I suddenly imagine it opening on the second floor and Uncle George standing there waiting to get on, the two of us face-to-face. I push the "2" button several times, hard, as though that will give me back control. My right eyelid begins to twitch; it feels as though it's going bang! bang! bang!— jerking my whole face around, but I know it's only going tic, tic, tic, not even noticeable unless you look for it.

The elevator stops. Second floor. The door slithers open.

The place hasn't changed as much as I thought. There's a thick carpet now; the room dividers, from behind which I can hear the thunder of typewriters and printers, are in different places, and there's a wall on the left making Marketing into a separate section; but as I look straight ahead what I see are the two offices I expected to see. Even from here I can read the names on the two doors. P. L. Levitt, Regional Manager. George Ferguson, Assistant Regional Manager.

The elevator doors are closing and again I have to step quickly between them. They bump clumsily against me, like blind old dogs. The receptionist, whose desk is beside the elevator, looks up at me.

"Can I help you?" The company has had a smile permanently glazed onto her face.

"I'm just here to see Mr. Levitt," I say, giving her a confident nod. I walk quickly away in case she asks me my name, if I have an appointment. There's another desk in front of Mr. Levitt's office, but no one's sitting at it. I pause there for only a second, and then I walk around behind it. When I raise my hand to knock on the door I'm surprised to see I'm not trembling at all. It's like someone else's hand, closed into a fist, directly in front of my eyes.

I knock loudly, three times. There's an ache in my chest from where air is collecting, breath I can't expel, as though I'm saving it for something. The door will open; what will I say? My throat is pulling tight, closed. Mr. Levitt will face someone struck dumb—

No answer. I knock again, three times. My hand begins to throb like a heart.

"Mr. Levitt's not *in*," says a territorial voice behind me. When I jerk around I see his secretary back at her desk, holding a cup of coffee and looking at me suspiciously, her mouth pleating in disapproval. She's a woman in her fifties or so with excessively red hair and thin as a stick although her make-up alone must weigh five pounds. "Do you have an appointment?" she demands, confident that I'll say no.

"No," I say, giving her my brightest preppy smile. "I just thought I'd, you know, drop by."

It disarms her a little; she'll have to be careful—I sound like a personal friend. She sets down her cup and says, "Is there anything I can help you with? Or if it's urgent you could see the Assistant Manager. He's in."

I look at Uncle George's closed door. *He's in.* My god. He could walk out here any minute. I cap my right hand, still fisted from when it was knocking on Mr. Levitt's door, with my left, to stop them both from shaking.

"Oh, no thanks," I say, backing away from her. My foot rattles the wastepaper basket. "Sorry." I look at the elevator, so far away, as it is in a dream when you're running from whatever's chasing you but your feet move too slowly and where you're going retreats.

And then I stop. Why should I run? Why not see him? *If it's urgent,* the secretary said. Well, it is. If I don't face him now I may never find the courage again. What's the worst that can happen—matter collides with antimatter and destroys us both. I'll risk it.

"Just a minute," I say. "Maybe I *will* see George."

The secretary gives me an ingratiating smile. *George,* I can see her thinking, *she must know him.* If she only knew how well. She goes up to Uncle George's door and taps on it lightly. "Mr. Ferguson? Someone to see you."

"Okay." I can hear his voice inside.

The secretary opens his door. I can go in. I steady myself for a moment on her desk, and then I walk up to the doorway, stand there.

"Hello, Uncle George."

He looks up, over a litter of beige file folders and computer print-outs that drip perforated squares over the edges of his desk. He's a lot fatter than I remember him from that Christmas two years ago. His face has the thick middle-aged look some people get, his cheeks pushing up into fleshy little embankments in front of his eyes, his head and neck starting to look like two balloons squeezing out of his collar, his necktie the string anchoring him to his desk. This is Mom's handsome older brother. This is the man who raped me. I simply look at him, my mind such a swirl of feelings—anger, loathing, revulsion. And suddenly fear, the worst and clearest one of all, fear that pounds at my chest and says run, run. I grab onto the door frame, as though I'm standing on a bus that's starting to move.

He can't hurt me. Not any more. Today I'm not thirteen. I swallow, a taste in my mouth of metal.

"Chris!" he says. "What's happened? Have they found Pat?"

I can only stare at him. What's he talking about? My mother. Of course. He thinks I'm here to bring him news. It's what I should have expected but didn't, that his first thought on seeing me would be concern over her, nothing even to do with me. And here I am, not thinking about her at all, thinking only of myself.

I almost give in. But no, goddamn him, I won't. I take a deep breath. I can feel the skin at the corners of my eyes, my mouth, pull tense, pull closed and mean, pockets I am zipping shut.

"There's no news. That's not why I'm here."

"Oh." He leans back again in his chair. "Well, how can I help you?" He twirls a pencil in his fingers, bounces the eraser tip lightly on one of the file folders. A cramped smile wedges itself between his nose and chin.

"I want to talk to you about what you did to me when I was thirteen. How you raped me."

His mouth drops like a chute I've pulled open. The pencil stops dead, the eraser pointing amazed at a stray paper clip.

"What are you talking about?" His voice is a harsh whisper. Behind me I can hear Mr. Levitt's secretary opening a drawer in her desk.

"You know what I'm talking about."

"For god's sake, come in and close the door."

I stand there for a moment, as though I'm thinking it over.

"I'll come in," I say, "but I won't close the door." I step inside, lean against the wall, cross my left foot over my right and balance it on my toes. The casual look. I hope he doesn't notice my shoulders shoved so tight against the wall it feels as if I'm denting it.

"Chris. For god's sake. What's the matter with you? What are you trying to do?" He hasn't moved at all. He's still clenching the pencil, upside-down, like a cigarette with the filter pointing the wrong way and you know he's going to light the wrong end.

"I've decided, Uncle George, that I'm not going to let you get away with it. You should have gone to jail for what you did to me. And I'm not going to pretend any more that it didn't happen. That's all."

"Oh, Chris, come on now." He sticks a gluey smile on his face. "That was such a long time ago."

"I wanted to kill you," I say. "Sometimes I still think about it. About killing you." My voice is suddenly so tense with hatred it's like a shard of glass slicing the air between us. He leans back from it. As though he were actually afraid.

"What do you want?" he says. "What the hell do you want?" His Adam's apple bounces quickly up and down, a marble in an elevator zooming between floors.

I think about it. For the first time, really, since I came here, I make myself be still and think about it. What do I want? I have to be sure I get it right.

"I want for it never to have happened. I want to have those years back the way they should have been. But that's not possible. So what I want instead is for Mom to know the truth. Right now that's all that matters to me. When she gets back you have to tell her."

"I can't do that," he says, his voice incredulous. He gives a little bark of laughter. "You think I'm crazy? What's this obsession you have with this, anyway? God, Chris, your mother's been kidnapped and all you can think about is getting revenge on me for some stupid thing that happened years ago." His voice rises and he looks nervously past me at the open door. I'm surprised he hasn't thought to get up and try to close it.

"I know you don't understand. I don't care if you do."

"Well, why should I do it? It doesn't make any sense. You tell her and see how far you get. She won't believe you."

I try to hold my face still and impassive, to give nothing away. But I can see that smug look climbing on his face, and I know he thinks I'm hesitating because I'm on the defensive, and he grabs the advantage.

"You know what I think it is?" he says. "I think it's not me you want to hurt as much as your mother."

"Why should I want to hurt her?"

"Because you always have. You were jealous of Mint, of your father, of me. Now you want to punish her."

"No. I just want her to know the truth." But something in me stumbles, something whispers, frightened, *Could he be right?* And Mint's voice from yesterday, *You were always picking fights*— I cut the thought off, denial like a tourniquet squeezing no, no. I can't let him get to me; it's a trick; he knows where I'm vulnerable, that's all; he's trying to use a little truth to erase a large lie. I can't let him see me unsure. I can't let him win.

"If I want to punish someone, Uncle George, it's you. You better believe it." I attach a little laugh which I hope he interprets as derisive.

"Well, it's sick," he says. "What you're doing, it's sick. After all this time. Just wanting me to suffer. Wanting revenge." He's trying another angle.

"It's not just revenge. It's wanting things to be right between Mom and me."

"But you still want to punish me. Isn't that right?"

"Yes, all right. So what? So I want to punish you. So I want revenge. What's wrong with that?"

"Everything. It's childish. It's immature. It's—there's this saying, *One who seeks revenge should dig two graves.*"

"Well, there's only one grave here and I didn't dig it and I'm not going to be the one in it."

"The saying *means,*" he says, trying to make me seem obtuse, "that revenge is self-destructive."

"Oh, yeah? Well, there's another saying. *Revenge is sweet.*" All those years as a smart-ass are paying off.

"What good will it do? Tell me—what good will it do?"

"It'll do *me* good—" I start to explain, and then I pull the words back. It's what he wants, to keep arguing, to find a weak spot, to make me feel guilty. "It just has to be this way," I say instead.

He looks at me, turning my words around in his head to see where he can slide in a wedge and crack them open. I keep my face closed up flat and tight.

"Well, I'm not going to tell her," he says finally. "That's all there is to it. I can't believe you thought I would." He waits for me to absorb his words, as though I were a cloth to soak up a spill.

And so here it is, his bottom line, and his face now looking up at me in triumph, a little smile actually twitching at his mouth because he wants me to know that he could have been arguing all along just as an exercise, an amusement even, because it wouldn't matter if he won or not since nothing was at stake, since at the end he would win regardless, just by saying no, a flat and easy refusal, impervious to argument.

"All right?" he says. He bounces the pencil twice on his desk. His smile widens a bit, becomes generous, kindly almost. Avuncular.

I take a deep breath, shift my posture against the wall. This is my only chance, my one weapon I brought with me. Murray, please be right.

"No," I say.

"No?" The smile drops away. He tamps his pencil once more on his desk.

"Actually, Uncle George, it wasn't you I came here to see. I'm only here because Mr. Levitt wasn't in. You can ask his secretary. I was knocking on his door and she said he was out and did I want to see you instead—"

"This has—"

I raise my voice and cut him off. "I came to see Mr. Levitt because I decided to tell him all about it. About how you raped me. How you raped your own niece. And if you don't tell Mom the truth, I'll come back, and I'll tell him."

He starts to say something again, but I don't care, I rush on, faster now. "And, oh yeah, you'll say he won't believe me, either, and maybe he won't, but he'll just never be *sure* about you any more, really sure. The next company picnic, you'll see him watching you out of the corner of his eye, afraid now to leave you alone with his grandchildren, even just for a minute. He'll remember me, that cute little girl you used to bring to the office, and ask himself why I would lie about something like this. And the papers are full of stories now about creeps like you, after all; you're sort of the fashionable perverts."

It gets to him. It really gets to him. I can see it on his face, the way it sags like a sheet between clothespins. Little pebbles of sweat are stuccoing his forehead. And oh, it's worth it, just for this moment, the expression on his face, oh, Murray, come look. Something like a long breath leaves me, loosens a muscle somewhere I've been keeping clenched tight for ten years.

"It would be awful for her, Chris," he says, his voice low, plaintive. He sags back in his seat, lets his pencil drop to the desk. Through his thinning hair his scalp is shining as though it's been buttered.

"I know," I say. "But if I were her I'd want to know. Because it's the truth."

"She needs me now, with the divorce and everything. I'm her best friend. You'll destroy that. She'll never trust me again."

"Better you than me." Oh, I am hard. I am rock. I am diamond.

"Why do you want to do this to me, Chris?" He sounds hurt, like someone who deserves sympathy. "Why do you hate me so much?"

"You raped me. It was the most horrible thing that ever happened to me."

"You must have liked it, Chris. Come on, admit it. You wanted it, too. Flaunting yourself in front of me all the time—"

"I never did! I was thirteen, for god's sake." It's another trick, the old blame-the-victim trick.

"You were pretty sexy for thirteen, kid."

"It was rape, you bastard, You know it."

"Well, I thought you wanted it. I thought you liked it. I swear I did. If I was wrong I'm sorry."

I'm sorry. Maybe that's what I've been wanting to hear from him, all these years, even today. But it's too late. I can't believe him. He's afraid, that's all. *I'm sorry* are just the words recommended in the corporation manual on how to manipulate people.

"I have to go," I say. "Maybe Dad's heard something by now." I straighten my purse on my shoulder and take a step toward the door. "I'll let you know about when I want you to tell her. I want to be there."

"What if she's dead?" he says, his voice cold. "You got some alternative punishment in mind?"

"I'll think of something," I say, matching him. I can be as brutal as he can. "I'll let you know. But she's not dead. Don't talk as if she were."

He sighs, lifts his hands a little in the air, lets them drop dully to his desk. A paper clip spurts out from under his fingers, embeds itself in a file folder.

"We both love her," he says. "At least we know that, whatever happens. Whatever's between us."

It's an unexpected thing for him to say, and because it's so nakedly true I can't do anything but nod and say quietly, "Yeah."

 And then, just for a second, I feel a nudge of pity for him, can hear him that night crying in the living room, can imagine his life all these years alone and lonely and waiting for the day I would step through his door and demand retribution. But it's just for a second. He is still my enemy. Pity is too dangerous a compromise.

Before he can read any of this on my face, I turn abruptly
and go. I can feel his eyes on my back, tangible as a hand. The
secretary looks up as I walk past, the brush from a bottle of
opaquing liquid in her hand, and gives me a cheery smile. If
she overheard anything she's good at disguising it.

The elevator is still there, and the doors stumble open
when I touch the button. I step inside, turn around. Directly
in front of me, at the end of the building, is Uncle George's
office. He sits behind his desk, cut off at the waist, a chunk of
torso in a grey suit jacket, a round fleshy face with eyes that
look now right into mine. The elevator doors close, two
hands clapping shut on an insect.

When I reach out to push L for Lobby my hand is shaking
so much I push P for Parking by mistake, and, as though I
can't push L as well, I let the elevator take me down to the
bottom floor.

I did it. I've beaten him. After all those years of smiling and
keeping silent, passing him the mashed potatoes at supper,
taking his presents and saying thank you, feigning gratitude
for his rides to school, watching my mother's easy affection
for him, all the time hating him so much my dreams were full
of his screams, his pain. God—could it really all be over now,
the monster so easily vanquished? As though I've been an
animal whose heel tugs back and back in the leg-hold trap
and I've gnawed to the white bone to get loose, but is it
possible that all I've ever needed to do was reach down and
pry open the jaws? Have I had that power all along? Well, if
we didn't have free will they'd have called it free won't.

The elevator grunts up from P for Parking, and this time it
stops at L for Lobby, and I step off. I'm giddy with relief,
free, safe. Laughter whoops lunatic out of me. A woman
carrying a briefcase enters the lobby from somewhere behind
me, and she stares at me as she goes over and waits for the
elevator. I look at her and laugh and laugh. She reaches up
and punches the button for the elevator again, several times.

I stumble out the door, my feet like a drunk's, forgetting
how to move. But outside the air smartens me up, and I start
to run, my purse flapping at my side like a third arm, until I
get back to Granville and the pub where Murray's waiting. I

lean against the wall, gasping, until my heart has slowed down to only about twice normal and then I go inside.

He's still at the table where I left him, although someone else is sitting across from him now, a young destroyed-looking guy who's talking away at him and gesticulating with a cigarette that flings ashes at anyone who walks by. Murray sees me and gives a relieved grin, but the kid only looks up at me with an annoyed expression and doesn't move.

"Tim was just leaving," Murray says. "Sit down."

"You know her?" The kid twitches his head in my direction.

"No, she's on a scavenger hunt and has to find a cripple."

The kid's eyes zing suspiciously from one to the other of us, but finally he gets up and backs away. "Shit," he says vaguely.

I grab the vacated chair. "Slut. Can't leave you alone for a minute."

Murray makes a face. "He wanted to know if he could borrow my wheelchair for a while. Jesus. I think he's had liposuction of the brain." He leans eagerly across the table. "So what *happened*?"

I tell him, everything I can remember, what Uncle George said, what I said, what the secretary said.

"And how do you feel?" he asks. "Better? Catharsized and all that?"

I think about it. Emotion recollected in tranquillity. Yes, I feel better. But. (What do you mean, *but*? Of course you feel better.)

"I feel better," I say.

"Well," Murray says, "praise the Lord and pass the beer."

But all the glasses are empty, and the waitress seems afraid to come near us. "It's all right," Murray shouts at her. "I'm only a hologram," but of course that just makes it worse, so finally I say, "Oh, what the hell. Let's blow this town."

"No gay jokes. If you don't mind."

It's only three o'clock but the traffic is starting to build. I'd forgotten rush hour in Vancouver is about four hours long. Oak Street is busy but we jerk along without more than a one-light wait at any intersection. (*You did it,* says the voice in my head. *You did it. But* is still there, deep down, a small whisper, but I don't let myself hear it; I listen to that voice gloating, *You did it.*)

Over the bridge we pick up speed but then the traffic backs up again and we move ahead only a foot at a time. The right lane is blocked off so we all have to squeeze left. I'm feeling magnanimous so I let in about four cars ahead of me. When we finally get to what's blocking the right lane we see it's only a truck whose sole purpose is to flash a big arrow directing us to the left, and after we pass it both lanes are clear again.

"Was that some experiment to test stupidity?" Murray asks.

"Probably," I say cheerfully. The traffic clots up again and we move ahead in little irregular surges.

Murray sighs. "Oh, well, I guess I'm in no hurry to get back to Tom's, anyway."

"I take it you aren't looking forward to seeing him again."

"Was Salieri looking forward to seeing Mozart again?"

"I guess that means no."

"Was John the Baptist looking forward to seeing Salome again? Was—"

"All right, all right. You could stay with us if you want."

"Well, no—I've got all my stuff at Tom's and everything."

"You really should talk to him about how you feel."

"I know. I'm just so uncomfortable about it."

"This from the man who advocates compusex."

"That's different. The machine is just sort of an intermediary. It's still straight sex."

"But you can't really be sure. I heard of a guy pretending to be a woman." I'm making that up, but it sounds plausible.

"Come on."

"Really. How would you know for sure?"

Murray groans. "What's the world coming to, if you can't even trust your computer?"

"You're just afraid of being gay yourself."

"Hey, of course. No wonder I always threw up on girls I slept with. And I thought it was bulimia." He sighs. "I've just never known anyone gay before. Let alone a good *friend.*"

"Well, that's the point, isn't it?" I say, exasperated. "Is he a good friend or not? Are you going to drop him just because he happens to be gay?"

He thinks about it for a moment, plucking at his seat belt with his thumb as though it were a guitar, and then he says, "Of course I won't. He's still a terrific guy. I'm lucky to know him. I'm being an asshole. Which is fortunate if you're full of shit." He turns and gives me a smile. I see he's even using his dimple. "So golly gee, Sigmund, thanks for straightening me out. So to speak. I'm, like, just terminally grateful."

"You're welcome." Maybe it *is* that easy for him—he can decide something intellectually and that's it, voilà, he feels different. The way Mint says it should be. Well, it hasn't worked like that for me. But something *has* worked, I think fiercely, my hands tightening on the wheel, something *has* changed. I can see Uncle George behind his desk as I told him and somehow ten years of rage began to slide off my back as though I were finally learning to stand upright.

The freeway squeezes us to a stop again, but then another peristaltic surge expels us at our exit and from there it's only a few minutes to Tom's.

"Well," Murray says, as I turn off the car.

"Well," I say. "Are you going to be all right here? Should I leave the meter running?"

"I'll be fine. But maybe I should fly back tomorrow. I kind of miss Edmonton, actually."

"Yeah. I should be in my English class right now. I haven't even read the novel we're starting."

"If God had meant for us to read novels he wouldn't have given us Cole's Notes."

I laugh.

"Sloth is much underrated," he insists. "Newton was sleeping when the apple fell on him. And I say that with all gravity."

"You're too much."

"Thank you. Flattery is the sincerest form of imitation."

"Well," I say, determined to stop him. "I should go, I guess."

"Maybe your dad's heard something this afternoon."

I nod. "I'll call you tonight, okay?"

"Well," Murray says.

"Well," I say. "Do not pick noses."

"What?" He shoves half his damned hand up his nose.

"Go away," I laugh.

"I know," he sighs. "Real estate values are dropping even as I sit here."

And then, without thinking about it, I slide over and give him a hug. It's awkward because the gearshift is in the way and I have to sort of attack him from the side. He sits there stiffly; I feel as though I'm holding a door. But just when I think I've made an awful mistake, his arms go around me and he hugs me back.

Finally I pull away a little, but our hands are still on each other's shoulders, and he's so close I can hardly focus on his face. His eyes are so surprisingly blue. I lean forward and kiss him on the mouth.

I can feel his shoulders tensing under my hands, but I don't let go, and after a second I feel him kissing me back, his arms tightening around me. My head feels light and airy, as though all it contained were bubbles, nothing capable of logical thought, brain cells melting into helium.

At last I draw back, turning my head quickly because I'm too embarrassed to look at him. I slide back over to my seat, the gearshift spiking me in the kidney.

"Well," says Murray. "That sure made me want to throw up."

I laugh nervously, pick at something brown stuck to the steering wheel. "I'll get your chair," I say. I fumble my way quickly out of the car, open the trunk and hoist the chair out. I have to try three times before I slam the trunk lid down hard enough for it to catch, and then I only stand there for a while with my palms pressed against it, as though I'm afraid it will suddenly fly up again into my face. When I wheel the chair around to the passenger side I see Murray's already pulled himself out of his seat and is propping himself up on the door frame, facing me. When I push the chair toward him he doesn't turn around, only keeps looking at me.

"Just be careful," he says.

I flex my fingers on the handles, watch them stretch out straight and determined, then coil back. "I'm always careful," I say.

"You know what I mean."

I nod. I don't look up.

"I won't get better."

I nod again. From the corner of my eye I see the door opening at Tom's house, and I know in a minute he'll be coming out, thinking Murray must need help, standing so awkwardly with the empty wheelchair facing him. I glance around, at the street, the other houses, in dumb desperation, looking for, I don't know, someplace to hide, maybe.

Murray's arm is starting to tremble from the pressure of supporting himself, and I butt the chair at him and say, "Sit down before you fall down."

"Yeah." But I haven't coaxed a smile from him. He turns around so that he can drop into the chair. I see Tom coming down the walk.

"It was just an impulse," I say. "We don't have to take it any further."

"I just want you to think about it, that's all."

Tom says something to us then, and we give him half-hearted answers, and he takes over the chair from me and starts wheeling Murray to the house. I take a few steps after him before I understand that of course I'm supposed to leave now.

"Call me." Murray's words blow back at me over his shoulder. Tom, not sure what he's supposed to do, stops and turns Murray back to face me.

I smile, reach up and shade my eyes from the sun. To them it probably looks like a salute. "All right," I say.

"On the phone," Murray says. "You know."

I nod, lower my hand. The sun slams into my eyes. "Keep your pecker up," I say.

Tom guffaws, and Murray laughs, too, I think, but I can't be sure. Finally Tom nudges the wheelchair a little, and when Murray doesn't resist he turns it around and starts pushing it up the walk.

I back away until I bump into my car, and I get in, close the door. I roll down the window, as though there's something more I should say, but my brain feels vacuumed out. I sit here numbly, not knowing what I should do. Start the car. Go home. Home is where when you go there they have to take you in. I turn the key in the ignition. The car lurches ahead, stalls, mercifully without hitting the vehicle in front of me, and I realize I've forgotten to put in the clutch. I glance over at Murray and Tom, who have turned to wave.

"It's the pedal on your left," Murray shouts.

By the time I finally drive away he's got Tom shouting stupid directions at me, too. "The steering wheel's the big round thing," I think I hear him say.

It isn't until I'm almost back on the freeway that I let myself think about what happened. *What happened:* as though I weren't an active participant.

It was just a *kiss,* for Pete's sake. No, it wasn't. It was more than that.

Maybe I'm just trying to prove something. To him, to myself? But surely I wouldn't want to use him like that. And surely the place for anything sexual to start is with liking someone. And I like Murray. I glance up into the rearview mirror, as though I could see him there, making rude comments about my driving, and I smile.

Still, he didn't act exactly overjoyed. But what did I expect, that he'd be thrilled and grateful? *Be careful,* he said. Yeah, I know. We can't pretend there's no MS, the mad wife waiting in the attic. My palms are sweaty, sliding on the wheel. I wipe them, one after the other, on my jeans.

Damn his stupid bloody disease, god *damn* it.

Maybe he's right to be so wary. How can I say for sure I could handle a sexual relationship with him as he gets worse and worse? How can I be sure I can even handle the friendship then?

We can't let the disease win. We're not a happy ending, we both know that. But we can't put our lives on hold waiting for a happy ending.

A car beeps at me, and I realize I'm sitting at a green light. I jerk ahead, although the traffic in front of me is stalled again.

Of course, maybe Murray was hesitating because he isn't interested—he has *Nadia,* remember. But I think he is. Interested. I think he wants to. He didn't throw up on me, after all. I look into the rearview mirror and smile again.

Well, when we're back in Edmonton we can see how it

goes. In a way I miss Edmonton the same as he does; I bitch about the cold, but it's where my life is. I've been happy enough there, living with Murray. And how long should I stay here, waiting, mindlessly waiting, and for what news? The horror of what's happened to Mom settles over me again like a sudden black blanket, stifling.

I won't think about it. You can choose what to think about. *Willy Loman is a tragic hero.* . . . I insert myself back into the freeway, inching along. No, it was one of the boys I'd decided to do. *The real tragic hero in* Death of a Salesman *is Biff, who realizes his uselessness in a society that . . .* something or other; Murray's written it down for me. Or should I do Happy, because he won't see the truth? I'll have to read that last scene between them and Linda again. Linda. What about Linda? If anyone suffers it's her. Her tragic flaw is just being a woman in the old-fashioned sense, the loyal wife to Willy, the good stay-at-home mother to the boys, and what does she get? A husband who screws around and finally leaves her in the cruellest way possible, children who disappoint her. The essay is assembling itself in my mind, topic sentences glowing at the beginning of paragraphs, quotations shuffling into place, the omnipotent "therefore" swaggering in with its conclusion.

I almost start to laugh. My mind is such a boil of personal chaos—Murray, Uncle George, my mother, my father, Mint—and in the middle of the cauldron is this intellectual calmness that writes me an essay. Well, it must be a good sign. It must mean some parts of the pot are cooling down.

As I'm pulling out of the Deas Tunnel it occurs to me that Linda Loman's life isn't all that different from my mother's.

I'm almost home. As I turn onto Zero Avenue I anticipate what's ahead, Dad staring at the TV set, waiting for the phone, the house thick with depression.

The sun is shining here, though, as it often does when it's raining in Vancouver; I can see it sucking leaves out on the willows, a lilt of green on the buffer of trees we share with the U.S. I remember one night Mint and me driving home from a

party, and somewhere along here we saw a white van parked
on the side of the road, and then someone came running from
out of the trees, from across the border, with a knapsack
which he tossed into the van and then dived in himself, the
van already moving, spitting gravel out at us from its rear tires
like some cornered animal. It frightened us for a moment, it
was all so sudden, and then Mint laughed and said, "Drugs,
they're smuggling drugs."

It seemed exciting, that something like this could be
happening just across the street from our dull suburban
house. "Don't tell Mom," Mint said, as though I would have.
"She'd want to move out tomorrow."

So it was our secret. The kind of secret brothers and sisters
can have with each other.

Well, I won't be nagging him any more to tell that awful
other secret, the one he finds impossible to face. And eventually I suppose I'll forgive him for his cowardice; I'll have
dinner with his wife and be an aunt to his children, and I'll
tell myself I have no right to be disappointed in him, to be
judgemental, that he is after all just stumbling through life the
best he is able. Eventually.

I pull into the driveway.

When I come into the kitchen, the first thing I see is the
sink piled full of popcorn. Then I see pieces of it everywhere,
on the stove, the counters, the floor, like huge flakes of snow.
It's so unexpected, the chaos of it, that I start to panic, sure it
must mean something dreadful.

"Dad?" I shout. "Dad!"

I hear him say something in the living room, and I rush in,
my heart thudding at my chest. He's sitting on the sofa,
watching TV, just as I pictured him, but in front of him on the
coffee table is an almost empty bottle of Scotch. Oh god, oh
god—he's heard she's dead—he'd never get drunk if he knew
he still had to answer the phone—

"Dad? You okay? Any news?"

He looks up at me, with a stiff unfocussed look. "Hi,
Chris. No news. No."

I sink down in the chair beside him, heavy first with relief
and then with despair. Maybe we'll never hear. Maybe this is

how it'll go on, day after horrible day. She will simply have disappeared and we'll never know what happened.

On the end table beside Dad is a huge pot of popcorn, and another bowl of it sits on the floor by his feet.

"All this popcorn," I say.

"It got out of control," he says. "I didn't think it would expand so much."

"How much did you use?"

"It didn't seem like a lot. A cup, maybe."

"Good grief, Dad."

"Have some," he says, holding the pot out to me. I take a handful, drop some on the floor but don't bother to pick it up. It tastes like nothing, like air.

I see Dad's made a fire in the fireplace, too, an odd thing to have done this time of the day, but I don't say anything about it. A log shifts a little like someone stirring in his sleep, and a spatter of sparks bounces off the grate.

A talk show is on TV, the interviewer asking giggly questions of a woman with long black hair and décolletage down to her pubes.

"Do people ever mistake you for your character?" the interviewer asks.

"Oh, all the *time,*" she twitters. "Once even *I* forgot!" And everyone laughs. Or maybe it's only a laugh track, another illusion. Sometimes the picture gives a little twitch and then turns from colour to black-and-white, but neither of us comments—it could be part of the program. Dad gazes at the screen as though it all made sense.

"Have a drink," he says, not taking his eyes from the set. "I've been bad. I'm probably drunk. I just couldn't stand sitting here, waiting, waiting, waiting."

"I know, Dad." I reach over and run my hand down his arm. "I shouldn't have stayed out so long. I'm sorry."

"It's okay," he says. "There's nothing you could have done."

"Still," I say.

"Oh. By the way. That constable phoned. Persky. I think he just wanted to talk to you." He gives me a nervous look, expecting, I suppose, that I'll be annoyed.

But I only laugh awkwardly and say, "I guess he finds me irresistible." I think of Murray. My face feels warm, as though I'm blushing.

"I guess so." Dad smiles, relieved. "So. Where did you go this afternoon?"

"Oh, just downtown. I went to see someone with whom I sort of had some old business to finish." I catch my breath, watching Dad out of the corner of my eye. Why did I tell him that? My heart starts to gallop, Silky racing for the door the second before it slams closed.

But Dad only nods in a disinterested way and keeps his eyes on the TV. My heart trots back to its usual speed.

Old business. The item on the agenda that has to be disposed of before the meeting can proceed, the item that keeps being tabled because nobody knows what to do with it. Well, not any more. The old business has been dealt with. I lean back in my chair, slowly, carefully, letting myself remember it all, what Uncle George said, what I said, even the nudge of doubt I felt later, the dangerous *but*. I'm a sorter in a factory looking for defective pieces. It's been several hours now; things have settled and cooled; the errors should start to show, the cracks in the argument. But still it feels right, little there I want to throw out and replace, nothing I need to fit in to make it work. I look at every accusation he made; they don't stand up, none of them.

I remember telling him I wanted to kill him. I don't any more. Maybe it's over, just like that, the hate like a blister on my heart, gone. What I feel for him right now is contempt. Contempt is better than hate. Contempt is something you feel when you're stronger than what you despise. Then I remember my lurch of pity for him as I was leaving his office, and, yes, even that is still there. But I'm not afraid of it now—what you pity is pitiable, pitiful. It's not an emotion that will weaken me.

When Mom gets home—

And of course there it is, the crack in the argument so big a whole book of rhetoric could fall in. Mom might not get home. My face turns itself away from that knowledge as though it's coming at me like a fist, as though it's something I only now have to understand. She has been gone for six days and the likelihood is that she's dead. There. That's it, the bottom line. I make myself look at the word, cold and absolute: dead. My mother is probably dead.

So what have I gained from confronting Uncle George? Maybe it was all just part of a pathetic denial—if I make him promise to confess to her she can't be dead—

And if she's not dead, and we do tell her—some present, some gift. Here, Mom, happy birthday, your brother raped your daughter. And even if she does believe it happened, she might still blame me, for seducing him, for being responsible just because I was there; in her eyes I'll be less the victim than the troublemaker, as I always was, without the good sense to keep my mouth shut—

Tears are starting down my cheeks, and I turn my head quickly so Dad won't see, and brush them away. It's all been a stupid waste, my seeing Uncle George. I'm still just a pathetic child crying over her mother's rejection; confronting Uncle George has solved nothing, nothing at all.

No. I clench my fingers on the sofa so hard they hurt. What I did today was the right thing. No matter what happens. Even if it's too late to make things right between my mother and me, this was still something I needed to do. For myself, no one else, myself. What Uncle George did to me is his dirty little secret, not mine, not any more.

I release my grip on the sofa, feel the panic subside. God. It's a struggle to make any headway: up the ladder of this bit of logic, down the snake of that one. But I *am* going to win. No snake is going to get the better of me.

My head is starting to hurt, the way it does when I stay up too late cramming for an exam. An intellectual kind of pain, I suppose. Not real. Not like— Oh, my mother: where are you? What have they done to you? Are you past feeling anything at all?

I scrape a piece of gluey popcorn off my palate with my thumbnail and drop it onto the coaster on the end table. I glance at Dad. He's lifting another drink to his lips, which open rather clumsily, as though he's been to the dentist and the freezing hasn't all come out. A drop of Scotch gets snagged at the corner of his mouth, runs about an inch down his chin before it disappears. He doesn't seem to notice. His eyes have a strangely inanimate look, like the eyes of statues.

The room starts to smell dusty and stale, the furnace getting ready to kick in. "You should get the vents vacuumed sometime, Dad," I say, rubbing my nose.

"I don't live here any more."

"Oh. I forgot."

We watch the TV. A serious man in a suit, talking about arms control, has replaced the actress in the interviewee seat. Comedy, tragedy, pictures in a box, muddling the important with the trivial. Next week it could be me on the show, for my two minutes' worth of entertainment value, lined up between the magic act and the aerobics instructor. "And what did it feel like, Chris, when you heard your mother'd been killed?"

I get up abruptly, go to the kitchen and pour myself a glass of wine. A big glass, a tumbler. Dad gets up, too, his knees cracking as he stands, and heads off down the hall to the bathroom. He carries his arms away from his sides, like an arthritic old man. I wander restlessly around the kitchen, gulping at my drink, opening cupboard doors as though I were looking for something. I clean up most of the popcorn—what's in the sink alone fills the garbage can—and then I soak a pot that's sitting on the counter and has something green and gummy stuck to the bottom. I poke a fork into Buddy's cage and amuse myself with the way he scolds and pecks at it; finally he turns around and shits on the damned thing, so then I have to clean it.

I pour myself more wine, go back into the living room where the TV is talking about diets and anorexia, pick up the remote control and switch around the channels. A lot of cartoons. Kids must be home from school. It's where I would head, first thing, the TV. It's a wonder I ever learned to read a book, have a thought that didn't come in square, flickering pictures.

I hesitate on a show that is a tour of the house of a multimillionaire somewhere, the voice-over gushy and sycophantic, talking about how many pounds of gold are in the wallpaper alone. Glass water-filled bubbles built into some of the walls are really aquariums of exotic fish. There are two

Rolls-Royces in the garage, driven by two chauffeurs wearing uniforms in colours matching their cars. I remember driving Dad's Lincoln. Is this really what we all want, money and luxury to the point of the grotesque? I think of the kidnappers and quickly push the button to another channel. Finally I leave the set on Channel 10, which is just running announcements and playing schmaltzy music.

When Dad comes back and sits down he doesn't say anything about the TV—maybe he doesn't even notice anything different. Still, I've no right to take away what he needs right now. I should at least try to talk to him.

"Have you and Yvonne thought of any names for the baby yet?"

He looks at me, confused. Okay, it's not the greatest question, Dad, but I'm trying.

"Yvonne has. Jeremy if it's a boy, I think. I can't remember what for a girl."

"You want a boy?"

He shrugs. "I suppose so. I think Yvonne does."

"Most people would rather have a boy," I say, setting my glass down with a harder thump than I intended.

"I didn't," Dad says. "I was glad you were a girl."

"Really? I never knew that."

"Sure," Dad says. "My sisters were terrific. My brothers were hell to raise. They took ten times as much work and now that Grandma's old and needs them, it's only the girls who care. No, I hoped Mint would be a girl, too."

"You're kidding."

"After he was born, of course, and he turned out to be so easy to get along with, I was glad he was a boy. But at first, no, I wanted nothing but girls."

"Well. That's surprising. I'm glad you told me."

"Why?"

"I always thought I was, well, not what you wanted."

"You were always what I wanted." He says it without any emphasis, as though it were so obvious it didn't need to be said. I can feel something cramping in my throat and I swallow several times before it goes away.

"What about Mom?" I ask. "Was I always what she wanted, too?"

He hesitates, the way you do when you want to phrase something unpleasant the kindest way possible. Shit. I should have left well enough alone.

"Your mother loved you," he says, looking at me. "It's just that she loved Mint best."

"Oh," I say.

"I'm sorry," he says, waving his hands clumsily in the air, as though he'd spilled his drink and didn't know how to mop it up. "I didn't put that very well. She loved you. I know that. But Mint was, he was, well, you know," he ends lamely.

"Yeah, I know." I take a swallow of wine. Dad runs his forefinger nervously back and forth under his watch band, as though he's told me some terrible secret I didn't already know.

Channel 10 is playing some Bob Dylan while the screen runs a notice about a revival meeting at the Redeemer Tabernacle. Pastor Bob will be talking on "Satan and the Virtuous Man." What's left of the log in the fireplace shifts, crumbling into coals and sending a last flare of light around the room.

"I was using the past tense," Dad says suddenly. "When I was talking about your mom. I was using the past tense."

"Oh. Well, that's because we were talking about when I was a kid." But of course I know what he means; I shouldn't pretend I don't. Past tense. Mother. Mom. Mommy. I drain my glass, a swallow so big I almost gag, lean my head against the chair back. Past tense. Everything is past tense, this flick of a moment, the blink of seconds I see on Dad's watch, past tense, and we're goddamn helpless against it.

I can feel my brain going sloppy and swampy with wine. Well, it deserves a rest. Whole years of my life have gone by with less exercise than I've given it today. I get up, vaguely, pick some dead leaves off the ivy that grows like wild hair on top of the buffet, and, because I'm standing up with a handful of dead leaves in my hand and have to dump them somewhere, I walk down the hall to the bathroom, drop them in the toilet. Then I prop my hands on the counter and look at myself for a long time in the mirror. Chris Duvalier. A billion years of evolution and here I am, present tense, a simple twist of DNA. I have my father's complexion, my mother's eyes. Sometimes I have Mint's smile. I'm pretty enough.

Your mother loved you. But she loved Mint best. Okay, I think. She loved Mint best, but she loved me, too. Is that so bad? I put the idea up on a shelf in the vanity, look at it for a while, like an odd gift you didn't like at first but hope you will learn to be fond of. She loved me, but she loved Mint best. She loved Mint best. But she loved me, too.

I smile at myself. If she loved me at all, that's pretty good. That's something to hold onto.

Then Dad is pounding at the door, his voice thick and muffled. ". . . the phone. About Mom."

P A T

The only difference between this motel and the last one is that the second bedroom here has no window of its own, so they did not tie me up last night. Chuck pushed his bed up against the door to my room instead, so it was blocked as tightly as if it had been bolted. Still, it felt wonderful, my own room, the freedom to stand or sit or lie down without being observed, to sleep without rope cutting into my wrists and twisting my arms over my head. Probably because my body needed it, I slept more soundly than I have since the beginning, and this morning I lie here in the dark and think that my head has mended itself surprisingly well; the throbbing is gone and my mind no longer feels it has had by-pass surgery. But my jaw feels worse, if anything, more swollen and sore, and I know I will cringe at what will look back at me in the mirror when they let me into the bathroom.

I lie here for half an hour at least, not turning the lamp on, just watching the brightening hem of light under the door, before I hear movement in the next room, Chuck coughing, the mumbled monosyllables of their conversation. They take turns in the bathroom, and the sound of running water makes me sit up and cross my legs from the sudden urging of my bladder. I lean over and feel under my pillow for the note I put here last night—the envelope from my purse on which I have written, "Help! Patricia Duvalier, kidnapped. Please— phone police. Two men, one named Bill. Green Chevrolet.

Returning to Vancouver or Burnaby." The maid will probably throw it in the garbage; she will have cleaned enough rooms to have no curiosity about the seedy things people leave behind. Even if it does reach the police it won't be much help. But it gives me a little feeling of power, knowing I have done what I could, that I have left a clue.

At last I can hear the bed being pulled away from in front of my door, and Chuck opens it and sticks his head in, squinting in the dark. He fumbles for the light switch on the wall and when the light flares in the room he is obviously startled to see me awake and sitting on the bed.

"Move it," he grunts.

I pick up my purse and sidle past him into the other room. Lyle is sitting hunched on his bed looking like a melting candle slowly slumping into a puddle of wax. He is wearing only pyjama bottoms, and as I walk past him I notice his shoulders are pocked with dozens of small moles, as though bits of gravel had embedded themselves in his skin. I look quickly away, embarrassed. He doesn't even seem to be aware I am here.

The room is bright with sunlight, and I realize it must be at least ten o'clock already. Time flies when you're having fun, my mother always used to say when she was depressed. I hurry into the bathroom and close and lock the door behind me. I avoid looking at myself in the mirror until I have urinated, and then I take a deep breath and raise my eyes. It is pretty awful. The woman in the mirror has a jaw that puffs out as though her mouth were stuffed with cloth, and my whole cheek has turned a mottled purple. I have make-up in my purse, I think suddenly; I could disguise the bruises at least, if not the swelling. But immediately I think how foolish that is, to worry about my appearance, Marie Antoinette on the guillotine wondering if her hair looks all right. Besides, it is probably better to look as I do: someone people will notice. The cut, I see, has scabbed over and looks like a thread of rusty spittle hanging from my lip. I wash my face cautiously. It doesn't improve things but at least I feel cleaner. My whole body smells. I wish I could take a bath.

Why not? I look at the tub, white and waiting, at the door closed and locked. If I hurry it should be okay. I quickly turn on the tap and am amazed at how much pressure there is, considering we are miles past Princeton. The tub should be full in a couple of minutes. I tug my comb through my hair and give my stale mouth a rinse, and by the time I slip off my dress and bra and panties and shoes the tub has filled. I step in and the water feels wonderful, an expensive gift someone has given me. I sink down, the water rising to my shoulders, lifting me almost from the bottom. Steam mists the walls, turns the mirror a fuzzy grey. I see my body spread in front of me like a long white scarf, not changed all that much from when I was a girl. Two children have nested in me, pushed their way out of me, but when I look down now I could be seeing myself at seventeen. It's a trick of vision, I suppose, the eyes not capable of registering the slow changes, the incremental betrayals of the flesh.

Because it *has* betrayed me. I am a body rejected by my husband. I have kept myself in shape, the way I have kept my house in shape; it was my job, a housewife, to keep us both attractive and functional, so what part of me shall I blame, which part is guilty of not pleasing? Perhaps it's the most shameful part of all, the brain—perhaps that is what Stewart looked at one day and found flabby and boring, out of fashion, out of shape. I lift my hands out of the water and press them, dripping, against my face. The water stirs around me, warm as blood, an opened vein.

No. His leaving was not my fault. I drop my hands into the water, clench them into fists, watch the bubbles spurt to the surface. I am sick of this, *sick* of it—I could be killed any moment, but still my thoughts come whining back to Stewart, Stewart, Stewart. It's stupid. It's pathetic.

It's a waste of time. And I don't have time to waste. I grab the washcloth and lather it until it can hold no more suds and I scrub at myself, my armpits and back and breasts, my crotch and my legs, washing away the dirt and smell of these last five days. The soap has a strong perfumey smell, and I breathe it in gratefully.

And suddenly the door glides open as though I hadn't locked it at all, and Chuck is standing in the doorway.

He is looking right at me. I am rigid with horror. My legs, by some instinct of their own, pull up toward my chest. I sink down into the tub as far as I can go but there is no hiding place; the water is murky with the soap and the dirt, but not impossible to see through. I glance down at myself and I can see everything he sees, my naked body, breasts and thighs, the triangle of pubic hair.

"Get out," I whisper. "Please."

He acts as if I had invited him to come in. He walks over to the sink right across from the tub and leans against the counter, folding his arms casually over his chest.

"I can do what I want," he says. He looks at me, looks at me, his eyes like wet stones. His face is as expressionless as if he were watching TV.

"Please let me alone," I say, trying to keep my voice from shaking. "Please leave and let me get dressed."

"Maybe I will and maybe I won't," he says. He reaches into his shirt pocket and slowly takes out his package of cigarettes. He knocks one out expertly, sticks it in his mouth and lights a match, all without taking his eyes off me. He inhales so deeply it's as though he were sucking me in, too.

"I'll call Lyle," I say. It is a risk, saying that, something I have been holding in reserve until I have nothing else to use.

His arms drop to his sides, and his expressionless face twists into rage. He kicks at the tub, jarring the water like an earthquake. I reach my arms up instinctively to cover my head, terrified the next blow will be aimed at my face.

"You fucking bitch," he breathes, bending down so he is level with me. He grabs my arm and twists it back so that I cry out, more in fear than pain. "It's you and Lyle, you and Lyle. Cunt. Fucking cunt."

He throws my arm down and scoops up a handful of water which he tosses in my face. I cringe back, my eyes squeezed shut, waiting for the rest of it. Panicky keening sounds I have never heard are stumbling up from my throat.

And then I hear him stand up. And walk out. I open my eyes. It's true. He's gone. His cigarette floats in the bathwater in front of me, but he is gone. I am faint with relief. Using Lyle's name worked. Chuck is still not ready for a confrontation with him. Lyle is still the one in charge.

I leap out of the tub, slurring the water onto the floor, and slam closed the door and lock it, although locks are obviously no impediment to Chuck if he really wants in. I towel dry as fast as I can, rush into my clothes. I am panting as if I had run a mile. I put the lid of the toilet seat down and sit on it, taking deep calming breaths. I can smell sweat on me as if I had never taken a bath—the sharp acrid smell of fear that is not like normal perspiration at all. Once it must have been strong enough to drive your enemies away, as it still is for skunks, a defensive tactic, an offensive tactic. I can feel myself becoming giddy, wanting to laugh. It's over, I say to myself, over.

But going back out will be hard. I have used up my one advantage and it may have saved me from rape but it has made Chuck hate me more than ever. And he is in the next room, waiting.

There is a kick at the door. "Come out of there," says Chuck. "Right now."

I have no choice but to comply, so I get up and go to the door, open it carefully. Chuck is standing at the entrance to my bedroom, his arms crossed again as they were in the bathroom. He is holding his jacket.

"Get your coat," he says.

I glance over at Lyle, who has gotten dressed now and stands at the window looking out, his back to me.

I edge over to my bedroom and past Chuck, looking over at my bed with its rumpled sheets, my message waiting under the pillow. I reach up to pull my coat from the hanger and I can hear the door close behind me. I don't turn around.

"No," I say, more to myself than to him.

"Yes," he says, and he moves quickly up behind me, pinning my arms with his, wrapping them around me and locking his hands together on my chest. He jerks me over to the bed, throws me onto it. My head bangs against the bedside table, stunning me for an instant. When I look up I see he has dropped his jacket to the floor and is unzipping his fly, slowly, in no hurry. He pushes his pants and shorts down together, steps out of them and walks over to the bed. I stare at his crotch like a girl, someone who has never seen male genitalia before. He has no erection, but I don't know if that will protect me or not.

I try to roll away from him but he has grabbed my arm and drops himself full-length onto me. I gasp from the weight, unable to get enough air. His hands are pushing my dress up around my waist, my breasts, and he jerks at my panties, trying to tear them but they won't, so he pushes them down around my knees, manages to work them down to and free of my feet.

"Lyle!" I scream. "Lyle!"

"Shut up," Chuck says, his mouth on my neck. "Bitch. Bitch. Shut up."

I am naked beneath him, naked, his testicles and penis, not yet erect but moving, grinding into my pubic area. He forces a knee between my legs, prying them apart. He has one of my arms pinned with his and my other is collapsed against my chest and pushing without much effect against his shoulder.

"Lyle! Help me!"

Chuck bites hard into my shoulder—I can feel his teeth through the fabric of my dress. I scream and scream.

Lyle. Lyle.

"He won't help you," Chuck says into my ear, so loudly and clearly that I know it is true. He gnaws at my throat.

And suddenly I am filled with such rage, rage as I have never known it. I pull free the hand squashed against my chest and close it into a fist, punch at his face. I try to remember what I saw Chris do, practising her moves from her self-defense class. I draw my hand back as far as I can and shove its heel hard up and against his nose. He jerks his head back, gives a grunt of surprise and pain, and it is enough to give me more leverage. I twist my knees together, heave them up and tumble him to the side. He still has my arm pinned, but I am able to struggle up onto one elbow.

He regains his balance and reaches for me again, and I know this time he will be prepared for me. I try to pry his fingers from my arm but it is useless; they only tighten more.

And then I see what I should aim for, what I accidentally kicked once on Stewart that sent him gasping on his knees to the floor. I've no time to think about it—my hand pounds down like a hammer into the rumpled nest of hair and soft flesh, up fast and again, harder this time.

I am astonished at the effect. Chuck screams, louder than I did, and pulls his knees up to his chest. His fingers fly loose from my arm as though their muscles had been severed, and he rolls down off the side of the bed onto the floor. I twist off the bed on the other side, kick off my panties, and run. My dress falls back down to my waist, snags around my hips.

My hands fumble with the door into the other room, and I throw a look behind me to see where Chuck is. He is still on his knees, not close enough to grab me. But in the instant my eyes photograph him I see also that he is reaching not toward me but toward his clothes on the floor, and my split second of relief turns to a sick fear because I know what he is reaching for, what is in the pocket of his jacket and against which I cannot fight and from which I cannot run.

The door flies open and I leap after it, slamming it shut behind me. I race across the room, stumbling and knocking over one of their suitcases, to the door to the outside. Lyle is standing by the window where he was before, only facing in now, and I can see immediately that he will probably not stop me. I can hear him sobbing, thick and uncontrollable moans of sound that tear like a seizure at his body. His thin arms are wrapped tightly around himself like rope. I spare him only a glance and then I am at the door, clawing at it, little pieces of noise breaking from my mouth. I twist at the doorknob and it moves easily, the door jerking inward. And stopping. The night chain is on. Frantically I push the door closed, pull at the chain which is difficult, which needs to be turned before it will slide.

Behind me I can hear the other door tear open. Without turning I can see Chuck there, still crouching, but the gun in his hand is steady and I know the bullet is starting on its way to me.

The chain rips out of its slot. My hand is on the doorknob, opening. I can hear Lyle shouting, "Don't, don't!" at me or at Chuck I don't know. The door is open and I propel myself forward, out, out, and behind me I can hear the shot, a second shot, something shattering, glass perhaps.

I am running as I never have before. My arms pump wildly for more speed; my feet slap at the walk. My dress is still jammed up around my hips, but I am glad of it; it gives me a longer stride. Perhaps he has hit me, I can't let myself even think about it; if I do, the pain and the bleeding will start. I must only run, run, send my body only that one desperate message.

It is a small motel and the manager's office is right in front of me. Chuck must be at the outer door by now, sighting his gun at my back. I'm at the door—I wrench the handle to open it. It is locked.

"No!" I shout, shaking the door. "Open up!"

Right in front of my eyes is a little card that says "Manager in #201." 201. Oh, God. I can't run around looking for 201. It's probably back behind me. I whirl around, sure Chuck will be there, but the walkway is empty. The door to our unit still seems to be open. He must have gone around to the back of the building to head me off. I look wildly for someplace to run. There is only the highway, cars sliding past oblivious to what they could be seeing if only they looked.

I can't stay here. It is too open, too vulnerable. So is the road, but at least it is farther away. I run toward it, across the small gravel parking lot, onto the black solidity of pavement. I look over my shoulder for Chuck, but I can't see him. There are some trees now, thick fir, and they hide me from the motel.

A car is coming toward me and I wave my arms frantically, but the driver swerves dramatically out of the way, pushing his horn at me as though it were his road and I a trespasser. The horn will have alerted Chuck; he will probably head back for the car, try to track me down that way. Perhaps it was a mistake to run from the motel, from where I am sure there are people, but I can't change my mind now. I stumble onto the shoulder of the road, down into the ditch. There are trees and hills on the other side, places to hide.

The water in the ditch is so cold it must barely be liquid; I have to clench my teeth to keep from crying out from the shock of it on my feet. When I look down I see I am only wearing one shoe. I am amazed not to have noticed until now. I can see my missing shoe lying in the motel room, and I feel such a leap of dumb affection for it I almost start to cry.

I climb up out of the ditch, tumble into a thick jumble of small trees and fallen branches. I shouldn't have looked down at my feet; now I am aware of nothing but my naked foot scraping over rocks and debris. I throw a quick look behind me, but the road cuts off my view and all I can see is the dirty sign flashing "Yellow Pines Motel—Vacancy." The trees thicken quickly and after only a few yards I am invisible from the road. I hunch down behind one of the biggest trees and try to rein in my mind which is still shouting *run, run, run*. My heart bangs fiercely at my chest; my mouth gapes, sucking in air, more air.

Is it possible I have made it? Is it possible I have actually escaped? I have to stop myself from leaping up and shouting, in sheer idiot triumph. Chuck is still out there, I remind myself, and he is the one with the gun. Huddled in the bush is not escape. But it's closer than it was, it's closer than it was, and Stewart, damn you, you just might have to be stuck with me coming home again.

That calms me down, for some reason, that unexpected surge of rage not against Chuck and Lyle but against Stewart. It was probably just adrenalin. But it felt good, right. Righteous anger. I'll have to remember that. But I've more important things to worry about now.

I realize that if I had been shot I should have felt something by now. Still, I check my arms and legs, feel around on my back and neck. When I touch my right shoulder my fingers come away bloody. I shudder. I *have* been hit. I examine the wound and the tear in the dress as carefully as I can, and then I remember Chuck, the sickening wet feel of his teeth, biting like an animal. Well, at least I haven't been shot. Human bites can be dangerous, though. Especially Chuck's. I imagine his saliva deadly as snake venom.

My naked foot is bleeding a little, too, from a cut from one of the branches. I press a little moss on it, and even though it still bleeds it feels better.

And what to do now? I can't sit here all day. Well, perhaps I can. I'll have to think about it.

I have run in the direction of Princeton, so that is probably the way I should keep heading, although I've no idea how far beyond the town I am—I wish I had paid more attention last night. But there will have to be a gas station or a house along the road eventually. I can try walking along in the bush, to see if it's possible, and duck down whenever I hear a car—it's so quiet here you can hear things coming half a mile away.

I limp back closer to the road and begin heading east. It's hard to move quickly because there are so many branches and bushes, but I grit my teeth and work my way along. To make things worse I notice I am heading uphill. Closer to town I know there will be a long downhill slope, but I don't know how far away that is. Suddenly a car comes around a corner and I am in plain sight. I lunge for cover, terrified, even though I could see immediately the car is not the green Chevrolet. Lying there, I laugh out loud, a madwoman's laugh. I have a vision of myself staying here forever, becoming more and more like the animals, wild, afraid of humans.

My foot is definitely unhappy now. It has some new cuts and bruises, and pressure makes it send back a shout of pain. I hop along as best I can, leaning on trees and rocks, but the shoe on my other foot is beginning to wear out, too. Its thin sole wasn't meant for hiking, and it has at least one hole. I take the shoe off and shake out some dirt and gravel. The insole still looks lumpy and I imagine there is more debris under it. When I lift it I can see a stone has worked up through the hole, and as I reach in to take it out, my fingers pull out as well a piece of crumpled purple and white paper.

I stare at it for several seconds before I recognize what it is. A little stutter of laughter jumps out of me. It's the ten-dollar bill I hid there so long ago I can hardly remember doing so. Money—what use is money here? It's just a piece of paper, nothing of value. I shove it back under the insole. It's padding, that's all, insulation. But it gives me an idea, and I gather some of the dead grass and some old leaves from the occasional deciduous tree and shove them as well into the shoe. There is hardly room for my foot now, but they give the sole more padding. If I start to get a blister I can always take them out.

But then I look at my other foot, the one that really needs attention because it doesn't even have a thin-soled shoe for protection. I gather a bit more grass and moss and leaves and pack them around the foot, but I've no way of keeping them there when I walk. I look around the forest for something to use as string, as twine, but there is nothing. What would Tarzan use? What would Rambo use? The forest looks back impassively. Perhaps I can tear a strip from my dress, I think suddenly, but even as I look down at it I can see a better plan, can see where the hem is drooping, and I pick up the end of the unravelling thread. When I pull at it, about four feet spin loose before it hits a knot and won't go any further. I lift up the hem and try to bite the thread off, but it's acrylic and my teeth just grate and slide. Finally I set it on a rock and hack at it with another stone with a sharper edge, and at last it snaps off. I feel as clever as Einstein. I shove a slice of hard bark under the bottom of my foot and then wrap the thread around and around everything, a bizarre shoe of grass and leaves and moss and bark. I knot the thread as tightly as I can. It will be an advantage having the acrylic kind—at least it won't break easily.

When I stand up the whole things feels lumpy and unstable, and my pride at my ingenuity dribbles away. But when I take a few limping steps, to my surprise the contraption does not fall off, and I can actually walk as well as before, only now with moss cushioning my sole.

I will have to get moving. I've stayed here too long as it is, and I doubt if I've come even half a mile so far. I struggle on, clambering over roots and rocks. A branch like a huge fist clubs me on the head, making me dizzy for a moment. It might be easier if I went further into the forest, where the vegetation is thinner because the big spruce block out so much light, but I am afraid of getting lost if I do not keep the road in sight. At least I seem to have reached the crest of the hill and now there's a predominantly downward slope for a while.

The ground in front of me crumbles abruptly away into a sharp ravine, and I can see immediately there is no way I can get across it. The ravine cuts back as far as I can see so it's unlikely I could walk around it, either. The only place I can go is back to the road. I look at it nervously for a while. Perhaps I should abandon this whole plan, should take my chances on the highway trying to flag somebody down. Surely eventually a car will stop; they can't all be like the man who honked at me and swerved past. Even if Chuck is cruising the highway looking for me, it might be worth the risk. But I am like a person in a long line-up at a store; even after you realize it is absurd to wait so long, that you should just leave, you stand there stupidly, thinking you have invested too much time to give up now. But I will have to give up, at least for the moment.

Then across the highway I can see the ravine seems to be no more than a small depression in the earth. Obviously I should just cross the road and resume my trek on the other side. I slide down into the ditch and then claw my way up the other slope. The highway is clear of traffic and I dash across, my makeshift shoe going bang, bang, bang on the pavement. I am just clear and sliding into the other ditch when I can hear the hiss of a car, and panic grabs at me because it sounds exactly like the Chevrolet. I drop into the ditch, flatten myself against the slope, my frightened breath wheezing out of me. I close my eyes as the car approaches, as though that will make me invisible, and then I can hear it whining past above me, not slowing, not stopping to let Chuck leap out to investigate the flutter of movement he has glimpsed at the edge of the road. But it might have been him. I don't raise my head to look after the car.

I stay in the ditch for several moments, squashed up against the bank, just in case the car comes back, but I hear only two different vehicles go by, so finally I pry my cramped fingers loose and climb up the other bank. A car goes past as I am halfway up, and I feel like an insect mounted for inspection on a wall. But it is not Chuck, I can see by glancing over my shoulder, just someone in a red sports car who doesn't care. I scramble to the top and dump myself back into the tangle of undergrowth. I lie there for a few grateful moments, feeling safe, and then I continue walking. The thread on my homemade shoe has loosened and some of the grass has fallen out, so I know it will not be long before the whole affair simply falls off. But it can't be much farther. Surely there will be a service station or something soon. If not, I suppose I will have to take my chances on the road.

Ahead of me the forest thins, and I have to move back deeper into it and away from the road, but then I see something wonderful: a trail. As I get closer, I can see that it is

probably a bit of the old highway, heavily overgrown now but
still making an easy path. I hobble along on it at several times
the speed I was able to make before. I try to imagine the
people who travelled here before me, people who might have
felt the road under their feet the way I do, before asphalt and
cars changed everything, removed people from the
landscape. The forest leans in on the road, the grass already
reclaiming over half of it: another generation and it will have
disappeared altogether, gone back to wilderness, the first
mystery.

The trail curves back toward the main highway and then
ends abruptly, a row of trees blocking it off as though they
had been planted there like a barricade. I move beyond them
reluctantly. It was so easy on the trail; blundering through the
pathless forest again will seem so much harder. But I have to
go on.

Suddenly there is a noise behind me, a branch snapping. I
whirl around, my eyes preparing for Chuck, the gun, the shot,
but I see only the trees, the occasional bird navigating
through the branches. My heart is beating madly and I can
feel the pulsing of sweat in my armpits. But I can see nothing,
nothing human at all, and finally I decide I have no choice
but to move on. I keep looking over my shoulder, more afraid
than I have been since the motel. Perhaps it isn't even Chuck
stalking me; perhaps it's a bear. I go cold inside my perspiration. Beside me a squirrel begins chattering with the determination of a machine gun.

My foot steps on something soft and damp, something it
recognizes immediately as different from rock, from soil,
from grass, and when I look down I see it is a dead bird. I
cannot stifle a moan of revulsion. Death. I think of Lyle. I
wonder what he is doing as Chuck is out hunting for me. I remember his face, the stark misery and despair of it, as I
rushed past him to the door. But I make my thoughts go hard
and unforgiving against him. He would have let Chuck do
anything he wanted to me. That makes him guilty, too. I
 don't want to remember that I felt something for him, in spite
of the way he hurt me yesterday. He was better than Chuck, I
know he was. He hated what he was doing. If he had been

Pity for Lyle

like Chuck I might have been dead days ago. Or wished I were. But at the end he betrayed me. I can see myself lying on the bed screaming his name and how he didn't come. If I survive, and if the police find them, I suppose I will see him again. I wonder what I will say to him then. *I liked you?*—my voice sad and touched with pity, or *How could you do that to me?*—angry, only angry. Perhaps both things. It's hard to imagine what I will feel when I go back to my house on Zero Avenue, when I am clean and healed. I think of that woman almost as someone I knew a long time ago, someone who has moved away. She could not conceive of such a woman as I am now, a woman kidnapped and assaulted and wandering through the bush stepping on dead birds, a woman wondering whether she should offer pity to her kidnapper.

A huge tractor-trailer wheezes by on the highway, going west, to the coast. It is the way I should be heading, home, not back the way I have come. But what is there for me at home, anyway? A husband who is divorcing me, a son with a family of his own, friends who were friends to a couple, who are pulling away from me now that I have no husband, now that I am only myself, alone. Perhaps I should just continue going east indefinitely, work my way up to Edmonton where Chris is, knock on her door, be someone she would no longer recognize, someone wild and new, and I would say, "I want us to be friends."

Friends. That is what I do want from Chris, I suppose. Not to be her mother, the one who judges. She has never forgiven me for being her mother. "Friends?"—I can hear her say it, her face tight and closed. "I don't think that's possible, Mother."

I push on, trying not to make noise, but I am sure I sound like a tractor plowing through the brush. I catch movements from the corners of my eyes, scurryings, but when I look there is always nothing there, a branch quivering, perhaps, a dead leaf settling back down, the mover itself already gone. I am sweaty with exertion. Who would have thought walking through here would be so hard?

A small gully dips in front of me, and I slide down it, my eyes already on the slight incline up the other side, but when I hit the bottom I see there is a stream pulsing rapidly past in front of me. I stare at it stupidly, as though I don't know what it is. It makes a sound like a baby gurgling. A real babbling brook. I am amused, I suppose, because it does not seem to pose a major obstacle, is only five or six feet across, not quite narrow enough to jump, but I should be able to cross with only one or two steps into the water. I go downstream a little way, to where it seems narrowest and where there is a rock I should be able to use as a stepping stone.

I take off my good shoe; my makeshift one would be too hard to tie back on, I decide, so it will just have to take its chance in the water. Carefully, I step in, my bare foot first. The water is like ice, and I let out a little whimper at the shock. And it's deeper and swifter than I expected. I teeter on one leg, my toes grabbing at the bottom like fingers, until I am confident I have my balance, and then I step onto the rock with my other foot. But the rock is slimy and not as flat as it looks, and my foot twists away from it, sending me thudding to my knees in the freezing water.

"Damn!" I hear myself saying. "Damn! Damn! Damn!"

When I struggle to my feet, I can feel the makeshift shoe pulling loose, and when I look down I can see the current taking it, the pieces coming apart, the sole of bark bobbing along like a small canoe. I have to stop myself from lurching after it, as though it were something of infinite value, something I must rescue regardless of risk. Watching it go, I almost begin to cry.

Clumsily, I wade ashore, almost falling again as the creek bed suddenly drops off and I step in up to my knees. I clamber up the bank, my teeth beginning to chatter from the cold. I can't believe that a few minutes ago I was hot and sweating. I cast a quick look behind me to make sure Chuck, like a hunter attracted to floundering prey, hasn't found me, but there is nothing across the creek that is human. I get to the top of the gully, still clutching my good shoe which I have somehow managed not to drop, and then limp away to the cover of some large trees. I dry myself a little with dead leaves and grass, although most of it only sticks to me. Well, this is nature, the forest the way it really is, not a picture, not scenery, but the real thing that bruises your feet and trips you up in icy streams. I suppose I'm lucky I didn't fall in completely. At least my dress hasn't gotten wet beyond a few inches at the hem, which I can wring out, more or less.

I feel so exhausted that when I find a sunny spot under one of the trees I sink down and lean my head gratefully back, let the sun flow over my face. Above me I can see a large bird, a hawk, perhaps, rowing slowly across the sky.

After a while I begin to pick the dead leaves and grass and branches from myself, although perhaps I shouldn't; it is good camouflage, the way animals survive, blending into their surroundings. I have been good at doing that all my life.

At least it is warm; my legs, my bruised face, suck up the sun like salve. I'm lucky—it could be freezing, snowing— March is always unpredictable here. I've seen a few scabs of snow clotting on the rocks and the north side of the trees, but nothing I couldn't walk around, and although the ground is damp it's not so waterlogged that my feet sink in. Still, there are few signs of spring, none of the fresh green that nudged out on the trees and lawns at home over a month ago. The crocuses will be blooming there now; daffodils will be pushing up their yellow snouts; people will be cleaning their yards and gardens, imposing civilization again, unlike here, the wilderness, where I have no rights, am something the forest would like to expel. Yet it feels so good just to sit here, the sun on my face.

The trees in this little grove are large, different from the pine that mostly make up the woods here. These are cedar, with thick trunks I can feel safe behind, like the trees in Bear Creek Park, where I used to take the children for picnics on Sundays when Stewart had to work. It must be ten years since I've been there.

It is so wonderfully warm. I pull my dress up a little and move my legs apart, let the sun touch the insides of my thighs.

Chuck's body pressing down on me, grinding into me.

Dear God. Oh, dear God. How could I not have believed her?

I slump back against the tree and close my eyes. When Chris came to me with her terrible story, why didn't I listen?

It is all as clear and obvious to me now as the sun on my body, as my own name. She told me the truth. About George. It was the truth.

For how long has that knowledge been there in me, squashed down by my fear and my horror? I remember myself standing in the kitchen, holding the colander with the pieces of broccoli falling witlessly to the floor, and looking down at her pale face turning away from my anger and disgust. Oh, Chris. Oh, my poor innocent daughter.

I open my eyes, look slowly down at myself, sprawled so gracelessly at the foot of this tree. My hands tremble in my lap—they seem alien, repulsive. I sit here for a long time, staring at them, my heart beating at my chest.

"Chris," I say. "Chris."

The worst is that a part of me is not shocked, as though I am only looking clearly and coldly at something I must have known, in some way, in some locked and hidden place, for a long time. Is it possible to know yet not know at the same time? Can one's own mind be capable of such deception?

The dinner with George in the restaurant a week or so after she told me, and how he started to tell me something and then began to cry and I thought it must be about his ex-wife. There must have been a voice that whispered a warning to me then, a voice I was too frightened to hear. Perhaps I smiled kindly at him, turned and asked the waitress for another coffee: incapable, simply incapable, of believing he could do such a thing, to his own niece, a child. And now? I can believe it now. This truth so ugly I know it means I will lose him, my brother, whom I have known and loved longer than anyone.

It is only Chris who matters. I have wronged her so deeply I can hardly bear to think of it. I lift up my hands, press them, hard, against my face. How could I have been such a fool; how could it have taken me ten years to understand? Is there anything I can say to her now that will make up for not believing her? Will she care enough to listen to me, at all?

At last I take a deep breath and pull myself up straighter against the tree. At least now I have recognized the truth, I say to myself, and, yes, there is a relief in that, as though something chasing me for years through a dim forest has finally caught up with me and it is only knowledge, handing me its red apple, and now my job is to repair all the damage my ignorance has done. I remember myself in the room in Burnaby shouting at the boarded-up window, "Why me?" but perhaps this is why, this moment. Well, I know life's not that logical. Although it's the way God is supposed to work— you suffer in order to find enlightenment.

I'll never know, I suppose, when or if I would have come to this moment if nothing had happened to me. Surely I would have. Surely. The truth has been inside me all along, after all; perhaps until now I did not think it possible to live with it.

I feel suddenly such a desperate leap of energy—I have to get home; I have to talk to Chris. Nothing else matters.

But first I must concentrate only on getting through this day alive. I've probably come less than two miles, and already the sun is leaning into the afternoon. The cedars pull in their arms as a sudden chilly breeze pushes at their elbows. If I don't keep moving I will be stuck here in the dark and cold, and somewhere behind me is Chuck, closing in. I look nervously around, but there are only the noises of the forest, indecipherable.

I grunt to my feet and stumble on. It takes me about fifteen minutes just to get past a large tree that has fallen, too big to climb over, so I have to walk around it, branches pawing at me; I can see their muscles in huge knots under the bark. I am so eager to get on that I find myself breaking into a jerky trot whenever I can, ignoring my feet which are going numb from the cold and the cuts, which I am afraid to even look at. A large bird I don't recognize swoops low over my head several times. "Get out! Get out!" it shouts.

"I will," I say out loud. "I will."

A bramble grabs hold of my dress and I have to rip the cloth to get free. I can see a tear in my arm, too, but I don't feel anything—it seems like only another rip in fabric, something unimportant, something that can be mended later.

I'm starting to feel thirsty. It was foolish not to have drunk from the stream, water coming straight from the mountains and probably more pure than what comes out of my taps at home, to have seen the stream only as an obstacle instead of something useful. Well, the water running in the ditches is probably just as safe. I have finally worked my way around the tree so I head back toward the road; I will slide down into the ditch and quickly scoop up some water. I won't need much.

I can see the road again. And suddenly, just visible around a bend, is what I have been looking for. A gas station.

I lean against a tree, dizzy with relief. Little animal sounds contract up from my throat. The first white explorers could not have felt more elated to see the Pacific. The station is not that far away, and as I clamber madly over rocks and underbrush, I can see there is a restaurant attached to the service station. There are (I count them) seven cars parked in front of the restaurant and a big truck filling up at the pumps. And people are walking around, people I will be able to talk to.

I am directly across from the filling station now. It's on the other side of the road, so I will have to risk the exposure of crossing back over again, but I've chanced it before so I can chance it again.

Still, I just stand here, looking across the road, hesitating. At this moment I am utterly free, not only of Chuck and Lyle, but also of that other life that is waiting for me across the road—what I must do about Chris and George, Stewart and the stupid bondage in which I am keeping myself to him. I glance down at myself, filthy and bruised and scratched but alive, and strong, a survivor. Where I am hurt I will heal, and scar tissue, the doctor told me once, is the strongest tissue in the body. I remember looking at myself in the bathtub such a short while ago and thinking my body had failed me, but it hasn't; it's only Stewart who's failed me.

The image of the room in Fiji flashes into my mind, but for the first time I can see myself in the scene, from the outside, a woman sitting on the bed filing her nails, her sudden pain and despair happening to her, not to me. I am no longer that woman. Who I am I guess I will find out now, when I walk across that highway and continue my life. If I have escaped from Chuck I can escape from anything.

So, get on with it, I tell myself impatiently; don't just stand here and be symbolic.

I limp forward, my naked foot cringing as it scrapes again against rocks and roots, my arms raised in front of me to fend off the last branches that reach at me, and then I am in the open. I look around, carefully, and then I slither into the ditch and hunch my way up the other side, although it is not easy, the incline is so steep and the damp earth breaks away in chunks in my fingers. But at last I am on the road and I stumble across it, the flat pavement like a surface I have forgotten how to walk on. I look around for Chuck, for the green Chevrolet, tensing for a bullet, a blow that will knock me to my knees. But there is no bullet, no man with a jumbled face suddenly leaping up in front of me.

The two men at the pumps stare at me, their mouths actually dropping open. The one filling his tank releases his pressure on the nozzle and it slides out of the opening; gas from the hose drizzles onto the ground. Well, I must be something to see, all right, my face with its huge purple jaw, my dress in dirty shreds, an epaulet of blood coagulating on my shoulder, one foot shoeless, my body covered with mud from the ditch—I don't care. I have survived. I don't want to look as though it has been easy.

"Hello," I say to the men, my voice as pleasant as if I were entertaining in my own living room. "I wonder if you could help me. I've been kidnapped, you see, and I've just escaped. The police are looking for me, and perhaps you could phone them for me?"

"Jesus Christ," says the man holding the hose. He hangs it up on the pump after several tries. "You bet, lady. The police. Sure, sure. You wanna come inside?"

"Yes, please," I say. "One of the kidnappers is still chasing me, I think, so I'd appreciate being able to stay out of sight. He has a gun," I add.

"Jesus Christ," says the man again, reaching out to take my arm and then drawing back as if I might break if he touched me. "Tim," he shouts at the other man who is standing right beside him, "phone the cops. Hurry up!"

The other man swallows and it seems to pull his mouth finally closed. "Yeah. Yeah," he says, and he runs over to the restaurant. The first man ushers me, moving his arms a little the way you would shoo chickens, not touching me, into a greasy-looking little office around the side of the service station. He pulls out a chair and holds it for me. It is miraculous there is a chair there, just now, because my legs are collapsing.

"Thank you," I don't forget to say. "Thank you very much."

"Would you like anything from the restaurant? A sandwich? Coffee?"

"A coffee would be lovely," I say. I gesture at the phone on the desk. "Do you think I might use the phone? To call my husband and tell him I'm all right? I promise I'll pay for the call."

"Oh, sure, sure. Of course." The man pulls the phone even closer to the edge of the desk, as if I would be incapable of reaching a few feet for it. Maybe I am. "I'll get your coffee." And he backs out of the office, a large strained smile that he means to be reassuring pulled taut across his face.

I pick up the phone, my fingers so numb they can hardly hold the receiver. I start to dial, my own number, my home, Stewart. But halfway through, my fingers fumble to a stop, and then they push down on the buttons that break the connection.

 Why should I call Stewart, the man who is leaving me? He can wait a little longer until he hears from me. It is Chris who is in my mind, Chris I need to talk to. Without letting myself think about what I will say, I dial her number in Edmonton, 1-403-432—am I remembering it correctly? I've called it so seldom. The phone rings, an empty bleat in my ear. She's probably in class. It was foolish to try her, anyway; the police will expect me to call Stewart so that is what I should do.

I hang up, but before I can pick the phone up again it rings, startling me so that my hand flies away from it as though I had been touching something on fire. It rings again, and I only stare at it stupidly. It's not my phone; I shouldn't answer. By the third ring I am thinking, against all reason, it's so loud surely Chuck will hear—

And even as his name enters my head the office door whips open and I give a terrified cry because I am sure it is him, he has found me, after all this, he has found me— But it is only the other gas station attendant, staring back at me, frightened.

"It's okay," he insists, "it's okay." He reaches cautiously for the phone, exaggerating his movements so I won't misconstrue them. "The call's for you," he says excitedly, before he even picks up the receiver. "It's the cops. I told them you were here." He picks up the phone, and says importantly, "Hello? . . . Yeah, yeah, she sure is. Right here. Sitting right here. Here she is."

He hands me the receiver, and when I am slow in taking it he draws it back a little and thrusts it at me again, as though I hadn't seen it.

"Thank you," I say, smiling up at him.

"You bet," he says. When I take the phone and say "Hello?" he whispers at me, "I'll let you talk," as though this would be an intimate and private conversation. Maybe it will be. He closes the door softly behind him.

"Mrs. Duvalier?" asks the voice at the other end. "This is Corporal Warnock. We're sure glad to hear you're all right."

"Yes," I say. "So am I." I take hold of the receiver more firmly. *I'm all right.* Yes. I really am.

"We'll have you home in no time."

"That will be a relief. I should tell you about the kidnappers. They were in the Yellow—"

"—Pines Motel," his voice overlaps mine. "We found them already."

"Both of them?" It doesn't seem possible. I imagine the police following Chuck into the woods, some wild shoot-out behind me I somehow didn't even hear.

"Yeah. The manager called us. One of them was dead. It looks like the other one had shot him."

"What?" I reach out and grab hold of the desk. It doesn't make sense. "Which one was it? The one that's . . . dead? Which one was it?"

"We haven't I.D.ed them yet. He was blond, though, I think."

"Lyle."

"Who?"

"Lyle. It's Lyle. Chuck was shooting at me and Lyle must have stepped in the way."

"That could be, Mrs. Duvalier. Now we'll be right there to pick you up—"

"And the other one," I say harshly, not letting him hang up. "How did you catch him?"

"Well, he was still there. In the motel room. Funny, really. He was just sitting there on the floor beside the other guy. The blond one. The one that was dead."

"I see."

The phone sags away from my ear and I can only faintly hear him say he will be here in ten minutes. "That's fine," I say absently.

I hang up and stare dully at my hand still limp on the receiver, at the long, rusty-looking scratch that puckers the skin on my wrist. Lyle is dead. I can hear him shout, "Don't, don't," and he must have rushed over from where he was by the window and the bullet heading for me hit him—I squeeze my eyes shut, twist my head to one side, trying not to see it, yet I have to. It's something I will have to see for the rest of my life. I feel a terrible sense of loss, and guilt. My hand pulls back from the phone and knocks the receiver off the hook but I only look at it, lying on the desk, its whine filling my ears like a siren.

And why didn't Chuck run? I can see myself clawing and clambering through the woods, terrified of him behind me, and now it seems like some pointless and grotesque joke, Chuck not chasing me at all, not caring about me any more at all. Why did he stay there with Lyle? I will never know the answers. Lyle is the one who could have explained it, and Lyle is dead. Sobs tear themselves loose in me, as though someone were picking me up by the neck and shaking me.

But I don't let myself give in to it; the police will be here soon and I can't let them find me crying. I take a deep breath. I have to prepare myself for their questions, and soon I will be home and there will be more questions, a story I will have to tell over and over. Chris. George. Stewart. It will take time to sort out the lies from the truth, but I will do it; I am not the same woman who looked up, terrified, from her television set five days ago.

I pick up the receiver, punch at the top buttons until I get a dial tone, and dial my own number.

The door opens and the man who went to get me coffee comes in with two cups, sets them both on the desk. "One's with cream and the other's black," he whispers. "I didn't know which you liked so I brought both." He pulls some sugar cubes and a spoon out of his jacket pocket. The pocket where Chuck would have kept his gun.

"Thanks," I am able to say. "Thanks so very much."

At home, the phone begins to ring.

Leona Gom was born in 1946 and grew up on an isolated farm in northern Alberta, where her parents were homesteaders. She received a B.Ed. and M.A. from the University of Alberta in Edmonton. After moving to Vancouver, she was editor and poetry editor for about ten years of the literary magazine *event*. She now lives in White Rock, B.C., and teaches at Kwantlen College.

Zero Avenue is Leona Gom's second novel. Her first novel, *Housebroken,* won the Ethel Wilson Fiction Prize in 1987. She has also published five volumes of poetry including *Land of the Peace,* which in 1980 won the Canadian Authors' Association award for the best book of poetry that year. Her writing has appeared in numerous anthologies, journals and literary magazines in Canada, the United States and Australia.